'Peak comfort read has been achieved'
Red

'One of the best in the genre'
The Sun

'Unashamedly cosy, with gentle humour and
a pleasingly eccentric amateur sleuth'
The Guardian

'A fabulously satisfying addition to
the canon of vintage crime'
Daily Express

'Highly amusing'
Evening Standard

'TP Fielden is a fabulous new voice and his dignified,
clever heroine is a compelling new character'
Daily Mail

'A golden age mystery'
Sunday Express

'Tremendous fun'

TP Field is a leading author, broadcaster and journalist. This is the fourth novel in the Miss Dimont Mystery series.

Died and Gone to Devon

TP Fielden

ONE PLACE. MANY STORIES

HQ
An imprint of HarperCollins*Publishers* Ltd
1 London Bridge Street
London SE1 9GF

This edition 2019

1
First published in Great Britain by
HQ, an imprint of HarperCollins*Publishers* Ltd 2019

Copyright © TP Fielden 2019

TP Fielden asserts the moral right to be
identified as the author of this work.
A catalogue record for this book is
available from the British Library.

ISBN: 978-00-08-24372-2

MIX
Paper from
responsible sources
FSC™ C007454

This book is produced from independently certified FSC™ paper
to ensure responsible forest management.

For more information visit: www.harpercollins.co.uk/green

This book is set in 11/15.5 pt. Sabon

Printed and bound in Great Britain by
CPI Group (UK) Ltd, Croydon, CR0 4YY

For
Julia Richards Ellis
– divine ancestral voice

PART ONE — WINTER

ONE

For a newspaper which went to such lengths to remind its readers of the forthcoming jollifications – ill-drawn holly wreaths garlanding the masthead on Page One, other pages adorned with large woodcut prints of Santas and sleighbells – the newsroom of the *Riviera Express* was decidedly lacking in Christmas cheer.

Above the sub-editors' table some optimist had hung a dispirited-looking mistletoe twig, but since most of the desk's occupants were too old or too ugly to kiss, as a gesture it seemed particularly hollow. Outside the editor's office a despondent-looking fir tree was already shedding its needles, while from the darkroom came the sounds of Terry Eagleton murdering 'Santa Bring My Baby Back To Me'. It wasn't a nice thing to hear.

Betty Featherstone was sitting on John Ross's desk, swinging her legs and listening to the old bore drone on about the glory days.

'Ayyyyy...' he said with a growl, 'it was just aboot this time o' year. The old King was dying, the worrld was waiting for the soond of muffled bells. Fleet Street had come to a standstill in anticipation. Ye're too young to know the name Hannen Swaffer, but let me tell you, girrlie, he was the finest – the greatest columnist ever. Hannen *Swaffer*!'

'Yes, I think I've heard the…'

'So old Swaff was sent off to Buckingham Palace to find out how things were going. He came back to the office and told the editor: *His Majesty must be slipping away. He didn't even recognise me.*'

'Ha, ha,' said Betty.

'You say that, girrlie, but I can tell you don't mean it.'

He was right. Betty was inspecting the run in her stocking, successfully dammed with a dollop of Cutex Rosy Pink nail varnish, and thinking about the WI Whist Drive report she had to finish before going-home time. Or rather, she wasn't thinking about it, using Ross and his interminable meanderings as an excuse not to.

Nobody told her, when she joined the *Riviera Express* from school, it could be this dull – and in the fortnight before Christmas, too! All she had to look forward to for the rest of the afternoon was writing up the tide tables, sorting out the church brass-cleaning roster, and finally doing something about the Bedlington Crochet Club's seasonal *chef d'oeuvre*, a knitted Madonna and child complete with manger, now lopsidedly adorning the font in St Margaret's Church.

'Ye jest don' get the quality of writer down here, girrlie. Now Cassandra of the *Daily Mirror* – that's quality for ye!'

As she half listened to the Glaswegian's monody she struggled to think of an intro. How many thousand stitches, she drearily thought, would it take to make a knitted Madonna? Wait a minute – I could turn that into the New Year quiz!

4

'Ye ever read his description of Liberace? So brilliant I know it by heart.'

'Liberace?'

'The singer, girrlie, the singer!'

Betty nodded absently. She was actually thinking about whether to take the train up to Exeter for the annual Pens 'n' Lens Club party – though it usually ended, like all journalistic gatherings with added lubricant, in backstabbing and recrimination. She hated it, too, when people she hadn't seen for a month or so asked after the wrong boyfriend. Betty got through men like a hot knife through butter, or it was the other way round.

Ross licked his lips and looked into the middle distance. '*This deadly winking, sniggering, snuggling, chromium-plated, scent-impregnated, luminous, quivering, giggling, fruit-flavoured, mincing, ice-covered heap of mother love*,' he recited. 'That's Cassandra for ye! Sheer genius! Ayyyy, girrlie, have you ever tried your hand at writing something like that? Ye ought, ye know.'

'The chap who typed that got sued. And his newspaper. And his editor. Are you suggesting we put that kind of stuff in the *Riviera Express*, Mr Ross?'

The chief sub suddenly found something more interesting to occupy his time.

Just then a heavy thudding noise proclaimed the approach of Rudyard Rhys, bewhiskered editor of the *Rivera Express*, stalking down the office in his heavy brogue shoes. You could tell that he too had yet to catch the Christmas spirit.

'Where *on earth* is everybody?' he snarled, though he knew perfectly well – they were all off doing their last-minute shopping and his newsroom was a wasteland.

'Where is my so-called chief reporter, Miss Dim?'

'She went off with her handbag,' said Betty disloyally. 'Didn't say where.'

'Anything in the diary for her?'

'No,' said Betty even more disloyally. In fact, Miss Dimont had told her before lunch, 'I'm going over to Wistman's Hotel to see Mrs Phipps. Back much later,' meaning opening-time. The newsgathering was over for this week, after all.

'Well, I've just had a call from Sir Frederick's office. He's giving a constituency workers' party and wants someone to cover it. Says his secretary forgot to send the invitation.'

'That'll mean the *Western Daily Press* turned him down. He always favours them.'

'Rr… rrr!' said the editor, who hated his more powerful daily rival.

'Anyway, Judy knows him. I don't.'

'It'll have to be you, Betty, it's on in an hour. Take that young Skinner fellow along with you.'

'I thought you said politics was beyond me,' said Betty, trying to get a rise out of her boss.

'Six o'clock, Con Club.' Rhys stumped back up the deserted newsroom. There were days when he barely held control of his newspaper and his best response to the doubters was to retreat into the office and slam the door. That showed them.

'Better slip on your party frock,' drawled Ross over his shoulder, 'Sir Fred likes a pretty girrl ye ken.'

He's seventy-five if he's a day, thought Betty with a shudder. On the other hand there were always young people eager to get on in politics hanging around his office and the party was sure to be fun. It solved the Pens 'n' Lens problem, too.

'I'm going to make the crocheted Madonna the New Year quiz,' she said decisively as she picked up her handbag from the desk and headed for the cloakroom.

'Ay ye would, ye would,' uttered Ross shaking his head and talking to his desk. If only he could pop out now for a quick drink with old Swaff and Cassandra in the Old Jawbones, what things they'd have to say to each other...

'He did the most unspeakable things with animals,' sighed Mrs Phipps, flipping ash into her coffee and throwing her ancient eyes up to the ceiling. 'Quite reprehensible. We had to send him away.'

Judy Dimont – runaway chief reporter and possibly one of the most accomplished journalists in the West Country with her sizzling shorthand, rat-a-tat-tat typing and fearless interview technique – turned to face the old Gaiety Girl. She'd driven out to join her friend for lunch but now, looking out of the window and watching the snow crawl up the glass with quite alarming speed, she began to realise her chances of escape from Dartmoor were diminishing by the minute.

'Your son-in-law, Geraldine? Guy? What did you do with him in the end?'

'Bundled him off to Tangier. With just enough money to keep him away.'

'Ah yes, I remember now.'

'They don't care how they treat their animals there. Beat their donkeys to death, then eat them. Or is it the other way round?'

'Did it do him any good?'

'It's a hard life when you have no money,' said Mrs Phipps,

looking round for a waiter, 'herding donkeys. Anyway, it prepared him for the jail sentence. Shocking for a mother to discover what a contemptible beast her daughter had married.[1] He had it coming.'

They were sitting at an upstairs window of Wistman's Hotel and the light was fading fast. Inside, the room was suffused with a magical glow from the fire, the candles, and the reflections from the many gilded mirrors on the walls. As the massive hall clock struck the quarter and the logs settled lower in the grate, the lines in Geraldine Phipps' old face gently evaporated until she became young again. Though approaching her eightieth year, she was still a beauty.

'You look lovely, Geraldine,' said Miss Dimont. 'Must be all that success!'

'They were barbarians,' laughed Mrs Phipps, looking back with relish on her triumphant summer as proprietor of the Pavilion Theatre. 'They came, they saw, they conquered! Raped and pillaged as well, I have no doubt! Come the spring, the Temple Regis birth rate will quadruple as a result.'

She said it with a joyous lilt to her voice, as if she personally had ordained the unwanted pregnancies which startled and divided Devon's prettiest seaside resort, in the wake of Danny Trouble and The Urge's riotous summer season at the end of the pier.

'Shocking,' said Miss Dimont, shaking her corkscrew curls in disbelief. Back in the holiday season, Britain's No. 1 beat group had grabbed the town by the scruff of its neck, shaken hard, and prepared it for the 1960s in spectacular fashion.

---

1 See *Resort To Murder*

Their six-week residency at the Pavilion, though marred by an untidy death or two, had saved the theatre from closure, and turned Mrs Phipps into an unlikely national celebrity.

DOWAGER'S DRUM-BEAT DRIVES OUT THE DODOS, yodelled Fleet Street's headline writers, though Miss Dimont's own publication, the *Riviera Express*, was less forthcoming in its support. The editor disapproved of beat groups, and he especially disapproved of lively old dames turning his bailiwick upside down.

The two friends spent lunch hopping from milestone to milestone in Mrs Phipps' eventful life, and though it was past three o'clock there seemed so much still left unsaid. Geraldine Phipps, who was spending Christmas at the hotel, was enjoying herself immensely and ordered a Whisky Mac for her reporter friend. Her own Plymouth gin had appeared as if by magic, for she was extravagant with tips.

Terry Eagleton, the chief photographer, had driven Miss Dimont out from Temple Regis in the Minor but then disappeared off to Widecombe-in-the-Moor, probably never to be seen again – the snows over Dartmoor now enveloping all and everything.

'I have the feeling I'll be staying the night,' said Miss Dimont as a heavy thud of snow, driven by the Dartmoor winds, hit the window with a crash. It was getting darker by the second.

'That's nice,' said Geraldine Phipps. 'Because I've got something I want to discuss with you.'

'Tell me first what you have planned for next season, Geraldine. At the Pavilion – is there something I can write about for the *Express*, since it looks like I'm stuck here till the snow plough comes through?' Judy looked out of the window but by now there was even less to see, Dartmoor's snows having seized the day and put it to bed.

The theatre's proprietress settled more comfortably in her chair, looked around at the darkening room festooned with ivy and fat white candles, and exhaled.

'Part of me yearns for Pearl Carr and Teddy Johnson,' she said, 'sweetly crooning tunesmiths. But frankly, dear, I've always adored a bit of danger – and those leather-jacket boys certainly provided that last summer!'

Miss Dimont recalled the singer Danny Trouble, who missed his mum terribly during the band's turbulent residency at the end of the pier – not too much danger there!

'But I wonder what my editor will say if you decide to throw a spanner in the works again next summer? Some people got very upset with all that racket you made, Geraldine.'

'What? That fellow Rhys? The buffoon who calls himself Rudyard?'

'He only changed his name when he thought he was going to be a novelist,' explained Judy. '*Richard* Rhys has less of a zing to it. Anyway, if not Pearl Carr, then who?'

'Before he was arrested, Gavin told me about a young man called Gene Vincent, rides on stage on his motorbike. Revs it up a bit, the girls go crazy! Then he starts to strip his leather off.'

'Geraldine!' cried Miss Dimont with feigned horror. 'You'll be eighty soon! Motorbikes? Strip-tease? At your age? What's the Mayor going to say?'

Mrs Phipps' finely painted lips crept into a wicked smile.

'My dear, when we Gaiety Girls appeared on stage way back when, it wasn't always a Salvation Army rally, you know. Some of us deliberately forgot to put on our frillies.'

'Surely not!'

'The can-can was a special favourite, just think. Very popular.'

'Honestly, Geraldine, you're a disgrace!'

'No, my dear, I'm not. I'm not pregnant.'

'I'm told there are eleven unwanted babies on the way. Those Urges and their urges.'

'They should have been more careful. Never happened in my days on the stage.'

'Really not?' said Miss Dimont. 'You do surprise me!'

'Well,' said Geraldine Phipps, gently reminding her lips of the gin glass, 'not unless it was necessary.'

'What d'you mean?'

'My dear, in my days at the Gaiety Theatre there were possibly as many as thirty or forty girls – dancers like me, darling – who married a lord. Some of them were well-born, but an awful lot of them weren't.'

'I don't follow.'

'The well-born ones would face no difficulty from the family should milord drop to one knee and pop the question. It was the others. The rule was – if in doubt, let nature take a hand.'

'You mean they got pregnant *deliberately*?'

'Cheaper to marry the gel than to defend a breach-of-promise action in court. You know how our noble families like to cling to their small change.'

Miss Dimont shook her head and took a sip of the Mac. It

breathed fire into her chest and brought a tear to her eye. The vast first-floor sitting room, stuffed with big leather chairs and polished mahogany side tables, had emptied. Either guests had retired for a nap or had wandered off to the library to find a thriller. From where she sat in the window, Miss Dimont could see that nobody was entering or leaving the hotel by the front door – indeed, the wide semi-circular drive had altogether disappeared under the snow.

'I'd better go and see if they have a room.'

'Don't worry,' smiled Geraldine. 'I had a word with Ethel while you were powdering your nose. You're just down the hall from me and they've found you some pyjamas and things.'

I ought to phone the office, Miss Dimont thought lazily. She stretched and turned towards the fire, the idea escaping her brain the second it had been formulated.

'So what is it you wanted to ask me about, Geraldine?'

'A murder, dear. A murder long ago. One which touched the royal family and could have created an unprecedented scandal, had it ever become known.'

'Good Lord!'

'It happened around Christmas time, I suppose that's what put the thought in my head. I'd forgotten all about it – but sitting here, seeing them putting up the decorations, getting out the punchbowl, brought it all back.'

'How fascinating, Geraldine.'

'I was there, Judy. I was there and it has puzzled and worried me ever since. I want you to solve it. *I need you to solve it!*'

TWO

Temple Regis, a mere twenty miles from the edge of Dartmoor, was enjoying very different seasonal weather. Here, the maritime climate meant that as the day faded, the darkening sky revealed its precious jewels one by one, stars so sharply defined you could almost pluck them and wear them round your neck. The evening was beautiful.

'Shall we go for a walk?' said Auriol Hedley, looking at the elegant old gentleman sitting in her kitchen chair, his legs neatly crossed and the shine on his brogues sparkling in the lamplight. 'The air's crisp, but if you wrap up warm it should be invigorating. We could go to the pub.'

'I say,' said her companion, 'what a wonderful idea!' as if nobody had ever thought of going to a pub before. Miss Dimont's uncle Arthur was like that – still a boy through and through, though the occasional arthritic twinge was a reminder that he no longer was.

'Come on, then.' Auriol was already in her ancient fur coat and whizzing Arthur's hat across the room. He caught it neatly and jammed it on his head. They let themselves out of the Seagull Café and set off through the deserted harbour just as the moon rose to light their way.

Out in the dark you could hear the crack of lines against the boat masts, and the sloosh of water slapping the sides of the craft anchored against the harbour wall. Towards the mouth of the estuary a few red lights moving slowly inland showed there was still life on the water, but otherwise it was silent.

'So glad you've come for Christmas, Arthur, always a joy to see you.'

'My final attempt to put Hugue and her mother together again,' he said, using the family name for his niece. 'After that I've pledged never to say another word.' Both shared a love for Miss Dimont, both were concerned at her evasion tactics when it came to Madame Dimont, Arthur's sister – both seemed powerless to intervene.

'Did Grace ask you to do something about it?'

'You know what she's like,' said Arthur, linking his arm through Auriol's. 'Grace is as difficult in her way as Huguette – two opposing forces. Grace says, *My daughter never sees me*, and then finds an excuse when I try to put them together. Huguette is naughty – never replies to her mother's letters and is always on a story or solving a murder or something, just when it looks like the two of them might meet.'

From across the harbour the old man and his companion suddenly heard the piping voices of young choirboys singing, in descant, a melodious chorus of 'Once in Royal David's City'.

'Cynical little brutes,' said Auriol briskly, stepping up the pace.

'I say, steady on,' panted Arthur. 'That's the spirit of Christmas you're giving a kicking! Where are the tidings of comfort and joy in your heart?'

'You don't know. I had them knocking on my door last night. When I opened up they were wearing choirboys' ruffs and had a candle in a milk bottle. Such innocence, such sweetness!'

'Well,' said the old boy, pulling his leather gloves tighter into his palms, 'think yourself lucky. In London I get nobody knocking on my door this time of year. No point in leaving a mince pie on the doorstep when you're on the eleventh floor of a mansion block. Personally, I think it's charming.'

Auriol did not agree. 'They stand there, singing and singing, looking at you with goo-goo grins, begging with their eyes to give them a hefty tip. And when you do, they don't stop singing, they keep on going in the hope you'll give 'em a bit more.'

'Good heavens, Auriol, are you by chance related to Ebenezer Scrooge?'

'Choirboys?' came the snorted reply. 'Extortionists!'

They pushed their way into the saloon bar of the Belvedere. Inside, there was a sense of repressed celebration – this was, after all, Bedlington, lordly neighbour of Temple Regis where beer is served only in half pints (and then with some disdain) while there were at least half a dozen different kinds of sherry on offer.

'Sherry?'

'Good lord, no!' said Arthur. 'A nice glass of whisky to keep the cold out, if you please. And you, Auriol?'

'Same.'

Since her retirement from Naval Intelligence, Auriol Hedley had made her home, and a thriving business, in the Seagull Café, perched enchantingly on the edge of Bedlington Harbour, and a magnet for the more genteel seaside visitor.

Auriol had put on a pound or two since her uniform days, but it suited her. '*La patronne mange ici,*' she explained airily to friends who came to try out her lardy cake and Welsh scones – and anyway, who was counting calories?

In winter, and especially around Christmas, there was little trade and plenty of time to think of other things.

'That's why I'm glad you're here, Arthur,' she said as her companion returned from the bar. 'I wanted to ask you about Sir Frederick Hungerford.'

'Freddy? We're both old Seale-Haynians, you know. Haven't seen him for years. He's your MP, isn't he?'

'Not for much longer. Standing down at the next election. Been here for yonks. You're not friends?'

'Far from it. We met only briefly, forty years ago, when I came back from the Front. Seale Hayne was an agricultural college but it was used as a hospital for chaps suffering from shell-shock. Well, we both had a bit of that. Freddy and I spent a few weeks in bath chairs lying next to each other, though we didn't get on awfully well.'

'*Rich, truculent, and litigious* said one newspaper when he announced his retirement,' said Auriol.

'Obviously no friend of yours either, then,' laughed Arthur.

'Well, he's charming enough when you meet him, that I will say. But soon to be replaced by an absolute poppet. It'll be something of a relief to have a real person as our MP instead of that…'

'Shall we have another?'

'Bit soon for me – you go on.'

'I wanted to talk to you about Huguette before she gets here. Keen to ask your advice. If we've finished with Freddy?'

'Well, that can wait. What about her?'

'You know her better than anyone.'

'Yes.'

'Her closest friend.'

'Yes.'

'Auriol, she's going round in circles. Her life seems to have become one long chase after the next sensation. It's this story, it's that headline. It's this crime and that murder. I feel she was made for better things.'

'Well, Arthur, I wonder whether I can agree with you about that. She distinguished herself in war service. She had a second career during the Cold War. She found a third career down here, working in local newspapers, away from the combat zone you might say. You might argue she has a fourth career solving the crimes she has since she started working on the *Express*. Is there something wrong with that? I should have thought you would have been proud of her.'

'Well, old girl, I am, I am! But…'

'Aha! This is Madame Dimont talking, Arthur, isn't it? You've been nobbled!'

Arthur looked at his empty glass and then up at the bar. He looked at the glass again but made no attempt to get up.

'Look, Auriol,' he said, 'you know that one day Huguette

will be very well off. Her father left everything to her mother when he died, but she is the eventual heir – after all, when Monsieur Dimont became ill she took over the diamond business and did wonders with it. Wonders! You might almost say she made more money than her father, and he was a shrewd one.'

'She knows all that. She doesn't need money, Arthur, she needs peace of mind. She found it working at the *Riviera Express*. She's got her cottage, her cat, her career.'

'Grace wants her to change her life. Give up the journalism business. Go to live in Essex and enjoy what is rightly hers.'

'Not *Essex*, Arthur!'

'You've been there, it's a lovely house. Right on the edge of the marshes. It needs to be lived in, have some life brought back to it.'

'But it's huge. She doesn't need all that – how many bedrooms, for heaven's sake!'

'Grace hates the thought of it going out of the family. She always hoped Hugue would marry.'

'Well,' said Auriol, 'you can tell her all this yourself when she gets here.'

The old boy looked shyly at his companion. 'I was rather hoping you'd say it for me. I do so hate rubbing her up the wrong way,' he said.

'And you – awarded the military Order of the British Empire!' laughed Auriol, planting an imaginary medal on his lapel. 'Sir Arthur Cowardy Custard!'

The old soldier rose to his feet and headed towards the bar looking perhaps a trifle green round the gills.

*

Hector Sirraway made quite a fuss when he first arrived in the public library on Fore Street. It was a small building, no bigger than the size of a large terraced house, but perfect for the needs of Temple Regis – during the summer months the residents were far too busy serving their guests, refugees from less attractive parts of Britain, to sit around reading. And in winter they were too busy repairing, and preparing, for the next season.

To say Temple Regents weren't bookish would do them an injustice, but it followed that their modest library needed only the smallest area reserved for reference work – and even then its one desk remained empty most of the year. Was it any surprise that this is where the Christmas tree should be placed when Advent came around?

Given their modest budget, Miss Greenway and Miss Atherton had done a wonderful job, lavishing the lofty conifer with love and, it might be said, the necessary splash of vulgarity. Everyone said what a marvellous sight it presented, with the exception of Mr Sirraway.

'What have you got that thing there for?' he asked starchily when he first showed up a month before Christmas. 'Can't you get rid of it?'

Since then, he'd been in every day, and his temper never seemed to improve. Miss Greenway had offered him her desk if he needed somewhere to sit, and even made him a nice cup of tea. But nothing budged Mr Sirraway from his hatred of the tree.

Or it could have been something else that bothered him, it was hard to tell. Tall, white-haired, with a pinched face and a permanent dewdrop at the end of his nose, it emerged from the few sentences he uttered that he was researching a book on the industrial buildings of Dartmoor.

'Fine time to come in and make a nuisance of himself,' muttered Miss Atherton on the fourth day. 'Why couldn't he wait till after Christmas?' But Miss Greenway loved to see her library used, whether by schoolchildren, housewives or scholars like Mr Sirraway. In fact, she especially liked Mr Sirraway's presence because very few asked much of the library, apart from a light novel or a Jane Austen and the occasional Shakespeare.

'We must show him what we're capable of,' she told her assistant, and so they did.

The two librarians watched with interest the growing pile of books their visitor ordered from the shelves. From an ancient leather satchel he drew large sheets of paper which looked like plans of some kind, spreading them out on an adjacent table, grunting and whispering to himself and only occasionally remembering to reach for a handkerchief for his nose.

Miss Greenway was inclined to look up to him – she adored learned people! – but Miss M had taken against.

'Rude, secretive – and you can tell he doesn't have a wife. Look at those socks!' One red, one grey – what wife would allow their man to go out dressed like that?

Mr Sirraway was oblivious to these whisperings. Though he originally demanded books on buildings from all over the moor, he seemed after the first couple of days to be concentrating on an area towards the eastern edge, nearest to Temple Regis. His interest stretched from tin mines to corn mills to peat cutting and even granite blasting – for such a large and barren place as the moor, it was extraordinary how many different ways there were to earn a living from it. He'd even demanded, and got, a book on warrening, the mass farming of rabbits.

But he remained unimpressed with the raw material he was being fed. 'Look at these charts – crude, outdated, and frankly inaccurate,' he barked, waving a lanky finger at some ancient roll of papers Miss Greensleeves had unearthed after considerable effort. 'How can you possibly present a case – an important case – using erroneous data like this?' But he seemed more to be arguing with himself than complaining about the service the librarians provided.

Over by the desk the occasional last-minuter would wander in, returning books before they collected a penny-ha'penny fine, but nobody lingered over the shelves – they were far too busy preparing for the festive season. As each one entered there would come through the door a mournful sound offering a reminder of the approach of Christmas.

'There's old Wilf, left behind again,' said Miss Greenway to Miss Atherton. 'I'd better take him a cup.'

The noise, like a cow calling for her calf, also wafted through the high window and irritated Mr Sirraway no end, but it wasn't likely to cease any time soon – Old Wilf was a stalwart of the Salvation Army silver band, whose gentle harmonies stirred up the Christmas spirit in the marketplace and encouraged everyone to dip into their pockets.

Wilf was old and lame now, and could no longer wander through the town with his bandmates, so they would set him up on a chair outside the library with his euphonium and leave him to it. Somehow 'Away In A Manger' tootled through his silver tubes lacked joy and encouraged sorrow. You could get tired of it pretty quickly.

'Thank heavens,' sighed Mr Sirraway finally, pushing his plans and his books away from him. 'That's that done!'

'Have you finished, sir?'

The scholar leaned back in his chair, stretched his legs and put his hands behind his neck. 'Finished.'

'Is there anything else we can get you?'

'Nothing.'

'Cup of tea?'

'Nothing.'

'Well, I hope we've been of service.' Miss Greenway wouldn't have minded if her little library got a mention in the author's acknowledgements when Mr Sirraway's book came out, but was too shy to ask what its title would be.

'Well, I'll be wishing you a Happy Christmas, then. May I ask when your book will be published?'

'I don't think a fir tree covered in tinsel has a place in an establishment of learning,' replied Sirraway, and with that walked out. As he opened the door they got a blast of Wilf's 'Hark the Herald Angels Sing'. It sounded more like someone sitting on a whoopee cushion.

'He's left a carrier bag behind,' said Miss Greenway later, tidying up the desk and taking the books back to their shelves. It was all a bit of a let-down, it had been quite exciting having someone so – well, *academic* – about the place.

'Let him come back for it, the miserable so-and-so,' said Miss Atherton. 'I'm not chasing after him.'

Miss Greenway was unconvinced. Maybe, too, she was still thinking about that mention in the acknowledgements.

She picked up the carrier bag and put it on the desk. 'I'll just look and see if there's an address. Though you could tell he's not local.'

'Not with those manners.'

There was little to give away the identity of the man who had colonised their small world over the past four days. Because he was conducting research and not taking books away from the library, there was no requirement for him to provide a driving licence or similar. And all there was in the bag was a large notebook with no name inside and a folder containing a large number of press cuttings.

'Mostly about Sir Freddy Hungerford,' said Miss Greenway, leafing through them. 'Maybe he works for him. Oh, and look, quite a few on Mirabel Clifford.'

'The one who's going to take over from Sir Freddy?'

There'd been quite a lot in the *Riviera Express* about Mrs Clifford. The decision to field a female candidate in the forthcoming general election had been a controversial one, mainly because women were rarely allowed to stand in winnable parliamentary seats. There were plenty of no-hope constituencies where they could go and stand on a soapbox, if that was their thing.

But the Liberal candidate, Helena Copplestone, had made a huge impression on a populus that was growing tired of a self-congratulatory MP with a preference for the cigar and brandy to be found in his St James's club; and there were real fears that when he retired, the Liberal would win the seat.

'She's prettier,' Miss Atherton said one lunchtime. 'She'll win it.'

'It's a bit more complicated than that,' countered Miss Greenway, though with precious little authority to back up her argument, for she had never voted. 'Think of all the good things Mirabel Clifford has done for Temple Regis!'

'Well,' said Miss Atherton, who could take a bleak view when she wanted, 'I can tell you if there are three women contesting this seat, it'll be a fight to the death. The death!'

THREE

There was something faintly ridiculous about Terry when he put a hat on. Obviously he never looked at himself in the mirror or he wouldn't do it.

The item in question was a deerstalker and he was wearing it with the flaps down. Out in Widecombe it had caused little comment – moorland folk have no dress code and offer little in the way of advice to incomers – but back in the office it was greeted with hilarity.

''Ello, Sherlock!'

'Found your way back from the North Pole, Terry? Dog-sled drawn by the hounds of the Baskervilles?'

Shopping done, the newsroom had filled up again just ahead of opening time. Most would be taking their Christmas cheer with them down to the Fortescue Arms, and Betty promised she'd come to join them as soon as she'd got the Con Club drinks party out of the way.

'Don't wear that if you're coming with me,' she sniped at Terry. 'It looks daft.'

'You wouldn't say that if you'd just been where I've been,'

snipped the snapper. 'Three-foot drifts. Had to leave Judy behind – she's snowed in.'

Betty was unimpressed. She rarely left Temple Regis, whose Riviera climate seldom permitted snow to fall on its rooftops; indeed it would be fair to say she never willingly exposed herself to the wilder elements – a tropical umbrella in her cocktail was more her idea of wet-weather gear.

'Bet she could have got back if she wanted,' she sniffed, cross at having to deputise for Judy. 'Come on!'

They walked over to the Con Club in silence. Terry was marvelling at the new lens he'd bought for his Leica, which promised to do some amazing things with snowflakes – he couldn't wait to get into the darkroom to see how well it'd done. Betty meanwhile was thinking about Graham Platt, who'd chucked her last week, saying he was thinking of taking holy orders.

Holy orders! If the bishop only knew what Graham…

'Let's make this snappy,' said Terry. With Betty on a job, it was he who issued the orders; with Miss Dimont things were a bit different. '*Friday Night Is Music Night*'s on the wireless.'

'Not half,' she agreed, 'fifteen minutes, tops. Then home for your programme.'

She knew Terry had a tin ear and couldn't even whistle the national anthem in tune, so obviously there was a girl waiting. You knew very little about Terry's private life – altogether a Mystery, as Betty labelled them when they didn't make a pass.

'Got a date, Ter?'

'Over there,' he rapped, heading through the crowd to where the sitting Member of Parliament for Temple Regis was, indeed, sitting.

Around Sir Frederick Hungerford were gathered the simple and the sycophantic of his party workers; everyone else with any sense had herded round the bar. A small but polite audience, they sat with vacant looks on their faces as the parliamentarian recalled a wartime exploit by which he'd single-handedly cut short the conflict by at least five years.

The old boy was looking tired, but then who could blame him? There'd been the lengthy business of being introduced to a lot of people he didn't know because his visits to the constituency were so severely rationed, and the tiresome ritual of shaking everybody's hand. Despite this, he put on a good show – well-practised in the art of flattery, he would repeat their names as if drinking in their identity, and then offer a whispered word. They went away on Cloud Nine.

'Don't think we've seen you here since last year,' challenged Betty; she voted Labour when she could be bothered. 'Of course, under your government, rail fares have increased so much people can't afford to travel down to Temple Regis like they used to. I expect you have the same difficulty – affording it, I mean.'

'Come over here and sit down,' smarmed Sir Frederick, 'I do like a woman with an independent mind.' He reached out and tickled her knee. 'Featherstone, you say? Related to the Featherstonehaughs of Arundel, by any chance?' He knew how to patronise a person all right – he could tell by her shoes that Betty had gone to the local secondary.

'How does it feel to be giving your last party?' riposted Betty, notebook flapping and eyes blazing. 'And *don't* do that, Sir Frederick. If you don't mind.'

The old boy settled back and eyed her with amusement.

'Must be a relief to be retiring,' went on Betty. 'So many calls on your time in London, so many people to see. You missed the annual fête back in the summer, I recall – they had to get Sam Brough to make the speech. You were very much missed.'

Sir Frederick's eyes were on Betty's knees. 'I think you must play tennis rather well,' he smiled, as if this were a compliment.

'Are you making the speech tonight? Or will it be Mrs Clifford? We've only got a moment,' she said, nodding towards her photographer, 'then we're off on a real story.'

This was unlike Betty – sharp, rude, insubordinate – maybe she was hoping there'd be a complaint and she wouldn't have to cover politics any more. After all, they were still talking about what Judy Dimont said and did at the Annual Conservative Ball two years ago!

'Clifford?' pondered Sir Frederick. 'That name seems familiar. Could swear I've heard it before somewhere.'

Betty fell for it. 'She's your successor, Sir Frederick! You're retiring, she's the new candidate. A much-respected figure…'

The MP's gaze turned to scorn. It said, of course I know who the woman is, I'm not a complete idiot. But one does not, in the presence of an honourable Member who has served his community loyally, unflinchingly, tirelessly, for thirty years mention some pipsqueak piece of fluff who's only been selected because she has nice curly hair and wears a skirt.

FLASH! Terry got a nice one in, Sir Fred's face a death-mask tinged with contempt. Of course the editor wouldn't put it in the paper – no chance. But it would make a nice addition to the Thank Heavens! board, usually reserved for the photos of less attractive bridal couples (as in 'Thank Heavens they found each other – nobody else would have them').

A pretty girl wandered by, heading for the bar. 'Over here!' ordered the MP. 'Just the sort!' The girl smiled vaguely but walked on.

'Over *here*!' he repeated, louder. 'Sit down, put your arm round my shoulder, smile at the camera!' The girl blushed timidly and tried to say something, but the MP was edging forward in his seat and sticking a fiendish grin on his face. 'Want your picture in the paper, don't you, sweetie?' he said through his practised smile. 'Look at the camera now. Young adoring party worker looks up to her hero Member!'

His victim did not directly respond but said to Terry. 'I... I... shouldn't be here. Don't put my picture in the paper, please!'

'Why ever *not*!' roared Sir Frederick.

'I'm not one of your party workers,' she said, getting up. 'I work behind the bar. And I vote *Liberal*.'

Unabashed, the old boy managed to get a tickle to the back of her knees before she scooted away.

'We've got all we need,' said Terry, who always maintained a cheerful demeanour no matter the circumstances – good photographers never sulk on duty.

'Can't stay for the speech,' said Betty to Sir Freddy. 'But I'll write that our outgoing MP hasn't a clue who his successor will be.'

'No you won't,' replied Sir Frederick with confidence. 'I've got your editor's home number.'

Good, thought Betty. No more politics for me, then.

*

'So you see,' Mrs Phipps was drawing on a Player's Navy Cut and her quite astonishing memory, both at the same time, 'Eglantine's only ambition was to marry a moat.'

Miss Dimont shook her head slightly, as if to clear it. They were sitting in the coffee room after breakfast, and her old friend's endless flood of reminiscence gushed on like a mountain stream.

'She had a thing about castles – there were one or two in her family, you know – and she thought the only way to show you'd married well was if, when you went home, you were surrounded by a moat. Preferably with a drawbridge to pull up.

'So she did – marry a moat, that is. She collared Sir Jefrye Waterford, but little did she know that in the wink of an eye he'd lose the lot – too many wagers, too much *crème de menthe*. Too many popsies.'

And were you one of those, thought Judy, and would that have been *while* he was married to Eglantine? She changed the subject.

'You were going to tell me, last night, your royal story.'

'I wonder how that particular tale escaped,' said Mrs Phipps, her eye travelling around the room to check if the drinks waiter was out of bed yet. 'We got talking about other things, I suppose. You really are terribly good company, Judy, it's such a pleasure to have the time to chat.'

'Why don't you call me Hugue, Geraldine? My close friends do.'

'Hugue?'

'Short for Huguette. I stopped using it at school because they used to call me Huge – I wasn't! Well, just a *little* bit, and only then sometimes… Judy's really a work name.'

'Why didn't you tell me before?' asked Mrs Phipps. 'We've known each other for years.'

Because most of the time we're talking about you, and there never seems to be the opportunity, Miss Dimont thought, but not unkindly. Mrs Phipps' stories were worth a guinea a minute and anyway, she was an actress – and who else do actresses talk about but themselves?

'I like it,' opined Mrs Phipps. 'French, of course.'

'Actually Belgian. My father was a diamond merchant in Antwerp, though my mother's English. I grew up there until I was four but what with the war… we moved to England when my father was imprisoned by the Germans.'

'Did he escape?'

'No, he couldn't. He was treated very badly and was never quite the same again. I did a year or two at university but then I took over a lot of the business from him – travelling around Europe, buying and selling. The diamond business is like a club for men – they think you know nothing. As a result I was quite successful.'

'Good Lord,' said Mrs Phipps. 'Then you must be quite well off.'

'Well,' said Miss Dimont, reflecting. 'There's a nice house in the Essex marshes, and we still have a tiny home in Ellezelles – that's where we come from – but I'm very happy down here.' And a million miles away from my overbearing mother, she thought with relief.

'So you…?'

'Let's talk about you. You were going to tell me a royal story.'

'It's rather a long one.'

'That's all right, it's my Saturday off. I'll get the bus back to Temple Regis after lunch, if the snow allows. What's it all about?'

A petite breakfast waitress was clearing away the coffee things, and Mrs Phipps fixed her with a commanding gaze, borrowed from when she played Lady Bracknell in, oh, 1934, was it? The Adelphi. And wonderful reviews, naturally...

'Would you kindly bring me a large Plymouth gin?' she said. It didn't sound like a request. The girl blinked, looked at the clock over the mantelpiece and the lifting morning light through the window, then bobbed and moved away.

Just look at her, thought Miss Dimont. She's eighty but her eyes are clear, her voice is strong, she carries herself in a commanding manner, and she oozes charm. What an extraordinary woman!

'I was too tall for the Prince of Wales,' began Mrs Phipps. 'He could be quite charming but he was such a pipsqueak. And he bleated if he didn't get his way – very unattractive in a man, don't you know.

'We were at the Embassy Club – it's where we all used to go, everyone knew everyone, of course. And I could see he'd been eyeing me up. His popsy at the time was Thelma Furness, though she wasn't there that night.

'He sent someone over to ask me to dance, which really is *not* the way to go about things, but he *was* the future king so I suppose he could please himself. We both got up and moved towards the dance floor but the moment we met, you could tell it would be a humiliation for him – I was nearly a foot taller, or so it seemed. We managed to scrape around the floor but he was very unhappy – never liked people showing up how short he was.'

'Did you lead, or did he?' asked Miss Dimont mischievously.

'Ha! Ha! I will say this, he had the grace to ask me back to his table and that's when it all began.'

'What, exactly?'

'Well, there was a group there, possibly ten, can't remember them all but Prince George was there – you know, the Duke of Kent, the one killed in the war – and he had some American girl in tow. There was Diana Cooper and her husband, as well as Lord Dudley, Lord Sefton, a few others and this girl Pansy Westerham.'

Mrs Phipps looked around the room but so far there was no sign of the gin. She plunged on.

'Pansy and I hit it off immediately – she raised one eyebrow as if to say, who's your short friend? We both started laughing and that was it. She was wonderful company, didn't care a hoot about anybody or anything – big blue eyes, wonderful figure, and funny as all get-out. We had lunch the next day and we were best friends from the word go.

'She was having a fling with one of the men at that table but wouldn't say who – she said it was complicated. But she told me everything else, I even knew his inside-leg measurement, dear!

'After we'd known each other a few weeks she confessed there was someone else – someone she didn't even like but was drawn to, fascinated by – he sounded quite nasty, actually. We'd meet most nights at the Embassy and she'd tell me little bits and pieces but actually, darling, I was only half listening – that nightclub was the most dazzling place on earth. Everybody who was anybody was there, and slap bang in the middle of it all were the Prince of Wales and Prince George and their côterie. Your eyes were out on stalks and of course, you were on the *qui vive* – I was between husbands at the time and you never knew who might come over and ask you to dance.'

'Apart from the Prince of Wales.'

'Ha! We never danced again – but I did have a go with Prince George – a lovely dancer and very manly with it. But he *knew* it, my dear, always a bit of a put-off.'

'Not always.'

'No, not always.'

There was a pause as they pursued their separate, pleasurable thoughts.

'So,' said Miss Dimont after a moment or two, 'was it Pansy you wanted to talk to me about?'

'I was just coming to that,' said Mrs Phipps, beaming as the waitress slid into view with a glass on a silver salver. 'Won't you have one?' The question was rhetorical.

'After a bit Pansy got very down. It was man-trouble all right, you can always tell, but she didn't want to discuss it. She just looked very strained and talked about the weather, that sort of thing.

'Then one day she wasn't there – pouf! Disappeared like I don't know what. She had a little house off Knightsbridge, and I called round a couple of times but there was never an answer. I telephoned, left messages, but nothing.

'I wondered if she'd run away with her bad man, but gossip soon got around our circle and nobody that we knew had left their wife, or absconded, done a bunk, so we were up a gumtree.'

'I think I know what's coming,' said Miss Dimont, leaning forward with interest.

'I expect you do, dear, what with your background in sleuthing. Anyway, they found her a fortnight later – dead in the street. She'd fallen from the top of her house – just behind Harrods, you know – and it was all very distressing. It turned out she had a husband who loved her dearly, she never told me about *him,* who lived in Paris. And there was a child she never mentioned either.'

'Sounds like you never knew her after all.'

'You're right, of course. Later I discovered she developed pashes on people but after a bit got bored and moved on. When I thought about it afterwards, I realised she must have been running away in her mind from something – the abandoned husband and child, I suppose. And what she wanted to do was to live inside other people's worlds. She wanted to open the door and take refuge in your house, as it were. She was delightful company, adorable, but all it covered up was unhappiness.'

'You think she killed herself?'

'Well, people took quite a lot of drugs back then – not like today, dear.' Mrs Phipps looked ruminatively into her gin glass. 'Morphine and cocaine and so on. Quite a lot of people killed themselves back then – but no.

'No, that's why I wanted to talk to you about her, Huguette – shall I call you that? I think she was murdered, and something inside me – even thirty years later – wants to find out what exactly happened.'

There were tears in her eyes. 'Will you help me? Do you think you could get to the bottom of it? Find out the truth?'

'Geraldine, think about it – how could I find anything out after all these years? There's been a world war, an atom bomb, who knows what.'

'But my dear, you're so clever! All those things you've seen and done!'

Judy Dimont got up. 'After all this time?' she repeated, gathering up her raffia bag. 'Geraldine, I would love to, but there's not a chance. Too much water under the bridge.'

The old woman looked forlornly into her gin.

'But now you've told me, I won't be able to think about anything else.'

FOUR

Monday morning was always unnerving at the *Riviera Express*. The weekend had gone by in a flash, and now there were only four days left to press day. An ancient accounts book, importantly renamed 'the diary', sat on a rickety table outside the editor's office and its entries were a strong indicator of the excitements ahead for the newspaper's readers on Friday.

MONDAY   Townswomen's Guild rededication
              TR rent Tribunal
              Bell-ringers' AGM, St Margaret's
TUESDAY   Mag Court
              Highways Committee
              Rural District Council
WEDNESDAY
THURSDAY   Mag Court
              Mothers Union jumble sale
              Lifeboat lift-out

The blank space against Wednesday was not unusual – it was early closing day and probably for that reason alone the world came to a halt in Temple Regis. Maybe it was the day people stayed at home for *Ray's A Laugh* on the wireless, but whatever the reason, it was unnerving to see how little news there was to harvest in the coming days – hence the nervous 11 a.m. weekly assembly over which the editor, Rudyard Rhys, grumpily presided.

His room was crowded with the flotsam and jetsam which staffed the editorial departments of local newspapers everywhere – retired servicemen, young hopefuls, failed theatricals like Ray Bennett, the arts editor, and people into whose background it was as well not to inquire too closely. They were a shifting community with little in common outside a good shorthand note.

One recent addition stood out a little uncomfortably. David Renishaw had appeared out of nowhere with an impressive sheaf of cuttings, an urgent self-confidence, impeccable manners, and the apparent capacity to oil his way through locked doors. As journalists went, he was a cut above.

Miss Dimont took against him in an instant.

'Too good to be true,' she said to her friend Auriol as they'd walked back from church the previous day. 'He's handsome, accomplished, go-getting – I don't understand what he's doing in Temple Regis when he should be in Fleet Street.'

'Woman trouble,' judged Auriol shrewdly.

'Apparently there's a wife in Canada. She's going to join him once he's settled in.'

'We'll see. How long's he been here?'

'Three weeks.'

'Going home for Christmas?'

'Can't afford it.'

'There, I told you.'

Miss Dimont ignored this. 'He's volunteered to do the Christmas rounds.' These entailed the reporter visiting the resort's hospital and hostel and nursing homes, then returning to the office to paint a rosy Yuletide picture of those less fortunate than himself. Normally Ray Bennett, lonely confirmed bachelor, did the job with loud moans of self-sacrifice, but he'd been ousted by Renishaw and was very upset about it. This Christmas he would have nothing to complain about.

Renishaw was sitting next to John Ross in the editor's office, with Peter Pomeroy as usual serving up the tea. There was a gaggle of other reporters, including one or two from the district offices, as well as Judy and Betty, until the room was full to the brim with journalistic talent. Why, then, with so many people, was it so difficult to fill the paper each week?

'What have you got, Judy?' Mr Rhys was in typically gangrenous form.

'Caring volunteers,' she said, absently – she was thinking about the long-dead Pansy Westerham.

'Rr… rrr.' The growl coming from behind the editor's whiskers indicating disapproval, disappointment, disbelief at so feeble an offering. It was no different to any Monday – if the town hall had burned down and His Worshipful had been caught halfway up the flagpole in his longjohns, it would have drawn the same reaction. If Brigitte Bardot had blown in and landed a kiss on Rudyard's cheek with the news she was moving to Temple Regis, it would have been no different. Nothing was ever good enough for the editor.

'Caring volunteers crisis,' Judy soldiered on, though she could tell he wasn't listening. 'This round of flu has meant that there's nobody fit enough, or free enough of germs, to visit those who need calling on over the Christmas period.'

'A wee job there for Ray, then,' said John Ross acidly, out of the corner of his mouth. 'He's been bellyachin' ever since you gave the Christmas calls to young Renishaw here.' He approved of the new arrival, whose copy came perfectly typed with no mistakes and an extra carbon included, just in case.

'OK,' agreed the editor. If he'd said the other thing there'd be nothing in the paper. 'Betty?'

Betty was doing a crossword and didn't realise immediately it was her turn. Judy gave her a nudge.

'Hairdressing night,' she said finally.

Everyone groaned.

'All the hairdressers are doing late-night opening so everyone can get their perms done for Christmas. I thought I could get mine done this week – picture story – help drum up trade.'

There was the traditional rustling of notebooks which accompanied stinkers like this, a vicious indicator that buried somewhere in their scribbled pages they had a better idea. But the editor nodded and the moment passed. 'Mr Renishaw?'

Miss Dimont looked up from her notebook and watched the newcomer's profile as he started to speak. His words came without hesitation in a low, urgent murmur and with no recourse to notes.

'I've been speaking to a member of the Chamber of Commerce,' he said. 'They're thinking of charging an entry fee to holidaymakers coming into Temple Regis – thruppence in the box at Regis Junction when you get out of the train, or one per cent on the bill in the hotels and guesthouses. He reckons that in three years it will have generated enough income to build a bridge from Todhempstead Sands out to Nether Island – which would then generate even more income from toll charges. It will bring a massive new wealth to Temple Regis *and* steal a march on Torquay and Paignton and all the others.'

You could have heard a pin drop. This was actually a very good story, brought in by a reporter who'd been here so little time he'd hadn't yet had the opportunity to find the Oddfellows' Hall. How on earth had he pulled it off?

'Rr… rrr,' rumbled Rudyard Rhys, 'first I've heard of it.' He usually got all the best stories down at the Con Club at lunch on Fridays, *after* the paper had been published. 'Who told you that?'

'Confidential source,' said Renishaw. This was not a phrase you ever heard at the *Express* – Temple Regis being the kind of town where everybody knew everybody else's business. And how had this newcomer, in so short a space of time, managed to find a contact prepared to confide a piece of information which could radically alter the town's fortunes and set it apart from its rivals on the English Riviera?

It beggared belief.

'So… are you saying people will be forced to *pay* to be allowed into Temple Regis?'

'That's about it,' replied Renishaw. He didn't seem to think it that peculiar.

'I can't think of another place in Britain that does that.'

'My source is an innovator, thinks differently from the rest of us. Says the town needs shaking up, or it's going to lose its custom to the bigger resorts. Look at what Teignmouth has been doing recently!'

'But – it's like paying to go into a shop!' said Peter Pomeroy scornfully. 'Who'd want to do that?'

Others in the conference, perhaps less forward-thinking, nodded in agreement. But Renishaw was unruffled: 'You all agree Temple Regis is the prettiest resort in Devon. Now's the time to test that theory. If people really *do* want to come here, what's an extra thruppence?'

There was a silence which could only be described as hostile.

'Very well,' said the editor, and just for a moment a wintry smile broke out on his bewhiskered face. Persuading young Renishaw to join the *Express* was the best thing he'd done in years. His choice, his decision, his triumph!

'See,' he crowed, turning to the bunch of deadbeats he'd also employed over the years, 'see how it's done? All you have to do is put yourselves out there, make your contacts, and they come running to you with their best stories. That's journalism for you!'

'Have you noticed that he has a bit of hair that springs up on the back of his head?' whispered Betty to Judy. 'It could do with a bit of smoothing down and I bet if he let me I could—'

'Married,' reminded Judy.

That shut Betty up. She had Certain Rules – though they didn't prevent her looking.

'How old is he, d'you think?'

'Mid-thirties. Still married, Betty.'

The news conference trundled on, with a depressing amount of time devoted to the fortunes of Regis Rangers, the local football team, and Plymouth Argyle, nearby giants of the turf. Betty went back to her crossword and Judy briefly focused her attention on the rogue curl on the back of David Renishaw's head.

She wasn't thinking about him, however – she'd already formed certain conclusions about this genius in their midst – she was thinking about Pansy Westerham.

'You wouldn't believe it,' Terry was saying, shaking his head in disbelief.

They were in the Minor, the only editorial vehicle the *Riviera Express* possessed. Mostly if you were a reporter you had to catch the bus or use Shanks's pony, though Miss Dimont was something of a legend in Temple Regis the way she manoeuvred Herbert, her trusty moped, around the town.

For a time she'd enjoyed the novelty of young reporter Valentine Waterford's tinny red bubble car – indeed, enjoyed the novelty of Valentine himself – but local newspapers have the careless habit of losing those most talented or attractive and one day he'd gone, never to be heard of again.

There was always Terry, though. He had a strong, sturdy profile, an enviable work ethic, an agile mind and a lust for perfection. He could also burble on about the most dreary topics, and his taste in clothes – witness the deerstalker – was nothing short of a crying shame.

'D'you know he spent forty years photographing snow-flakes,' droned Terry. 'The pictures are incredible – specially when you consider they were taken using a plate camera attached to a microscope.' They were off to the cottage hospital to see what they could work up on the Caring Volunteers crisis.

'Mm,' responded Miss Dimont, the sound from her closed lips a dipthong of apparent interest and barely concealed boredom. She was careful never to encourage him.

'The only way he could capture them – this is the 1890s, Judy – was by catching the flakes on a piece of black velvet. Wilson Bentley – what a genius! That's why I got the new filter for the Leica and, Judy, while you were holed up with that old biddy in Wistman's Hotel I managed to capture a few.'

'Oh?' A fleeting moment of interest.

'Didn't really work – too much sunlight. You see, when you photograph snow there are no shadows...' and on he rambled. Judy looked out of the window as they climbed the hill and came down the other side to Ruggleswick, where the cottage hospital was to be found.

At the lookout point halfway down the hill, Terry stopped the Minor and switched off the engine. He quite often did this when they came out this way, just to stare in amazement at the view. For Terry, the shifting light on the water was a technical challenge never to be mastered, and this morning's brilliant sunshine, despite the proximity of Christmas, threw up extra hurdles.

For Miss Dimont the seascape recalled memories and moments, captured like flowers pressed into a book, forgotten, only to be rediscovered by chance. The inexorable roll of the waves diminished life's hurts and filled one's heart with new hope. There would come a moment, when the sun shone on water on a winter's day like this, when she would forget about Eric Hedley. But not quite yet.

'This chap Renishaw,' said Terry, breaking into her thoughts. ''E's good.'

Miss Dimont swivelled her head round to look at the photographer. 'You think so?'

'We went out last week and I've never seen anyone work so fast. Brilliant. 'E won't last long at the *Express,* far too good for the likes of us.'

Judy took this personally. She had a sharp eye for a story and was – until Mr Renishaw appeared – the best interviewer in the West Country. She could create a story out of a handful of dust.

'Did he tell you what he's doing down here, sharing that towering talent with us lesser mortals?'

'Something about wanting a change. I think he worked in Fleet Street for a bit. Or maybe he was on one of the nationals in Canada. A bit vague. We spent most of the time talking about ballroom dancing.'

'What would you know about *that,*' snapped Judy, memories of bruised toes flooding back.

'You'd be surprised.'

'Coffee?' They often brought a Thermos on trips away from the office – it was nice, once you were out, to stay out.

'I wanted to ask you something – but Terry, don't go all technical on me. Just a simple answer.' She poured the coffee into two tin mugs and the Minor's windows started to steam up. Glimpsing the silhouette of their heads together, a passer-by might think they were lovers.

'What?'

'I'd like to find some photographs of a woman who died, oh, thirty years ago. She was a socialite, very glamorous, but

45

only appeared on the scene for a very short time before she fell off a roof and was killed.'

Terry looked at her keenly. 'Killed? D'you mean murdered?'

'I have no idea. But yes, it could be. On the other hand she may just have been depressed, or taken drugs – I don't know. But I want to know more about her, and to do that I need to see what she looked like.'

'Socialite, you say?'

'Yes.'

'Two places you go, then. The *Illustrated London News* has the best society picture library. Failing that, the Press Association. Or possibly *Tatler*.'

'I thought of that – but how do you ask?'

'Leave it to me. Hadn't we better get on?'

They rolled down the hill into Ruggleswick, parked outside the cottage hospital and were greeted by the Matron, Miss Stanway.

What followed was standard fare for the *Express* and any other local newspaper – a sad tale of the current flu epidemic leaving the town shorn of its crop of volunteers who traditionally swarmed in around Christmas to cheer up the lonely or those abandoned by their families.

In forthright tones Miss Stanway issued the plea that those more comfortably placed in the community might put their seasonal priorities to one side and step forward to fill the gap, while Miss Dimont's flawless shorthand took down every word. Terry took a picture of Matron standing in her hospital ward, and managed to capture the poignancy of the story by snapping her with a shaft of light behind her left shoulder, pouring down onto a bed whose occupant had turned her head away, as if in despair.

It's what made Terry brilliant. He may not be able to do *The Times* crossword and heaven knows when he last opened a book. His love of music was eccentric, and as for his dancing! It infuriated Miss Dimont that someone who wandered through life so immune to its glories could come up with the perfect picture to illustrate her story. How *did* he manage it?

When they came outside the sun had gone. The seascape had turned grey and nightfall was marching rapidly towards them, even though it was not yet four o'clock. A flock of seagulls suddenly took an interest and circled overhead, noisily beseeching these two isolated human beings to eat something and leave behind the remains.

Miss Dimont felt unnerved by how close they dared to come and rapidly got back in the Minor. Terry stopped to take a shot of them, but when he got in the car started complaining he'd got his stop wrong, or something. When he'd finished whinnying Miss Dimont asked if he'd drive her over to Bedlington.

'Not going back to the office to type it up? That's not like you, Judy.'

'My uncle's staying with Auriol. We're all going to have a not-so-nice evening together.'

'Isn't he staying with you?'

'He doesn't like cats.' Mulligatawny would have to do without her tonight.

'Why not-so-nice?' Terry was full of questions today.

'Because he's doing his best – yet again – to get my mother and I together in the same room.'

Terry knew a lot about the redoubtable Madame Dimont, who despite her English birth still insisted on being addressed that way, supporting her demand with a flimsy Belgian accent. Ever since her arrival at the *Riviera Express* Judy had filled empty conversational moments in the Minor regaling Terry with the Madame's awfulness and the avalanche of reproving letters with which Grace Dimont bombarded her only child.

'She's coming for Christmas,' she confessed. 'Staying at the Grand. Won't stay with me because there's no room service and no flock of adoring servants. She hates cats, too, just like Arthur – between them they must have had a sadly deprived childhood.'

'But you'll give her Christmas lunch at your house?'

'That's what we're going to discuss. How to make the best of a bad job. You don't want to come and join the party on Christmas Day, Terry?' For a moment she looked almost vulnerable.

'Not ruddy likely,' said Terry, starting up the motor. 'How long is it since you saw her? Your mother?'

'Oh…' answered Miss Dimont looking out of the window, not wanting to think about it anymore. 'Look, those seagulls are following us.'

'Nothin' better to do.'

'Get a move on, then!' She didn't like the way they tracked the car's progress, like enemy bombers.

'I'll talk to some mates when I get back to the office,' said Terry, sensing her alarm, changing the subject. 'See if we can find some pics of that woman you was interested in. What's her name by the way?'

'Pansy Westerham.'

'Say again?'

'Pansy Westerham.'

'That's odd,' said Terry. 'That's the very name David Renishaw mentioned in this car the other day. There can't be two of them, surely?'

'*What?* Can you say that again Terry? Very slowly?'

FIVE

In the Palm Court of the Grand Hotel, two men sat looking distantly at each other. Frank Topham perched uncomfortably in a small chair with bamboo legs, balancing a cup of tea on his bony knees, while opposite sat the small but cocky figure of Rex Inkpen.

'I really can't do anything to help,' the policeman said.

'My newspaper would be very grateful to you. Cover your expenses, kind of thing.'

Inspector Topham looked blankly at him. 'I didn't hear that,' he said. 'And I think now if you'll excuse me...' and he started to get to his feet.

The one thing to be said about the old copper was that he was incorruptible. It wasn't the first time Fleet Street had promised to buy him a nice holiday or a small boat – heaven knows, when Gerald Hennessy was murdered, he could have retired on the promises made by the visiting press corps!

An old soldier with a distinguished war record, Topham knew the law and believed in it. It's just that he wasn't very good at viewing it from the other end of the telescope – the view adopted by the criminals, large and small, who occasionally wafted through Temple Regis.

He sat there in his shiny shoes with his brilliantined hair looking very much as he was – an upright, honest, decent fellow with insufficient guile to see life the way criminals did. It made him a wonderful fellow but a poor detective.

Rex Inkpen, chief crime reporter for the *News Chronicle*, was probably a better sleuth, though as a human being, less upright. Behind his wire-framed spectacles lurked a devious mind only partially camouflaged by his earnest look and feigned diffidence.

Inspector Topham's visits to the Grand were usually confined to the private bar, where he could consume a pint of Portlemouth without being bothered, but it was his duty to see what the national press were getting up to when they swung into town, and so here he sat with his cup of tea and a plate of biscuits.

Only now he was on his feet. He was too old to be bribed!

'Sit down, sit down... sorry, I think you must have misunderstood,' said Inkpen smoothly. 'It's just that many of your fellow policemen feel... undervalued, as you might say. All those hours they put in, all the danger, all the anxiety if they don't get things right. It's nice when someone outside the Force values what they do – and that's all that the *Chronicle*'s trying to do, Frank.'

The detective did not like being addressed by his first name, but had the good manners to sit down again.

'Look,' Topham explained, 'we have enough trouble from the local press. They dog my footsteps' – he was thinking of one in particular – 'and pass judgement on my results.

Ill-informed judgement which puts up the backs of the general public.' *And* the Chief Constable, too.

'Honestly,' said Inkpen, a word he misused often, 'Frank, it's a way of saying thank you. We come down here and write a feature spread about you – about how this sleepy little resort has a disproportionate number of crimes, and yet you have a fantastic success rate in clearing things up.'

It's Christmas, thought Inkpen, when all right-minded criminals go on holiday. There's nothing for me to write about, and my editor gets very angry if he sees me with my feet on the desk telephoning my girlfriend at the company's expense – so please say yes, or I'll get put on general duties.

Say yes, and I can spend a week at the Grand, buying you drinks and telling you what a nice fellow you are – and at the end of it I'll make you a hero and at the same time make enough profit on my expenses to pay for the Christmas presents.

'Well, maybe,' said Topham, who hated the idea but had been getting grief recently from the Chief Constable about the size of his department. 'But you do understand, Mr Inkpen, you may not pay me a brass farthing. You can make a contribution to the Widows and Orphans Fund.'

'I assure you it'll be a generous one,' lied Inkpen. 'And thank you.'

He picked up his notebook. 'So, just to get started I want to talk to you about the Patrikis case. Then that double murder involving the beat group, and of course the tragic death of Gerald Hennessy – what a fine actor he was, too!'

'It was his widow I felt sorry for,' said Topham, relaxing. He had a soft spot for Prudence Aubrey, the widow, and it wasn't just because she knew his old commanding officer.

'Our greatest screen actor,' purred Inkpen. He'd got the old boy going now.

'Mm.'

'But let's start with the Patrikis case. Extraordinary to have a woman shot dead in a holiday camp. A mystery woman too – no clues – how did you unravel that one?'

Suddenly Topham was on his feet again. He could see where this was going, and the prospect did not please. Each of the cases Inkpen mentioned had been solved – not by him, but by the infuriating Miss Dimont and her ragbag collection of followers. Any further discussion of these famous cases could only draw attention to that.

'Look Mr... er... Inkpen,' he said. 'I'd better just check with the Chief Constable that he approves of the nation's attention being drawn to the, er... *unusual* level of capital crime in Temple Regis. Maybe we can talk later today, or tomorrow...'

'That's absolutely fine,' smiled Inkpen. 'I fancy a stroll along the front before tea. I'll drop into your office tomorrow morning.'

And if I'm not there, it'll be because of the *unusual* level of crime I have to attend to, thought Topham. This was a terrible idea and I don't know why I agreed to meet you in the first place. After all, and to put it bluntly, you're a journalist.

Both men picked up their hats.

'Just one thing,' said Inkpen. 'Have you had any calls from Interpol in the past couple of weeks?'

The Inspector didn't like to admit he'd *never* had a call from Interpol, and only knew of their existence by reading Inspector Maigret.

'There's something going on which might affect your manor,' said Inkpen conspiratorially.

'Is *that* why you're here? Not for this so-called heartwarming feature on Temple Regis and its fearless detectives?'

'Oh – no, no, no!' laughed Inkpen, fluttering his notebook as though a dead moth might drop out. 'Not at all, Inspector, I assure you – I'm here to write a wonderful piece about your great successes.'

Since when did a Sunday newspaper write anything nice about anybody? thought the copper, and jammed his trilby on his head.

'So, Interpol?'

'If we have, it's a police matter,' replied Topham gruffly, and marched off down the hotel's thickly carpeted corridor.

His polished boots did not take him far. As Inkpen sloped off towards the front door and the bracing sea air, Topham made a sharp left wheel into the private bar.

'Afternoon, Sid.'

'You're a bit early, Frank, it's only half past four. I'm not supposed to be serving for another hour.'

'Call it a leftover from lunch,' said Topham, ever practical. 'Have you had any press men in here in the last couple of days?'

'I bleedin' wish they would,' said Sid, reaching for Topham's pewter tankard. 'Things are a bit quiet.'

'Well, get yourself ready, I have the feeling we're in for a visit.'

At this, Sid brightened. When something juicy happened in Temple Regis – which, to be honest, was quite often – Fleet Street's finest would roll into his hotel, take over the bars and the restaurant, and spend money like it was going out of fashion.

'What is it this time?' said Sid, levelling off the Portlemouth and handing it to his old comrade.

'Murderer on the loose, an Interpol special. Complicated story.'

'He's here in Temple Regis?'

'Could be. Could be staying in the hotel. Keep your eyes peeled.'

'Come on, Frank, you're joking me! A murderer, here?'

'I think it's a wild goose chase, Sid. Chap from the *News Chronicle* with nothing better to do with his expenses sheet than get away from the office and loll around here for a few days. *He could be in Cornwall*, he says to me. Could be in Timbuktu, Sid!'

'Yers.'

'Even offered me money.'

'They're all bent,' replied Sid disloyally, for Fleet Street's finest had boosted his takings to record levels in the past couple of years.

'Yes – but that's not what he wants. He's looking for something else.'

'Yers.'

And I wish I knew what the hell it was.

The crisis meeting over the arrival of Mme Grace Dimont hadn't gone well. Auriol Hedley had made a delicious supper of chicken fricassée, Uncle Arthur had brought in some exceptionally fine wine. Both were looking forward to the arrival of Judy, whom they loved dearly, but it was all a bit of a disaster.

Grumpy, evasive, unco-operative, the reporter was at her very worst. She arrived in a rainstorm and spent a disproportionate amount of time drying her hair and shaking out her mackintosh. She knew what was coming.

'Here's your Whisky Mac,' said Auriol, all too aware what these signals meant.

'Why you live all the way out here by the dockside I really don't know,' grumbled her old friend. 'If you lived in town it'd be so much drier. So much more *convenient*.'

She's looking for a fight, thought Auriol. 'Let's get this over with, then we can relax. Christmas – with your mother.'

The rest of the evening went badly. Auriol heard Judy's arguments, but using the superior firepower of a brain which had launched a dozen successful wartime sorties, outgunned her friend's objections. Arthur, under the thumb of his sister, pleaded her case with eloquence.

'This is an ambush,' said Judy after an hour. 'No point in my saying no – you can't hear me! Why not just let sleeping dogs lie? You know that if she comes down here she'll only find fault, it's in her nature!'

And so the arguments swirled: the widow, grieving the loss of her only child against the grown woman, still treated like a child. The old lady, alone in the wastes of East Anglia, versus the younger woman liberated by the freedom that only the English Riviera – and a distance of two hundred and fifty miles – could provide. Irritation pitted against deep contentment.

Next morning, with Judy back at work, Auriol and Arthur faced each other over a late breakfast.

'It's not going to work. They'll be at each other's throats from the get-go.'

'Oh, I don't know, old thing,' said Arthur, ever the peace-maker. 'Give 'em time and a nice Christmas lunch and I'm sure all will be well.'

'Don't you see? That's just when things turn turtle – a heavy meal, several glasses of wine, and out come the recriminations!'

'Six of one and half a dozen of the other,' sighed Arthur. He looked wonderfully elegant in his brogues and flannels.

'What she said last night about her mother! Really doesn't bear repeating!'

'You have to remember, her father locked up in a German prison camp, Grace still a young girl struggling to bring up her small child *and* everything else! She did her best – she just found it easier to order every aspect of Hugue's life rather than allow her to make choices. And as a formula it worked so well she never saw any reason to change it.'

'Those letters she sends her – nothing short of harassment!'

'She's getting old,' said Arthur, smiling lazily, 'we're all getting old. She wants Hugue back at home, looking after the place. After all, what's to be done with it when Grace goes?'

Auriol took off her apron and smoothed back her fine black hair. 'Arthur, she's fifty. Young enough to enjoy a long life ahead, old enough to know what she wants to do with it. She loves it here in Temple Regis and doesn't want any more – she's got her job, her cottage, her cat and that pestilential moped Herbert.'

'No husband, though.'

'Neither have I, Arthur – do I look the worse for it?'

'My dear, the very opposite – if I were young again! But Huguette...'

'Still loves my brother. Hero-worships him, even though he was a bit of a fool. Too devil-may-care, too Johnny-head-in-the air.'

'She's had her admirers.'

'We all have, Arthur, our lives are what we choose them to be.'

The old boy looked at his hostess and smiled. If ever there was a woman in her prime it was Auriol – she was secretive about her life, but can never have been short of admirers.

'So then, Grace,' he said. 'What are we to do?'

'Christmas at the Grand,' said Auriol firmly. 'Then if there's the need to escape, it can be done.'

'Very well then,' said Arthur, 'and now I'm going to see a man about a dog. Back this evening.'

'Glad you said that, I have work to do. Have a lovely day, Arthur!'

SIX

Betty hated it when Judy found an excuse to skip Magistrates Court. The chief reporter's shorthand was better, her concentration sharper, her ability to sift the contents of grey interminable proceedings and find a nugget of interest somewhere in the debris, all seemed so effortless. But for Betty, it was a penance.

Every Tuesday and Thursday since time immemorial, the duty reporter from the *Express* put on hat and coat and trudged across Fore Street and round the corner to the pretty redbrick Edwardian building, adorned with its nicely stained glass and rash of oak panelling – the same old journey, taken so often, you wondered why there wasn't a groove in the pavement.

But this moment of freedom – the joy of exercise and window-shopping and bumping into friends and acquaintances – was cut short once you entered the building. There, slumped in the featureless front hall, was the menu of the day: a collection of drunks, petty thieves and nuisances – men too free with their fists and women too free with their wares (though the *Express* studiously ignored the latter, however fruity the case). Their misdeeds would be judged and, if only Betty could stay awake, reported in print next Friday.

The editor, Mr Rhys, had a difficult battle on his hands. Often a story of great national interest would emerge from these proceedings, but any article which suggested in some way that Temple Regis had lost its moral compass was instantly strangled to death, consigned to an obscure corner of the *Express* somewhere below the gardening column.

This led some, his staff included, to protest that Rudyard Rhys had no right to call himself a journalist, and should have stuck to his previous career as a failed novelist. But in fairness to the bewhiskered old procrastinator, he was subject to the desire of the city fathers and especially their sovereign, the Mayor Sam Brough, to keep things clean. This was a view shared by his proprietor, who owned a lot of property in Temple Regis and didn't wish to see its value fall through injurious headlines. If men fought in the streets, if ladies of the night beckoned you into the murky depths of Bosun's Alley, these were matters for municipal self-regulation – not national fascination.

It made life difficult for Miss Dimont who, since her arrival fresh from secret Cold War duties a few years back, had seen journalism as a refreshing way of shedding light on a community, good or bad. In Temple Regis there'd been a number of questionable deaths – but the Coroner, Dr Rudkin, often managed to pass these off as 'accidental'. He too believed in the Temple Regis idyll.

In court, however, justice still had to be done – and seen to be done. Since the departure of the Hon Mrs Marchbank and her habit of detaining anyone with so much as a nasty look on their face, the magistrates' bench had behaved itself pretty well. But a dreary long day in their presence was not dissimilar to a jail sentence, and Betty sat down on the reporters' bench with a desolate thump.

The door behind the bench burst open and Mr Thurlestone, the magistrates' clerk, issued his clarion call, 'Be upstanding!' as he swished down to his desk, all black gown and tabs and disreputable wig.

In filed a bewildered-looking couple of Worships who should surely be spending their days in a rest home, and the chief magistrate, Colonel de Saumaurez, who at least looked as though he knew which day of the week it was.

Proceedings got under way with the usual squabbles between publicans who wanted to extend their licensing hours and the magistrates, who didn't go to pubs but drank wine in their dining rooms at home. To them, the idea of a man putting a glass to his lips after 10.30 p.m. was a crime in itself.

Then it was onto the main course.

'Call Hector Sirraway.'

A tall white-haired man was led up the steps from the cells and entered the dock.

'Are you Hector Ransome Sirraway?'

'I am.'

'Hector Sirraway, you are charged that on the night of the twelfth of December you did cause a public nuisance in Harberton Square. You are further charged that in resisting arrest you assaulted a police officer. How do you plead?'

'Not guilty.'

'Sit down. Sergeant?'

The comfortably proportioned Sergeant Stanbridge rose to his feet and prepared to deliver a damning indictment of Mr Sirraway's inexcusable behaviour.

'Did the constable get his helmet back?' asked Colonel de Saumarez, fatally disclosing prior knowledge of the case. Nobody took a blind bit of notice.

'I believe so, Your Worship,' said Stanbridge, nodding.

'Very well. Proceed.'

'Your Worships, this is a simple case. On the night in question, the accused took up position outside the Conservative Association building in Harberton Square on the occasion of Sir Frederick Hungerford's annual Christmas party. As guests arrived, he began shouting and carrying on and despite a polite request to pipe down, he took no notice and shouted even louder.

'Police Constable Staverton arrived at the scene and warned the accused that he would be causing a public order offence if he did not immediately stop. That's when the accused knocked off his helmet.'

The magistrates were still sufficiently awake to smile at this.

'The accused was arrested and bailed to appear today before Your Worships.'

Colonel de Saumaurez eyed the man in the dock. He did not look like the usual sort of ruffian the town had to put up with.

'Mr Sirraway, you have pleaded not guilty to these charges. What have you to say?'

'I have a statement to make to the court.'

'No, no!' barked Thurlestone, the magistrates' clerk. 'No statement! You are being given an opportunity to speak in your own defence. Do, I pray, stick to that!'

Sirraway stared at the clerk's ancient wig and, unblinking, pulled out a piece of paper from his pocket.

'As I was saying,' he continued firmly.

'No, no, *no*! No statement!'

'Your Worships, last night I spent a good hour checking the position with *Stone's Justices Manual*, and I am within my rights, in responding to the clerk's question, to make a statement.'

Mr Thurlestone did not like this one bit.

'On the night in question it is true I stood outside the Conservative Hall in order to make a peaceful protest. I alerted the party faithful entering the building that their Member of Parliament is guilty of a number of illegal acts which...'

'No, no, *no*!' shouted an infuriated Thurleston, the wig on his head waggling. 'You can't say anything like that!'

'Court privilege,' said Sirraway, reaching for a handkerchief to wipe his nose. He'd certainly done his homework.

'I really don't think we need...' said the Colonel, who'd had dinner with Sir Freddy only the other week.

'...guilty of a number of malfeasances inconsistent with the public office he has held for the past forty years. In simple terms I pointed out to the party workers that their MP was a crook, is a crook, has always been a crook.'

'That's enough!' snapped de Saumaurez. 'I'm ordering you to put that piece of paper away! Anything else to say?'

'It's jolly easy to knock a copper's hat off his napper. Have you ever tried, Your Worship?'

The chief magistrate growled through gritted teeth. 'Anything known?'

'Nothing, sir,' said Sergeant Stanbridge.

'Fined ten shillings. Bound over to keep the peace – and I mean that, Mr Sirraway, keep the peace – for a year.'

'It's *Professor* Sirraway,' warbled the man joyously over his shoulder as he was bundled away.

Such a moment is always a testing time for the reporter. Your duty is both to cover the rest of the court proceedings, but also to chase up anything that could make a bigger story which might shine its light from under the hedge clippings of the gardening column. An impossible dilemma for Betty when, as on this occasion, there was no other reporter in court. Should she go out and chase the professor, if that's what he was, and lose the next three cases while she interviewed him and called the office to get a photographer round, or should she carry on drooping over her notebook, inspecting her split ends and waiting for the endless day to be over?

Boldly, she decided on action. Gathering up her things she made for the door under the furious gaze of Mr Thurlestone, who knew his proceedings had been abandoned by the Fourth Estate and that whatever secrets the man Sirraway had been prevented from airing by the Colonel would now go before a greater court, that of public opinion.

'Just a moment!' called Betty as she emerged into the front hall. Sirraway was making a quick-march out of the building. 'Mr... er... *Professor...*!'

'Can I help?' The man who'd been so beastly about the Christmas tree in the public library seemed perfectly charming, if more than a little odd.

'Betty Featherstone, *Riviera Express*. I was there at the Conservative Hall the other night. I didn't see you, though.'

'You arrived at approximately 5.39 p.m.,' said the Prof. 'With a photographer.'

'Yes, yes I did. But I didn't...'

'I thought I recognised you while I was in the dock,' he went on. 'But I wasn't sure. You've changed your hair.'

'Oh,' blushed Betty, 'd'you like it?'

The professor did not say. Instead he explained that he started his protest almost as soon as Betty entered the building, then went on until about 6 p.m., by which time his throat was hoarse, his wrists were bound, and a police constable was chasing his helmet down the gutter.

'It gave me time enough to let the party faithful know the worst.'

'And what is it they need to know?' She had her notebook out and nodded with her head to a nearby bench.

'I came to give Sir Frederick Hungerford a bloody nose for Christmas,' said Sirraway in lordly fashion. 'Perhaps you'd like to help me do that.'

'Oh!' said Betty. She could smell a big exclusive, even though she didn't know the details yet, and *how* she loved to see her name in big print on Page One!

'Won't you come and have a cup of tea in Lovely Mary's?' she smiled, touching her newly permed hair and secretly blessing M'sieur Alphonse for his finesse.

'Will ya no' look at this rubbish,' spat John Ross. He'd adopted his customary posture in the chief sub-editor's chair, lolling sideways and flipping bits of copy paper over his shoulder as he read and rejected them. His foot pushed the bottom drawer of his desk back and forth, and from within you could hear the rattle of a half-empty bottle of Black and White whisky.

A couple of junior reporters looked up, then hastily down again. They may only have been here since leaving school in the summer, but already they'd learned the perils of being sucked into Ross's vortex of cynicism and derision.

'Betty Featherstone at her vairy worrrst! Listen to this:

FOND FAREWELL TO TEMPLE'S
TREMENDOUS SIR FREDDY.

'Friends, admirers and well-wishers gathered at the Temple Regis Conservative Club at the week-end to give a rousing send-off to Sir Frederick Hungerford, who steps down as the town's MP next spring.

'Sir Freddy, as he is known, has for forty years served the constituency with distinction and dedication. His place as Conservative candidate at the general election will be taken by Mrs Mirabel Clifford, a prominent Temple Regis solicitor whose Market Square practice was established in 1950.

'A much-loved figure in the...

'I canna go *orn*,' wailed the chief sub-editor. 'Did the man write it himself? I canna imagine anyone else getting it so wrong!'

He got up and stalked over to the juniors' desk. 'I'll expect better of ye when it's yeur turn to write about politics. This man – he's turned himself into a *saint*.'

There followed a lengthy monologue along the lines of how this businessman's son had reinvented himself as a member of the aristocracy, and even now was awaiting the call to the House of Lords as reward for the years of his devoted service in the bars of Westminster and Whitehall.

Hungerford, ranted Ross, never visited the constituency, discouraged visitors to the House of Commons, served on no parliamentary committees, and spent a lot of time toadying round the fringes of royalty. His service to self-promotion was exemplary, however.

'Betty!' he yelled, but to no avail – she was having her hair done. Again. She'd taken the wiser course of action and written a chunk of syrupy prose rather than the mutinous squib she'd threatened Sir Freddy with on Friday night. The editor liked Betty and gave her extra big bylines on Page One – why rock that particular boat?

With a grunt Ross picked up the pieces of copy paper he'd scattered to the four winds and shoved them viciously on the spike. 'Picture caption only,' he ordered one of his underlings. If Freddy Hungerford lived by the oxygen of publicity, he could suffocate as far as John Ross was concerned.

'Next!'

It was Tuesday morning, and though the *Riviera Express* described itself as a 'news' paper, most of what would appear on its pages this coming weekend was already sewn up – Renishaw's entry-fee piece for Page One and a small picture of Betty having her hair done with a turn to Page Two. Page Three top, Judy's hospital crisis. Then, through the rest of the newspaper, the customary smorgasbord of inconsequence and run-of-the-mill which each week was lapped up by the readership.

There was a piece on a new operating table at the local vet's, an item about lost anchors in Bedlington Harbour, and a picture story on an irritating child prodigy who would go far (and the sooner the better). The centrepiece, as always, was Athene Madrigale's glorious page of predictions for the coming week:

> **Sagittarius – Oh, how lucky you were to be born under this sign. Nothing but sunshine for you all week!**

> **Cancer – Someone has prepared a big surprise for you. Be patient, it may take a while to appear, but what pleasure it will bring!**

> **Capricorn – All your troubles are behind you now. Start thinking about your holidays!**

If there was a ring of familiarity to these soothing phrases – indeed, if any reader had a sharp enough memory – Athene might easily be accused of self-plagiarism. But no right-minded Temple Regent would do that, for she was a much-loved figure in the town with her long flowing robes a kaleidoscope of colours, her iron-grey hair tied back with a blue paper flower and, often as not, odd shoes on her feet. When Athene spoke – whether in print or on the rare occasions she granted an audience – the world slowed its frantic spin and everything in it seemed all right again.

Only slowly had Rudyard Rhys come to realise what an asset this ethereal figure was to his publication, but when he tried to make Athene his agony aunt – offering tea and sympathy, solving problems, restarting people's lives – she was driven to despair. For Athene discovered, when given her first batch of readers' letters, that there is no solution to some problems – indeed, to most problems. And being Athene, she could not bear to face that eternal truth.

So instead she now doubled as Aunty Jill, writing the Kiddies' Korner which featured the birthday photographs of some of the ugliest children in the West Country. This, too, was a great success – they loved her and, having no children of her own, she loved them.

A centre-spread of photographs sent in by readers, a welter of wedding reports, a raft of local district news, and pages and pages of football reports, made up the rest of the wholesome mix which constituted the *Riviera Express*. That was enough for its readership – leave the scandal to the Sunday papers!

Temple Flower Club – Our demonstrator for the evening was Mrs Lydia Sabey, a florist from Dartmouth, and her exhibit was titled Going Dutch. She started off with a copper urn and created an arrangement depicting the Dutch artists using coral and red dahlias, cosmos, red trailing amaranthus, berries and grapes...

Riviera Writers' Group – Mrs Bellairs read her first piece since joining the group and held us spellbound with her account of a Christmas party with a twist – she took us on a visit to a stately home with dark-panelled walls, hidden chambers and relics belonging to a persecuted Catholic priest. She then proceeded to find herself trapped between time dimensions...

Bedlington Social Club – Mrs Bantham led the meeting and introduced our speaker, Mrs Havering from Torquay. Her first recital was the Devon Alphabet, never heard by any of us before!

Occasionally there was room in the *Express* for something meatier, and certainly the goings-on down at the Magistrates Court could provide enough spice to fill the paper several times over. But as an editor Rhys lived cautiously, caught between angry city fathers desperate that nothing should besmirch the town's reputation, and underlings desperate to tap out the truth on their Olivettis and Remingtons. It was the city fathers who invariably prevailed.

In the far corner of the newsroom by the window overlooking the brewery, a tremendous thundering could be heard. It was the newcomer David Renishaw, evidently putting the finishing touches to what was destined to be the bombshell Page One splash – that Temple Regis would soon be charging holidaymakers for the privilege of walking its gilded streets.

The rate at which you could hear the 'ting' from the carriage return showed just how rapidly Renishaw worked, with barely a pause to consult his shorthand notes. Such industry in a weekly newspaper was unusual and, to be frank, unnerving: if you were lucky enough to get the splash, you could save up writing it till Thursday morning – this was only Tuesday!

SEVEN

With a final flourish, Renishaw wrenched out the last sheet of copy paper and walked it over to the subs' desk. Just then Miss Dimont came through the door and they engaged in that embarrassed sidestepping dance which comes from two people bent on achieving their destination without giving way to the other.

'After you,' said Renishaw finally. There wasn't much of a smile on his face.

'How are you getting on, David? We haven't had a chance for a chat. You're a very busy man.'

'Fine, thank you, Miss Dimont.'

'Judy.'

'Actually isn't it – Huguette?'

How the hell does he know that? thought Miss Dimont but replied with a forced smile, 'Most people find it easier to call me Judy.'

'I'm just handing this in and then perhaps there's time for a chinwag,' said Renishaw.

'Come and have a cup of tea, I'll put the kettle on.'

As Miss Dimont spooned Lipton's best Pekoe Tips into

the pot, she watched the reporter and John Ross in earnest discussion. Ross was smiling, nodding, fingering the copy paper – quite a contrast from his usual Arctic welcome to a new piece of news. Then the two men laughed and Renishaw walked over to Judy's desk.

'Just talking about the old days. Great to find a kindred spirit,' he said.

'You worked in Fleet Street?'

'Oh, all over the place,' said Renishaw, his eyes skimming over Judy's notebook, unashamedly attempting to translate the upside-down shorthand.

'You're enjoying Temple Regis? Have you got somewhere nice to stay?'

'Staying with Lovely Mary – you know, the Signal Box Café lady.'

I know her very well, thought Miss Dimont – but obviously not *that* well. Why didn't she tell me she'd got a lodger? One whose desk is not ten yards away from mine? I've only spent most lunchtimes at her place over the past five years, why didn't she tell me?

'How lovely,' she said, not meaning it. 'And then... Mrs Renishaw? Is she coming to join you down here?'

Her question really was – are you planning to stay in Temple Regis, Mr Cuckoo? What are you *really* doing here? What are you hoping to achieve?

'Why don't we have a drink later?' he replied. 'I don't much myself, but since I've been here I discover that most social activity takes place in close proximity to liquor.'

His body was wiry, eyes clear, complexion fresh – so unlike most local reporters of his age who were already allowing the middle-age spread to develop, learning new ways to comb their receding hair. He really is quite handsome, thought Miss Dimont, the eyes are a very sharp blue.

'Why not?' said Judy. Maybe then I can ask you about Pansy Westerham – or is it you who's going to be asking *me* about her? What a strange fellow you are.

'The Nelson, at six?'

'We usually go to the Old Jawbones or the Fort.'

'The Nelson's very comfortable. But then you know that, of course – you were in there at Easter.'

How on earth would you know *that*, thought Miss Dimont – Easter was months and months ago, long before you arrived in Temple Regis, and who would you ask in there who knew me, and how would they remember from all that time ago?

Renishaw smiled knowingly. 'Man called Lamb,' he explained. 'You took pity on him. Bit of an old soak – well, that's putting it mildly – hadn't quite got enough change to buy his whisky. You got out your purse and coughed up. He hasn't forgotten.'

It still doesn't make sense, thought Judy. Why would a man, who clearly doesn't drink, spend time in a pub in the company of a sad old down-and-out long enough to learn I once gave him ninepence so he could make it a double?

'See you there at six,' she said. 'I've got to write up the Caring Volunteers story.'

'If you need any help,' said Renishaw, and sat down in Betty's chair opposite.

'Er, no thank you. I think I've got all I…'

'Did you talk to Hugh Radipole?'

'No, I did not,' said Judy, taking out her crossness by

ratcheting copy paper viciously into the Remington Quiet-Riter. She banged the space bar several times as if to say, go away, I'm busy now.

'Only I think you should,' said Renishaw, smoothly. 'I told him about the crisis and he responded very positively. He said he'd put on a party at the Marine Hotel for all those who volunteer this year. Pop in and see an oldie, get rewarded with a cocktail. That should take care of the problem.'

Dammit, thought Miss D, this is my story – go away and leave me to it!

'See you at six, David,' she said, as sweetly as she could, and shoving her spectacles up her nose, began to type furiously.

The Caring Volunteers piece should have come easily. She'd already thought of the introductory paragraph – always the hardest bit – but suddenly it didn't seem to work any more. She decided to carry on typing in the hope the story would come good – she'd have to retype the whole thing, but better for the moment to press on – but eventually after rapping out a few more paragraphs she ground to a halt.

Renishaw! The smug way he'd sat himself down and told her how to do her job! He hadn't been rude, hadn't been patronising, but now she knew she'd have to ring up Hugh Radipole, get a couple of extra quotes, include the whole thing about cocktails in return for care, and rewrite the entire story just as Renishaw had dictated. The cheek of the man!

At the same time, at the back of her mind was the unsettling matter of Pansy Westerham. And then again, that old soak Lamb. When you collected these together with the Caring Volunteers, it suddenly seemed as if Renishaw had deliberately plugged himself into her life.

But why?

'Miss Dim!' the editor's voice trailed out from his office, a combination of tired regret and impending retribution. 'Here please!'

She walked, not particularly quickly, across the office.

'Yes, Richard?' She addressed him just as she'd done during those intense days in the War Office. No matter he now called himself Rudyard after a failed attempt to reinvent himself as a novelist; he would always remain the erratic naval officer who, though older, was junior to her in the spying game they conducted from that cold uncarpeted basement deep below Whitehall.

They'd known each other for twenty years but now their roles were reversed, and Judy worked for Rudyard – Richard – Rhys. It was not an arrangement which suited either.

'Freddy Hungerford,' grunted her editor. 'There's been a complaint. Where *were* you on Friday?'

Drinking cocktails with a fascinating old lady, a lady who at a very late stage in life decided to make herself a fortune by putting young men on a stage who stripped themselves to the waist and shouted into microphones. Who went around getting young girls in the family way, and then left town.

'I got stuck out at Wistman's Hotel. Snowed in – had to spend the night.'

'I hope you're not thinking of putting that on your expenses. There's nothing in the diary to say you should've been out there.'

'I went to interview Mrs Phipps to see if I could get a piece out of her about next year's season at the Pavilion Theatre.' It was a lie, but lies never count when it's the editor.

'I don't want any more rubbish about noisy beat groups – look at all the trouble they caused last summer,' grumbled Rhys.

'She's thinking of Pearl Carr and Teddy Johnson.'

'Who?'

'Pasty-faced woman, man with a straw boater and bow tie. They croon sickly songs at each other.'

'That sounds a bit more like it.'

Actually, Mr Editor, she's going to have Gene Vincent – ripping off his leather jacket as he mounts the stage at full revs on his Triumph Bonneville. That'll increase your heart rate a bit when he hits town.

'Rr… rrr. Anyway, Freddy Hungerford – apparently Betty rubbed him up the wrong way at the Con Club on Friday night – when *you* should have been there, Miss Dim – and he wants an apology.'

'Don't call me that! I've told you, Richard, I am Miss Dimont, or I am Judy. I am not the other thing, and well you know it. Anyway, Betty's at M'sieur Alphonse having her perm done, she can pop over to the club the moment she's finished, it's only round the corner.'

'No,' said Rhys, fishing in his pocket for a box of matches and not meeting her gaze, 'I want you to go.'

'And apologise for something Betty said?'

'You can do it better than her.'

'For heaven's sake, Richard! What did she say, anyway, to upset the old goat?'

'I have no idea. Just get round there and smooth him down.'

'And have his hand up my skirt? No thanks! He's retiring

in the spring and finally we're going to be represented by a woman who's diligent, caring, and knows what she's doing.'

'Not necessarily. Could be the Liberal who wins.'

'Same thing – she's a good candidate too.'

'I suppose you would say that of the Labour contender as well.'

'Certainly! It would just be nice to have an MP who actually turned up here occasionally and cared what went on in the constituency.'

Rhys lit his pipe and a foul smell instantly filled the room. 'Off you go. Smooth him down. Find some story to write. I see John Ross spiked the piece Betty wrote; there has to be something else worth saying.'

'I suppose you mean his forthcoming peerage? That the lazy good-for-nothing has bought himself a coronet and an ermine robe?'

'Don't be so impertinent!' snapped the editor. 'You're the chief reporter on this newspaper and my personal representative – an apology from you will go a long way. Hop round there now!'

'Just got to finish the Caring Volunteers story first, Richard.'

'Oh *bugger* the volunteers and their blithering care. Get round to the Con Club and get down on your knees!'

'I don't sleep much, do you?' he was saying.

Miss Dimont could take it or leave it, but it was Mulligatawny who needed the requisite seven-and-a-half hours, trapping her feet under the eiderdown and prompting dreams of having been manacled and thrown into a dungeon.

'I have the usual quota.'

They'd met in The Nelson but there was a bit of a scuffle going on so they'd come outside until it was sorted out. Apparently, the Tuesday night crowd tended to get a bit excitable.

'I find the thoughts keep coming and it seems a waste not to get them down on paper,' David Renishaw went on. 'How about you?'

Miss Dimont found his conversational style a little alarming. Though he offered nuggets about his life, each sentence ended with an interrogative, as if he were trying to break into her house and steal her valuables.

'Rest is essential in our job,' she said, firmly. 'Otherwise you lose concentration.'

She didn't know why she was saying this, but Renishaw unnerved her. She was trying to get to the bottom of why he was here in Temple Regis, what he was running away from (that surely had to be the case?), and why he was interested in Pansy Westerham and her violent death all those years ago.

They were sitting outside The Nelson on a wooden bench. A small green square hemmed by fishermen's cottages lay in front of them, illuminated by the winking lights of the neighbourhood Christmas tree. It was extraordinarily warm and as she unbuttoned her coat, Judy thought of dear Geraldine Phipps, still up on Dartmoor in Wistman's Hotel, looking out of her window towards the snow-capped Hell's Tor a mile distant.

'Extraordinary, the meterological variances in the area,' said Renishaw, looking up at the sky. It was if he was reading her mind. 'Sun, snow – all at the same time.'

'I was with a friend at the weekend, over in Brawbridge.

Snowed in. She needed an extra Plymouth gin to keep out the cold.'

'That wouldn't be Geraldine Phipps, by any chance?' asked Renishaw quickly, turning towards her.

In the glow cast from the Christmas tree he seemed strikingly handsome, but of course that was probably the light. She'd decided on first sight he was not to be trusted.

'Let's talk about you, David. It seems extraordinary that someone as gifted as you should want to come and work on the *Riviera Express*. How so, may I ask?'

'I needed a change.'

'From what?' Good, now it's me asking the questions, she thought.

'Canada isn't all it's cracked up to be.'

'Meaning?'

'Land of infinite promise. You work hard, you get ahead. You don't like one place, you go to another. Nobody bothers you, asking questions.'

'Like me, you mean? Asking questions?'

He looked up at the sky again, smoothing back his hair, tamping down the irritating curl. 'You're an exceptionally clever woman, Judy, I don't mind you asking. It's all the others – with their official forms and their fact-checking and their overbearing manner...' his voice trailed off.

This seemed a bit of a contradiction, but I'll leave it lying where it is for the moment, thought Judy. 'So what do you do while the rest of us are wasting our lives snoozing?'

'Think up things.'

'Such as?'

'Well, everyone has a novel in them, so sometimes I tap

away at that. It started out as an autobiography but in every-body's life there are bits which are plain boring, or you don't want to revisit, and you need to skip if it's going to be at all readable. So in the end it was just easier to change the names and make it into a novel.'

'How's it going?'

'I've called it *On the Road to Calgary*.'

'Would that be a tribute to Jack Kerouac? Or do you think you'll end up being crucified?'

Renishaw turned to face her and leaned forward. She caught a whiff of something exotic – was it his hair cream? – and involuntarily drew a deep breath.

'Calgary, Alberta. Where they have a stampede. I worked there for a time on the *Calgary Horn*. Cattle country. It's a bit like the wild west out there – you're an instant star if you can lassoo a chuckwagon to your ten-gallon six-shooter.'

'Ha, ha!'

'Fabulous people.'

'Rather different from Temple Regis.'

'I've travelled a lot. Something always seems to make me want to move on.'

'And Mrs Renishaw…?'

'Who can say?'

'Anything else you do in the wee small hours?'

'I started an organisation called Underdog. When you're working on a paper you hear all sorts of things – you know that yourself, Judy – people with genuine grievances against their boss, or their neighbours, or the police. Sometimes as a reporter there's nothing you can write to help them – the laws of libel and so forth – but a telephone call, or a foot in the door, from someone who's not afraid of authority can work wonders.'

'I don't quite follow.'

'A stiff talking to. A reminder of the complainant's rights. A suggestion that they should think twice before bothering the little person again.'

'That sounds like issuing a threat.'

'I wouldn't say that, Judy,' he replied with a smile. 'And anyway, don't tell me that during the war you didn't use threats to get what you wanted.'

Now how do you know about *that*? thought Judy. I never talk about my war work.

'Mr Rhys is an old friend,' explained Renishaw.

'I doubt he told you anything about his war work,' said Judy coldly.

'There are ways,' said Renishaw with a nod. He really was supremely arrogant – so self-assured, so careless how he stepped. This whole conversation is not about sleep, or Geraldine Phipps, or the weather, or lassooing cattle in Canada. It's about him putting me in my place, demonstrating his supremacy, indicating he knows yards more than he will ever share. What's it all about?

'I still don't understand why you chose Temple Regis.' And I do wish you'd hurry up and choose somewhere else, you're bothering me.

'I was working in Fleet Street after I arrived from Canada. I didn't like the atmosphere. I like fresh air, a small community.'

And now you're here in Temple Regis, are you going to go round knocking on people's doors, telling them they can't do this and they can't do that? Is that part of a journalist's job?

'You mentioned Geraldine Phipps.' She wasn't going to do this, it felt as if she was handing Renishaw an advantage, allowing him to extract more information from her than she'd get from him, but she couldn't resist.

'Isn't she wonderful?'

'It does seem strange you know her *and* Mr Rhys. You, all the way from Calgary via Fleet Street, knowing two people who to my certain knowledge have never met. That's an extraordinary coincidence wouldn't you say, David?'

'Not really. She knew my mother. I was walking past the pier on my first day here and she was just coming out of the theatre door. Hadn't seen her for years.'

How strange, thought Miss Dimont. How strange that two women whom I call my close friends – Geraldine, and Lovely Mary – both know about you, and yet don't mention your name to me. I know we as human beings have a habit of making and keeping secrets but really, I work on the same paper as David Renishaw! I'm his chief reporter! Why haven't they mentioned him to me? What is the mystery about this man?

Pushing these thoughts to one side, she ploughed on. 'And then, Pansy Westerham. I was a bit surprised about that – that you knew her name, and when I'd just been talking to Geraldine about her.'

'Simple. My mother knew her too. They were all thick as thieves back in the old days. I brought up her name and it set Geraldine reminiscing. She does that quite a lot, doesn't she?'

And why ever not, she's had an extraordinary life. And now the prospect of Gene Vincent, roaring his motorbike on stage next summer – there's no stopping her!

'She's adorable,' Judy agreed. 'Well, I think I ought to be going.'

'Oh, come on, we've only just got here. It's fun – forget the fisticuffs earlier, they were just horsing around. You'll find there's real life here at The Nelson.'

'I think that's why we don't come here.'

'Then I've got a wonderful surprise for you,' said Renishaw, getting up and taking her hand. 'Come along!'

Inside the pub, the crammed bar where they'd arrived an hour before was now empty. 'Come on,' said her fellow reporter, and pushed her through a side door. In this room, once a coach shed, cobwebs swung from the ceiling. An overpowering smell of dust and horse dung came up from under the feet of a crowd gathered in one corner.

Nearby, a makeshift bar was making light work of replenishing people's glasses, while next to it an old fellow stood on a chair shouting. There was a tall box on a bench with half a dozen shelves, around which a group of men, their sleeves rolled up, were busying themselves. What with the dust and the jostling crowd, it was difficult to gather what was going on.

'What *is* this?' asked Judy. He hadn't let go of her hand.

'Wait and see,' he said and strode forward to the bar.

'FYVTAWUNNERTHESIX,' bellowed the man, red-faced and clearly loving every moment. 'AAAAAY-VANSTHETOOOO.'

In a moment Renishaw was back with a ginger beer for Judy and one for himself.

'*What is this?*' he heard her shout, the noise was getting beyond a joke.

'You've never seen this before? It's mouse-racing.'

'It's *what*?'

'MOUSE-RACING,' yelled Renishaw, but his words disappeared into thin air.

Miss Dimont had bolted.

EIGHT

Though adored by many, there were a few who disliked Athene Madrigale intensely; and they tended to be the ones who worked closest to her.

This wasn't to say that Devon's finest soothsayer was anything other than lovely. Miss Dimont felt instantly better if she could spot Athene across the newsroom, half hidden behind her lopsided bamboo screen adorned with ostrich feathers and silk scarves, staring at the ceiling for inspiration and puffing gently on a Craven 'A'. She lit up the room with her clouds of smoke, her oddity and originality.

No, it was the sub-editors, the down-table reporters, the photographers and, of course, the printers, whose lordly attitude towards all was a bit of a disgrace – these were the ones who sneered at her ethereal presence.

'Call that work?' one would say to another. 'Dreaming up rubbish like *Capricorn is rising – oh what a glorious week you'll have!* To think we struggle to fill the newspaper with real news and she just sits there making it up.'

It was no coincidence that in the newsroom the editor's placard, near to Athene's desk, had had its message:

MAKE IT FAST
MAKE IT ACCURATE

Augmented thus:

... MAKE IT UP

Mercifully, serene Miss Madrigale was above such common slights, and anyway at the moment she had too much on her hands to worry about trifles. Apart from her weekly column – the first item everyone turned to when they paid their sixpence for the *Express* on Friday mornings – there was her children's page.

Nobody knew where Athene came from; she seemed to pre-date most of the shifting population which made up the *Express*'s editorial staff. To be fair to Rudyard Rhys, when he took the editor's chair he started to promote his astrologer, printing little teases on Page One, and found himself rewarded by an increase in circulation. For him, Athene could do no wrong.

Even the sunny-natured Miss Dimont found this vexing while out and about in town plying her trade, to be confronted by townsfolk eagerly demanding – 'Do you actually *know* Athene? Could you give her a message from me?' – just at the point where she, Judy, was breaking a murder or worse. There was a special magic about Athene; and it was just as well they were friends, for there was quite a lot to be jealous about when the plaudits came to be handed out.

One of the unbelievers was John Ross, whose job it was to make up the *Athene Predicts...* page. His rugged Gorbals childhood had not permitted glimpses of an azure-coloured future.

'What's *this*?' he growled, holding a sheet of Athene's lightly scented copy paper at arm's length.

CAPRICORN – FULL STEAM AHEAD

The frustrations of last month will resolve themselves. Those things you tried to restore to some semblance of beauty from their shabby former selves will now look radiant, even if that means yourself. And – whatever you do – watch your aura!

'What's that *mean*?'

'It's rather nice,' said Denise Hopton, a new sub-editor fresh from university, speaking from the bottom end of the huge wooden desk they occupied. 'She writes well, doesn't she?'

Ross looked up sharply at the newcomer, and from under his foot came the agitated rattling of the whisky bottle.

'This,' he said with a contemptuous sneer, as if he need add no further explanation.

PISCES – HARMONY replaces the nasty little rash-like irritations of November. Personal achievement, expression and success are all on the cards, undoubtedly as the result of the special effort you made to say what you think. Satisfactory adjustments will be made. Some aspects you thought you'd put in a drawer need minor adjustment, but this really is the last of them. Postpone new projects until after Christmas.

'I give that A for Admirable,' said the young girl, who was not in the slightest bit frightened of the old warhorse.

'I give it G for Gobbledegook. Or mebbe S for—'

'She's lovely. *And* the wonderful tea she makes!'

'Aaaaayyy…' growled Ross, 'ye wouldnae know. Ye're young, ye didna have to break windows and rip out phones to get your space in the paper. Ye didna have to lie and cheat and rob because your news editor told ye to. But now here we are with this… this… *gobbledegook* filling one of our best pages, week after week. When we have important news to impart.'

'News? Like this?' said Denise, faintly lifting the copy paper she was subbing.

```
At the November meeting of Regis WI, Mrs
Inchbald gave a thrilling demonstration
of seven new ways to make wallpaper lamp-
shades, and just in time for Christmas!
She…
```

'Ayyy, ye may mock, but that's what sells our newspaper, girrlie – real life! Not made up fiffle-faffle!'

'These lampshades look pretty fiffly-faffly to me, Mr Ross.' There was a keen intelligence about the girl. She wouldn't last long.

Just then the teleprinter behind Ross's desk sprang into life. Its rattle was rarely heard except when an away football match was played and no reporter sent to cover it; or, less often, when the Sovereign died. Apart from that it usually slumbered in the corner, an expensive piece of journalistic vanity which convinced all that the *Express* was not only in touch with the rest of the country, but the rest of the world.

'Denise,' said Ross without lifting his head. He could easily have reached the paper spitting its way out of the machine, whereas she had to get up and walk from the other end of the desk – but that's the price you pay for contradicting your chief sub-editor. 'And – milk, two sugars, while you're about it.'

The girl tore off the short missive sent from the Press Association, then took it off to the tea station, where she ostentatiously read it while waiting for the kettle to boil.

'Hmm, this seems a good one,' she said, rattling the paper, almost to herself but loud enough for Ross to hear.

'Give it here, girrlie, I'll be the judge o' that.'

'Was that one sugar or two?' She was in no hurry to humour him.

Finally she brought over the cup and placed it on top of the PA snapful, as it was known, gently sloshing the contents so half the message from London was obliterated. 'Oh, sorry about that – would you like a biscuit?'

Maybe John Ross was finally losing his power to mesmerise. He pulled out the damp communique and read:

```
PA Parly snapful — Sir Frederick
Hungerford MP Temple Regis has disap-
peared after being attacked in street
near Westminster home. Broken nose,
badly bruised, hands stamped on. Attacker
escapes. Full story 1 hr.
```

'Well, he'll nae be hiding out in Temple Regis while he recuperates,' sneered Ross. 'Broken bones heal so much better in the South of France, one finds – doesn't one?' He finished the sentence in a cod upper-class accent.

'Good story, though,' he added, licking his lips. 'Where's Judy, for heaven's sake!'

Uncle Arthur was back from London. Though his home was high above a leafy garden square in a comfortable mansion-block flat, he seemed to have taken a shine to the seaside, or was it more that he'd taken a shine to his hostess, Auriol Hedley?

'Out of the way, Arthur,' she said bossily, 'Christmas or not, this café is still open. There may not be many customers but you know that old wartime phrase *we never shut* – well, that's me.'

'You've got new coffee.'

'Yes, and you can't have any more. Haven't you something to do – go and polish your shoes or something?' She looked efficient this morning, the crisply laundered white apron as smart as the naval uniform she had once worn.

'Chap I met in the club last night,' said Arthur, neatly rearranging his long legs and staring at his twinkling brogues, 'was talking to me about Freddy Hungerford – you know, you were mentioning him the other night.'

'Ah yes.' She couldn't remember why.

'Apparently a hooligan attacked him in the street. It was seen by several witnesses and someone called the police, but by the time they got there, he'd disappeared.'

'Where was this?'

'Near the House of Commons.'

'Well, I expect he picked himself up, dusted himself down, and found his way across the road to Annie's Bar.'

'Well, yes, you would suppose that. But I heard on the radio this morning he hasn't been seen since.'

'Who? Hungerford?'

'The very same.'

'I've known many a man go missing inexplicably, Arthur. It usually only means one thing.'

'Oh, hah! I suppose you're right. He's a rum 'un, though.'

'I thought you only knew him after the First War, when you were recuperating together.'

'Oh, chaps tell me things.'

'What do they tell you?' Business was slack this morning, there was time for a chat.

'I don't know if you recall but there was a fad for motor-racing at Brooklands between the wars. Huge great old Bentleys, and of course I had my Lagonda…'

'I know about the Lagonda, Arthur.' It was as well to stop him in his tracks when he started droning on about cars.

'Freddy Hungerford – more money than sense – decided to impress his latest girlfriend by attempting the Blue Riband trophy. He bought himself a brand-new Sunbeam and there was an epic battle between him and Count Zborowski which Freddy lost. A bad loser, that man – the word went around. Zborowski was a complete gentleman about it, though. Even if he did drive a Bugatti.'

'You'll be talking about carburettors and double-declutching next, Arthur – anything in this for me?'

The old boy's face expressed mild surprise. He had a

tale or two in his repertoire about double-declutching, as it happened. Most people were fascinated.

'Well, Hungerford then. He got a reputation as a womaniser. Though he was married, he had girlfriends who overlapped each other like planks on a clinker-built boat. Not so much love-'em-and-leave-'em as love-'em-and-shove-'em. He was a bit brutal, don't you know. Not many friends as a result.'

Come on, thought Auriol, haven't got all day.

'What made me think of it was back in those days, one of his girlfriends went missing. Now *he's* gone missing. Bit of a coincidence, that.'

Auriol sat down opposite him. Much water had flowed under the bridge since she quit her post in Naval Intelligence, but though sometimes she was called on in an unofficial capacity to help her ex-bosses, there was nothing much going on at the moment. A mystery always intrigued her, just as it did her best friend.

'Tell me more.'

'Wish I could remember her name, something to do with Kent – Maidstone? Dover? Anyhow it was long ago – doesn't really matter now. What my chap at the club told me in confidence was that Hungerford won't be getting his peerage.'

'Peerage?'

'Apparently he only agreed to step down as your MP in return for getting a seat in the House of Lords. My chap,' added Arthur, just a shade boastfully, 'is already there. In fact, his family, for generations…'

'Yes, yes, Arthur, you have friends in high places. But what about Hungerford's peerage?'

'Well, he likes being in Parliament and had no intention

of standing down. The local party are fed up with him and fixed it so he would get a peerage; that way he'd be out of their hair and they could get a proper person to represent them in Parliament, and he could snooze away the rest of his life in the Lords.'

Auriol made a snort of disgust.

'Everything was fixed up and he even chose his title – Lord Downpark – while they chose a new candidate. I hear she's a woman,' added Arthur with a slightly amused chuckle.

'And a wonderful one, too. You should see what she's said and done since she became the candidate.'

'Well, you would know,' said Arthur, retreating hastily. 'Anyway, here's what I wanted to tell you – everything was going ahead quite smoothly when a royal personage got to hear about it and suddenly – pouf! – no more Lord Downpark.'

'Heavens!' exclaimed Auriol. 'I didn't know the royal family interfered in politics!'

'They don't,' said Arthur quickly, though his expression seemed to say different. 'Anyway, Sir Freddy he will now remain and he can kiss goodbye to the old ermine.'

'But why, if it'd all been fixed up?'

'I was told it went this way. Hungerford qualified on all counts – long service as an MP, no divorce, no criminal record, no bankruptcy, general support for the government when his party was in power. All that sort of thing – should have been a dead cert.'

'So what went wrong?'

'I think probably because he's a dislikeable fellow.'

'That hasn't stopped others from becoming lords, in fact I'd say the vast majority are a bunch of—'

'Now, now, Auriol! Anyway, it finally got to the ears of a Certain Person. The Person heard that Hungerford was having his head measured for a coronet, and the Person put their foot down.'

'Her foot.'

'If you like.'

'So what now?'

'Well,' said Arthur, getting up and walking over to the window. The day had suddenly gone, and though it was barely four o'clock it was almost pitch-black. The lights of a late fishing boat bounced across the water as it came to rest on the harbour pontoon.

'Well,' he repeated, 'I wonder whether this disappearance isn't something to do with losing his peerage. He can be an ugly customer when he wants – I remember the way he treated those lovely nurses back at Seale Hayne. We'd all come back from the Front, all of us in a pretty poor shape and delighted to have the attention of these lovely angelic beings looking after us. But he was awful to them, bullying them around, shocking behaviour – I wonder if he isn't a bit free with his fists.'

'You said it was Hungerford who was attacked.'

'Takes two to start a fight, Auriol.'

'How would you know, Arthur? I bet you've never hit anybody in your life.'

'Just saying,' came the reply. He was inspecting the polish on his brogues. 'It all fits together.'

'It doesn't make sense,' said Auriol after a moment's thought. 'Look, I'm shutting up shop now, why don't we go back to the cottage? You can put your feet up for an hour before supper.'

As the couple strolled companionably back through the deserted harbour, the conversation swung round to Miss Dimont again.

'You know, I do agree with Grace that she should give up this reporting lark,' said Arthur. 'She has responsibilities to face up to. There's the house, the business, the investments, all that to think about. She's having a lot of fun down here, I know, and of course there's you as her friend. But, you know, there's always room for you up there in Essex – wouldn't you fancy a change of scene?'

Auriol stopped in a pool of watery light cast by a harbour wall lantern. She looked up and smiled. 'Your sister is very persuasive, Arthur, but this is one battle she won't win – Hugue will never leave Temple Regis.'

'Never?'

'It's her safe haven. While I stayed on in Naval Intelligence after the war she, as you know, shifted to another branch.'

'Military Intelligence.'

'You don't know that.'

'A little birdy told me,' laughed Arthur. 'Oh, come off it! Of course it was – all that capering about in Europe.'

'It wasn't capering, Arthur. It was pretty awful – the Cold War was a war just as much as 1939–45 had been. She went through some gruelling times, I can tell you.'

'Well, yes.'

'In the end, she had to leave. She had to change her way of life.'

'Well, yes, I…'

'You remember she came down here to stay with me.'

'That was when I was in South America.'

'Well, I can tell you now, it took a year before she could get up with a smile on her face. After that she started to look around and found this vacancy on the *Express*. They were taking just about anybody on then, and certainly she knew nothing about journalism – but she got down to it and turned herself into a brilliant reporter.

'Temple Regis is her safety blanket, her happy home, the place where she feels safe. Mme Dimont can huff and puff as much as she likes, but Hugue will stay here, I guarantee you that.

'And anyway, what would that chap Terry do without her?'

NINE

The sudden disappearance of Sir Frederick Hungerford got a mixed reception from his constituents. For a start it was too close to Christmas for anybody to really concentrate, just when there was shopping to be done and preparations made.

Then again, though Sir Freddy may have claimed to represent Devon's prettiest resort, not everybody voted for him. Indeed, securing only twenty-nine per cent of the electorate's votes could hardly be called a landslide victory when seventy-one per cent of townsfolk remained opposed or indifferent to his languid charm. Furthermore, there was a whole generation who'd never even seen him, his travel arrangements being what they were – ample sunshine on the beaches of his town, but for some reason preferring the sands of Monte Carlo.

There were those like Betty who'd come too close to the old boy, only to step swiftly away from his nimble fingers. And others who had tried but failed to get Hungerford interested in some dispute or local issue.

But not everyone felt this way. The party faithful liked his patrician look, his superior manner, his Rolls-Royce and his cigars. They liked the party he stood for, even if they didn't much care for him, and such was their atavistic loathing of all other political parties they put their faith in him.

To these, it came as a great shock to hear that such a beloved figure – one so distinguished, one so dedicated! – could be subjected to a hooligan's attack in broad daylight. And then to disappear! What could it mean? Who could have abducted him? And why?

These thoughts eventually crossed the mind of the Chief Constable and, summoning Inspector Topham, ordered the detective to get on a train to London and find out first-hand from Scotland Yard what had happened, what was happening now, and what their plans were in the immediate future.

'Don't take any nonsense from them this time,' said his boss, leaning back in his chair and stirring his tea. 'You remember the Digby Jenkinson affair where they led you up the garden path.'

'I could have solved it twice over,' protested Topham, 'if I'd been given the information they had.'

'My very point,' said the CC. 'They didn't tell you anything. Not a sausage. And they won't tell you anything now, down the end of the telephone. Get up there and badger them – Sir Freddy is *our* property, not theirs!'

'Happened on their manor.'

'Get the 4.30, and keep me informed!'

Over at the *Express* the journalistic machine sprang into action. With a creaking sound the door of the editor's office opened and Rudyard Rhys peered out onto the editorial floor.

'Conference!' he bellowed and turned back into his den.

'Where's Judy? Where's Renishaw?' he barked when all

were assembled. 'Where are my highly paid reporters when I need them!'

Peter Pomeroy, his deputy, said soothingly: 'Remember Betty did an interview with Hungerford only the other day.'

Betty, sitting at the back of the gathering, instinctively ducked her head and started scribbling in her notebook. Her recent brush with the MP meant that she had, by default, become the 'expert' on him – everyone in the building would now look to her to answer all the unanswerable questions about what happened and why.

She hadn't a clue.

'I barely spoke to him,' she said defiantly into her notebook.

'Rr... rrr,' growled Rhys, 'this is Page One stuff, Betty. I want everything you've got!'

'You mean how he tickled my knees?'

'Rr... rrrrr!' growled the editor, reaching for his filthy pipe and scraping at it viciously with a pencil. 'Just remember, Betty, Freddy Hungerford has served this town with distinction for forty years. Why, only the other night – the celebrations for all that he's done – you were *there*, Betty. Give me lots of that!'

'And the fellow who did the one-man protest? Can I add that in? How he wanted to give Sir Freddy a bloody nose for Christmas? How Sir Freddy...' she quickly whizzed back through her notebook to find the court proceedings. 'How he is... *guilty of a number of malfeasances inconsistent with the public office he has held for the past forty years*? How he *was a crook, is a crook, has always been a crook*?'

'Just a minute,' said a commanding voice from the doorway,

'can you say that again?' It was David Renishaw, just back from a job with Terry.

Betty repeated the quotation, adding the background to the court case she'd attended only yesterday morning. 'I don't know how true any of it is,' she added, looking at Renishaw's hair and wanting to give it a pat. 'We went and had a cup of tea in Lovely Mary's and he may have a point, but I warn you, Mr Rhys, he's definitely odd.'

'What's this man's name?' Renishaw's voice carried such authority you might swear that he was the editor, not Rhys.

'Hector Sirraway.'

'Never heard of him.'

Well, no surprise there, thought Betty, you've only been here five minutes. You may have discovered a plot to charge people to visit Temple Regis but that doesn't make you the Oracle.

'Is he local?'

'He's a foreigner. Lives in North Devon.'

This drew a titter from the assembled journalists, none of whom had a clue what was going on with Sir Freddy and sat in fear of being asked their opinion of how to develop the story. Mostly, like Betty, they kept their eyes down, though now Renishaw was showing an interest Betty herself had perked up quite a bit.

'So what's his beef? What's he got against our beloved MP?'

This was more like it! Betty had the information that nobody else had – and maybe suddenly she *was* the 'expert' – even if what was in her notebook was just hearsay ramblings from a man not entirely of this planet.

'He's a Professor of Industrial Archaeology. He specialises in the potteries of Staffordshire, but his family has lived in Hatherleigh for generations,' she began, importantly. 'Still has a house there.'

'He was arrested for causing a disturbance outside Sir Freddy's party last Friday. He was in court yesterday and bound over to keep the peace – I didn't write the story up because we don't do bound-overs.'

'Rr... rrr,' uttered the editor dustily. Clearly this edict needed to be reviewed.

'I took him for a cup of tea after the court let him go, but nothing he told me could be used in a piece. Mostly angry ramblings about Sir Freddy's corrupt ways, as he saw them. I didn't stay long, he's definitely a bit peculiar.'

Renishaw now sat himself down on the edge of the editor's hallowed desk. The room waited for an explosion which never came – what *was* it about this man which allowed him to bulldoze his way through all that was sacrosanct?

'What, specifically, were his allegations?' asked the reporter.

Betty consulted her notes. 'He said, and here I quote, that *Dartmoor is a vast tract of land which remained untouched for centuries. But then they discovered tin. Slowly other things in the moor were discovered and exploited – granite, china clay, peat, warrening. And every time someone discovered a new way of making money out of what people had viewed as a worthless piece of countryside, portions of the moor were bought up or stolen to build factories on.'*

She was glad she'd been sitting at the table in Lovely Mary's when she interviewed Sirraway – her shorthand when standing up was often illegible by the time she got it back to the office.

'Professor Sirraway gave me a lengthy lecture of how these money-making ventures had flourished during and after the Industrial Revolution, but most of which had now disappeared.'

A heavy silence had settled over her colleagues, some of whom might even have fallen asleep, and certainly she could see a glazed look in her editor's eye. She struggled to bring her narrative to a conclusion.

'Sirraway's point was that over the past century, the owners of these places slowly gave up and walked away. And that for the past forty years Sir Freddy had been acquiring – usually by devious means – many of these substantial properties on the moor, without anybody noticing.

'It was only when the professor started investigating his own family's property history that he discovered they'd once owned several mills, but that Hungerford had somehow acquired the land title to them. Straightforward theft, he said.'

'Has he tried to get them back?' asked Renishaw.

'He told me he's been researching and double-checking to make sure he was right. Then he went to see Sir Freddy in the House of Commons and confronted him – there was a terrible row, and he was thrown out. He was warned he'd be arrested if he set foot in the Palace of Westminster again. That's why he protested outside the Con Club last weekend.'

'When he got arrested.'

'And let off with a caution.'

'Tell me,' said Renishaw, 'do you think he'd be capable of physically attacking Hungerford? Do you think it was him in the street in Westminster?'

Betty thought about it for a moment.

'He's a very strange man, very edgy, very irritable. And he's got a huge grudge, obviously. Yes, it could be him.'

'What about abducting the man? Is he capable of that?'

'Shouldn't have thought so. He's tall and weedy and quite old.'

'With an accomplice?'

'Well, yes,' said Betty, enjoying the moment, 'I don't see why not.'

There was a lengthy pause.

'I'm going up to Hatherleigh,' said Renishaw without deigning to consult his editor. 'That's just the sort of out-of-the-way place where you could hide someone you'd kidnapped. Where's Terry?'

The Riviera Express – the luxury Pullman steam train, not to be confused with the *Riviera Express*, newspaper of record – served the most delicious teacakes. They were just one of the many delights of travelling up from Temple Regis on the great, groaning, shining monster that daily plied its trade between the West Country and Paddington Station.

Owd Bert, the dining-car steward, always had a friendly word and a special seat for Miss Dimont on her journeys to town – he'd been serving cakes and buns on his silver salvers since the end of the war, and knew just about everybody who'd travelled on the Express more than twice.

'Got a seat ready for 'ee, and a nice cuppa on its way,' he beamed as she wandered into the carriage.

In summer, when you caught the 4.30, you watched the light slowly go down as you slid on ribbons of steel towards the capital city, the passing scenery a rich kaleidoscope of colour and memory. In winter if you looked out of the window, all you caught was your own reflection. Miss Dimont gave a perfunctory adjustment to her curls, pushed the spectacles back up her nose and got out the notebook from her raffia bag.

'Shall I draw the curtains, Miss?'

'No, thank you, Bert – look, there's a beautiful moon!'

But Bert didn't look; he was more concerned with the state of his teacakes. He could tell where you were at any stage in the two-hundred-mile journey, he'd done it so often he didn't need to look out.

The moon sliced the black silhouettes of trees, and the clouds outside raced, but instead of engaging in their interplay Miss Dimont leaned forward and started to doodle, hoping the flow of her pencil would cause her brain to start working. The instruction to get aboard the 4.30 to Paddington was clear and abrupt – Peter Pomeroy may be the sweetest man in the world, but as he described the editor's displeasure at her no-show at conference, she could judge from his tone that things weren't going well.

'You've got a friend in the House of Commons,' Peter said. 'Get in there, see what people are saying. We need five hundred words from you by lunchtime tomorrow.'

'I doubt there'll be anybody left,' Judy had replied from the warmth of the cottage hospital where she'd gone to check up on the volunteers. 'All gone home for Christmas.'

'Just get up there and give us what you can. David Renishaw's gone over to Hatherleigh – the man who was baiting Sir Freddy about dodgy property deals lives up there, he thinks there may be something in that.'

'Good Lord, quite unlike Mr Rhys to want to send someone all the way to North Devon. Think of the cost of the petrol!'

'It wasn't his idea,' said Peter in a flat tone.

The teacakes going cold beside her, Miss Dimont started to make notes in the hope inspiration would come. But as the Riviera Express pulled out of Exeter and took up its steady momentum, her thoughts started to wander.

Is it only ten years since I was in Berlin? she thought. It seems both longer ago and more recent – certainly I can recall every last detail of the job I had to do. Yet the things that happened, the people we lost, makes you want to put the memories in a drawer – wrap them in tissue paper, tie a ribbon round them, lock the drawer.

And throw away the key.

Yet sometimes, when Miss Dimont was caught unawares, the drawer would unlock itself and beckon her to take her Cold War memories back again. And there was nothing she could do to stop herself.

'Summat wrong with they teacakes, Miss?'

'Oh… sorry, Owd Bert, I was miles away.'

'Reminiscing?'

What a clever observer of humankind you are, thought Miss Dimont. 'Yes, alas. Sometimes memories are good things, sometimes not. Don't you think?'

'I lost every lars friend I had at Monte Cassino,' said Owd Bert slowly, perfectly understanding her mood. 'I could never make any more after that. They died all around me, mown down, there was nothing I could do to stop it. It went on and on for weeks. You don' want to go makin new friends after that.'

There was a long pause. 'I'll bring you some fresh.'

She'd done it – gone to Berlin – for Eric, the crazy lovely foolish man who gave his life away in the last days of war. His photograph still shone from her mantelpiece, his eyes telling her he was glad she'd found peace in Temple Regis. He was as alive today in her memory as he had ever been, while part of her had died with him.

The moon had risen and Bert's new pot helped to melt those thoughts. Memory is such a dangerous thing, thought Judy, maybe it's better never to open it up. Don't keep a diary, don't keep a scrapbook, burn all the photographs, never see people who were part of that past. Keep forging forward in life and whatever you do, don't ever look back.

She looked down into her cup.

'No surprise to find you here,' said a gruff voice.

Judy looked up, dabbing her eyes with her napkin. 'Inspector Topham!' she said with a smile. She felt a flood of relief to see him. 'Won't you join me for a cup of tea?'

The old policeman smiled and sat down. 'No prizes for guessing we're on the same mission,' he said. 'And no prizes for thinking we'll both come away empty-handed.'

'Freddy Hungerford? The storm will have passed by the time we get to Paddington. I've been sent by a trigger-happy editor, what about you?'

Topham looked at her. 'I am very near retirement,' he said, putting his big hands on the table. 'I'd like to think we know each other well enough for us to have a private conversation which won't embarrass me at a later date. Do I make myself clear, Miss Dimont?'

'One lump or two, Frank, dear?'

He took off his hat and brushed his hair back with his

hands. 'The Chief Constable sent me. I don't know if he expects me to find Sir Freddy sitting in his club drinking port, but I can tell you now I won't. He wants me to keep abreast of developments in London, but Scotland Yard aren't going to tell me any more than they're going to tell you – sweet Fanny Adams is all I'll get. To them, all local police are a bit of a joke, and last time I came up on something like this they spent the whole time talking to me as if they'd got a pot of clotted cream in their mouth.'

'They haven't done so strikingly well themselves, have they, in finding a lost MP? Is the theory that he's been kidnapped?'

'What else? You don't get roughed up in the street then push off without making a complaint. Not if you're a knight of the realm you don't. What I can't understand is why these thugs attacked him, then carted him away. Why not grab him then do whatever you're going to do once you've got him out of public view?'

This was wonderful stuff. Old Topham assumed Judy knew the facts of the case whereas until this moment her grasp had been confined to two or three bare sentences from Peter Pomeroy on the blower.

'Between us,' said the copper, stirring his tea, 'the most likely candidate is a fellow who's been causing him trouble locally. Lives up Hatherleigh way. He'll be in custody by the time we get off the train. But if he has an alibi, there's nothing more my department can do – it's up to the Met.'

His eyes dropped to the knives and forks jingling on the tablecloth as the express hurtled over a set of points. 'May I have one of your teacakes?'

'You certainly may, Frank. As many as you like.'

TEN

Despite her prediction, the House of Commons was still busy and with surprising ease Miss Dimont found herself in the library where an old friend from Admiralty days, April Needham, awaited her.

'I can't be long, Judy, I've got a dinner engagement. What can I do for you?'

'I've been sent up here to do a story on the disappearance of Sir Frederick Hungerford.'

'Huh!' said April. '*That* old poodlefaker! He can stay disappeared as far as I'm concerned.'

'You know him?'

'When you work here you get to know most of them. Not that he ever comes in – most MPs have to bone up on their subject before speaking, so we see a lot of them, but not Hungerford. He's such a know-it-all. No, it's in the corridors and on the stairs you have to watch out for him – wandering hands.'

'I'm in a bit of a spot, April. I've been sent up here to find out something – anything – and I've got less than twenty-four hours to do it. I tried ringing Sir Freddy's office in the hope somebody would be there, but no luck. Got any thoughts?'

'Well,' said April, putting on her coat. 'You're welcome to stay here as long as you like – just sign the book when you leave. But without wanting to sound too negative, I don't think you'll find the answer to a missing person inquiry buried in the shelves of this library, wide-ranging though it be.'

'Do you know who his friends were in Parliament?'

'Anybody with a title. Sorry, Judy – must dash!' Slinging her handbag over her shoulder, April walked over to the door and shut it behind her.

A moment later it opened again.

'I think you may be in luck. There's a woman in the reading room next door who, if I'm not mistaken, is the candidate hoping to take Hungerford's place at the election. She's very keen. Comes in at odd times and is reading up all sorts of things – I hope she gets in, just the sort we need in here.'

'Is it Mirabel Clifford?' The trouble was that, in Temple Regis, all three main parties were fielding female parliamentary candidates.

'The very one. Byee!'

Miss Dimont followed her friend out into a large grey room dotted with leather sofas, upright chairs, and mahogany tables with reading lamps on them. A dozen people were doing what the room was designed for – reading – while a handful more were snoozing until it was time for dinner. In the far corner, bathed in a pool of light, sat an earnest-looking woman with urchin-cut hair and a serious expression.

'Er, Mrs Clifford? I don't think we've met, and I must say it's a surprise to find you here. Judy Dimont, chief reporter of the *Riviera Express*.'

The woman looked up and eyed her shrewdly, estimating whether she faced friend or foe. 'Hello,' she replied, neither a welcome nor a rebuff.

'May I sit down?'

'As you can see I'm busy, but yes. I've met your photographer, of course – Mr Eagleton, is it? Very nice. But your editor seems to be determined not to mention the upcoming election in his pages until the campaign starts.'

'When will that be?'

'In about six weeks – just waiting till the dust settles after the New Year, then off we go. I'm just mugging up on a few things before we go out and start kissing babies.'

She's attractive, thought Miss D. Clever, purposeful, nicely dressed but not bossy. She'd certainly be an improvement on the present incumbent.

'Well, I hope we shall see much more of each other,' said Judy warmly. 'But the reason I'm here is Sir Freddy.'

Mrs Clifford shot her a suspicious look. 'You've come all the way up from Temple Regis to ask me about Sir Freddy?'

Well, no actually, thought Miss Dimont, I hope you haven't already caught the politician's disease of assuming the story is always about *you*. I'm sitting here opposite you because I'm desperate for a line – any line – on Sir Freddy which will give me something new for my newspaper's front page. Please say something which I can offer my editor tomorrow morning. Please!

'Actually, I was just passing,' she lied, but with a purpose – it took the pressure off the interviewee. 'A friend works in the House library and I dropped in to see her. Just as I was leaving I spotted you in the corner here, and it seemed an appropriate moment to come and introduce myself.'

'Because I'd really prefer my name and the present Member's not to be bracketed in the same story,' continued Mrs Clifford, very firmly.

Good Lord she's sharp, thought Judy. Keeping her distance. Doesn't want to be tarred with the same brush.

'Well, in this place,' said Judy, waving her hand upward towards the carved stone ceiling, 'there's such a thing as off the record. You help me with my inquiries in return for my promise not to name you.'

'No thanks.'

'It's an accepted custom.'

'Look,' said Mirabel Clifford, 'and you may *not* quote me on this. The way things are going, my party is going to lose the seat they've held for forty years. It'll be me who takes the blame for that, even though – as I'm sure you're only too aware – the love affair between the present Member and his constituents went stale years ago, and this is the natural consequence.'

'Yes but…'

'It's his unpopularity, his negligence, which will cause me to lose the seat. I'm a solicitor, Miss Dimont, and a widow. I have two children whom I rarely see at the moment. I've worked hard over the past few years to prepare myself for Sir Freddy's retirement, at considerable cost to my private and personal life. Do you have a husband?'

'No, I…'

'Neither do I, nor do I have time for one. I believe, very passionately, that women have a right to a voice in politics and yet how many MPs in this place are women?'

'Twenty-four,' said Judy.

'Oh,' said the solicitor, looking anew at her questioner. 'Well, thank heavens at least one person has taken notice of that fact! We make up more than half the population, but have less than four per cent of the membership of this House.'

She stood up. 'The 1960s are just around the corner, but there are no High Court judges who are women – no surgeons, no vicars or bishops. No chairmen of major public companies, heads of the armed services – the list is endless of the things we don't do.

'And so, Miss Dimont, you will see how precious this forthcoming election is to me. My job is to turn over the apple cart – make a change, make things better, alter the direction this country is going in.'

'Sir Freddy...' reminded Judy, though she knew it was futile.

'I want nothing to do with him. I hope he's OK for Lady Hungerford's sake and I hope they find him soon, but I keep my distance. I'm not going to say a thing.'

'I understand you didn't go to his Christmas party last weekend.'

'Wasn't invited. But I wouldn't have gone anyhow.'

My goodness you are resolute, thought Miss Dimont. And look at you – you have a lovely face, pretty clothes, a studied elegance and a responsible job – for some women that would be enough. But here you are, scratching away trying to climb aboard this male-dominated juggernaut just so you can make a change.

'Well, it's been a pleasure meeting you,' said Judy getting up. 'I'll be seeing a lot more of you once the election is announced, and I wish you luck.'

'What do you think of my chances? At the election? You're a reporter, you're out and about meeting people – what are people saying?'

'Mostly they're talking about Christmas,' said Judy, frankly. 'After the next edition of the *Riviera Express* they'll be hotly debating the idea of an entrance fee being imposed on visitors to Temple Regis – asking whether it'll offend people and kill business off, or increase the town's prestige and set it apart from its rivals on the English Riviera.'

'Good Lord,' exclaimed Mirabel Clifford, 'where did *that* come from?'

'Well,' said Judy, neatly turning the tables, 'you wouldn't enter an off-the-record agreement with me so it's only fair our arrangement is evenly balanced. You can read about it on Friday in the *Riviera Express*. Because of this hoo-hah over Sir Freddy it'll probably be on Page Three with a turn to Page Four. A snip at only sixpence a copy, highly recommended.'

The lawyer looked at the reporter with a long and even gaze. 'OK,' she said after a long delay, 'OK.'

Leaning forward she scribbled something on her notepad, tore off the page, and handed it without a word to Judy. It said:

Mrs Baines
35 Ebury Street
SW1

'Is this…? Er, what exactly…?' stumbled Judy. Mrs Clifford looked at her and smiled.

'Could you just give me a clue?'

The prospective parliamentary candidate for Temple Regis shook her head slightly and continued to smile.

Otherwise her face registered nothing.

It was ten o'clock by the time Miss Dimont found her way to the lower end of Belgravia. A sharp wind blew down the long street, shining black and wet from an earlier shower. In the distance two Belisha beacons flashed pools of light over the pedestrian crossing while further down, a policeman in his mackintosh cape ambled slowly, counting the minutes till the end of his shift.

It was the hour in London when everything comes to a halt – people have gone wherever they're going and are busy having a good time, or else they've gone home and are listening to *Ray's a Laugh* on the radio. Soon the city would come to life again, at chucking-out time or when theatregoers emerged from the latest musical, but just now there was an eerie silence.

Far away you could just hear the grinding of gears at Victoria Bus Station as travellers set off on their long journeys through the night, but here in Ebury Street all was still – no traffic, no people.

Number 35 was like all the others – a terrace house with a Georgian frontage, not too smart but not unattractive. Its stucco front, painted a regulation ivory, gave no clue as to what lay inside. Miss Dimont had absolutely no idea why she was here, standing outside, looking at a tarnished doorknocker, but like all good journalists she had been driven by the story which lured her, urged her, onwards. And now she had to face the consequences.

Feeling a trifle apprehensive, she stepped forward and knocked.

There was a lengthy pause, but eventually the door was opened by a plumpish woman in a cream silk dressing gown. She looked at Miss Dimont but said nothing.

'Mrs Baines, I…'

'I had your lot round here earlier,' said the woman, irritably. 'I'm fed up with being bothered – can't you go and find another victim somewhere else – preferably the North Pole? Go away!'

'*Who* came earlier?' barked Judy, surprising herself with her vehemence. Not David Renishaw, surely? Or that infuriating man from the *News Chronicle*?

'Go. Away.'

'No, no, please – just tell me who it was!'

The woman shifted the weight on her feet. Miss Dimont could see through the open toes of her slippers that she had a taste for adventurous nail varnish.

'Don't tell me you're from a rival organisation?' she snorted. 'Not Jehovah's Witnesses? What are you – Salvation Army? Well, I can tell you it's too late for my salvation, dear, so why don't you just push off?'

She had a soft face but her voice was tired. Miss Dimont stepped forward – this was the now-or-never moment.

'Sir Frederick Hungerford,' she said forcefully. It was the only card she had left to play – she had no idea who this woman was, what her connection to the story was, but there was nowhere else to go and this was the last throw of the dice.

The woman started and her jaw dropped. 'Are you – Press?' she hissed.

'Yes.'

'How on earth…?' Her pink marshmallow face had turned white.

Miss Dimont took another step forward – they were now within striking distance of each other – but just as she wondered what her next question would be, a fruity voice from a back room called, 'Who is it, Millicent? What do they want?'

I don't believe it, thought the reporter, I've just got my scoop! A senior Member of Parliament has been missing for two days after being attacked in the street, and I've found him. He hasn't been kidnapped, he's with his… lady friend!

Her brain moved swiftly. 'Judy Dimont, chief reporter of the *Riviera Express*. Just come to make sure Sir Freddy's all right. Might I have a word?'

What she didn't say was 'Judy Dimont, chief reporter of the *Riviera Express*. What the devil does this man think he's playing at? Missing for two days, headlines in all the newspapers, people thinking he's been kidnapped, police looking everywhere for him, and here he is hiding in the bosom of his popsy!'

The woman had adopted the stance of a doorman at The Ritz – undesirables were not going to pass through her portals. But just then the gentleman in question came up behind her, curious to know what was going on. He did not like what he saw.

'What the devil are *you* doing here?' he blustered, recognising Judy instantly.

'I might say the same, Sir Frederick.' What the devil are you doing here when the whole world is looking for you? 'Don't you realise the police…?'

The politician stuck his head out of the door and looked quickly up and down the street. 'You'd better come in,' he said angrily. 'Wipe your feet.'

How impertinent, thought Miss D, deliberately stepping over the doormat. When she entered the sitting room it appeared to be garlanded in feathers and shawls – a bit like Athene's little corner back at the *Express*, but without the spirituality.

Sir Freddy took up position with his back to a large ornate mirror, a towering presence in the small room with a large whisky glass in his hand. 'Sit down!' he thundered, and in the confined space his words sounded like cannon fire.

'I'm not going to ask what you're doing here, Miss, er...' he began. 'I'm just going to say a few words to you, and then you can get right back on the train down to Temple Regis.'

The reporter fished out the notebook from her raffia bag without a word.

'Put that *away*!' he ordered. 'Just listen to what I have to say, then get out. Millie, you push off for a minute while I talk to this... person.'

He's shameless, thought Miss Dimont, he's going to bluff this out.

'I don't know how you found this address,' he began, 'but I consider it an invasion of my privacy. Everyone – MPs included – is entitled to a small corner of their lives which remains a personal matter. I expect you have jumped to conclusions in discovering me here, but you may well be incorrect in your assumptions. I do not need to remind you of the laws of libel.

'Furthermore,' he blustered on, 'I have the telephone

numbers of your proprietor and your editor and I shall be ringing them the moment you leave. You will *not* write about my presence here, and if you do, you can expect the worst.'

Miss Dimont was unabashed. 'Your private life is your private life,' she lied, 'but you seem to be overlooking something, Sir Frederick. You've been missing for two days, the police are out looking for you and, by extension, for the people they suppose abducted you. Yet here you are, apparently unharmed, having a comfortable evening in. Does Lady Hungerford know you're safe?'

'You leave Lady Hungerford out of this!' he bellowed. 'She's not… not a well woman.'

'Well, just tell me this, and I'll go. What happened outside the House of Commons, and what are you doing here when people are looking for you everywhere?'

'How did you find this address?' Hungerford demanded. His fist tightened around the whisky glass.

If only you knew, thought Judy. 'I have my sources,' she replied, using the age-old response reporters give when they a) have found out something by accident, b) paid someone to blab, or c) been struck by a bolt of divine providence.

'Well,' said the MP, 'I'll give you credit. Nobody else has managed it. Last thing I expected was to be rumbled by my local rag.'

'We don't call it a rag. It's a newspaper.'

'Good for wrapping fish and chips, that's all. That editor of yours, Rhys, what a complete waste of…'

'He's a very distinguished journalist,' snapped Judy, surprised to hear herself saying it. 'He balances the interests of the community. He puts things in the paper and you wonder why, equally he leaves things out and you wonder why. But it's a successful formula. Above all his goal is harmony and well-being.'

Actually, that's true, she thought to herself in surprise. He may dither, he may dissemble, but his newspaper is very popular, and if his choices sometimes appear bizarre then maybe he's entitled to have made those choices.

'He'll do as I say,' said Sir Freddy with a sneer. 'This is a complicated business and I'm not having it upset by the interference of a local… *rag*.' He repeated the word slowly, deliberately.

'Well, you go ahead and call him,' said Judy. 'Right now Inspector Topham of the local CID is over at Scotland Yard – I came up on the train with him – and the first thing I shall do when I leave here is telephone to let him know you're well.'

Although, thought Judy, I may not do that tonight. I first want to get my story in print and I don't want Scotland Yard stealing my thunder.

The MP did not like the sound of this. He poured himself another whisky and sat down. He did not offer Judy a glass.

'All right, all right,' he said eventually. 'I *will* talk to you, off the record.'

Not something your successor is prepared do, Judy thought mischievously. Watch out for the whoppers!

'I will admit that my disappearance is not what it seems. I can't tell you why, but I *can* tell you what happened. If I do, will you hold off telling the police until late tomorrow?'

Willingly, thought Judy. It suits me just fine – I get my '*Express* Discovers Missing MP' scoop, and you hand yourself in. 'It depends,' she said, slowly. The man was too much of a bully to give in easily.

'Let me put it to you this way,' went on Sir Freddy, flashing a practised smile. 'Certain things have occurred which will have an effect on the rest of my career. It has made life very difficult indeed, and I am seeking to adjust things. I need time, and I need not to be disturbed.'

'What things?'

The MP looked at her witheringly. 'I'd hazard a guess and say you know nothing about politics.'

'Would she like a cup of tea?' Millie put her blonde head round the door, curious to know what was going on, not whether Judy was thirsty.

'Yes,' said Judy, wishing to prolong the moment.

'No,' said Hungerford, wishing her out of the house.

'I'll just get myself one, then.'

'Mrs Baines,' said Sir Freddy, 'has been a great comfort at this difficult time. I trust you will understand the need for discretion.'

'But... what actually happened?' burst out Judy. 'Why are you here? Hiding? Police looking everywhere for you? The whole country turned upside down by your apparent kidnapping?'

'Are we off the record?' said Sir Freddy, finally handing her a glass of whisky.

ELEVEN

Pushy though he was, the one thing to be said for David Renishaw was he knew when to leave well alone. He might be able to show Rudyard Rhys how to run a newspaper but he had better sense than to tell Terry when to point his camera.

They were sitting outside a sprawling thatched cottage in Hatherleigh, the 'foreign' part of Devon, which it turned out was every bit as beguiling as its Riviera cousins to the south and west. Both men had done the usual – knocked on the door, peered through the windows, lifted the dustbin lids, interviewed the cat – but each attempt at winkling out Hector Sirraway met with the same defeat.

'We'll wait,' said Renishaw. So both settled back in the Morris Minor and looked out of the window.

When that got boring, Terry got out his camera and started polishing it. Renishaw took out a notebook and started scribbling. The minutes dragged.

An hour later, nothing had changed. Doorstepping is a jaw-crackingly dull business and rarely leads to an improvement in relations between those who undertake it.

'You like this suit?' said Terry. 'Hepworth's, seven guineas. I thought I'd splash out.'

'A bit shiny.'

'That's what adds the class.'

They resumed their silence.

'Did you bring a Thermos?' said Terry, after half an hour.

'No.'

'I think I'll switch the engine on, get a bit of heat going.'

'Good idea.'

Another hour passed.

'Won't be long before the pub opens.'

'Mm.'

'What d'you think?' said Terry.

'Give it another hour.'

They waited.

Terry spent most of the time pondering the merits of a new lens hood he was thinking of buying, while Renishaw appeared to be writing the new *War and Peace* – his pen never stopped moving. Finally, Terry could bear it no longer:

'*You* seem to be busy.'

'I can't bear to waste time,' said Renishaw, without looking up. 'Life's too short, you have to keep adding to the things you've done, brick upon brick, stone upon stone, before they come to take you away.'

Terry wasn't quite sure what he meant by this. 'Is that a story you're writing?'

'You might say so. In a manner of speaking.'

Well, thanks, thought Terry, I'm fed up with this doorstep malarkey and I'm fed up with you. I've never known the time pass so slowly. Bring back old Judy any time, at least we could have a good argument!

'Time to go,' he said finally, and since he was in the driver's seat it looked like he'd get his way. 'And anyway, it was a pretty useless idea coming up here in the first place. If this Sirraway chap attacked the MP and kidnapped him in London, how was he going to get him all the way down here? It's over two hundred miles.'

Renishaw turned to him. His eyes were bright with an overabundance of intelligence and to be frank, just a little bit spooky. 'Not so useless, Terry. You see, if he is what I think he is, Hector Sirraway has plans for our local MP. And where better to hide him than down here?'

'Yes but…'

'He told Betty his family still owns a load of old buildings on and around Dartmoor. He has an abnormal grudge against Sir Freddy. If he wanted to do something with him – maybe make an example, I don't know – then this is the place to bring him.'

'No, but…'

'We don't know for certain he kidnapped Sir Freddy – it could be someone else – but he's the one who, as we've seen, bears him a grudge enough to want to denounce him in court and to bellow in the street that he's ten different shades of horrible. I think he's got a screw loose and, whatever he's done with that man, he'll come back here sooner or later to rest up.'

Terry couldn't deny the logic of this but was fed up anyway; it was an hour's drive back to Temple Regis and darkness had fallen. He turned the ignition key.

'Wait!' Renishaw suddenly jumped out of the car and raced over towards the cottage. Terry flipped on the lights and behind the five-bar gate you could just see two spectacled eyes blinking in the near darkness. He watched as Renishaw wrenched open the gate and got the professor by the lapels.

'What've you done with him? Where is he?' shouted the reporter.

'Get off me! Get away!' cried Sirraway in a shrill voice, pulling away. He made for the back door but Renishaw grabbed him again and managed to land a couple of punches on the professor's back before he jumped inside the door and slammed it.

'I'm calling the police! Nine-nine-nine! I'm calling them now!' shouted the muffled voice on the other side of the door. Renishaw shot forward and wrestled with the handle – for a man so slightly built, he certainly was muscular.

'Leave it off!' shouted Terry, running over. 'You're scaring him! Can't you see he's frightened?'

'Frightened? I should say so!' shouted Renishaw, shouldering the door. 'He's a kidnapper! Kidnapper! They're all cowards at heart!'

Even to Terry this seemed a little extreme, and as Renishaw shouldered the door again, Terry could see a strange look in his eye.

'Leave off! Leave it out!' he ordered, pulling Renishaw away roughly. 'You've gone too far! Too far! Get back in the car – I'll take care of this.'

He strode round to the front door, his movements caught in the glare of the Minor's headlights, before adopting the time-honoured doorstep tradition of kneeling down, lifting the letterbox and calling through it.

'Mr Sirraway, sir! Sorry about that, a bit of a misunder-standing! We're from the *Riviera Express* – can we have a word?'

Silence.

'Only take a minute.' Terry's knees were a bit gyppy, he couldn't stay down there for long. 'Just a quick word.'

'Go *away*!'

'I'm a colleague of Betty – you know, the blonde reporter. With the hairdo. She said how helpful you were.'

The door opened a fraction. 'I told her all I wanted to say. What are you after? Why did that man attack me?'

'My colleague is… he can get a bit jumpy. Not used to our ways. I'm very sorry,' said Terry. Before the minute was up he was inside the door and saying just the one spoonful, thank you, while Renishaw sat shivering outside in the Minor.

'Now, Mr Sirraway.'

'Professor.'

'Yers. Have you been to London?'

'As a matter of fact I go quite often. Why do you ask?'

'No, I mean have you *just come back* from London?'

'Why do you ask?' Now that the upset had subsided, the professor seemed more interested in his tea than anything else. He was stirring it with a pencil he'd taken from his top pocket.

'Just asking,' said Terry, thinking quickly. 'Betty will want to know.'

'She's very nice,' said the Prof, absently. 'I told her all I…'

'She'll want to know where you've been the past forty-eight hours.'

'Why?'

Terry was stumped for a moment. 'For the… the… report she's doing on you.'

'Ah, yes. Well, if you really want to know I have an old friend up in Ilfracombe. Been up there to stay. I've been very upset by the court case business – they had no right, you know. Why, under the Riot Act of 1714…'

'Yers, yers,' said Terry, lifting his Leica. 'Just taking a quick test shot.'

That old lie. Once he'd taken a test shot from one angle, he took another from above, then one from the side. 'Hmm, seems to be working OK,' he muttered to himself, 'I've been havin' a bit of a problem with it.'

'You're not going to take my photograph, are you? Because I'd prefer it if you…'

'Nah, nah,' said Terry soothingly. 'It's just a bit of a habit o' mine.'

'Well, is that all you want? Because I've got some clearing up to do.'

Oh, have you, thought Terry. Getting a sandwich for the prisoner? 'And where would that be?'

'Where?' The professor scratched his head.

'Out there… in your…' Terry had been only half listening to David Renishaw's theory, so he pointed vaguely – 'outhouses?'

'I don't have any outhouses.'

'Old buildings.'

'No.'

'Sheds.'

'I'm sorry, I don't follow. I was trying to say I've got to push the carpet-sweeper round, it's the Hatherleigh Bridge Club in an hour.'

The light was beginning to dawn. 'So you haven't got any outbuildings? Haven't been to London? Not recently? When did you last go?'

'The Proms. Elgar's *Dream of Gerontius* – you know, it's quite an extraordinary piece of…'

'The Proms are in the summer, aren't they?'

'Yes, of course.'

'Haven't been up since?'

'No. If you'd like to give that young Betty a recommendation for next year, though, they'll be doing Mahler Three in the second week. Sure to be a riot.'

'I'll leave you in peace then, Prof.'

'Send Betty my warmest regards. Tell her I'm sorry about her hair.'

But Terry was gone, into the Minor and revving it up as hard as he could before sharply letting in the clutch and heading back to civilisation.

'Wait a minute, wait a minute,' said Renishaw, who on the outward journey had been in charge of proceedings. 'Where d'you think you're going?'

'Wasn't him,' said Terry, his jaw jutting out. He was a bit fed up with this reporter.

'How d'you know?'

'Instinct, mate. Instinct and experience.'

There were many sterling qualities to Betty Featherstone. She was attractive, bright but not too much so, and energetic. She played hockey every Saturday and had the leg muscles to prove it.

She was good at her job and had a smile for everyone. If

there were occasional errors with her hair, or a mishap in her choice of clothes, it was nothing that a bit of inspiration couldn't put right.

But she was nosy.

In the world of journalism, surely this is a good thing – it's no use being mildly interested in something, you really have to turn over every stone when you cover a story. But there are limits – and there have to be times when you switch off the nosiness and just become a well-mannered human being again.

Betty couldn't.

There'd been the time when, on the instructions of Mr Rhys, she'd gone rifling through Judy Dimont's notebook to discover what was going on in the Gerald Hennessy affair. It didn't do her much good – she could read the words but couldn't interpret their significance – but she did enjoy the thrill of seeing something she shouldn't.

Now she was sitting at the desk assigned to David Renishaw and her fingers were itchy. Its surface was neat – oilcloth cover neatly folded over the Imperial Standard typewriter, mug with pencils. And a spike – the nasty curved instrument on which you impaled a carbon copy of your story once typed up – together with a couple of notebooks already crammed to bursting with a tight, neat Pitman's shorthand despite the brief time the new reporter had been here.

The drawers were locked.

Betty finished off writing a filler for the graveyard, the nickname given to the centre-spread of pages devoted to adverts for local businesses dressed up to look like news, and had been using Renishaw's typewriter even though there was nothing wrong with hers. It felt comfy sitting at his desk.

She tried the top drawer again, just to make sure. It rattled but refused to open. Looking round to see if anyone was watching, she leaned down to the bottom drawer and gave it a yank. It opened to reveal a pair of clean socks. This was an old trick – you then reach inside the bottom drawer, push up the one above and slide it out, and repeat the process till you get to the top.

Would it be a terrible indictment of her character to say that Betty was obsessive in her determination to find out all she could about David Renishaw? That she didn't mind using underhand methods to achieve her goal?

Yes, it would and no, she didn't.

The next drawer up contained a foolscap folder. Inside was a neat pile of typing paper bearing all the hallmarks of a half-finished book. Moving on up, Betty found a few letters and some chewing-gum packets. The top drawer, with its lock, proved more tricky. Betty was not unversed in the art of breaking and entering office equipment, and with the aid of a paper knife she released the unwilling victim in no time at all.

Whatever she was hoping to find, it came as a disappointment to discover no more than a few sheaves of paper, yellowing press cuttings, an old passport with its top corner clipped off and a packet of rubber bands.

'Finished that filler?' asked Denise, the new sub-editor, who'd wandered up behind her.

'Wha—' replied Betty, startled at being found out. 'Y… yes, here it is.' She looked at the girl and did not like what she saw: her features were too regular, her clothes well co-ordinated, and anyway someone said she'd been to university.

'Thanks.' Maybe Denise hadn't noticed the burglar's look on Betty's face, or maybe she was still too new to work out what was going on with Betty seated at Renishaw's desk. Betty breathed a sigh and turned back to her task.

Now her work was done for the day and Renishaw and Terry were safely miles away in Hatherleigh, she felt safe in taking out the contents of the top drawer and sifting through them.

What was she looking for – a photograph of Mrs Renishaw? Snaps of the children? Whatever it was, the first thing she turned up was a series of roneo'd pages clipped together with the banner:

The Tannville Trumpet

NEW ORGANISATION
FIGHTS INJUSTICE

ran the headline, with the sub-deck beneath:

OPERATION UNDERDOG

It began:

```
Working from offices in seven provinces,
without pay, 182 volunteers take up the
cudgels for the little man.
    'I'm from Underdog,' I said to the man
behind the desk.
```

```
Annoyance writhed across his face.
'You again? Get out of here,' he
snapped. 'The man's been fired and that's
the end of it.'
    But it wasn't the end of it. And after
two more visits from Underdog - an organi-
sation I created to take up the cudgels
for anyone getting a raw deal - the man
behind the desk gave in and grudgingly
reinstated the timekeeper he'd fired
unjustly six months earlier.
```

Betty started to skim-read. It was a lengthy, deftly written and tightly argued piece about how Underdog's knights in shining armour would come riding to the rescue if you were the victim of mistreatment or had been bypassed, overlooked, bilked or threatened.

As she read, Betty realised that the publication in her hand was a home-produced newspaper for a prison somewhere in the middle of Canada. Her eye strayed to the bottom of the piece to reveal Renishaw's name and a dateline from just eighteen months ago.

It all seemed very odd. Renishaw claimed in the piece to have worked for newspapers, first in England and then Canada, but from the content of the article it was clear that by now he was running a full-time organisation hellbent on pinning down those who oppressed:

```
It's no fun being an underdog. It is like
being in a deep, dark pit. You see the top
```

slowly closing over your head and desperately you fling up a hand for help. But
there is nobody there.

From now on, Underdog is there.

She shuffled through the rest of the contents of the drawer,
but there was far too much material for her to be able to
concentrate on – she'd have to come back after work, claiming to be writing up an evening job if anyone happened to
come into the office.

Her original quest, to discover a picture of Mrs Renishaw
(if, indeed, there *was* a Mrs Renishaw), had failed. There was
nothing personal to offer any clues to the enigmatic reporter
and yet she needed to know more. He'd invited Judy out for
a drink – surely it must be Betty's turn next?

The problem for Betty was she had Certain Rules. But did
those rules extend to a non-existent wife in a country three
thousand miles away? That was a matter which required much
consideration, because David needed looking after – that much
was clear from the hair springing up on the top of his head.

'Ach, dreamin' your life away – as usual,' said the nasty
old Scotsman with the pot belly and the bottle of whisky,
approaching at speed from the subs' desk. 'Here's something
for ye to do,' and he dropped a piece of paper on her typewriter.

EVERLASTING LIGHTBULBS!!!

proclaimed the public relations handout.

'There's a gap in the graveyard,' said Ross. 'Fill it. Five

pars on *Why Don't Lightbulbs Last As Long As They Used To?* Take the info from this handout and give the comp'ny a plug at the bottom – nae too much, ye mind, just a mention.'

It was at moments like this that she longed to get away. Oh, to be Betty Featherstone of the *Daily Mail* – Featherstone of Fleet Street! – her credentials were good enough, why couldn't she break away, get out of the stagnant backwater that was Temple Regis?

'Have you noticed how brilliantly the sun is shining?' cooed Athene, as she wafted past on the way to her desk. 'So magical, the sky... what a glorious day – a miracle when we're less than a week to Christmas!'

Time to go! thought Betty, as she jammed a wad of copy paper and carbons into the typewriter.

```
Do you ever feel that lightbulbs don't
last as long as they used to?
```

she hammered angrily.

```
A new survey shows that four out of five
households...
```

Her mind drifted away as she rewrote the lies and deceits the advertising agency had come up with to promote a lightbulb that was as likely to last for ever as it was for hell to freeze over this Christmas.

TWELVE

Sir Frederick Hungerford KBE was a man of his word. When Miss Dimont finally left the Ebury Street house, clutching her scoop to her chest and brimming with the joys of life, he did indeed lift the telephone just as he said he would. Only it was not Judy's editor or proprietor that she rang, but another number.

The result of that call took up a huge slab of the *Daily Herald's* front page next morning.

THE TRAGEDY THAT NEARLY KILLED ME

Missing MP found by the **Herald**

'I was in deep despair,' says Sir Freddy

Safe and well – pledges to fight on for constituents

by Guy Brace, Chief Reporter

Missing MP Sir Frederick Hungerford was found safe and well by the *Daily Herald* last night. He said he had suffered 'a mighty breakdown'.

Sir Frederick, 72, has been missing since he was seen in an altercation with an unknown man on Westminster Bridge. Scotland Yard says there is no cause for further alarm and that the case file has been closed.

Reunited with his wife Griselda, Sir Freddy confessed that he went into hiding after the fracas, which was witnessed by several passers-by.

'I suddenly cracked,' he told the *Herald*. 'Sometimes you can take the problems of your constituents too personally. But I'm all right now.'

The veteran backbencher said he had been approached after a constituency party which was held last weekend in Temple Regis, Devon.

'This person – I cannot name them – told me a story of such gut-wrenching personal tragedy that I found myself unable to think of anything else. I became so upset by it that when a member of my staff, who was walking with me towards the House of Commons, mentioned something which I considered trivial by comparison, I'm afraid there were fisticuffs,' he confessed. 'Fortunately my assistant does not bear a grudge and we have made it up.'

Sir Freddy says he then felt so ashamed of his behaviour he went into hiding. But after seeing a doctor who convinced him that his breakdown was 'emotional, not mental', Sir Freddy said he would be reporting back for work today.

'My constituents come first, second and third in my life. I love them. But I will try to maintain a

balanced viewpoint from now on,' he said, adding his apologies for any distress he may have caused.

He*(turn to page 3)*

Miss Dimont read it on the train travelling back to Temple Regis next morning.

'Pack of lies!' she cried aloud. 'Complete nonsense!' She was sitting in a compartment at the front of the Pullman train, and what with the thundering of the steam engine and the fact she had the compartment all to herself, she could voice her thoughts as loud as she liked without anyone thinking she was mad.

'What an absolute fraud! And what a fool he made of me!'

She went over the conversation of the night before, not for the first time. The bullying, hectoring MP had first ordered her to do his bidding by keeping quiet. Then, when that didn't work, he gave her a glass of whisky and told her the whole story – how he'd been beaten up by the same employee because the man was overworked and was not being given extra time off for Christmas – 'We have a lot on at this time of year and he frankly wasn't pulling his weight. We were walking towards the House and I decided he had to be fired. I told him his time was up, and gave him a few home truths, and the chap completely lost his grip and let me have it with his fists.'

'Why didn't you report him? And why then did you run away?' Judy had pressed.

'He's the son of an old colleague, I couldn't have him arrested,' replied the MP smoothly. 'I knew he'd clear out his desk and vamoose, and that would be the end of the matter.'

'But why then disappear?'

'Look,' said Sir Freddy, pushing his face towards hers. She could smell the whisky. 'The bruises – look at them! Millie covered them up with some of her make-up, but I didn't want tongues wagging in the House, so I thought I'd take a couple of days off. No harm done!'

Miss Dimont compared this version of events with the one described to the *Daily Herald*'s Guy Brace. Both were lies, compounded by the photo of Sir Freddy sitting happily in the company of, not the woman who opened the door last night, but Lady Hungerford.

He must have phoned the *Herald* the moment I left the house, she thought, and arranged for Brace to meet him at the marital home. Only a short taxi ride away from his popsy, after all.

But what does it mean? What's it all about?

A steward with a trolley rolled by her door and she beckoned him in. 'Black coffee and some ginger biscuits, please.'

As she dunked the biscuits and watched the countryside race by, she puzzled over the true purpose of Sir Freddy's subterfuge. There was no point in continuing to be angry with him – he'd double-crossed her, and that was an end to it. There might come a day when the situation would turn to her advantage – maybe when he retired. That wasn't very long away, after all.

No – what could it all be about? Was it to do with that protest outside the Con Club last weekend which Betty had been writing about? Could it be the odd professor who'd attacked him, only he didn't want to admit it because of some business between them? Could it have been Millicent's husband – supposing she had one?

Certainly, there'd been a fracas outside the House of

Commons involving Sir Freddy – there were eye-witnesses, after all. She rather wished, now the mystery had been solved by the obliging *Daily Herald*, that Inspector Topham was on the train so she could compare notes. But he was not; she'd walked up and down the corridors and there'd been no sign of his bulky frame.

And why, now she was thinking about the police angle, was Scotland Yard saying the case was closed? It was obvious Sir Freddy was telling a pack of lies and surely they must know that – why drop the case? Surely they should at the very least be interviewing his assailant?

And then what part did Mirabel Clifford have to play in all this? Could it somehow be connected to her?

On the face of it Mirabel was beyond reproach – a solicitor devoted to her job, who did her best to look after her family, then used up all her spare time in nursing a parliamentary constituency which there was no guarantee would be hers.

She seemed the kind of person Miss Dimont could easily befriend – brainy, charming, hardworking, and with the betterment of the community as her goal.

But then Mrs Clifford had given away the fact that Sir Freddy had a lady friend, and knew enough about the woman to be able to pass on her name and address. Did she have spies? Was her ambition secretly to ruin Sir Freddy's reputation? Was this the sort of behaviour to be expected from a future member of the House of Commons?

Indeed, was the amiable Mirabel Clifford not quite so lovely as she seemed?

Crisscrossing Miss Dimont's mind as the train pulled out of Exeter on its final run into Regis Junction was the shadowy figure of David Renishaw. Somehow since he'd arrived in the office things had changed, and not for the better. The old pecking order had been upset and though she rightly went by the title of chief reporter, Judy could see that in Mr Rhys's eyes, there was a new top dog – someone he could trust to come up with scoops like the entry-fee business. He'd only been here five minutes – who knew what he'd come up with after a few weeks?

The thought made her unhappy – her track record at the *Riviera Express* had been exemplary, but when men got together… well, maybe it was time to move on.

Or, was it time to call it a day anyway, give in to her mother's constant demands and go home to Essex, far from her cherished Devon, and take up the diamond trade again? There was nothing she wanted less, but maybe the choice was about to be made for her – maybe Rudyard Rhys's prayers had been answered, and he'd finally found a replacement for her.

'Next stop – Regis Junction for Temple Regis! Don't forget yer bucket and spade!' came the chirpy announcement over the tannoy. She looked out of the window as the train eased slowly to a halt and there at the end of the platform, she spotted the waiting figure of Terry Eagleton.

No sight could have made her happier.

'Terry!'

'Urs.'

A quick double-take: 'What's that you're wearing?'

'Don't *you* start,' he said, cranking up the Minor. The winter sunshine through the windscreen made his Hepworth's seven-guinea miracle shine like bauble on a Christmas tree.

'Well, you look very smart,' said Miss Dimont in placatory

tones, though she asked herself what they'd say when he strolled into the Old Jawbones wearing it – it really was a stinker.

A pause, then they both started talking at once. Terry was desperate to tell her about Renishaw's startling assault on the mad professor while Judy wanted to unload the treachery of Freddy Hungerford and the anguish of her lost scoop.

Who should go first?

'Lovely Mary's,' they agreed simultaneously, and Terry energetically steered the Minor towards the Signal Box Café. Once ensconced in its steamy interior, overlooking the railway line and only a hair's breadth from the passing locomotives, the frustrations of the past twenty-four hours gently eased. Though first Miss Dimont had a point to make.

'Mary,' she said commandingly as the sweet-faced proprietress brought them fish and chips twice, extra chips for Terry, 'Mary!'

'Yes, maid?'

'How long have we known each other?'

''Arf a lifetime, my darlin'!'

'And you know where I work, don't you?'

Mary scratched her head with the pencil she kept behind her ear. She lived up to her name at such moments – there was something particularly adorable about her features, even when her hair was anyhow and the orders were stacking up in the kitchen.

''Course I does!'

'Well, Mary,' said Judy with a touch of asperity, 'I'm just a bit surprised you never told me our new reporter is your lodger. I mean, he works in my office! Didn't you think I'd be interested in knowing that?'

Mary's eyes flicked to the door as more customers pushed their way in. It was a particularly busy lunchtime, what with the monthly cattle market and everything. 'Din' he tell you?' she asked, surprised.

'No, he didn't.'

'Oh. Well, he bin with us a fortnight. Was in the Station Hotel for the first week then moved over when he heard I had a vacancy. Is he permanent-like?'

Not if I have my way, thought Miss Dimont.

Terry was chewing his chips and looking out of the window. 'Bit secretive, is 'e?' he said to his reflection.

'You could say that,' said Mary slowly, then compressed her lips. If there was one thing about her, it was loyalty – she wasn't going to gossip about her lodger, even to Judy and Terry. She wiped the table with her cloth and whisked away.

'A rum 'un,' said Terry, and told the story of yesterday's action-packed trip to Hatherleigh. ''E takes things personal. 'E thought the Prof had kidnapped old Hungerford, and he wanted to perform a citizen's arrest. What *is* a citizen's arrest, anyway?'

'An action legitimised by section 24(A)2 of the Police and Criminal Evidence Act,' said Judy automatically. 'You're allowed to collar someone who you believe has committed a crime.'

'You allowed to beat 'im up?'

'No, Terry, no. You're supposed to arrest them and take them to a police station wrapped in cotton wool.'

'All I can say is your Mr Renishaw doesn't think he needs the police. Yesterday he was judge, jury *and* bleedin' executioner. I had to put him in the car a bit forceful-like.'

Miss Dimont nodded her approval. 'Well, as I told you,

Sir Freddy was never abducted. But he *was* attacked – I saw the bruises. Could Sirraway have done that?'

Terry thought about it. 'Yes, he could. He was definitely not at home when Hungerford was attacked – he said he'd gone to stay with a friend in Ilfracombe, but he could easily have been in London. And he's certainly got a bee in his bonnet about Hungerford – I couldn't get to the bottom of it all; he was rambling on a bit about stolen property, but I think that was because he was in shock after Renishaw attacked him. Don't you think I should tell Mr Rhys?'

'That a member of the public had been assaulted by a member of his reporting staff?'

'Well, don't you?'

Judy itched to say yes – looks like old Rudyard's got it wrong again, she thought. Just like his whopping mistakes over the Vicar's Longboat Party, and the Temple Regis Tennis Scandal, and the football pools farrago. Just when he thinks he's on top of this editing malarkey he goes and slips on another banana skin. One more trick like that and our Mr Renishaw will be on his way back to Canada.

Or jail.

'He took me mouse-racing,' she said. 'You know how much I hate…'

''S why you have that Mulligatawny,' said Terry, though he was more interested in a green-liveried locomotive that was trundling by the window. 'Look at that, Judy – an absolutely pristine 4-6-2 Class 8P, that is!'

'Oh, for heaven's sake, Terry, you and your steam engines! Have you read the papers today?'

'Might have.' This meant no.

'Well, I think, to keep on top of all this, you need to know about Sir Freddy and his popsy.'

'Hold on a min',' said Terry, and pushing his plate aside he reached into his camera bag and brought out a large buff envelope. 'You were asking about Pansy Westerham.'

Judy had forgotten all about it. 'Yes, but not now, Ter—'

'I had to call in a favour or two from a chum at the Press Association. Here y'are,' and with that he triumphantly slid half a dozen black-and-white prints onto the café table.

Only her innate good manners forced the chief reporter to turn her attention from a present-day political crisis involving a well-known politician to an obscure event which occurred twenty-five years before, the sum of which was a brittle blonde socialite spending most of her life in nightclubs and falling from the roof of a Knightsbridge house.

Well, perhaps that was unkind. Perhaps Pansy Westerham had been a lovely person, much adored, much missed. Certainly, Geraldine Phipps spoke up for her, while admitting that Pansy was not the friend to her that she had been to Pansy. Whatever Mrs W's pluses and minuses, here was all there was left of her – a handful of photographs which comprised her entire epitaph.

The wrinkled prints had gone brown with age. Each, according to librarian tradition, had a little paper tag pasted on the back with a typewritten caption giving the date and location.

THE ROYAL ACADEMY SUMMER EXHIBITION, JUNE 5 1935. L-R, LADY DIANA COOPER, MISS MARGARET WHIGHAM, LORD ANDREW CAVENDISH, MRS PANSY WESTERHAM.

LADIES' DAY AT ROYAL ASCOT, JUNE 14 1934. L-R, THE DUCHESS OF FIFE, THE EARL OF CRAVEN, LADY PORCHESTER, MRS PANSY WESTERHAM, THE MAHARANEE OF JAIPUR.

Miss Dimont found the images irresistible. They spoke of a time when women of a certain class would don as many jewels as they could muster and step into a satin gown before setting sail into the night. Perhaps they did it still, thought Miss Dimont, I wouldn't know – *do* people wear extravagant jewels any more? Not down here in Devon they don't!

'Oh look!' she exclaimed to Terry, who'd got a magnifying glass out and was professionally absorbing the whole content of the pictures – not just the hairdos – and making the occasional note. 'Look, Terry, here's Mrs Phipps!'

FIRST NIGHT, *THE TRANSATLANTIC EXPRESS*, ADELPHI THEATRE, PICCADILLY. L-R, JAMES DONAHUE, MISS BARBARA HUTTON, THE MARQUESS OF MILFORD HAVEN, MISS GERALDINE BEAUREGARD, MRS PANSY WESTERHAM.

'Geraldine!' exclaimed Judy. 'How incredibly glamorous she was! Just look at those legs! And how wonderful to take the name Beauregard for the stage!'

'Are you lookin' at this Miss Westerham?' said Terry sternly. 'Or just stargazing? This Pansy looks a pretty cold fish to me. Strained, not natural, looks like she's wearing a mask.'

His trained eye was spot on. Though the backdrops and the clothes and the jewels and the hair changed from picture to picture, one thing remained static – and that was Pansy's face. Crowned by a thatch of blonde hair, she was a thing of immense beauty with chiselled cheekbones and a square-cut jaw. The lips were full, the eyes wide – but her expression never changed, frozen as it was in a mixture of surprise and disdain.

'She's at all these parties but she's not enjoying herself,' observed Terry.

'Geraldine described her as the life and soul,' said Judy, 'but you're right. It's as if when a photographer hoves into view, she sets her features and they never change. As if she believes the camera can see inside her and she is determined not to let it.'

Lovely Mary brought an extra cup of tea; she was feeling a bit regretful she hadn't told Judy about David Renishaw.

'What do these pictures tell you, Ter?'

'Absolutely nothing. A bunch of stuck-up socialites putting on their best face for the camera. 'Er included.'

'I fear you're right. But Pansy doesn't look as though she belongs to them, she's always standing apart from the group. As if she doesn't really want to be there. It's all a big mystery. I know Mrs Phipps has high hopes of me finding something out about this case but I don't know, Terry, it's all so long ago.'

'Tell me about Sir Freddy instead, then,' said Terry resignedly, scooping up the prints and putting them back in his folder. 'I know you're dying to.'

THIRTEEN

It was Monday again, time for the dreaded weekly conference. But for once this was a joyous occasion – Christmas Day was on Thursday, which meant no newspaper. The conference was therefore given over to a stern tongue-lashing from the editor.

'Let there be no slacking,' hectored Rhys, looking with disdain upon his scurvy crew. 'I want a full working week from you all – the early pages drawn up even earlier, pictures filed, captions sorted, and then we'll leave the news pages over till next week. Obviously there'll be a great deal of Boxing Day sport, so that'll take up the space left by those lily-livered advertisers who don't believe our paper will be read over the Christmas break.'

'Ayyyy…' growled John Ross from the back of the room, 'and how rrrrr… right they would be.'

The editor feigned not to hear this and pressed on with his plan for reporters to make their New Year resolution to clear their desks of debris and smarten themselves up. In her notebook Miss Dimont practised the shorthand signs for 'hopeless' and 'futile', thus giving the appearance of taking notes while devoting her agile mind to the question of Freddy Hungerford.

The meeting broke up with little achieved and Judy returned to the newsroom.

'David Renishaw,' said Betty, shifting to her side of the desk – she had the irritating habit of occupying other people's chairs, just to see what the view was like from where they sat.

'Why weren't you in conference?'

'Late night, the alarm didn't go off.' With a faint blush she straightened her unruly hair. 'Now… David Renishaw…'

'Yes?'

'Not what he seems,' said Betty.

'I think we've gathered that.'

'No, I mean – *really* not what he seems.' She was itching to tell someone about Operation Underdog, but wasn't yet ready to confess to having riffled through the reporter's drawers.

'When you interviewed Sir Freddy the other day,' said Miss Dimont, oblivious to the world scoop Betty was incubating, 'did he strike you as being a little odd?'

'No more than usual,' replied Betty, 'a pat on the backside, the usual. Honestly, Judy – the colossal nerve of the man! Horrendous! Thank heavens he's going!'

'I agree with that,' said Judy, and told the story of Millie Barnes and the black eye covered by her make-up, which cheered Betty up – she was having to go home to her parents for Christmas and wasn't looking forward to it.

'The whole thing seemed so contrived – the punch-up in the street,' said Judy, puzzling. 'It just seems really odd.'

'There must be a dozen women who'd like to do that,' said Betty, 'give him what-for. I wouldn't mind a go myself.'

'Was there anything, though, that struck you as unusual about his behaviour that night?'

'Well, yes,' said Betty after a moment's thought. 'I thought it was a joke at first, but when I mentioned Mirabel Clifford's name he refused to acknowledge her existence. That seemed very strange – the election's only a few months away, surely he wants his party to win?'

'Not necessarily,' said Judy. 'I get the feeling it's more a case of *après moi le déluge* – he wants everyone to fail, so that in the history books his lengthy reign in Temple Regis will seem even more magnificent.'

'Well, if he knows who his successor is – and I bet he does,' said Betty, 'I reckon he must hate her guts to not even mention her in his farewell speech to the party workers.'

Judy made a mental note to tackle Mirabel Clifford again, once she returned to Temple Regis.

'But now – David Renishaw,' said Betty, bringing the conversation back to square one. She was brimming over with her secret.

'Where is he? He should have been in conference.'

'He's gone to test-drive the new office car.'

'*New… office car*? I haven't heard anything about that…!'

'He persuaded Mr Rhys we needed another car. So that he could get around the circulation area more easily. He was complaining about being stuck in the Minor with Terry, after that trip up to Hatherleigh.'

Miss Dimont was furious. First, being stuck in the Minor with Terry could be a penance, but one which all reporters had to put up with. He smelled nice but heavens, he could be boring if he got on one of his hobby-horses. Surely, if anyone was going to get a new office car, it should be the chief reporter!

Second, she'd asked Rudyard Rhys a dozen times if the newspaper could have more transport and he always said no on budgetary grounds – why was Renishaw able to persuade him when she couldn't?

And third, did it mean that she would have to continue whizzing round town on Herbert? He was a joy to ride in the summer months, but a vicious companion in the wet and cold. For a moment it made her think fondly of Valentine Waterford and his old tin bubble car[2], though you didn't want to be seen getting in and out of it in a skirt.

'I'm going *out*!' she said crossly and swept up her raffia bag.

Judy stepped into the street without thinking where she was going – there were a few small gifts still to get, she could do that. Or she could go over to Lovely Mary's for a cup of coffee, but that was sure to bring up the vexed question of Renishaw again.

Or she could hop on Herbert and go over to Bedlington to see Auriol – but she was due there this evening for the final showdown on Grace Dimont's arrival in town tomorrow, and she saw no reason to hasten that particular conversation.

Her footsteps took her towards the Market Square, where a huge Christmas tree dominated the canvas-topped stalls underneath. She eased her way into the crowd, shoppers eagerly snapping up last-minute purchases they'd regret the moment they got home, and for a moment gave up her

---

2 See *Resort To Murder*

thoughts to the sheer pleasure of seeing the red faces and bright eyes of the crowds.

'Hello.'

Standing before her was Mirabel Clifford with a wry smile on her face.

'Did you go carol singing with Sir Freddy in Ebury Street?' quizzed the solicitor, tongue-in-cheek. 'I saw something in the *Daily Herald* next day – was that you?'

'Yes. No.'

'Why don't you come into the office and have a cup of tea? I don't have a client for another hour or so.'

'That would be lovely.' The two women stepped across the square to where an important-looking portico announced the premises of Clifford & Co., Solicitors.

'I felt it was tempting fate to talk to you in the Commons Library,' began Mrs Clifford, once they'd settled in her wood-panelled office. 'I'm not an MP yet, and as I indicated, there's every chance I won't get elected – it didn't seem the time or place. But over the weekend I had the chance to think about our encounter and as long as I feel I can trust you, there are probably some things you ought to know.'

'About Sir Freddy?'

'Can I trust you?'

'That's a difficult one to answer. Supposing you tell me something I might find out by other means? If I were then to print it, you'd accuse me of having double-crossed you.'

'Point taken. Well, then, shall we come to what might be called an uneasy understanding?'

I like her, thought Miss Dimont. She's savvy.

'I've been having a problem with a man called Sirraway,' said the lawyer. 'He's been pestering me with complaints about Sir Freddy and I wonder if you know anything about him.'

'A little. What sort of complaints?'

'Well, it started out with him sending me a fairly comprehensive report on some less-than-legitimate property deals – all a very long time ago, but on the face of it decidedly shady.'

'Do you know he made an appearance in court before Colonel de Saumaurez the other day?'

'Yes, I'd heard that. The man's a nuisance, no question. No, the reason I mention him is because he then went further, sending in letters accusing Sir Freddy of a number of acts of embezzlement over the years, mainly from women who, according to Sirraway, were Sir Freddy's lady friends.'

Miss Dimont put down her teacup. 'I don't know about that,' she said, 'but in my experience he's not a man you'd leave your handbag with.' She was still seething over being scooped by the *Daily Herald*.

Mirabel Clifford reached into a drawer and brought out a sheaf of letters. 'He names names, and these are quite well-known women, those that are still alive.' She scratched her head. 'There seem to be an awful lot of them.'

'I wonder how he found all that out? Probably not even true – he just seems intent on stirring up trouble for Sir Freddy, by the sound of it.'

'I agree. But it puts me in a difficult position. You could say Sirraway has a bee in his bonnet, you might also say he's a bit of a crackpot, but he seems determined to bring all this into the open. And he's leaning on me to denounce Sir Freddy.'

'Can't you just ignore him?'

'Not altogether. If, when the election is announced, he comes out in public and says that Sir Freddy's successor – me – is hiding secrets about his murky past, how's that going to look? As if in some way I am in collusion with him. And you know what some people think – that all politicians are corrupt. As I explained the other night, I've got an uphill struggle as it is to convince the electorate they should vote for me.'

Miss Dimont smiled. 'I have the feeling you're going to ask me for help,' she said.

Mirabel's eyelids flickered. 'I hadn't thought of that,' she said shortly. 'I just asked you in for a cup of tea because of that chance meeting at Westminster the other night. I thought we might get along.

'But,' she added, 'since you mention it, I confess I'm not sure what to do. This man seems determined to ruin Sir Freddy's reputation, and he wants to use me as the weapon to destroy him. By giving me all this information he's drawing me in, implicating me somehow. As a solicitor I can handle it; as a politician it makes me vulnerable.'

'You could complain to the police.'

'That would be very unwise. He's not threatening me in any way that you could put your finger on, though I *do* feel threatened, I must confess. And of course he can say what he likes in court – about me, about Sir Freddy, using court privilege.'

'Which he's already done.'

'So I gather. The man's a loose cannon, quite likely to cause a great deal of damage.'

'Look,' said Judy, 'I'm not quite sure how to put this. You know me – well, you hardly know me at all – but what you do know is that I'm a reporter. But I also have certain other, um, skills. It seems to me that you need to discover whether what Professor Sirraway is claiming is actually true. I might be able to help there. If it *is* true, you might like to see that set in print before the election's announced so as to put as much distance as possible between you and the sitting MP.'

'Dangerous,' said Mirabel, 'if it comes back to me – *Prospective candidate stabs her predecessor in the back* – I can see the headlines now. And anyway I can't see the *Riviera Express* ever wanting to wash Sir Freddy's dirty linen in public.'

'Ah,' said Miss Dimont. 'That is where our Fleet Street brethren come in. We give the story to someone like Guy Brace on the *Daily Herald* or a chap called Inkpen on the *News Chronicle* – both of them would lap it up. I agree, my editor would never attack our sitting MP.'

'And the purpose of all this would be?'

'I think you've been put in a very difficult position. You hold information on your predecessor which, if it became known, could damage your chances at the election. If you do nothing, you risk being blackened by Professor Sirraway – has he got some kind of down on you?'

'I have no idea. I do know, or I believe, that he is slightly unhinged.'

'Well,' said Miss Dimont. 'It looks as though he means to let out all this information into the public domain. If *he* does it, he could accuse you of being part of the cover-up.

If on the other hand my Fleet Street friends Mr Brace and Mr Inkpen get the story, Sirraway's goal is achieved without implicating you.'

'So to save my own skin I stab Sir Freddy in the back? I'm not that kind of person.'

'It's going to happen anyway.'

Mirabel got up and walked to the window. Out in the Market Square the Christmas festivities were under way with a group of Morris dancers kicking up their heels to some squeezebox music, but when she turned back her face was puckered with indecision.

'There may be nothing to all this,' said Judy. 'Why don't you let me take these letters away and do some digging, see whether I can find anything out?'

'Oh, *will* you?'

Terry was in the darkroom, where all photographers hide when they want to avoid being sent out on a story. There is something mystical about the dark black space which brings a cathedral, or monastery, to mind – a place where, when the door was shut and the red light on, journalists of the writing variety are wise to keep away.

He was disappointed that the Pansy Westerham pictures, borrowed from his chum at the Press Association, had stirred so little interest in Miss Dimont. And after all that effort! Now he sat, once again, at the print table with a large magnifying glass staring at the ancient prints, willing them to speak to him.

Terry was usually very good at interpreting still images, recreating in his mind the circumstances which led up to that moment, frozen in time now, when these disparate people were drawn together at the photographer's behest. But today he could get nothing from these assorted tableaux – it was as if the dead hand of Pansy had killed all clues stone dead.

She looks gorgeous, he thought, but she looks troubled. He went through the prints once more, but they refused to communicate. Idly he turned them over and read out the typed captions, but each gave no more than a bald statement of who the figures were, left to right, with a date and the venue. Some had a rubber stamp – PUBLISHED, DAILY EXPRESS or PUBLISHED, THE TIMES COURT PAGE – but there was nothing else.

'Nothing,' grunted Terry, picking up the envelope and shovelling the prints back in – they'd have to go back to Fleet Street this afternoon. As he was doing so, he spotted a small piece of paper which had got itself stuck in the gum on the envelope flap. Obviously it had been shovelled into the package with the prints and got stuck to the interior. He pulled it out gently and saw it was a clipping from the *London Gazette*, the daily register of important matters whose only readers were newspaper librarians.

WESTERHAM, Mrs E.L.P. of 6 Hans Crescent, London SW1, and Paris. Personal bankruptcy etc., etc., etc.

The *Gazette* clipping was dated 15 July 1934. On the back was a rubber stamp:

DEAD 15 July 1934.

FOURTEEN

'So if we all pull together,' said Auriol briskly, 'we should see this through.'

She was greeted with blank stares; Miss Dimont and Uncle Arthur did not share her optimism.

'You sound just like you did in that Admiralty basement, all those years ago,' snipped Judy. 'Ready to consign others to a risky enterprise, giving them the cheery pat on the back before you parachuted them off into oblivion.'

'That's a bit harsh,' said Arthur deprecatingly. 'It's only your *mother* coming for Christmas. And she's not even staying with you.'

'All right,' said Judy, her eyes flicking from side to side, 'as long as we're all in this together.'

'Couldn't be easier,' said Auriol authoritatively. 'She's coming down on the afternoon train on Wednesday. Arthur will meet her and take her to the Grand Hotel, see her to her room and have a cup of tea and a chat. At six o'clock you and I arrive and we have cocktails and dinner. An early night.

'Then, on Christmas Day we meet for drinks in the Palm Court, exchange of presents, lunch, Grace goes off for a snooze. Arthur picks her up at six, she comes here for a light supper, then back to the hotel.'

'You've got this beautifully organised, Auriol,' said Arthur admiringly. Despite the minefield ahead he was rather looking forward to the family get-together. Since the death of his wife, his was a rather solitary existence.

'Then,' continued Auriol, 'on Boxing Day we collect her up, give her a glass of sherry and bundle her back on the train. Job done.'

'Let's have a drink,' said Judy quickly, picking up the whisky decanter. They were in Auriol's sitting room and it looked like the worst was over, for now. Thanks to Auriol, Grace Dimont's state visit would go like clockwork, as long as nobody said the wrong thing.

'Why *is* Christmas so stressful?' asked Judy plaintively. 'I feel as though I want to murder somebody.'

'Go ahead,' urged Auriol. 'You're so brilliant you could solve the case all by yourself.'

They all laughed; the pressure was easing but hadn't completely disappeared. 'What have you been doing, Hugue?' asked Arthur, as a way of changing the subject.

'More digging on Sir Freddy Hungerford,' said Judy. 'I had an interesting chat this morning with someone – apparently, he had a reputation in the early days for fleecing rich women.'

'Oh yes,' said Arthur, 'I know all about that.'

'Really?' said Judy archly. 'You do surprise me, Arthur! When we talked about him before, you said you'd had nothing to do with him after your spell in hospital together.'

'You asked if I knew him,' said Arthur defensively. 'I rightly said I didn't. You didn't ask if I knew *about* him.'

Judy topped up his glass grudgingly. 'So…?'

'Man was a rascal,' said Arthur. 'He married that German woman but always had someone else on the go – always rich, always a bit daft, usually a widow. He used to encourage them to buy racehorses, or invest in some get-rich-quick scheme. He'd use them and then drop them once he'd squeezed them dry. His wife had no money; he made his fortune out of all those others.'

'Were there lots of them? I've been given a document which lists some of them – haven't had a chance to look it over yet. I wonder if you'd have a squint and see whether any of it sounds familiar. There's a man who seems hellbent on ruining Hungerford's reputation.'

'Too late for that,' said Arthur complacently. 'Man was a rotter from the day he was born.'

'And he's dragging his replacement, Mirabel Clifford, into it as well,' said Judy.

'Really?' said Auriol, her ears pricking up. 'I've known her for years. Did some conveyancing for me when I first came down here. Very reliable, very charming, and just the sort of person we should have representing us in Parliament, no matter what your political preferences are. A terribly good egg.'

Isn't it marvellous how we all live inside our own little world, thought Miss Dimont. First Lovely Mary not telling me about Renishaw being her lodger. And now Auriol! I've known Auriol since the days of war, she has been my truest friend, we share secrets that nobody else could ever know – and yet I didn't know she knew Mirabel Clifford.

'I didn't know you knew—'

'Oh yes,' said Auriol in the slightly bossy way she occasionally deployed back in the Admiralty days. 'Haven't seen her recently but we were quite close once.'

'Well, since you're such good friends,' said Judy with a touch of asperity, 'it may interest you to know this eccentric figure, Professor Sirraway, appears to be determined to torpedo Mirabel Clifford *and* Freddy Hungerford, both at the same time.

'I mean, Sir Freddy's probably fair game – but Mirabel? Maybe he's got a bee in his bonnet about politicians, I don't know – but this campaign of his seems to be more than just getting back some old buildings Sir Freddy snitched years and years ago.'

'Poor Mirabel!' Auriol shook her head.

Arthur was loving this – here he was, in the thick of it once again! At his age, much of what went on in the world was beginning to pass him by. Often, though he had *The Times* delivered every day, he'd do no more than scan the Court Circular to see which of his friends had died, and check the runners and riders in the 2.30 at Newmarket. The birth of beat music had eluded him, and he had yet to travel on a jet plane. But when it came to Freddy Hungerford, suddenly he was the fount of all knowledge – the gossip in the back bar at his club had made sure of that.

'Eloise Cavendish,' he said with a beam.

'Yes?' said Judy and Auriol in unison.

'You remember – her husband was Governor-General of Australia. He might have been prime minister, only people are so dashed dismissive of titles when it comes to politics.'

'She was much younger,' recalled Auriol, 'Eloise.'

'A beauty,' nodded Arthur, 'but a bit dim. When her husband died he left her two houses, a safe full of jewels, and a tidy sum in the bank. Freddy Hungerford swallowed the lot.'

'What d'you mean?'

'His harebrained schemes for making money – *I know a chap who knows a chap who can double your fortune* kind of thing, and of course Eloise fell for it. Usually it was someone who Freddy owed money to who'd end up rich, while he and his lady friend sunk slowly further in the mud.

'He had a house and a wife to keep up. And being an MP costs a packet, too. So he fleeced Eloise for all she'd got, then dropped her. I believe she lives in a bungalow in Bexhill now.'

'*Bexhill!*' chorused his audience, shuddering.

'She wasn't the only one. So I think probably your man – what's his name, Solloway? – has got it right.'

'Looks like Freddy got his hands on several fortunes, then. What a beast!' said Auriol. 'Supper, everyone? Or we could go out.'

'Let's stay here,' said Judy, 'it's a lovely fire.'

Auriol lit candles and fished out cutlery. Judy was delving in her raffia bag for the document Mrs Clifford had handed over earlier. Pausing to sip her drink, she laid it on the table and pushed her spectacles up her nose.

'You're right,' she said to Arthur, riffling through its numerous pages. 'Sirraway names Eloise Cavendish. He seems to agree pretty much with what you were saying.'

She looked up. 'I wonder what he's trying to achieve? Either he has a case against Hungerford with regard to those buildings, or he doesn't. I can't see why he's bothering with all this.'

'It's personal,' said Auriol. 'Who else has he got in there?'

Judy took a sip of her whisky and flipped the pages. 'Half of the ladies in *Debrett's*, by the look of it. But there's too much here to go through just when we're about to have supper. It's mostly handwritten and I'll need a magnifying glass.'

'I've got one in the drawer.'

'No, Auriol, it can wait. I have the feeling that it'll be the same old story, several times over.'

Uncle Arthur clinched it. 'Top up, anyone?' he said.

Despite the editor's insistence that work should not be abandoned simply because there wasn't a paper this week, the newsroom was deserted. It was Betty's moment to pounce.

'What are you doing for Christmas, David?' she asked, turning her headlights on the reporter who, judging by the look on his face, was busy typing something terribly important.

'Mm-huh?' he said, looking up briefly. Before Betty could answer, his head was back down and he was hammering away again.

'Mrs Renishaw coming to join you? Or will you be going away?' The thing you could always say about Betty, she was dogged.

He finished his typing with a flourish, and pulled the paper noisily out from the Imperial Standard.

'Oh,' he said vaguely. 'The, er…'

'Mrs Renishaw,' pressed Betty.

'Ah, yes.'

I wonder what *that* can mean thought Betty, but didn't pursue it. She had other questions to ask.

'Some tea? I'm just making a pot.'

'No, thanks,' said Renishaw. 'Do you know Inspector Topham, the CID man?'

'Yes, a lovely old thing. Due for retirement soon.'

'I wonder what's the best way to approach him. I've just been writing out a report on this Professor Sirraway. I think I've discovered something which... well, let me put it this way,' he said, as if Betty wasn't bright enough to grasp the import of his findings, 'I think the man poses a risk to public safety and something should be done about him.'

'Oh, I don't think so,' said Betty, giving the matter her full consideration for all of two seconds. 'He's a bit odd, but safe enough. I had a long chat with him, you see. He keeps bees – I think that's always a good sign, don't you?'

'Betty,' said Renishaw, 'the man's got a screw loose! You didn't give him your address, did you?'

Betty couldn't remember. She gave it to most gentlemen who asked.

'I... I think you're wrong, David. I think he's got a grievance against our MP, that's all. And from what he told me it sounds like he has a point.

She paused, gathering herself for the onslaught ahead.

'I think, in this case,' she finally continued, 'that's it's the Prof who's the *underdog* here. And our paper should be looking into his claims and giving him the support he clearly wants. I'm all for the *underdog*, aren't you, David?'

A wintry smile spread over Renishaw's face. 'You're cleverer than I thought, Betty,' he replied slowly.

Was that an insult or a compliment? And – what exactly did it mean? She'd chosen her words carefully to show she knew something about him – maybe. But not so much as to give away the fact she'd been going through his drawers and making a note of his bank account details.

'Ha, ha!' she said eventually.

Renishaw got up and came around to sit on the corner of her desk, swinging his leg and looking down at her. 'What do you know about underdogs?' he asked sweetly, but his eyes had narrowed.

'Well,' said Betty, who was not easily intimidated, 'I'd say in that man Sirraway, you have a case in point. He's been pushed around by a man who has all the power and all the connections.

'He told me he'd been to see Sir Freddy on a number of occasions but he was always kept waiting, never given the chance to put his case. Which was, by the way, that the MP had stolen a number of buildings which rightfully were his. That he knew of other examples of what he called *this wholesale theft*, and that he knew one or two things about Sir Freddy's private life as well.'

'What sort of things?' said Renishaw, suddenly sitting up straight and looking alert. '*Who* was he talking about?'

Betty felt rather pleased with herself. When Renishaw first arrived at the *Express* it wasn't difficult to see he'd written her off, whether as a woman or as a reporter she couldn't tell. Now, all of a sudden, he was paying her very close attention indeed.

Wasn't it shrewd of her that day to have plucked up her courage, left the courtroom, and chased after Professor

Sirraway? She was now not only the *Express*'s expert on the local MP, but on his tormentor, too!

'He's an underdog, David,' she said, looking him straight in the eye. 'I get the impression those are the kind of people you stand up for.'

'I do. More than you can ever know, Betty.'

'Well, you should be sticking up for him! Rather than that old goat Hungerford. Saying he's a menace, wanting to get Inspector Topham to investigate him – that's not sticking up for the underdog, is it?'

'Forgive me if I say so, Betty,' replied Renishaw smoothly, 'you haven't a clue what you're talking about.'

Betty jumped up. 'Are you a journalist, David?' she said, challengingly. 'Or are you something else? And anyway what are you doing here in Temple Regis – about the most unlikely place in the world for someone with your skills? I can tell how you look down on everyone here, from Mr Rhys to Judy, from me to... to... John Ross over there!' She pointed her finger at the abandoned subs' desk with its forlorn sprig of mistletoe and its tawdry piles of waste paper.

'Actually, John and I get on rather well,' said Renishaw, taking this outburst in his stride. 'We've quite a lot of friends in common from old Fleet Street days.'

'Were you *ever* in Fleet Street?'

'Why are you suddenly so interested in my past? About my work, my wife, where I come from? And... this word you keep bandying around... *underdogs*?'

Well, thought Betty, this is making Christmas a lot more exciting than I thought it could ever be! She looked round the newsroom, but there were now even fewer people dotted about its furthermost reaches than before.

'The cleaners came while you were out,' she said. Thinking, this much you learn when you enter journalism – if you can't put out a convincing lie when you need to, you've no right to be in the job in the first place.

'Yes, they came by as they always do at this time of year. They go through the desks to make sure there's no flammable liquid or other stuff left lying around while the building's empty over the holiday period. They have pass-keys, they go through everybody's drawers. Strange, I know, but true.'

Renishaw gave her another of his wintry smiles and waited for her to go on. He's waiting for me to stumble, she thought, but I can pull this off. I can!

'They took everything out of your desk and just left it lying about. So careless! Since I had a minute I straightened everything up and put it all back for you.'

'And while you were at it, you just happened to read what was in there.'

'Well, no. Looks like you're writing a book – that's private, I wouldn't look at that.'

'But you saw the prison newsletter, the one with the article about Operation Underdog.'

'You could hardly miss it,' replied Betty, giving her untruth every last ounce of personal conviction. 'Sitting there on top of the pile! Which is what prompted me to ask you these questions – what *is* Operation Underdog? And have you brought it to Temple Regis with some ulterior motive in mind?

'Are you a journalist, or are you something else? If so,

what are you? And what are you doing in Temple Regis? What's the jail connection? Are you trying to put someone in jail – Professor Sirraway, perhaps? Or trying to get someone out?'

Betty felt exhilarated at having got all this out in a single coherent line of questioning. But then she had to go and let the side down.

'And,' she added, 'is there *really* a Mrs Renishaw? Or did you just make that up?'

FIFTEEN

The way Sid polished a glass was remarkable – he put more effort into bringing it to a perfect finish than it took to swallow the contents. But in his domain, the back bar of the Grand Hotel, he brought his soldierly ways to everything – the shining silver ashtrays, the plumped-up cushions, the neat arrangement of newspapers and magazines on the console tables.

He was a diligent worker, and an even more diligent listener.

'So you see, Frank,' he said, pulling the Portlemouth beer-tap with caution, 'I thought I'd better let you know.'

'Much obliged, Sid. Tell me again, only slower, and don't leave anything out.'

Those years in the desert had left a lasting imprint on both characters. Sid was glad of his hotel uniform, a reassuring emblem of order and rank. His white tunic was immaculately pressed, its gold buttons polished to a dazzling sheen, with the small gold-wire epaulettes adding just the right amount of dignity. The medal-ribbons, discreet enough, told their own story.

Inspector Topham never wanted to don a uniform again,

and tried hard never to think about what he'd seen in battle. Wearing a suit, a waistcoat and a felt hat relieved him of memory.

Yet the two were drawn together by their history, sharing a brotherhood not easily expressed in words.

Deeds, though, were something else, and Sid had been keeping his ears open.

'I heard 'im on the blower out in the corridor,' he said. 'Saying it was a good 'un, so good he'd prob'ly have to stay here over Christmas. He'd already called his lady friend and told her to get on the train.'

He leaned over the bar. 'Interpol, 'e says. Interpol's closing in. They'll be here in a few days, 'e said, but I need to be ahead of them. 'E was asking for they down t'other end of phone to authorise a huge sum of money.'

'Bribery, like?' said Topham.

'Like a bath tap you can't switch off. The money, I mean. 'E asked for a thousand, and judging from the smile on his face when he came back in 'ere, he'd got it.'

'Go on,' said the copper, gazing deep into his Portlemouth.

'The gist of it was, 'e didn't know the name of the chap Interpol was after and 'e needed to grease a few palms to find out. There'd been a murder. Interpol was on the murderer's tail, and they were homing in on Temple Regis.'

'Wait a minute, wait a minute,' said the Inspector, 'how does he know all this? I haven't had a word from Interpol!'

'Chum in Scotland Yard.'

'Oh, *them*,' spat the copper. 'They treat us like hayseeds, never give us the time of day. When I was up in London on that goose-chase involving the MP, they talked to me as if I was the village idiot.'

'Anyway,' said Sid, oblivious to inter-force rivalry but very keen on his priceless nugget of information, 'Mr Inkpen said 'e needed to grease a few palms.

'But,' he went on, 'this is the point, Frank. 'E said it would be the icing on the Christmas cake, this Interpol lark. 'E said when they pounced, it would make the front page for weeks and weeks. Temple Regis, the Murder Capital of Great Britain! 'E was reeling off all those murders – Hennessy, the beauty queen, Larsson, and that Patr—'

'I know, I know,' snarled Topham. 'No need to remind me, Sid! But it's ridiculous – how can I possibly investigate a crime when I don't know the name of the victim, and I don't know the name of the perpetrator?'

Sid put down the glass he'd been polishing.

'If nobody's officially informed you, it's not your problem,' he said cheerily. 'Let 'em come, I say, and just stand well back.' He was wondering whether Interpol could afford the Grand's bar prices.

'It's a bit more complicated than that,' said Topham. 'If Interpol come in here and make an arrest, that little toad Inkpen is going to drag all the other cases in when he writes his story. How's that going to make me look, with two years to retirement? What's the Chief Constable going to say? I don't want to end up on traffic duty, Sid, just when they should be sending out to the engraver's with my gold watch.'

'Tell you what, Frank,' said Sid, looking over the copper's shoulder. 'Back in the old days in the desert you used to say

Meet fire with fire – remember? Here's your chance to do just that, mate.'

Topham span round to see Rex Inkpen loping cheerily towards the bar.

'Ah, Frank!' said the reporter, just a trifle patronisingly. 'Have you thought over our little chat? It's not too late to change your mind – I'd be so happy to get you and the missus away on a nice sunny holiday somewhere.'

'Plenty of sunshine in Temple Regis,' growled Topham.

'Not this time of year. What's that – a pint of Portlemouth?'

'No, thanks.'

'Pint of Portlemouth, please, Sid, and a large VAT 69. On my tab. So what d'you say, Frank – have you ever been to the Canaries?'

'I've been to hotter places than that, Mr Inkpen.'

'You have only to say the word. But meantime I'm ready to lob a nice donation to the Widows and Orphans Fund in return for your memoirs. Why don't we go and sit down?'

The two men, with very different goals in mind, made their way to the other end of the bar and slid onto a red plush banquette. Sid tiptoed over with a silver platter.

'I know your game,' said the policeman, pushing the crisps away. 'You're here to make a monkey out of me, but it ain't going to happen.'

The reporter stretched out his legs and looked across the table. 'Don't know what you're talking about,' he lied. 'You've done a great job here and my newspaper wants to tell the rest of the country what an amazing achievement you CID boys have chalked up in Temple Regis.'

'If you turn that story on its head,' riposted Topham, 'it

comes out as, *What an amazing place Temple Regis is – more dead bodies floating about than round the* Titanic.'

'Ha! Ha!'

'And if you think you're going to come in here and show us up, you've got another think coming.'

'You've got it all wrong.'

'Oh yes?' said the policeman heatedly. 'You think I don't know about your Interpol line?'

'Well, I was only asking you over our nice cup of tea together whether they'd been in touch.'

Topham stared at him hard. 'About the murder. About the murderer on the loose. About the murderer on the loose holed up in Temple Regis.'

'Ah!' said Inkpen with a conspiratorial smile. 'So they *have* been in touch, then!'

I wish I were a better chess player, thought Topham, I need to know what move to make next. He thinks I know more than I do while I haven't a clue as to how much he knows. He has the advantage, while he thinks I have the advantage.

'I have the advantage over you,' he said experimentally. 'I know what's going on, while you're footling about trying to make a story for your newspaper. Why don't you tell me what you know, and I'll try to fill in the gaps?'

For a moment Inkpen looked startled. 'From what I'd been told, I got the impression the Temple Regis police had been kept in the dark. Deliberate strategy to reduce the risk of leaks.'

'You're a journalist,' said Topham. 'And a Fleet Street journalist at that. You can have no idea what goes on at a local level, when all you do is spend your time and money buying drinks for your chums in Scotland Yard.'

'Fair to me, Frank, I'm now spending time with you. *And* I've just bought you a pint.'

Topham looked at the glass of Danegeld in front of him. He'd promised himself he wouldn't touch a drop when Sid brought it over, but he'd been so intent on their conversation there was now only a third of it left.

'Tell me what you know, then. If you want my help.'

'Cooee, Inspector!' called a melodious voice from the doorway. 'Missed you on the train coming home! What a waste of time all that was!'

It was Miss Dimont: 'Can I join you? Just been in to check on the arrangements for my mother, she's staying here for Christmas.'

The policeman was furious. Just when he thought he was going to get something out of Inkpen, the nosiest woman in Temple Regis turns up and spoils the moment.

'Bit busy just now,' he said, shortly.

Miss Dimont ignored this. 'A pint of the usual, is it? And what would your gentleman friend like?'

'We're just doing some business,' said Inkpen in superior tones. 'If you'll excuse...'

'Now, Frank,' reprimanded Judy, 'I have not met this gentleman before. But I have a very sharp nose, and the odour rising from his side of the table suggests to me he is a reporter. What's more, he is not a reporter from anywhere round these parts. And so I deduce from his demeanour and his clothes that he is from Fleet Street.'

'Very clever. I'm Inkpen, *News Chronicle*. And you are?'

'Your country cousin. Judy Dimont, chief reporter on the *Riviera Express*. Isn't it usual for you lot to drop in and pay us a courtesy call when you're in town? Weren't you thinking of coming by the office to say hello?'

'Didn't want to bother you.' When he smiled and showed his teeth, Inkpen looked particularly vulpine.

'We like to keep tabs on what's going on. Not unreasonably. Are you here about Sir Freddy Hungerford?'

'Sir Fredd—?'

'MP,' said Judy crisply. 'Beaten up in the street, went missing. Found safe at home, nobody the worse for wear, soon to go to the House of Lords. End of story.'

'Ah yes, I believe I saw something…'

'It was Page One of the *Daily Herald*. You read the papers, do you, Mr Inkpen?' She was bristling at his breach of protocol, invading her home turf without letting anyone know. She decided to lob in a hand grenade.

'Or perhaps you've come about the mistress? The *News Chronicle* likes that kind of juicy story, doesn't it?'

'What mistress?' Inkpen was caught off-guard. Was he missing a scoop?

'Share and share alike,' said Judy, turning to wave three fingers at Sid – a Portlemouth, whatever Inkpen's sluicing down, ginger beer for me – 'tell me first what brings you to this joyous part of the world.'

Inkpen and Topham looked at each other. The big-time crime reporter most certainly wasn't about to share his great scoop with someone from a local rag. On the other hand, the policeman could see the advantage of getting the Interpol story out into the open.

'He's got a murderer on the loose,' said Frank with satisfaction, swallowing the rest of his pint.

'Oh yes?' said Judy. She didn't sound all that impressed.

'Mr Inkpen here is hot on the tail of a man who Interpol are desperate to get their hands on. He's hiding out here in Temple Regis.'

'Oh really? D'you think the population is safe, Inspector?'

'Or he could be in Cornwall,' added Topham sardonically. 'Or Timbuktu.'

'Ah. Less chance of our Christmas being spoiled then. If he's in Cornwall. Who's the miscreant, Mr Inkpen?'

'Call me Rex. I can't tell you that.'

I can't tell you that because I haven't got a clue. I was in the Lamb of God, round the back of the Yard, with old Charlie Berry the other night. It was late, we'd had a few; he mentioned they'd heard from Interpol HQ that their boys were coming down to Temple Regis, looking for a chappie who'd topped somebody. But then he clammed up. So I did some checking in the cuttings library and discovered there'd been a few murders down here, pretty good ones, and on that basis convinced my bosses I had a huge scoop on my hands.

'Oh go on,' smiled Judy, pushing the whisky glass encouragingly towards him. 'Give me a hint.'

I wish I could, dear. If this old copper doesn't open up and tell me what he knows, I'm going to spend Christmas in this very expensive hotel agonising about what the desk is going to say when I tell them the story doesn't stand up. And then, when they look at my expenses sheet…

'I don't think I should.'

'Come on, then, Inspector Topham – *you* tell me. The story's going to come out sooner or later, and a word or two from you will allow me to write about Temple Regis

CID's involvement. Don't want all the glory going to those foreigners coming in and invading our pitch!'

Both men looked at her, mute. Neither of them had a clue what to say next but neither would admit it.

'Tell me about the mistress,' said Inkpen, jinking sideways.

Shall I? thought Judy. It's a story which will never get printed in the *Riviera Express* – how would Temple Regis look to the outside world if we revealed their long-serving MP was a liar and cheat? And that was only as far as his marriage was concerned – there was all the other business involving Professor Sirraway, the illegal property deals, outrageously helping himself to other people's possessions. And then the way he'd made his fortune by bleeding dry a succession of feeble women.

Why not tell? she thought. Why should a man like Hungerford get away with appearing to be such an upstanding pillar of the community when he was rotten to the core?

'Where do you stand on the matter of hypocrisy, Mr Inkpen?'

'Ha, ha. Good one. I work for a Sunday newspaper.'

'Seriously. Your answer will determine whether I tell you what I know about Sir Frederick Hungerford and his popsy.' And then you can tell me about Interpol, so make it good.

Inkpen took off his wire-framed spectacles and huffed on them. He polished them, then continued to stare at them as if they were to blame for any shortcomings in his answer. He really was a bit of a ham.

'The public has a right to know,' he intoned, as though this exonerated all Fleet Street's misdeeds at a single throw. 'Whoever's in the public eye – actor, judge, politician, financier

– if they pretend they're something they're not, if they hide their baser instincts behind a veneer of respectability, we're entitled to know.

'It's all a game. They know they've done wrong, they're hoping they'll get away with it, but at the same time they're completely aware of the consequences if they get caught.

'It's a game for us, too. For every hypocrite we nail, there are a thousand more who get away with it – the curates in the vestry, the businessmen bilking their investors, every director in the theatre with a casting couch. People complain about what we write, but our type of newspaper sells more than the others, which proves there's a public appetite for it.

'You can call it retribution, the little man getting his revenge on the people beyond his reach – the ones who end up rich, famous and titled while they do not. And whyever not? The libel laws don't allow us to write what's not true, and what we are doing is entirely legal. And, you might say, just and proper. A suitable corrective.'

'So you're all knights in shining armour – how noble!' said Miss Dimont, drily. 'Not a guttersnipe amongst you!'

'Tell me about the mistress.'

'Mmm. I just need time to reflect on the consequences. The trouble with you Fleet Street boys is you live a hermetically sealed existence, cut off from the people you write about. Down here, we live in a community – we're here this year, next year, *and* the year after that. We walk through the streets and bump into the people we've written about. They can come up and complain if they don't like it. And they do! That makes the game, as you call it, adopt a different set of rules.'

Inkpen gulped his whisky. You could tell he was getting bored with all this.

'The national press,' he said importantly, 'serves the nation. *Your* job, down here, is to write up the flower shows. Tell me about the mistress.'

The contempt in his voice ensured Judy would most certainly *not* be telling him about the mistress, now or ever, but she was far too clever to let her anger show.

'In just a minute,' she said sweetly. 'But why don't you go first, Rex? Tell us about Interpol, do!'

There was a pause.

We're stuck, thought Inkpen.

Stuck, thought Topham.

'Hello,' said Terry. He had the deerstalker with him, but he'd had the good taste to take it off when entering the Grand.

'What are *you* doing here?' said Miss Dimont irritatedly. She was about to land a huge scoop for next week's paper – **INTERPOL IN TEMPLE REGIS MANHUNT** – no need for photographers to come pushing their lenses in!

'You'd better put this on,' said the photographer, tossing the hat in her direction. 'And get out your magnifying glass and pipe.'

'What d'you mean?'

'We've got a dead body, Sherlock. Get yer skates on!'

'Wait a minute,' said Inspector Topham, scrambling to his feet, 'wait a minute! I don't know anything about a dead body!'

'Down the library. One of the old ladies who works there. Fell off a ladder. Your lads are already there, Frank

– they didn't know where you were so they just got on with it.'

'Suspicious, is it?'

'Miss Greenway was afraid of heights. It was the other librarian – Miss Atherton – who used to put the books back on the high shelves. She called in and told Sergeant Gull she couldn't understand what on earth she was doing up a ladder. He alerted your boys, and off they went.'

All three – Topham, Miss Dimont, Terry – rose to their feet simultaneously. Inkpen looked at his watch, then his empty whisky glass. 'Let me know if it's anything exciting,' he said lazily, and sat down again. 'Sid!'

Sod, thought Topham.

The library was only a two-minute drive in the Minor. The police surgeon had already come and gone but the body of poor Miss Greenway was still there, decently covered with the sheets of brown paper which wrapped the parcels of books sent by publishers. The atmosphere in the library, usually so calm, so tranquil, seemed jangled and disjointed.

'Happened around 5 p.m.,' said one of Topham's faceless officers. Miss Dimont, who bumped into these fellows quite often, was not enamoured. There are nice policemen and there are nasty policemen, and this lot didn't fall into the first category – she couldn't understand why someone as upright as old Topham could abide them.

The Inspector himself had arrived ahead of them and was pacing round the book-lined room, all gilt and brown and crimson in the half light. 'You shouldn't be in here!' he barked at Judy and Terry.

'Too late,' trilled the reporter, 'won't be a jiffy, Inspector. Might I have a quick look?' she added to one of the faceless ones.

Disobligingly the man drew back a sheet of paper to reveal the head and shoulders of Miss Greenway. The poor lady's eyes were open and her features were set in an undeniable look of horror. Her body was splayed in such a dramatic fashion it was as if some giant had picked it up and thrown it down with angry force.

'She was always very keen on archaeology,' said Judy, gently replacing the brown paper after a quick look. 'I once had a lovely chat with her about tombs.'

'Well, now she'll be able...' said Terry jovially, about to state the obvious.

'Don't say it!' snapped his reporter. Terry tutted and wandered off to see if there were any books on Rolleiflexes.

'She'd done such a nice job with the Christmas tree, too. Although – look, Inspector – what a mess she made of it when she went down. How sad, if she could see it now.'

'Nah,' said the faceless one, who didn't like clever women and liked to show his superiority, 'the Christmas tree's over *there*. She fell off the ladder over *here*.'

That did, in fairness, momentarily silence Temple Regis's supersleuth.

'Come on now, off you go,' snapped Topham, 'you shouldn't be in here anyway. If there's anything to say, I'll make a statement in the morning.'

Terry and Judy made their way out of the library. 'Such a dedicated person too. She loved books so much it's as if they loved her back.'

Terry put on his hat. 'See you at the police station tomorrow, then,' he said. 'For Topham's statement.'

'Erm...' said Judy, slowing in her tracks. 'Er... I can't... won't be able... er...'

Terry wasn't really listening. 'Ten o'clock, OK?'

'I... can't... come,' said Judy. 'It'll have to be Betty. Or Renishaw.'

'Why ever not?'

'My mother. She'll be here tomorrow and I have to make all sorts of...'

'Only take ten minutes.'

'No, I can't, Terry! You don't understand!'

'Judy, for heaven's sake! If I don't understand about you and your mother by now I never will. How long have we been travelling round in that Minor together? Years, Judy, years! And every so often out comes your mother into the conversation. She's this, she's that, she's writing you letters. What's the problem?'

'You don't know. You've never met her. If you had...'

'After all you've been through, the war and that, I don't understand – what's the problem?'

Heaven knows, thought Judy. She's a difficult woman – a *very* difficult woman. But maybe the fault lies with me – if I treated her differently in the first place, stood up to her rather than running away, she wouldn't be such a millstone round my neck.

Maybe if I answered the letters, if I went to visit occasionally, if I allowed her into my life – made her come down here and stay in Temple Regis – it wouldn't be this way.

In any case, is she so wrong in wanting me to go back to

live in Essex? It's a lovely house, even if I don't want to live there. The countryside is beautiful, even if it's not a patch on Devon. It's nearer to London and the life I once had.

'So you won't be working tomorrow?'

'I can't.'

'I'll get Renishaw then. If there's anything suspicious about the old lady's death, he'll be all over it like a rash. He's hot as mustard, you know. If a bit trigger-happy.'

Miss Dimont turned and looked down the hill towards the *Riviera Express* offices. Down there, in the jumbled disarray of the newsroom, among the battered Remingtons and Underwoods and the discarded carbon copies and filled-up notebooks, alongside Betty and John Ross and Athene and even, for heaven's sake, Rudyard Rhys! – lay her life. The shocks of war and the evils of espionage had been laid to rest, slowly, with each successive edition of the *Express* since she came by accident to Temple Regis all those years ago. The days of being a brilliant young tyro in the international gem market were even further away, lost in the fog. *Now* was her life, *here* was her life…

She turned back to look at Terry – standing there like a mastiff straining at the leash, eager to get on with the big story. The multi-coloured Christmas lights flooding out from the market square framed his strong body, painting it brilliantly with their messages of goodwill. For a moment he looked invincible.

'Terry, would you mind hugging me? Just for a moment?'

END of PART ONE

PART TWO – SUMMER

SIXTEEN

Spring had given way to early summer. Herbert was released from his tarpaulin shroud and warned he had a busy season ahead of him. Terry came over to change the spark plug and check the tyres before giving him a clean bill of health.

In and around Temple Regis, nature had joyously come to life. The roads leading into town were foaming with cow parsley, while on garden walls red campion and speedwell made their debut and swifts jetted their way through the streets.

Temple Regis took a quick glimpse in the mirror to make sure it was looking its best, then prepared itself for the onslaught of the holiday season. The streets were swept, the kiosks on the Promenade given a fresh coat of paint, and the beaches stripped of the winter's flotsam and jetsam.

The Ways and Means Committee put away their knitting and dominoes and agreed a busy plan of activities to make sure each visitor was made to feel specially welcome. Estate agents printed up extra sales brochures, encouraging holidaymakers to dream the dream that, one day, they'd come down to Temple Regis and never go home again.

Nobody ever mentioned the unduly high mortality rate which kept Miss Dimont on her toes – indeed the Coroner, Dr Rudkin, went out of his way never to use the word 'murder' either in conversation or in his court. He lived in dread of the headline BRITAIN'S TOP MURDER RESORT appearing in one of the grubbier Sunday newspapers – but even his greatest supporters were surprised by the speedy way he brushed the death, some months ago, of the dedicated librarian Miss Greenway under the carpet. Despite promising clues and some energetic spadework by Miss Dimont, the mystery of Miss Greenway's fall from the top of a library ladder remained just that.

But by then all considerations had been pushed aside by the arrival of Grace Dimont at the Grand Hotel. This momentous event carried all the drama, anxiety, contention and pathos of a Second Coming; even old Uncle Arthur had become nervous at the prospect. 'For Heaven's sake, Captain Intrepid, she's your kid sister!' warbled Auriol, who was in a not much better state.

But it was Auriol's planning that saw them through. From the moment of her arrival, the fiery dragon with her extraordinary Belgian accent was treated like royalty – a lavish dispersal of tips made sure of that. The chilled champagne in her room, the winter roses, the latest glossy magazines, and a complimentary box of chocolates from the management left absolutely nothing for her to complain about.

'*Quelle horreur!*' were the first words she uttered as she settled in. 'Ze quality of marzipan has deteriorated *abominably* since ze war. Zese chocolates! And zey call zis ze *Grand* Hotel?'

Mother, mother, thought Miss Dimont despairingly, why do you carry on like this? You're more English than I am – at least I'm the daughter of a Belgian, you merely married one. Look at your brother Arthur, English as they come – why the airs and graces, the silly accent? You're rich, you've led an interesting life, who are you trying to impress?

But it was part of Grace Dimont's indomitable spirit that, always, she must be right while others were to be found wanting. She criticised Arthur's shoes ('like a lounge lizard's') and jibbed at Auriol's Chistmas hairdo – a sweep of dark hair flying up from her forehead like a cresting wave. 'You really should take a trip to Paris, my dear, to pick up some tips. A woman of your age… all or nothing now.'

The quartet managed to stagger its way through the early stages, though only through the iron self-restraint exercised by all but one of their number; Madame Dimont never saw any reason to hold back.

'And you too, Huguette, now the bloom of youth has flown – who will look after you, living alone as you do?'

'You live alone, Maman.'

'I have help, dear. You have a cat and a moped, not quite the same.'

The moment they'd all dreaded came just before Christmas lunch. They were sitting in the Palm Court and the wine waiter Peter Potts was making sure everyone's glass was topped up. The royal visitor had had her cushions plumped and a cigarette placed in her ivory holder.

'… coming back to live with me at Tillingham. You're too old for these silly reporter games, Huguette. You earn no money, you live in a tiny cottage, you have no husband and no life to speak of.'

'I really don't think we… look, Maman, it's almost time for lunch!'

'If Auriol would like to come too, there's that nice flat over the stables. It's empty, just waiting for a lick of paint…'

Auriol shook her head graciously. 'My life is here, though it's a very generous offer and thank you. The Essex marshes may be beautiful, Grace, but they lack the *adventure* we have down here – and every day, the sea so remarkable, so beguiling.'

Mme Dimont exploded. 'We have sea in Essex, too!'

'Not the same. Not the magic blue. We used to have this joke, Hugue and I, when she first came down here, that we'd died and gone to Devon. If only you were to stay for a week or two you'd see it for yourself…'

Judy shot her a furious warning glance.

'…I'm sure you'd see just how glorious it all is. But of course,' Auriol said, catching Judy's eye and quickly dismissing the idea, 'you're always very busy. Travelling here and there. No time to explore Devon.'

'*C'est vrai!* I shall be back in Belgium next week – I still have the gatehouse at Ellezelles, though as you know the main house is a nunnery now. What your father would have said!' laughed Grace, turning to Judy. 'A man who devoted himself to beautiful women all his life. His house a nunnery!'

'I think he would be pleased.'

'He would be *appalled*. Come back with me to Tillingham!'

'No, Maman, I have my job here, and my way of life.'

'No income to speak of. No man. A cat for company! What sort of life is *zat*, Huguette?'

And so it descended, very rapidly, into recrimination. Arthur and Auriol looked on uncomfortably while mother and daughter got it off their chest, their voices resonating down the Palm Court and into the dining room where the serving staff, smiles fixed, stood by on the alert. Words were spoken, accusations levelled, viewpoints overstated and repeated, only louder, before the two warring factions were pulled apart and safe, and dependable Auriol put everybody back on the straight and narrow.

'I doubt she'll be down here again any time soon,' she whispered to Judy as her mother stamped off to powder her nose.

'Or I to Tillingham.'

'Well,' sighed Auriol, 'that *was* an awful lot of effort for not very much.'

'Cleared the air,' said Arthur, uncrossing his legs authoritatively, as if he'd done something useful. 'Who's for oysters?'

And so, as the month of May shone brightly over Temple Regis, everything was set fair for a bumper year's takings. Why the Prime Minister chose that particular moment to announce a general election, nobody knew nor cared. Whatever need the nation had for an injection of new blood into the body politic, Temple Regis had more pressing priorities: in a word, cash. And people gadding about with loudspeakers strapped to their car roof, stopping people they didn't know in the street and arguing the toss, and generally getting tribal, was all bad for the resort's income stream.

Miss Dimont sat writing an opinion page article about this for the *Riviera Express,* deploring the distractions an election brought while offering no beneficial shift of government policy to those who lived locally. Privately, being a new-broom sort of person, she felt the election was a good thing – but she was under strict instructions from Rudyard Rhys to defer to the wishes and prejudices of the townsfolk.

'At last, an end to the reign of ghastly Sir Frederick Hungerford,' she said to Athene as they sat alone in the newsroom at the end of the day. Athene had made some special tea and was thinking about writing a poem while Judy tugged the disingenuous diatribe from her Remington QuietRiter and fluttered the carbon paper into her waste bin.

'Did you say that, dear, in your piece?'

'Of course not. As far as the *Express* is concerned, the man's a saint.'

'That's rather harsh, Judy – not like you!'

'It was that business at Christmas.'

'When poor Sir Freddy was attacked in the street? I thought that was an awful shame. At his age!'

'It was all the other things, the things that didn't get into the paper, Athene. You know, sometimes I feel the *Express* is like an iceberg – ninety per cent of what it knows about what goes on in this town is hidden below the surface, never to be seen.'

'Probably just as well,' said Athene absently, tucking the blue paper rose back into her unruly hair. She had put the poem to one side after an experimental line or two and was thinking about how to break the news to local Sagittarians that they were in for a bumpy ride next week.

'Anyway, if we have to have a general election, at least we have the best of all choices ahead,' Judy went on. 'Women candidates standing for all three political parties – just think of that!'

'Very nice, dear. D'you like this tea? My friend at Lipton's let me have a small packet to try out.'

'The only constituency in Britain to field three women – it's a breakthrough! And it means we'll have a woman Member of Parliament to represent us, no matter who wins. A miracle!'

'Won't make any difference,' said Athene with a sigh. 'They disappear to Westminster and you never see them again.'

'I can't speak for the other two, but I can tell you Mirabel Clifford isn't like that. She's determined to do the right thing by the town after all those years of Sir Freddy being the absentee landlord.'

'You really like her, don't you?'

'I do, Athene, but more than that, I admire her. She's tough but she's straight – well, almost,' she added, remembering the scribbled piece of paper with the name and address of Sir Freddy's popsy. 'The other candidates are excellent, too, but there's something special about Mirabel. And one thing you *would* like – she's nice.'

'Sagittarius rising.'

'How d'you know that?'

'I just sense it.'

I wonder whether your astral powers are strong enough to tell whether she'll win, thought Judy. There's sure to be a backlash at the ballot box against Sir Freddy, however good she is.

There was a faint rustle behind them: 'Hello, you two.' It was Denise Hopton, the sub-editor. 'Glad to catch you – I've just handed in my notice, I'll be off at the end of the week. Hooray!'

'Heavens,' said Judy, 'that's a bolt out of the blue! Why? Where? What are you going to do?'

'I've got a job working for Lilian Smee, the Labour candidate.'

'Are you Labour?'

'I most certainly am!'

'Well, she's worked hard and is very impressive. But Labour candidates don't usually stand much of a chance in Devon – what'll you do if she doesn't get elected?'

'Ah, but she will!' said Denise, perching herself on a corner of the desk. In her six months at the *Riviera Express* she'd shown real promise and, what's more, broken in pieces John Ross's scornful view of women in the office. He now looked across the desk at her with what passed in Glasgow for adoration.

'People are sick of the old ways,' said Denise. 'This clapped-out old warhorse who's been there since the year dot. They want someone young, fresh – ready to fight for those who need it most.'

'You could be describing Mirabel Clifford.'

Denise laughed. 'Yes! Aren't we lucky? And the Liberal candidate's pretty good, too. It'll be an exciting contest for once, but there's not a chance Mrs Clifford will win – she represents the party of Sir Frederick Hungerford. Not a good look!'

'I rather fancy her chances,' said Judy, smiling back, challenging.

'We'll have to see.'

'But what'll you do if she doesn't win? Will you come back here?'

'I went to see Mr Rhys this afternoon. He doesn't like his staff to be seen taking sides politically, so I think the answer to that is no. I thought I'd chance my arm in Fleet Street, see if I can get a night shift or two, see how it goes.'

Quite right, thought Miss Dimont. You're young, you're very bright, don't take any nonsense, and are prepared to take risks – just what's needed in the national press.

'So what did you make of your time here with us?' she said.

Denise looked around, slowly surveying the newsroom. Over in the far corner David Renishaw had slipped behind his desk and was sitting there, turning over the pages of a notebook.

'The *Express*? It's like the estuary out there,' said Denise, nodding at the receding tide she could see from the upstairs window. 'Conflicting currents, dangerous waters.'

'What d'you mean, exactly?'

'The old versus the new. Shafts of brilliance, but big puddles of stick-in-the-mud. Ingrained prejudice versus vaulting ambition.'

Good Lord, thought Judy, you *have* been thinking a lot about it.

'So it comes down to a question of which wagon do you hitch yourself to?' went on Denise. 'I expect it's the same in any office – I wouldn't know, I came here straight from university. Do you side with the editor when you know he's wrong, or court danger by siding with Mr Renishaw over there, when you know he's right?'

'He's not always right.'

'Mostly he is.'

'Not always.'

Sensing alarm bells, Denise knew better than to contradict. 'Anyway, it's been interesting and I've learned a lot.'

'*And* tamed John Ross.'

'Oh, *him*!' You could tell she didn't like that idea.

'He'll miss you. You're very good at your job.'

'Oh, he'll find another galley slave.' Denise smiled and wandered off in the direction of Renishaw. Since his great scoop about entry fees for Temple Regis, he'd become curiously withdrawn. There were no more invitations for Judy to the pub, no more mouse-racing, in fact the pair barely spoke. If he had a big story, Renishaw didn't wait for the Monday conference but slipped into the editor's office where they would discuss the idea behind a closed door.

Rudyard Rhys, after hearing about Renishaw's attack on Professor Sirraway, suddenly became far less enthusiastic about his new signing, and to the casual observer the new reporter appeared to be drifting into the nether world occupied by many a middle-aged journalist on local newspapers whose career had iced over, never to thaw.

He'd never taken the trouble to say a word to Athene, though their desks were close, but having studied him through her ostrich-feather screen, she decided she didn't mind – his aura was too green.

Betty and he had walked out a few times, but nothing much came of it. He explained away his passion for righting injustice – the Underdog years – as being triggered by boredom, 'and so would you be, stuck in Ontario, wondering what the hell brought you there in the first place.' It turned out that there *was* a Mrs Renishaw, but that she'd declined his offer of a new start on the English Riviera, and divorced him instead.

He sat alone at his desk, neither welcoming nor rejecting the approach of the young and clever Denise, lost in the pages of his notebook.

Judy glanced at him as she gathered up her things and aimed towards the car park where the faithful Herbert waited, but as she reached the back door, the heat and smell of early summer made her reconsider.

'An ice cream by the bandstand,' she said to herself with a smile.

By the time she got there, the Regis Brass Ensemble was parping its way through a selection of Gilbert and Sullivan tunes – a little rusty after the winter break, but showing promise. Judy sat on a bench, notebook in lap, thinking about nothing in particular but hoping that an idea for a story might come to her. It was certainly true that since Renishaw's arrival everyone had upped their game, trying harder to produce something fresh for the news pages.

'Hello, Judy, what a glorious evening.' It was Mirabel Clifford.

'Your last evening off,' said Miss Dimont with a smile, 'before the storm clouds break. Have you got a moment to enjoy the sun and the band?'

'Just what I need! We're already working full-tilt on the election – I came down here for a breather.'

'Well, I'll be reporting your every move, obviously. *And* those of the other candidates!'

'Ah yes, the impartiality of the Press! Except that when Sir Freddy reigned, your Mr Rhys was a bit niggardly in giving space to his opponents.'

'Duty. I don't think he was a big fan any more than anyone else.'

'And yet Hungerford reigned supreme, for years and years and years. That's the hurdle I now face – showing the electorate I'm not him.'

Judy recalled Betty's tale of the Christmas party where the MP pretended not to know the name of his successor. 'Did he send you his best wishes when the election was announced?'

'Not a dicky bird.'

For a few moments the two women talked over the events which had brought them together at the time of the attack on Sir Freddy. His whitewash interview with the *Daily Herald* had turned the whole disappearance into a damp squib, and what with a scandal involving the film star Diana Dors, Hungerford's name had been pushed out of the public prints overnight.

At the same time the unwelcome attentions of Professor Sirraway suddenly ceased and, as always, the world moved on. But the two events had opened up between Miss Dimont and the solicitor-candidate a mutual respect; they'd occasionally lunched together, and though Miss Dimont had no political preferences, she hoped Mirabel would succeed.

'How's Mulligatawny?' Not a politician's question, but woman-to-woman.

'Lost his good manners. Trips me up whenever I come through the door, bawls at me as though I've trodden on his paws when I've done no such thing, and refuses virtually everything I offer him to eat. And then he sleeps on my pillow when I'm at work.'

'That's males for you.'

'Yes. And no.'

They laughed.

'How do you feel about this election, then?' said Judy. 'And by the way I'm not interviewing you – just curious. You've given up a huge amount of your private life to do something you believe in, it seems to me, and from what I gather you've no ambition to get on the gravy train and become a minister, any of that. What's in it for you?'

'What this town needs is a woman's touch,' replied Mirabel. 'Less huff-and-puff, more action. If I'm elected, I'll spend equal amounts of time here in the constituency and in the House of Commons. Show the men how the job should be done.'

'And your chances? Of getting to Westminster?'

'Funnily enough, the thing I fear the most is if that ghoul Freddy Hungerford opens his mouth. Doesn't matter if he says something for me or against me, it's just his poisonous braying that could spoil my chances.'

She paused. 'I don't think I've ever said this of anybody – but if you asked me, I'd say I hated him. And if there were no laws in this land, I tell you, Judy, I would happily kill him.'

SEVENTEEN

Betty was standing at the back of the crowd craning her neck – Temple Regis could get a bit star-struck when someone as famous as Fanny Cradock visited town and the Press, well, they could just stand in the queue along with everyone else.

'And I had my hair done specially,' she complained to Terry, who was waiting his moment to lunge forward in typical press-cameraman style. 'Plus I paid a fortune for these shoes in Clark's. You didn't even notice!'

'I wondered what was different,' said Terry, turning to look at her for the first time. 'It looks like you had your hair done on a hillside. Tilt your head to the left a bit, girl – go on, that'll straighten it up.'

'That's the last time I have a perm! I'm going to let it go natural from now on – fifteen-and-six, it cost!'

The crowd was getting restless. Granted that Suds & Duds was the first launderette ever to open its doors in town, and it was always a treat to see someone special come and cut a ribbon – but these were busy people, what with the holiday season coming on, and quite a few of them were getting restless.

'Fifteen minutes,' grumbled one woman to another.

'And the rest! She's always late, I heard,' replied her companion. 'A prima donna, she is.'

Betty overheard this. She didn't know much about Mrs Cradock because she never watched TV, but Fanny was one of the most famous people in the land so the wait was to be expected. As she stood there she realised her shoes were too tight – it should have been the next half size up, like the shop assistant said.

Time ticked by, and finally a craggy-faced diva made her entrance into Fore Street, waving like Queen Victoria from the back of an open-top Daimler. Sam Brough, weighed down by his mayoral chain and with a tendency to self-abasement in the presence of celebrity, opened the car door and bowed as if Mrs Cradock were, indeed, the sovereign.

'Gin and Dubonnet waiting inside, madam,' whispered His Worship.

'Will this take long?' answered the cook in a tired drawl. Then, only as an afterthought, she turned to face the crowd and acknowledge their cheers with a curt wave.

'Come in, come in! May I introduce Dudley Fensome, the proprietor? We're so proud to have a launderette at last – there was quite some resistance from the die-hard brigade.'

'I can quite see why,' said Mrs C, looking with disdain around the delightfully painted shop and its shining machines. 'In my generation one didn't talk about laundry, it just arrived – open your drawer and it's there. Now, people want to make a song and dance about it, have parties and knees-ups and who knows what. What next? A communal lavatory for us all to meet and chat?'

Following Terry's lead, Betty got herself inside the shop with her notebook at the ready, but so far there was little to report. As she turned away from the star of the show, Betty glimpsed a look of keening regret on Dud Fensome's face; he and she had a bit of previous.

Well, a lot, actually.

'Hello, Betty.'

'Congratulations, Dud. You've done really well. And I love the name – very clever. So now you have a shop *and* Fanny Cradock!'

'She's a friend of my aunt's. Well, I wouldn't say friend, quite,' he replied, looking in trepidation over his shoulder. 'My aunt is actually a very nice person.'

'Whereas…'

'I gather Mrs Cradock's always like this. You don't know the nightmare I had getting her here.'

'Are you *serious*?' The celebrity's corncrake voice barged its way into their conversation. 'Put some laundry – in a *washing machine*?'

'If it's not too much trouble,' Terry was saying politely, 'tells the story neatly for the cameras. Don't worry, it's quite clean.'

Mrs Cradock turned to face him with an ugly curl to her lip. 'I have a *woman* who does that for me,' she grated. 'What would she think if she were to see me doing that? No doubt she'd have me up before her trades union! That's all the workers want to do these days, isn't it, gang up together and make trouble for those who've the money and the good grace to employ them?'

Betty wasn't quite sure whether to take notes or not

– suddenly this was terribly good, if not quite the story she'd been sent to cover.

'Go on,' urged Terry. 'Put the washing in.' He could see she wasn't going to.

'No.'

'Go on! I'll send a print to your woman, saying you promised me you'd never lift another piece of dirty linen in your life.'

'No need, she knows that. Where's my Dubonnet?'

Sam Brough was so nervous he managed to spill the cocktail over his brass chain, but one swift swallow had the effect of oil on troubled water and after a hurried whisper in Fanny's ear, Terry got what he wanted.

That was the miracle of Terry, he never took no for an answer – and people could be as important as they liked, it made no difference. Terry always won.

'You're brilliant, Ter.'

'That Mr Fensome likes your hair, even if nobody else does.'

'Oh, *please*!'

'Go on, he does. You could do worse, you know. First-ever launderette owner in Temple Regis – he'll be on the town council next!'

'Keep up, Terry. He's yesterday's news, that one.'

'Ah.'

'Are you interviewing me?' Fanny Cradock burst in on their conversation. She was wearing lilac gloves with a handbag to match, but her shoes were not very nice and the hat was a disaster.

'No, I think I've got it all,' said Betty. 'But may I say, Mrs

Cradock, that your fans out there will be disappointed if you don't go out and sign some autographs. A lot of them have been waiting here since breakfast.'

'Well, they can wait! The trouble with all these people is that they want you, heart and soul – you try to be nice to them, and all they want to do is paw you about and ask personal questions.'

'Well,' said Betty, bristling, 'you *are* a household name. You come out of their television sets, I'm told, every Thursday night. Telling them how to cook and how your husband Johnnie is good for nothing except pouring the drinks – they feel as though they know you. That you're part of the family.'

'They don't know me at all!' shuddered Mrs Cradock. 'I'm a very private person!'

'Come on, Betty, we've already taken up too much of this lady's time,' said Terry impatiently.

'You aren't going to interview me?' rasped Fanny.

'Not today, thank you,' replied Betty. She'd get it in the neck from Rudyard Rhys – he was hoping for a nice spread across Pages Four and Five – but he'd have to whistle for it. A picture caption, no more – that's all she deserved, the old dragon!

'Are… are you going, Betty?' said Dud hesitantly, seeing Terry packing his camera away.

'Don't worry, Dudley, we'll give you some nice coverage. Good luck with the old monster, don't let her drink you dry.'

'I don't suppose you're free on Saturday?'

'Now, Dud, you know what we agreed.'

Reporter and photographer hurried out of Suds & Duds into the May sunshine and made their way back to the office.

Behind them the crowd waited, hoping shortly to shake the hand of the most famous person to come to Temple Regis this year. But as each moment passed, their chances grew slimmer while indoors the TV star was doing magic tricks with the Dubonnet bottle.

'I wonder what other famous celebrities we're in for this summer,' said Terry dourly. 'And whether they're all going to be as charming as 'er.'

'We were going to have Gene Vincent over at the Pavilion Theatre, but he can't come. Such a shame – I wanted to see him tear his leather jacket off.'

'I'll take mine off if you like,' volunteered Terry. 'Who've we got instead?'

'Well, I know Mrs Phipps was thinking of Pearl Carr and Teddy Johnson.'

'Better than a cup of Horlicks,' said Terry dismissively. 'They'll have the audience asleep in five minutes flat.'

'But she changed her mind and we're going to have Marty Wilde.'

'And his Wildcats?'

'The whole cats' home for all I know.'

The chief perpetrator of civil unrest in Temple Regis lit a Player's Navy Cut and exhaled the first puff straight into her gin glass. Mrs Phipps, nearing her ninth decade, looked with scorn on convention and on those who, in these changing times, struggled to maintain pre-war peace and gentility.

Her management of the Pavilion Theatre since the departure of Ray Cattermole, her erstwhile companion and partner in business, had been lively and lucrative. Not surprisingly for a woman who once lifted her skirts as a Gaiety Girl, she needed the constant stimulus of new ideas.

And if not new ideas, then interesting old ones. 'When you came to see me before Christmas,' she said, chidingly, 'we had such a lovely time. But, darling, you *did* promise me you'd find out about dear Pansy Westerham.'

'I did, I did,' replied Miss Dimont, 'and I'm sorry, Geraldine. Life's been rather hectic.'

'Well, I've done some of your sleuthing for you,' said the old girl triumphantly. 'I bumped into Bobbety Thurloe the other day and, d'you know, he's got such a wonderful memory *and* he's nearly ninety!'

You're not doing so badly yourself, thought Judy, though it would be rude to draw attention to your advancing years.

'I thought he was dead.'

'Let me tell you what he said, and then you can judge for yourself. He told me what Pansy couldn't – that she was having an affair with the Prince of Wales's brother, Prince George!'

'I think you mentioned…'

'Of course, it all fits now. I first met her in the Embassy Club and in those days she would sit on the edge of the royal table – you know, the one just down from the bandstand. In a place like that, people move around talking to this person, then that, then they go on the dancefloor and disappear in the crowd.

'Now I come to think of it, she was always near Prince George – oh, he was gorgeous, darling, and not at all like his pipsqueak older brother! Tall and – how shall I put it? – *muscular*. Do you know the phrase NSIT?'

'Not Safe In Taxis,' said Judy, who'd known one or two like that herself.

'The phrase was invented for Georgy. I danced with him a couple of times myself and – well, let's just say he left you in no doubt.'

'Of?'

'*You* know.'

'Oh! Ha! Ha! Wasn't he married?'

'What difference does that make? So were most of the women. In those days, husbands thought it their bounden duty to lay down their wife for their country.'

'Good Lord.' Now I sound like Uncle Arthur, thought Judy.

'Anyway, Bobbety Thurloe told me that Pansy was desperately in love with Prince George. They'd met in Paris and she chased him back to London and set up home there. He'd been in hot water with girls before, but now he was newly married and supposed to be a reformed character. So it was all very hush-hush.'

'I saw some photographs of her,' said Judy. 'She always seemed to look as if she was under some kind of strain.'

'As I think I told you, apparently she'd left behind her child – a boy, I think. She never told me about that – at the time she was determinedly playing the role of rich bachelor girl. I rather envied her; she had a lovely house behind Harrods, small but beautifully done.'

'So what happened to her?'

'Well, that's just it. What I hoped you'd be able to find out for me. She was standing on the balcony of an upstairs room, and fell. Bobbety said it happened the day she was made bankrupt. None of us knew about *that*, of course.'

'But you said she was rich?'

'Whatever she had, she'd gone through the lot.'

'Well, what a very sad tale,' said Judy, her mind starting to think about her next job – she'd only popped in for a quick cup of coffee.

'No, but here's the interesting bit – Bobbety said she was murdered. That, of course, was the rumour at the time – that's why I asked you to try and find something out about it. You know all about murders, after all.'

Apparently not, thought Judy.

'It was just a rumour, though – the word went round the Embassy Club and we all ooh'ed and aah'ed, but it must have been around the time of the abdication or something – anyway, it soon got swept away by another scandal, and poor Pansy was forgotten about. The funeral was held in Esher and that was the end of it.'

'Why did you ask me about her, then, when we were at Wistman's Hotel?'

'Oh, I'd been stuck there by myself for a couple of days with nothing to do – not like here,' she said, looking around at the disorder of her manager's office. 'And Pansy came to mind. I really liked her, and I think she took to me. I felt somehow she was the victim of an injustice – not because I knew she'd been killed, I didn't know that then – but because she'd been forgotten. I thought you could discover...'

Judy shifted uncomfortably in her chair.

'Sorry, Geraldine. Did Bobbety Thurloe say anything else?'

'He explained the whole thing. Georgy's love affairs were a bit of a nuisance to the royal family – he was always getting into hot water. One particular girl who clung too tight had a visit from some very determined characters from the Palace, and pretty soon she was on a boat to France. Another was offered who knows how much money to do a flit, and she did.

'Bobbety said these people appeared to be gentlemen, but weren't – they could be ruthless when necessary. They visited Pansy in the dead of night and told her several things – first that now Georgy was married, her continued presence was an embarrassment and would cease forthwith. Second that in any case, now she'd been made bankrupt, she couldn't be seen in royal circles. And third, something about telling her husband.'

'All grounds for her to want to do away with herself, you think, especially the bankruptcy?'

'Not really. All Bobbety would say is those royal henchmen talked softly but carried a big stick, if you know what I mean. He's convinced she was murdered.'

'How long was she in London?'

'Oh, only a couple of years, I think.'

'So she must have arrived quite soon after Prince George's wedding – think of that!'

'Men,' said Geraldine. The word, as it emerged from her carmine lips, was weighted with a lifetime's experience.

'Well, women, too,' said Judy. 'They're not the—'

'Yes, you're right, of course. I think, with Pansy, there may have been someone else. Not because I *know* there was, it's just the way she'd make appointments – we'd meet at Gunter's for tea every Tuesday and Thursday – and sometimes she just wouldn't show up. Or she'd turn up late and all hot and bothered – *you* know.'

'So she left behind a husband in Paris, and a child, and

just upped sticks to come to London to chase after a royal prince? And then had someone else on the side?'

'It would appear so.' Mrs Phipps was enjoying this hugely.

'And either she took her own life, or it was taken by those gentlemen with the big stick?'

'Yes.'

'Couldn't have been anything to do with the other man in her life?'

'Ah. A very good point. No reason why not, I suppose. But since I don't know who that was…'

'I'm intrigued,' said Miss Dimont. 'And I'm sorry I haven't done anything about it – domestic affairs got in the way, I simply won't bore you. May I talk to your Bobbety? Do you think he'll see me?'

'Of course he will. You know he lives out near Tavistock, I'll telephone him and make an arrangement. But aren't you busy, dear, with this election?'

'That's the day job,' said Miss Dimont distantly. 'Murder is much more interesting!'

EIGHTEEN

Any hopes Miss Dimont may have had of pushing the day job to one side evaporated the moment she walked out of the Pavilion Theatre. Racing towards her along the promenade was Denise, the soon-to-be liberated sub-editor.

'Judy! What luck! Come and see!'

'What is it?'

'An impromptu catfight. Your favoured candidate, Mirabel Clifford, versus mine, Lilian Smee. They were both out canvassing and bumped into each other. They're at it right now, with Round One to Lilian. I was just off to see if I could find Terry.'

'Carry on, then. Unless you'd rather come and join in the fireworks – I doubt you'll find Terry in a hurry.'

'Oh, well – in that case…!'

She's clever, thought Miss Dimont as they hurried back along the Promenade to a large gathering by the bandstand. Maybe she's going to be a politician herself one day – self-assured, still young enough to believe one political party can make less of a mess of it than another.

As they neared the crowd, the two candidates were

shouting slogans at each other in much the way politicians do and to an unbiased eye they seemed evenly matched.

'Unfit to govern!' hooted Lilian Smee into a megaphone.

'Cannot be trusted – just look at their record!' cried Mrs Clifford, not to be outdone.

Well, that's good, thought Miss Dimont – whoever wins will serve us well. And we haven't even seen the Liberal candidate yet!

'L – A – B – O – U – R!' shouted Denise, getting straight into the spirit of things. Miss Dimont stood back, weighing up what each candidate was saying, stripping away the hopeless promises and the scornful asides. Where Lilian has passion, Mirabel has reason, she judged. And when Mirabel spoke the crowd listened, whereas when Lilian spoke, the crowd cheered. It was almost as if the two opponents were boxing by different rules.

But I do admire Mirabel, she thought. Her strong chin, her clear eye, her ability to take a joke against herself (Lilian was good with her poisoned darts) – she has the makings of a prime minister. No matter that we only have twenty-five women in the House of Commons, maybe this election will finally change things.

For heaven's sake, it's been thirty years since Margaret Bondfield became the first female cabinet minister – isn't it time we hurried things along a bit? We've had the vote long enough – it's time our voices were heard!

Denise was wasting no time in making sure hers was. 'OUT! OUT! OUT!' she was shouting, with an exuberance that the fusty old Rudyard Rhys would have deplored. Judy got out her notebook and scribbled a few hieroglyphs before yelling in Denise's ear, 'Enjoy yourself! I'm going back to the office!'

'Denise'll be in a bit later,' Judy lied to John Ross as she seated herself behind the Remington QuietRiter. 'Had to go to the doctor.'

'Ay well. Mebbe the thought of leaving us has proved too much. Enfeebled her.'

'On the contrary, John. Leaving the *Riviera Express* is probably the most liberating thing that could have happened to her. She feels free.'

'*Wummin!*' barked the chief sub, angrily yanking open his bottom drawer and rattling his whisky bottle.

'Mr Rhys!' called Judy, as she spied her editor sliding into his office. 'May I have brief word?'

Rhys nodded and she followed his tweed-suited figure with its too-short trousers into the editor's office.

'I've just seen Mirabel Clifford out canvassing,' she began, 'a lively time had by all down on the Promenade! But in amongst all the cut and thrust, she said something quite important – she said she was going to give up her legal practice if elected, so as to concentrate on her constituents.'

'Rr… rrr,' said the editor, who was bemused by the thought of women politicians.

'I think that's pretty important, don't you? She's spent twenty years building up that practice in Temple Regis, but she's prepared to throw it away to concentrate on the town.'

'A useful stunt,' said Rhys. 'Let's see if she does.'

'Well, it's a good line to kick off our election coverage.'

'Watch the balance,' replied Rhys, nodding his assent,

'equal coverage for all the candidates. Even if we want Mrs Clifford to win.'

Judy had her nose in her notebook as she made her way back to her desk, but when she looked up there was David Renishaw, plonked in her chair looking as if he'd taken possession.

'David.'

'Hello, Judy, I was wondering if you'd like to go for a drink this evening.'

No thanks, thought Judy.

Little had changed between the pair in the months since Renishaw's arrival. The pair maintained a competitive distance, like two heavyweight boxers retiring to their corner between editions, only to come out sparring for the Page One splash each week. Renishaw was good, but so too was Miss Dimont; and so the paper prospered from this needle match, even if their personal relationship did not.

'Well, I...'

'Just some things I'd like to chat over. I may be moving on soon.'

'Moving...?'

'Time to skedaddle. Pastures new. I'm a bit of a rolling stone, you may have gathered that.'

'But David, you've only been here, what, six months?'

'The *Riviera Express* isn't quite my speed, Judy, I see that now.'

Why ever did you think it was in the first place? thought Miss Dimont. You're a square peg in a round hole, and have been since the day you arrived.

'Where are you going?'

'I have a number of ideas.'

'So you don't have a job to go to?'

'I live simply, Judy, I don't have to work all the time.'

Miss Dimont sat down at the desk opposite, pushing aside the debris. Betty's hair curlers – really! Couldn't she do all that before coming into the office?

'Well, you're an extremely accomplished journalist, David. You won't have any difficulty.'

'I want you to put in a good word with old Rhys. I'll need a decent reference.'

Wait a minute, thought Judy… this hasn't got anything to do with Denise leaving the paper? Two resignations in two days is the kind of coincidence that never happens at the *Riviera Express*, normally a place where clapped-out old journalistic carthorses come to rest their bones.

'It was Denise's resignation that prompted it,' said Renishaw, reading her mind as usual – that's why she hated talking to him. 'I thought, I've been here too long.'

'Most people wouldn't start thinking that till they'd clocked up at least twenty years.'

'I might go back to London. Or France. I once lived there as well.'

'Really? I worked in Paris before the war – whereabouts?'

'A place called Saint Cloud. In some ways I wish I'd never left.'

'What an *interesting* life you've led, David. I knew some people in Saint Cloud – diamond merchants.' Her statement was more of a question – Saint Cloud is a place for very rich people: are *you* very rich, you conundrum? With your cheap suits and your funny haircut and your ability to pick and choose where and when you want to work?

'Ah!' said the reporter, quickly getting up. 'I wasn't there long. Must be getting along. Not a word to anyone – I haven't finally made up my mind. But if I do, will you speak to old Rhys? I know you were once very close.'

'I wouldn't put it quite like that.'

'I didn't mean it that way. You'll come and have a drink?'

'Only as long as no mice are involved.'

They went to The Albion. 'Is this where you come? I never see you in the Fort or the Jawbones,' said Judy.

'Too much drinking in those places.'

'The point of them, surely. Pubs are where people can get pent-up emotions off their chests without too much damage being done. Though, David, I will be frank and say there's little evidence of that in you.'

'What d'you mean?'

'You're a pretty controlled person, on top of your feelings, in charge. Most journalists aren't like that – they're free and easy with their opinions and their hearts, they're passionate and pompous, flawed and regretful, and always looking for a better way. You're none of those things, so how come you strayed into this profession?'

And why, thought Miss Dimont, am I bothering to ask you this just when you're doing us all a favour and walking out of the *Riviera Express*? I should just be grateful that you're off, and of course I'll give generously to your leaving present – but why am I sitting with you in the bar of The Albion, ginger beer for me, tomato juice for you?

He looked at her without saying anything, in no hurry to give anything away, and suddenly Judy was determined to get it out of him – the mystery of where he came from, why he was there.

She decided to go for the old soft-soap technique: 'You know, you made everybody feel pretty nervous when you first showed up.'

'Did I?' The faintest smile curled round his mouth.

'Those news stories you brought in – they changed the game. Sent everyone scuttling for the bunker. You were frighteningly good.'

I *will* make you talk, she thought, I *will* get to the bottom of your story before you fly away. After the way you showed the rest of us up, making people who'd enjoyed working here for years sit at their desks consumed by guilt jealousy and an overpowering sense of inadequacy.

'Were *you* frightened?' asked Renishaw, levelling his gaze at her.

'Not me. Others. Betty. Why did you come here?'

'Let's talk about Geraldine Phipps instead.'

'I thought we were talking about the office.'

'I think we were talking about *me*. But since your conversational technique seems to consist of question, question, question, I thought I'd switch tack.'

'Is that a polite way of saying I'm nosy? I *am* a journalist, after all.'

And in my different way, every bit as good as you, Mr Smarty Pants.

'I'm curious to know about Geraldine. She knew a friend of my mother, a woman called Pansy Westerham, but when I went to see her she claimed she couldn't remember Pansy at all.'

'I think I know the reason why. Mrs Westerham had a most unconventional life – a bit too unconventional for common chatter.'

'Hah! Is that a snub? Did you just say, I know something about her which I'm not going to tell you because I am enjoying withholding information from you?'

'You might say that.'

Renishaw's face reddened. 'Tell me!' he demanded. 'All I'm trying to do is get some information about my mother! She was a friend of Pansy, Pansy was a friend of Geraldine, Pansy must have talked to Geraldine about her! That's not common chatter, as you snootily put it, it's simple information about a member of my family.'

'Calm down, David! I wasn't talking about your mother, I was talking about a possible reason why Geraldine doesn't want to talk to you about Pansy.'

'OK, OK. Would you, d'you think, have a word with Geraldine and ask if she'd see me?'

'Is it urgent?'

Renishaw looked into his tomato juice. 'My mother went missing. She was in London, mixing with all these people, and one day she went missing and was never found. I was twelve. I want to know what happened, and maybe Geraldine knows something – maybe she knows something without knowing she knows, if you see what I mean.'

He's handsome, thought Miss Dimont, but looks aren't enough. To be attractive to women you have to have the personality to go with it. But David, you don't have that – you're like an automaton, fixed always and only on what you want to get out of someone.

'I'll have a word with her. What do you know about Pansy Westerham?'

'What?' The question startled Renishaw and he took a moment to answer. 'There were some letters from her. To my mother. You can understand, if you're a certain age and your mother is taken away from you, you tend to focus on whatever's left behind. Little things suddenly mean a lot.'

'It must have been a long time ago – how old are you now?'

'Thirty-seven.'

'Why's it suddenly so urgent?'

'It's not *urgent*,' replied Renishaw. 'It's just that… from what I learn of you, you have a mother who's everywhere – if she's not actually in your presence then you're talking about her or thinking about her, or trying to avoid her. Why, Terry told me you even…'

'Oh, did he now! Tell me, David, since you've been here in Temple Regis, have you spent *all* your spare time going round snooping into other people's lives?'

'Is that a polite way of saying I'm nosy? I *am* a journalist, after all,' he echoed back.

'Ha, ha. Point taken.'

'My point is, you know about your mother,' continued Renishaw. 'You know *all* about her. I know nothing about mine, beyond the age of twelve. D'you see?'

'I'm going to have a glass of whisky, I've drunk enough ginger beer to float a lifeboat. Will you join me?'

It was a subtle challenge – drink alcohol with me and I will be your friend, don't and I won't. How many times had that stunt been pulled in this pub?

'I really don't ever… I…'

'Go on.'

'OK.' Renishaw's face looked green at the prospect.

'Tell me about Saint Cloud. Is that where you grew up?'

'Why don't we talk first about your growing up?' He manfully sipped at the whisky, but now she realised how ridiculous her insistence had been – just point-scoring, trying to gain the advantage over this slippery eel.

'Look, you don't have to drink that if you don't want. Pour it into my glass.'

'No, no… it's just as a general rule I avoid alcohol.'

'Well, since you ask, I came to Britain when I was four, when Germany invaded Belgium during the First World War. My father was a prisoner of war but came over to join us after the Armistice, and he carried on his business in the diamond trade from our home in Kent. I went to school and did a year and a half at university, but by then my father wasn't so well, so he sent me off round Europe as his courier.'

'Buying and selling diamonds is a man's business, surely?'

'I was in my early twenties and looked young and foolish and – well, as a strategy it worked rather well. They thought I knew nothing, but my father had taught me all he knew and we pulled off some extraordinary deals.'

'So it was never your ambition to become a journalist.'

'Not then. I was having too much fun – Paris, Rome, Berlin, Belgrade, everywhere!'

'Lots of love affairs?'

'Mind your own business. The reason why I asked you about Saint Cloud is because I lived in Paris for a year, and stayed mostly in the house of my father's business contact Monsieur Schonberg, on the Rue de la Faisanderie. I wonder if you know where that is – quite an elaborate house with eagles on the gates, near the park.'

Renishaw took a large gulp of whisky. 'It's not a period I care to recall.' He thought for a moment, then added: 'We didn't live like that. My father was the concierge for the Palace Hotel. It was a lowly position but he made a great deal of money from the various tips and inducements that came with the job.'

'He was English? Renishaw's a fine old English name.'

'Half. His mother was French. But his wife – my mother – was English. A bit of a lost soul, so I gather. But back to you – why did you give it up, the diamond trade? Sounds like you were pretty successful.'

'With the help of others, yes. The war came along and… well, the rest is rather a long story. A long period in the service of the government. Then eight or nine years ago I came down here and, by luck, got a job as a junior reporter on the *Express*.'

'And now you're *chief* reporter. Have you never thought of moving on and up?' The way he said it was odd – was he jealous of her title, did he want it for himself, was he leaving because she'd got it?

'I'm very happy here. As I sense you will be very happy *not* to be here.'

'Other things to do.'

'So I imagine. Well, I'll be sorry to see you go,' she lied, 'but I'll be frank and say you've been a bit of a cuckoo in the nest.'

'People always seem to say that.'

'One thing that's always puzzled me.'

'Yes?'

'You remember just after you came here, Sir Freddy Hungerford was beaten up in the street in Westminster? Some people thought it might have been that strange professor who did it, and you and Terry went up to Hatherleigh to try to find him.'

'Yes, I remember.'

'Terry told me you attacked him. It doesn't seem like you at all, very out of character – what was all that about?'

'Why do you ask?'

'Because,' said Judy, 'I can't think of another single incidence where a reporter has become so personally involved in a story that they got into a fist-fight over it. Not one.'

'Terry's got it wrong. It was dark, I left the car to go in search of the man. Professor Sirraway. He attacked me – viciously. I've never known anything like it. He looks a bit old and weedy but he's got extraordinary hidden strength. I thought he was going to kill me.'

'So you fought back?'

'Exactly. Terry couldn't see what was going on because he was still in the car. Eventually he came over and separated us but you know, Judy, that man might have killed me. He's mad!'

'You think so?'

'I looked into his alibi after that little dust-up and, you know, he had no proof he was in Ilfracombe on the day Hungerford was attacked. He's got a real thing about Hungerford having stolen valuable real estate from his family – I really truly believe the man is a danger and should be locked up.'

Well, yes, thought Judy, only that's not how Terry

remembers the dust-up in Hatherleigh. He had the headlights on and even though he was still in the driving seat, he could see you. And he says you launched an attack on Sirraway when all the man was trying to do was get into his house. It was you who attacked *him*, not the other way around. The whole thing remains a mystery.

Just like you, Mr Renishaw.

NINETEEN

It took a surprisingly long time to find the body. With each succeeding hour, anxiety grew and hope diminished, to the point where the brave smiles had withered and the reassuring nods between the searchers had faded completely away.

Nobody could imagine what had happened to one of the most prominent people in Temple Regis, but then nobody thought of the lighthouse.

And why would they? The Templeton Light stood, massive and reassuring, out on the Temple Rock after which the town was named. Its octagonal tower had stood sentry duty for two centuries, warning ships of the deadly rocks scattered around the mouth of the estuary.

It wasn't until mid-morning the next day that a swarm of seagulls, shouting out their tragic discovery, finally drove someone to think of taking a look – and even then, if it hadn't been for the observant hiker's strong binoculars, the search would have lasted days longer.

They found the body splayed out on the gallery deck, the head resting against the iron guard rail. The blood from the stomach wound had partially dried, but a trained eye could see there would have been no chance of saving her once the knife went in.

Once she might have been prime minister. Now all Mirabel Clifford would be remembered for was this bizarre end to a promising life – her face drenched in spindrift, her sensible suit of clothes ruined for ever, her handbag still over her wrist.

'Tragic,' said Inspector Topham, holding his hat in the wind. He was thinking, it's worse when you know the person. Of the murders he'd been obliged to investigate since he arrived in Devon, none were known to him personally. Back beyond that, the war years, he'd known a fair number, and somehow this death brought all those alive again. He wanted to go home, talk it over with his wife, gather comfort from her.

Instead he allowed the age-old responses to take charge. 'Have you finished?' he said to the police doctor. The man nodded, got off his knees and wiped his hands.

'Bring her inside, then,' he ordered the uniformed constables standing behind him, 'and go down and take a look around for the weapon. There's a good chance whoever did this will have just chucked it over the side. Careful as you go.'

He moved inside to the lantern room and turned back to look at the sea. Waves angrily beat the rocks beneath, demanding his attention, but he barely noticed. Man is a mystery, he thought, a riddle to be solved, and I will never achieve it.

'What on earth is *she* doing here?' asked the lighthouse keeper, more annoyed than shocked.

'You know who she is?'

'I do,' said the man, looking down at the body. 'Mrs

Clifford. She was due to come here tomorrow to have her photograph taken – I went into town a couple of days ago to arrange it all. Publicity for her, publicity for us too. We rely on donations.'

'You weren't here yesterday?'

'My quarters are in the cottage down below, but during the day, if the weather's fine, I go home. I live in Ferry Lane. She must have come here yesterday afternoon while I was in town.'

'You don't lock the lighthouse up?'

The man gave him an old-fashioned look. 'Lock up a *lighthouse* – are you serious?'

'Basic security,' said Topham, importantly.

'Look, mate,' said the keeper, irritated, 'I've worked here nigh on thirty years. My dad were keeper before me and my great uncle afore that. Never in this century, or the last, has there been a case of someone trying to break into the lighthouse. Never—' he looked down unbelievingly, '—has anybody found a body out on the deck – or anywhere else, come to that.'

Topham realised how ridiculous his question must have seemed. 'I have to establish the facts. How she got here, who was with her, who saw them. You have an assistant, I take it?'

'Yers, Abraham. And before you ask, it was his half day yesterday. He went to see his sister.'

'So the lighthouse was left unguarded. And unlocked.'

'Look, mate, if I was you I'd get a move on trying to find out who did this, instead of wasting time giving me a lecture!'

'Who knows about the routine here?'

'Well, my bosses at Trinity House, obviously. A few of the

lifeboat boys – Abraham and me use their bar when we're in town. Nobody else much.' He counted on his fingers. 'Our wives, our children, the occasional visitor but we don' encourage that many, we're not a tourist attraction.' He thought again for a moment. 'Oh, we had a fellow the other day, said he's doing a book on lighthouses, he came and had a look around.'

Topham stiffened slightly. 'Name?'

'You'd have to ask Abraham, I wasn't 'ere.'

'Well, thank you, I expect…'

'Wait, wait – are you goin' to clear this away? I can't have dead bodies hanging around the lantern room.'

Topham didn't like his tone. 'What time's sunset?'

'It'll be 8.43 p.m,' came the instant reply.

'A good few hours yet, before you'll be swinging that ruddy great light around then,' the policeman said gruffly. 'She'll stay here until we're good and ready to move her.'

It was nothing short of chaos back in the editor's office.

'Where's Renishaw? Where's Terry?' barked Rudyard Rhys. 'What on earth are they doing? Why aren't they here?'

'Ice cream factory,' said Peter Pomeroy helpfully. 'They've got a new flavour out next week.'

'*Ice cream?* When we've got a murder on our hands?'

'Won't be murrther when Rudkin gets his hands on it,' said John Ross silkily. 'He'll have it down as a sprained ankle by the time he's finished wi' the inquest.'

'I'll get out there now,' said Miss Dimont. Her response was instant – measured, guarded, masking whatever feelings she may have at the loss of a friend. From the days of her time in Naval Intelligence, it had always been that way. 'Go over on Herbert. Terry can follow in the Minor.'

'No, I want Renishaw on it. You go and take over at the ice cream factory.'

'No, thank you, Mr Rhys.' Her response was defiant, a warning.

'*No?*'

'Renishaw will have all the information by now – and a free ice lolly too, no doubt, it's not exactly a complicated story. He can write it up in no time at all. May I remind you, Mr Rhys, that *I* am still the chief reporter round here, and it's my story? As you're aware, I knew the dead woman.'

The editor sat down at his desk and ran his hands through his hair. 'I was just trying to spare you the anguish,' he said, refusing to meet her eyes. Even editors lie.

'Nonsense! You just think David Renishaw will get you a better story. Send in the men – that's your attitude, always has been. When I think back…'

She was not allowed to finish the sentence. 'I'm *not* sending you,' rasped the editor, 'because you let your other activities get in the way when you're supposed to be covering events for the *Express*.'

'What do you mean, Richard? Are you saying I'm unprofessional?'

'All you ever want to do is play detective. I'm fed up with it.'

'Well, I'm going anyway. Renishaw can follow if he wants to. Tell Terry where I've gone and while you're at it, please thank him for topping up Herbert's petrol.'

It was a calculated act. On the one hand it was a sackable

offence to disobey your editor; on the other Judy knew he'd never do it. Whatever their relationship, and it was far from easy, they shared too much past history for Rhys ever to think of dismissing her.

Curious though, she thought, as she stowed the raffia bag and climbed aboard her trusty steed. When they worked together during the war, Rhys sometimes showed he was made of the right stuff – but here in Temple Regis, he'd become a slave to the newspaper owner's every whim. Caution was the owner's watchword, and so it had become his.

But not hers. 'Show me the way!' she ordered Herbert defiantly, and took off at breakneck speed.

The coast road out of Temple Regis rose spectacularly to a point where you could see the whole of Nelson's Bay at a sweep. Ahead in the distance stood the massive Templeton Rock with its distinguished-looking octagonal tower and despite the loss of her friend, Miss Dimont's spirits lifted with every yard Herbert advanced, so beautiful was it all. *This* is why I can never leave, she thought, as a flight of terns swooped over her head and plummeted over the cliff edge towards the foam beneath.

When she turned off the main road, however, the path out to Templeton Light was more of a rough-hewn track, causing Herbert to judder like a bucking bronco. 'All right, old fellow,' she said, 'I'll leave you here. Enjoy the view.'

She got off and walked up towards the lighthouse. Around a corner came a stretcher party bearing a shrouded lifeless body, with Inspector Topham and his men bringing up the rear. She stepped respectfully to one side to allow the ambulancemen past, then nipped back in front of the policeman so he was obliged to come to a halt.

'Come on, now,' he snarled, 'there'll be a statement. You'll get it.'

'It *is* Mirabel Clifford?'

'Yes.'

'And she did not die by accident?'

'No.'

'May I ask how she died?'

'You may.'

Here we go again, thought Judy, the same old routine. Question, no answer – question, no answer. 'Oh, come on, Inspector! You may as well tell me now. Why wait till we get back to the police station?'

Topham couldn't think of an answer to that, but holding an impromptu press conference as the corpse was being trundled away seemed somehow inappropriate. 'Come in at teatime.'

Judy stepped back to allow Topham to move off but just as she did so, a young constable raced up to his boss with an urgent look on his face.

'Sir! Sir! We've found the knife, sir!'

Topham's lip curled as he looked down at Miss Dimont. 'There's your first clue,' he said in a surly fashion. 'I wonder if you can work out what happened now.'

'Run over by a double-decker?' quipped Judy, but her heart lurched and she suddenly felt terribly sick.

She watched the corpse disappear on its stretcher and with a flood of relief glimpsed Terry, discreetly framing his shots while keeping a respectful distance. It was at moments like this that she recognised he could, when he wanted, show tact and diplomacy. She caught up with him just as he was changing film.

'Just going to go down to the lighthouse and get a couple there,' he said briskly. 'I don't suppose there's any visible evidence?'

'No idea,' said Judy, 'I didn't get that far. I'll come with you.'

'Get a move on, then.'

'Where's Renishaw?'

'Gone to see the editor. He's got some theory about this killing.'

'Has he now!' said Judy, struggling to keep up with the photographer's swift pace. 'I wonder what *that* can be!'

'No idea,' said Terry, crossly. 'He wouldn't dream of sharing anything like that with an 'umble photographer. Come on!'

They rounded a corner to be confronted by a lone constable, barring the way and generally ready to make a nuisance of himself. 'It's OK,' they chorused, 'Inspector Topham said we could.'

A trick that had worked before and, as it turned out, worked again now. They walked on up to the foot of the great white tower, and Terry pulled open the door. 'No point in waiting for an invitation,' he said, and in that moment Judy saw him afresh.

Terry was strong, he was resolute, he didn't do *The Times* crossword, but in every other respect he was just a bit of a miracle.

She gave him a rapturous smile.

The thought that had formed in Miss Dimont's mind – who on earth would want to kill such an upright citizen, one with such a promising future? – had seemingly taken hold of David Renishaw, too.

'It can only be him,' he said to Rudyard Rhys.

'I don't see why,' grunted the editor. He hated being confronted with anything awkward, and the idea that his newspaper knew the identity of a killer before the police did created yet another problem that would probably never go away; relations between the *Riviera Express* and the local police being tricky, even at the best of times.

'Don't get involved,' he advised his reporter. 'If you feel that strongly about it, I suggest you go and see Inspector Topham. There are procedures.'

'The way the police work around here, it'll take a month of Sundays before they do anything about it – you know that. Let me go up to Hatherleigh and see what Sirraway has to say.'

Rhys took out his filthy old pipe and started scraping away at it. 'You didn't actually distinguish yourself last time you were up there. Terry told me all about it. I didn't say anything because you were still very new on the staff, and I put it down to overenthusiasm. But I don't think I can let you go there again.'

'Look,' urged Renishaw, 'first of all, it was Sirraway who started it. Second, he's a dangerous lunatic – look at those attacks he made on Freddy Hungerford – and third, he was seen hanging round one of Mirabel Clifford's political meetings only a couple of days ago.'

'Who saw him?'

'Denise.'

'Denise who?'

'One of your sub-editors, Mr Rhys. You know, the one with dark hair.'

'Ah yes, the fish out of water.'

'If you say so, but she told me…'

Rhys struck a match so forcibly it broke in his fingers. 'She's no longer part of the staff, David.'

'She still has eyes and ears.'

'Rr… rrr. I want you to go and relieve Miss Dimont over at the lighthouse. Use your outstanding reporting skills to see what you can find out there. Go on, off with you.'

'You've got this all wrong,' replied Renishaw, angry now. 'Here we have the chance to have a real scoop, not some second-hand piece of information processed through the dim brain of the local constabulary! Judy's perfectly capable of covering that end of things.'

Rhys rose out of his chair. 'Defying your editor and refusing to cover a story is a sackable offence,' he said slowly. 'I'm sorry, David, things haven't turned out as I hoped they would when you first came here.'

'Come on, old boy. You sit at your desk and you make decisions, and they're usually the wrong ones. You're a decent enough fellow but you're hesitant and easily distracted. You're motivated by fear more than curiosity, and you don't seem to have the capacity to see that the people who work for you may have talent, may actually know something. I'd be tempted to ask whether you've ever covered a news story yourself, but if I rose to that temptation the answer would certainly be "no". The story's Sirraway – Sirraway, Mr Rhys, don't you see!'

The editor was suddenly very calm. 'You're an exceptionally

good reporter, Renishaw, but despite your talent you're no good if you won't do as you're told. *I expect my staff to obey me!*'

Renishaw looked mildly at the bewhiskered fellow in his tweed suit. 'Are you firing me?' he asked quietly.

'You're firing yourself. Do as I say, or go.'

Renishaw looked at him for a moment, shrugged his shoulders, and walked out.

The telephone on the editor's desk rang. 'Mr Rhys, it's Freddy Hungerford.'

'Ah, Sir Frederick. What a terrible business.'

'And just when I'd come down from London to offer dear Miriam a helping hand.'

'Mirabel, Sir Frederick.'

'Mm? Ah yes, yes… Anyway, I'm ringing up to let you know that, with the full support of the constituency party, I'm taking up the cudgels on Miriam's behalf and will stand for re-election in her place.'

'Really? She's been dead less than forty-eight hours.'

'I know, but it's as well to get these things settled quickly. Don't want our opponents taking advantage of a political vacuum.'

'Surely they'll delay the election? There's very little doubt that a candidate for political office in Westminster has been murdered. Surely a ballot can't go ahead until that's been cleared up?'

'I think you'll find,' said Sir Freddy smoothly, 'that parliamentary statute dictates that if such a tragedy were to take place at a by-election, the ballot *could* be stopped. But when it's a general election, you can't have the death of a single candidate, no matter the circumstances, upset the whole apple cart. No, we fight on!'

Rhys stood awkwardly over his desk, trying to take notes from a standing position. It would be nice to say his shorthand was a bit rusty, but he'd never actually bothered to learn it.

'Well, good luck,' he said. 'But there's just one thing. It's been widely discussed in the town that you were to take a seat in the House of Lords as a reward for your many years' service. What will happen to your peerage?'

'It'll have to wait for me. I'm not ready to give up the ghost just yet.'

'Well, as I say, good luck. I've made a note of what you've said – when will you make your first speech?'

'Tonight. Outside the Town Hall. Have a reporter there, there's a good chap.'

Rudyard Rhys did not reply, but gently replaced the receiver just as Miss Dimont walked in. He glared at her.

'You know it's a sackable offence, disobeying your editor?' He omitted to say he had used the same phrase not ten minutes before – people might assume he'd lost control of his staff.

Judy looked at him. 'I bring news from Templeton Rock. Mirabel Clifford was knifed to death.'

'Good God. And now I have news for you – Sir Freddy is stepping into her shoes.'

'What? He can't do that! Surely they must postpone the election out of respect?'

'He says not. He'll be making his first speech tonight and I'd like you to be there.'

'The peerage we've all been waiting for him to announce?'

'It's on hold. He's got the backing of the local committee to stand for one more term.'

Miss Dimont snorted. 'Well, *that'll* give a boost to Lilian Smee – *and* the Liberal candidate, too!'

'On the contrary. When news gets out about Mrs Clifford being killed, I quite expect that people will rally to her cause. I imagine Freddy will increase his majority, if not double it.'

'We'll see. Meanwhile, what's going on with David Renishaw? I passed him in the street and he was fuming. You've sent him out to Templeton Rock, I gather, but I got all there is to be had from the crime scene when I was out there. Terry's got some excellent pictures, by the way – including the body being carted away.'

'Can't use those.'

'You might think again when you see them.'

'Rr… rrr.'

'David said he needed to go up and find Professor Sirraway but you told him he couldn't.'

'You *know* what happened up there last time.'

'Well, yes. On the other hand, David may have a point. I didn't tell you this at the time, because there wasn't any way we could print it – but Mirabel Clifford told me that Sirraway had been blackmailing her.'

'Blackmail?'

'He sent her a huge file on Sir Freddy alleging a large number of illegal business dealings, but also some damaging personal matters too. He said if she didn't make them public, she would in effect be withholding important information on a public figure – she, a solicitor – and all because she hoped to inherit Hungerford's seat in Parliament.

'Sirraway then said that when he finally exposed Hungerford, he'd publicly accuse her of being complicit in the cover-up. Making sure Sir Freddy got his peerage, and she got his seat.'

'The man must be mad.'

'That's what David says.'

'Hmm. Are you sure it wasn't Sirraway who attacked David?'

'Well, Terry was there. At the time he said he was certain that David started it, but as we were coming back from Templeton Rock just now I asked him again, and he said he wasn't sure any more – it was very dark, and both men were behind a five-barred gate. He could see what was going on, but the gate was in the way. He said it was more from the sound of Sirraway's voice that he worked out who'd started it – but by the time he got there, they were each giving the other as good as they got.'

'So you're saying this professor is unbalanced, with a grievance against politicians, and prone to violence?'

'That of itself doesn't give us a murder suspect. But in the absence of anything else I'd go along with David's idea of putting some tough questions to Sirraway.'

'No, no, no! We mustn't get involved! We're a local newspaper, we're here to serve the community, not to catch criminals! I advise you to go and talk to Inspector Topham – let him know about Sirraway's blackmail attempts. Leave it to the professionals, for heaven's sake, Judy! Let's stay out of it!'

'Oh yes? Who do you want to win this election? The Labour woman? The Liberal? Or Sir Freddy?'

Rhys squirmed in his chair. 'You know we're impartial. Our stance is *may the best man win*.'

'*Man?* For heaven's sake, Richard!'

'Rr... rrr... you know what I mean.'

'Do I? My guess is that however awful Hungerford is, you'd rather him than one of these other candidates. If that's the case, ask yourself what are the consequences of going to the police with Sirraway's blackmail attempts. If you tell Inspector Topham about Hungerford stealing people's land and buildings, *and* the extortion racket he ran on ladies of high birth pre-war, he'll be duty-bound to investigate.

'If Sirraway's right in his accusations – and even if he did kill Mirabel Clifford – Freddy Hungerford would have to be brought to court. Then, if he's found guilty, you'd find yourself with a by-election here, with the absolute guarantee of a Labour or Liberal woman representing Temple Regis. Is that what you want?'

'Rr... rrr,' said Rhys. He sounded as though he'd swallowed a fish bone.

'I think, of the options available, you should let David Renishaw loose on Sirraway.'

Rhys was wondering whether it was another sackable offence, offering your editor advice which he was forced to take, even though he'd ordered the opposite.

'Get him back from the lighthouse, and brief him,' he sighed. 'And don't let me see you for at least the next twenty-four hours.'

TWENTY

Betty was putting on her make-up – Angel Face foundation, Maybelline mascara, pink Revlon non-smear lipstick – and singing the lines of her favourite song:

> *'Hey hey, set me free*
> *Stupid Cupid*
> *Stop picking on me...'*

She'd been thinking about Dud and the surprise success of his new business venture. He looked somehow different – not the grizzly bear who'd forced her to go platinum blonde just because he had a thing about Kim Novak. He seemed more alert, more focused – and richer!

And you could tell from the soppy look on his face the other day he was as smitten as ever. But as she applied the finishing the touches, Betty kept coming back to those sombre, wise words, *Never look back*, that she'd read in Athene's column last week. No matter they were directed at the Scorpios of this world, and Betty was Aquarius – still they rang true. Athene always hit the target dead-centre.

As Terry pointed out, Dud was on his way. It was brave of him to open a launderette when the snobs in town said it would lower the tone – bringing your dirty washing out in public was a backward step in the town's social advancement, they said. They did not care for Dud and his lofty ambitions.

Though it was too soon to be absolutely certain, it looked like he had a hit on his hands. Shrewdly he'd put piped music in, so that his clientele could listen to Craig Douglas and Tommy Steele while being driven dizzy by the many revolutions of his machines, and he'd opened up the back room with nice tables and chairs so there was an Espresso machine with lovely frothy coffee.

She could do worse. And yet, and yet... it only took a decent story on the front page of the *Express,* with the nice big byline Mr Rhys always awarded her, to set her mind racing to Fleet Street and fame.

Her thoughts slid to David Renishaw, who'd become something of a hero figure. They had walked out a few times, and though nothing much had come of it – beyond discovering there was no longer a Mrs Renishaw – they would still occasionally meet, two singletons in a world that seemed filled with couples. Over supper at The Chinese Singing Teacher, Betty confessed her thirst for fame and Fleet Street in the hope David could offer some advice.

'Don't worry,' said Renishaw. 'When the time is right, they'll come and find you.' Meaning, I don't think you'll make it, Betty, though I could be wrong.

'I don't want to wait any longer, David. The jobs are going to younger and younger women these days and...' She didn't finish, because it would only lead to her blabbing how old she was. She always did that with a man; no wonder her love life was such a rocky path.

'Well, I...' began Renishaw.

'...and I'll be twenty-seven next birthday.' She paused. Here the more intuitive of her dates would jump in to assure her she didn't look a day over twenty-four, but David wasn't like that. He was tough, steely, deeply absorbed in his own thoughts. And obviously I look every day of twenty-seven to him.

'You don't think I should write in with a few ideas? I mean, this whole Professor Sirraway business would definitely make something for *The Sunday Times*, don't you think? With your help we—'

'Betty, the man's mad. Don't go near him – he's going to kill somebody one of these days!'

She thought about this as she blotted her lipstick – despite Revlon's promises, it *did* smear, all over your coffee cups and fags and chaps' collars – but it was hard to see what Renishaw was getting at; she'd spent time chatting to the professor all that time ago and though he certainly had something to get off his chest, he struck her as a talker, not a doer.

Betty was an expert there, when it came to men and their talk. Maybe she would settle for Dud, though a large part of her would prefer to run away with Renishaw and fight to the last ditch for the rights of the underdog.

He'd ordered her not to tell anybody about what she'd found in his desk drawer, and she'd agreed – but, being Betty, she then had to whizz back and take a second look. This time she found a file on Freddy Hungerford which hadn't been there before, together with lots of notes in a shorthand she couldn't decipher – Gregg, she supposed.

No question, Renishaw was a mystery and, she had to

confess, a disquieting one. It was his secretiveness, and the bees in his bonnet – Sirraway, and now Freddy Hungerford – and the way he pushed all other pleasures and pastimes aside. It made him uncomfortable company, but was that any surprise, when you hung around with the champion of the underdog?

She stared into the mirror then tilted her head slightly, which had the rewarding effect of levelling the perm up. Satisfied with her preparations for the day, she strode out into the newsroom.

'Who's doing the Austerity Lunch?' hollered John Ross, keen to shovel the dreary event into one of his early pages.

'Not me!' chorused Betty and Judy simultaneously. It was possibly the worst job in the diary: a bunch of earnest do-gooders giving up the price of a meal to sit down with a celebrity speaker and eat gruel. The people were dull, their sense of martyrdom insufferable, and the food was abysmal.

'I did it last time,' said Betty, looking daggers at Judy.

'Only because you owed me one. It's your turn, Betty, and anyway I have to go and see Frank Topham.'

'Oh Lord. Who's the guest bore this time, then?'

'He sounds jolly – the Reverend Tubby Clayton. He founded Toc H, you know – a bit god-squad, but the time should sail by. Look, here's the leaflet for this month's talk.' She plunked down a roneo'd sheet which set out Tubby's talking points:

- Friendship (To love widely)
- Service (To build bravely)
- Fair-mindedness (To think fairly)

'Fun, fun, fun!' taunted Judy.

'I can't eat what they dish out, it's foul.'

'Have a sandwich before you go.'

To stifle further protest, Judy picked up her bag and marched purposefully out of the newsroom. The walk through the town was, as usual, a complete delight and she arrived at the police station with her spirits lifted, if not her expectations.

'Nothing really to add,' said Topham, predictably. 'Mrs Clifford was killed, you know that. With a knife, you know that. Day before yesterday, you know that. The killer is still at large and police are using every effort within their powers to identify and detain him.'

'Him?'

'We assume so.'

'Motive?'

'Ah, there you are driving me into the arms of speculation, Miss Dimont. We are following up several leads.'

'Meaning you haven't a clue.'

'If I hadn't known you as long as I have, I'd call that impertinent.'

Better than incompetent, which is what you lot are, thought Judy. 'Can I just establish that Mrs Clifford was due to make an appearance at the Templeton Light as part of her election campaigning?'

'Correct.'

'But that was one or two days ahead – why would she go there in advance, when she must have had her hands full elsewhere?'

'That I cannot say.'

'The murder weapon?'

'A professional fish-gutting knife, probably stolen from the dockside.'

'Oh,' shuddered Judy the woman, not the reporter, 'how horrible!'

'Very upsetting,' conceded Topham. 'That's not for publication, by the way.'

'And there was nobody manning the Light when she arrived, no witness?'

'Doesn't take a genius to work out that their job is at night, Miss Dimont. The two men were both in town.'

'What's happened to her children?'

'Leave them out of this,' warned Topham. 'Again not for publication, they're with their aunt in Surrey.'

'Inquest?'

'Next Thursday.'

'Anything else I should know?'

'As you can imagine, I'm rather busy,' said Topham absently, gathering up his papers and rising from his desk. 'I think you know the way out by now.'

Judy wandered slowly back to the office trying to piece together what had happened, if not why. Mirabel Clifford had planned to go to the lighthouse for a photo-opp – a way of displaying her interest in the lives of others while giving photographers the opportunity to picture her somewhere more attractive than sitting at her office desk.

These events take a few minutes only, and need little preparation – why did she come out to the lighthouse two days prior to the event? And who was with her?

As she strolled into Fore Street she could see ahead a crowd standing in a semi-circle round a tall individual, and as she drew closer she could make out the brilliantined head of Sir Freddy Hungerford, talking nineteen to the dozen and pumping his fist to emphasise each point.

Rudyard Rhys had ignored the MP's instruction to send a reporter to his hustings, and told his staff he was in no hurry to oblige the politician, but her innate curiosity led Judy to join the crowd. She hadn't seen Hungerford since he'd double-crossed her in the house of his mistress before Christmas. She was curious to see what effect he was having on the electorate – could the Hungerford magic weave one last spell after all the years of neglect?

The answer was yes and no. The old faithfuls cheered him, but the younger voters were tossing him some sharp questions.

'And that's about it, my friends,' Hungerford was saying. 'I'm expected at another meeting down by the lifeboat, if anybody wants to come along. I say the same thing over and over again, but it improves with the telling.'

A few laughed politely. 'But I can't finish without paying tribute again to Miriam... er... er... and the tireless work she put into preparing for this election. Nothing would give me greater pleasure than if she was standing here.'

'And you was warming your arse in the House of Lords,' shouted an unbeliever. Hungerford was far too smooth an operator, and bowed his head as if in deference to the oafish interruption.

Judy had her notebook out but there was little to report, she'd arrived too late. As the MP shook some hands and separated himself from the crowd, she was approached by a pink-cheeked man in a striped suit.

'Local press, is it?'

Judy looked him up and down. 'In a manner of speaking.' She always regarded with caution men who wore pinstripes in the country.

'Hamish Madden, what a pleasure to meet you.'

I'm not sure that's mutual. 'Judy Dimont, *Riviera Express*. You're with Sir Freddy, I take it.'

'*With* Sir Freddy, and *for* Sir Freddy! Look at him – younger than springtime, I don't know how he does it!' The way he said it, she wondered if he'd been drinking.

'You didn't waste much time getting down here.'

'We came down to support Mirabel.'

'He calls her Miriam.'

'Ha! Ha!' cried the man, 'Freddy's pet name for her!'

'Pet name? Not so long ago he didn't even know who she was.'

'Ha! Ha!' whooped the man. 'You *are* funny! I hope you're going to give him a good write-up, he relies on the local press you know – he'd be nowhere without it!'

'Nor we without him.'

'Ha! Ha! It's so good to meet you, Miss er…' There were flecks of spittle at the corners of his mouth. 'Are you coming on to the lifeboat station? A few words, press the flesh, then we'll all go for a jolly good lunch somewhere.'

'An excellent idea,' replied Judy, nodding. 'We need to keep up with what's going on in Sir Freddy's campaign. But before we do, there are a couple of questions I'd like to ask, just to catch up with the changeover of candidate.' She looked at his pink cheeks. 'I don't know if you know it, but the Fortescue Arms here has a lovely little upstairs bar overlooking the square. You can spare ten minutes, I take it?'

The pinstripe man's eyes looked greedily at the inn sign. 'My treat,' he said winningly. 'Sir Fred's given me an unlimited budget.'

'To bribe the local press?'

'What? Oh! Ha, ha!'

From where Judy sat, while Hamish Madden busied himself with the drinks, she could look down on the Market Square where only months before Mirabel Clifford had sought her out, taken her back to her office, and shared the secrets of genial Sir Freddy's vast fortune. Now she was dead, and the great wheel of the body politic had rolled over her corpse, leaving her memory crushed and, all too soon, to be forgotten.

'Cheer-ho!' said Madden as he brought the drinks back. He'd had an extra one at the bar.

'So you're part of the hustings team, taken on to steer him round the constituency?'

'Yes indeed!'

'Just as well – it's been so long since Sir Frederick was here he'll need reminding where the Town Hall is.'

'Oh, ho ho! You *are* funny.'

'No, Mr Madden, I merely repeat what a lot of people in Temple Regis feel – that he's a rotten MP who can't be bothered to come and meet the people who elected him. They expect better.'

'Well, they're wrong. I work with Sir Freddy in the Commons. It's often a fractious relationship because he cares very much about the constituency but there are so many other calls on his time – business, diplomacy, and so forth. He travels a great deal and devotes himself – *devotes* himself – to charitable work. There aren't enough hours in the day, and it's my job to keep him on the straight and narrow, balance up his workload.' He took a satisfied gulp.

This is nice for you, thought Miss Dimont, for a moment in your life you're allowed to talk about yourself. How you help to make the MP into the great figure he appears in public. And how many more of you are there in the House of Commons?

'I don't know about you,' said Judy, eyeing his glass, 'but the heat out there is making me thirsty. Let me get you a refill.' If he continues drinking at this rate, my purse will be empty in no time.

'Well, if you insist. I've got a slate going, just put it on that.'

'Well, that's very kind.' He was obviously in no rush to join his master and the lifeboatmen, or indeed ever move from his seat again. We could be here for some time, thought Judy.

She returned from the bar to find Madden looking thirsty and careworn – she noticed for the first time that the shirt he was wearing was not fresh, and the knot in his tie was awry.

'Must be hard work, keeping up with Sir Freddy,' she said encouragingly.

'Well, he's an unforgiving taskmaster but I feel I owe it to him. I went through a bad patch a couple of years ago and he helped me out. So now I'm his slave. Ha! Ha!'

Judy was thinking of Mirabel. 'Do you know the name Hector Sirraway?'

'Do I *not*. He's been pursuing this vendetta against Sir Freddy for the past few months, it's terrible. Sending letters, talking to people, turning up to meetings and disrupting them – what a ghastly fellow. They really ought to lock him up.'

'Have you been to the police?'

Madden drew back, looking at her sideways. 'I thought we were talking about the smooth transition of the candidacy from Mirabel Clifford back to Sir Freddy. What's this about?'

'Well, there are certain things going on here… it's difficult, Hamish. I may call you Hamish?'

'Yes, yes, of course. What things?'

'I happen to know Sirraway was attempting to blackmail Sir Freddy. I know certain things which haven't come out into the open and which I feel sure Sir Freddy wouldn't want, either. But since the issue is between him and the professor, surely the simplest solution would be to call in the police? It might help clear up one or two other things as well.'

'Well, since you know these things, I'll be frank. No point in going to the police because what Sirraway claims isn't – how can I put it? – it isn't exactly wrong.'

'The land deals? The acquisition of other people's property?'

'All I will say is, may not be wrong. Another?'

Crikey, we've only been here fifteen minutes and he's on his third. Or is it fourth?

'Yes, please.' This man Madden is going to make me very drunk and I'm going to regret it, but he's slowly opening up – who knows where this may go?

Miss Dimont thrilled at the challenge – can I get him to say enough before I get so drunk I forget it all? I can't make notes, after all.

'There! Doubles!' cried Madden, returning. 'Saves the tiresome business of getting up every five minutes.'

'Shouldn't you be down at the lifeboat station?'

'Freddy's got his secretary there to hold his hand. Delia. And here I am working hard on his behalf, doing my duty chatting up the local press. Ha! Ha!' He sniffed his glass and looked at Judy over its rim. 'We were saying?'

'So Professor Sirraway won't leave him alone. Tell me, was it him who hit Sir Freddy outside the House of Commons? Nobody ever got to the bottom of that.'

'It was me, actually.' Madden's cheeks had, if anything, grown pinker and he seemed rather proud of his confession.

'What? You assaulted your own employer in the street?'

'We're not on the record, are we? You're not going to print this?'

'Just background,' said Judy reassuringly. 'In-fill. You know, it's wonderful to hear what life's like at Westminster behind the scenes. Usually all we get is what the politicians want us to hear. This is fascinating – do go on!'

'Well,' said Madden, rising to the bait, 'as long as we're off the record. . . It was all a bit of a stunt which didn't quite come off.'

'But you're still working for him?'

'Oh yes, he couldn't get by without me. Actually, he paid me to do it – to hit him and run away. Outside St Stephen's Entrance. I had to make sure there was no policeman patrolling around before I did it, but there had to be witnesses.'

Judy leaned forward. 'I've never heard anything remotely like this in the whole of my career. A distinguished MP actually *pays* one of his staff to assault him?'

'That's about the size of it.'

'Tell me, please, what on earth's behind it.'

Madden looked tremendously pleased with himself. Once again they were talking about him, not the man in whose shadow he had long walked. 'I need two promises from you first.'

'What are they?'

'That you'll write something nice about him so I can say I set it up. And that you promise not to repeat the next bit until the day you die.'

'I will – I'll do both.' And I'll uncross my fingers under the table before they stick together.

'I hit him too hard. I suppose I then got carried away and knocked him about a bit.'

'I saw the evidence. You broke his nose.'

'He'd just had some terribly bad news and he wanted some sympathy. So it was arranged that he would walk out of St Stephen's Entrance, I would come up and biff him, the press would get to hear about it and then they would write nice things about what a wonderful old trouper he was.'

'Sorry,' said Judy, shaking her head slightly, 'I don't follow.'

'He'd decided to stay on as MP for Temple Regis, and he wanted the press behind him.'

'But his successor had already been announced! Mirabel Clifford!'

'I don't think he ever took that seriously. Women – in Parliament?' Madden emitted a heehawing noise.

'But she'd been selected! Chosen! Announced! She was ready to get going the moment the election was called!'

'Freddy has been MP for this constituency since the Norman Conquest. A word or two in the right ear would have sorted that out – Mrs Clifford would have withdrawn on health grounds or some such, with the promise she could stand again next time.'

'That's a disgrace!'

'Politics, my dear,' said Hamish Madden, leaning across the table and staring at her unevenly, 'is the art of the possible. It's what you can get away with that counts – and make no mistake, Sir Freddy would have got away with it.'

'So why didn't he?'

'Ah, as I said. This is where I hold up my hand and say *mea culpa*. The plan was that after I floored him he would get up, jump in a taxi, go home, and call the Press Association. They would come round and he would describe the assault, while making sure everyone understood he was such a devoted MP he wouldn't take a day off work, and he would be in Westminster, taking care of his constituents, the following day.'

Madden took a long gulp of whisky and put down the empty glass.

'That's when it *really* went wrong. I gave him what for, and he went down pretty hard. I think he must have been a bit concussed because instead of giving the taxi driver his home address, he gave him the address of Mrs... oh, I won't say the name... a friend.'

Judy looked at him shrewdly. 'Mrs Baines of 35 Ebury Street.'

'How... how do you know that?'

'I dropped in to see them both quite soon after your fisti-cuffs. He didn't tell you?'

'Not a dickybird.'

'He gave me his exclusive account of what'd happened in front of the House of Commons in Mrs Baines' parlour.

I went away to write it up for the *Riviera Express,* but the moment I left he hopped in a cab and went home to Lady Hungerford. From there he went back to Plan A, calling the *Daily Herald* and giving them his sob-story. That got him the sympathetic press he'd hoped for.'

'It certainly did – page one everywhere!'

'So why didn't he go ahead with his plan to grab the seat back from Mrs Clifford?'

'Ah,' said Madden. 'His mistake. He called the party chairman from Mrs Baines' house and he wasn't available, and so he left Mrs Baines' number. When the chairman called back and Mrs Baines answered – and with what followed in the press the next day – the chairman put two and two together. There's been a nationwide hunt on for Sir Freddy, and there he was, hiding in his lady friend's house. The local branch took rather a dim view of that and told him they were sticking with Mrs Clifford.'

'But why? Why this extraordinary rigmarole? Why did he want to hang onto his position when he had a seat in the House of Lords waiting for him?'

'Ah,' said Madden, his words slurring now. 'What I told you, about his having had bad news. A certain person in a certain Palace spreading ridiculous ideas about him, making life very difficult for the poor chap. Apparently to do with something that happened pre-war, I don't know the details.'

'Let me guess. He had a hand in the violent death of a married woman.'

'I wouldn't know anything about that,' said Madden, without turning a hair. 'I say, this is awfully jolly – shall we have another? Only could you get it? My legs feel a bit wobbly.'

TWENTY-ONE

Dickie Valentine was on the radio. His cloying tones did nothing for Miss Dimont's king-sized hangover.

'*Just as soon as they can make the guilty one confess*
I know exactly what I'm gonna do…
'*Who's bound to be the guilty one, who?*
The finger of suspicion points at you…'

The trouble is, she thought as she switched the radio off, the finger of suspicion points at nobody. Yesterday, as she sat in the Ladies at the back of the Fort desperately trying to scribble down everything Madden had told her, the revelation had come in a blinding flash.

Sir Freddy Hungerford had killed his political rival in order to keep his seat at Westminster.

But, as the dawn rose and she fought her way out of her tangled bed to trip over Mulligatawny, she realised what a mad idea it had been. Oh, ouch! Too much booze!

She rubbed her forehead and tried to think. On the grounds of *cui bono* – who benefits? – a wily political specimen like Hungerford would realise he'd be the first suspect. Plus how would he, at his age, haul a grown woman against her will up the winding staircase of the Templeton Light, then stick a knife in her?

The whole thing was preposterous, and while she waited for the kettle to boil, Judy wondered what other clues or leads from the loose-tongued Hamish Madden she'd managed to get down in her impeccable shorthand.

She opened her notebook. And couldn't read a word.

How many whiskies did I drink? she wondered, bumping into the kitchen table and spilling her tea. 'Oh, *Mull*! Get out of my way! Go and catch a mouse!'

She unlatched the front door to let him out, and brought in the milk and her copy of *The Times*. Then she sat down ignoring both. It can only be Sirraway, she thought – Sirraway! We know of no other person who'd got anything against Mirabel.

But even as she tried to put the pieces of the jigsaw together, she realised they didn't fit. Sirraway had a motive – perhaps – to kill Sir Freddy, who'd rebuffed every approach the professor had ever made. If he'd stolen that land, Sirraway could prove it in court – certainly an easier route to satisfaction than death.

But that was Hungerford – Mirabel Clifford had done Sirraway no harm. She'd treated him gently when he sent her threatening letters even though, if she'd wanted, she could have directed the full force of the law against him. And Betty – who, after all, had got to know him – said Sirraway was peculiar, but harmless.

No, someone else killed Mirabel. It was all very upsetting – the more so because the hangover refused to allow Judy to hold a thought in her head for more than a moment.

The doorbell rang.

'Morning, Hugue, I brought you the first ranunculus from the garden – aren't they glorious?'

'Lovely of you to come all this way, Auriol, but I don't think I can face the fish market this morning.' It was their Friday morning arrangement, once a month.

'You look wretched. Is it flu?'

'Whisky. Make more tea, talk to me.'

Auriol scrambled some eggs and they went out to eat them in the garden under the blossoming apple tree.

'So you see – Mirabel. Sirraway. Freddy Hungerford. You'll have to help.'

'I knew about his peerage being blocked,' confessed Auriol. 'I suppose I should have told you, but Hugue, we always have *so* much to talk about when we see each other, I forgot.'

'How did you know? Not that it really makes much difference.'

'Arthur told me – heard it from some chap at his club. Apparently, a word came down from the Palace, and Hungerford's name was quietly taken off the list. Something to do with Prince George – you know, the Queen's uncle. He was a terribly naughty fellow and got tangled up in all sorts of things. It was one of his women.'

Judy turned her head slowly. 'Something's coming back to me. Sorry, it's this hangover. Can you remember any more?'

'Apparently, Hungerford milked this woman for all she'd got – he had a hold over her because he knew about her affair with the prince, and used it to suck her money away. She was made bankrupt, and then committed suicide.'

'Pansy Westerham!'

'Sorry?'

'Her name wasn't Pansy Westerham, by any chance?'

'Couldn't say. I don't think Arthur mentioned it.'

As the tea and Auriol's company restored her jangled grey matter, Miss Dimont put to one side her concerns about the death of Mirabel Clifford and focused instead on what she'd learned from Mrs Phipps – that Pansy Westerham was a married woman with a child who'd left her husband behind and come to London, where she'd used her considerable fortune to get close to the royal circle.

She'd fallen from a house, but her friend Bobbety Thurloe said was it was murder. If it *was* murder, as Mrs Phipps implied, it could have been the men who talked softly and carried the big stick. But lodged in the corner of Miss Dimont's mind was the mention of the other man in Pansy's life.

Could that man have been Freddy Hungerford? Could Pansy have been one of his rich dupes? Could he have taken all her money and, in despair, had she thrown herself from the roof of her house?

'Unravel this, Auriol,' she said, watching as Mulligatawny stalked slowly down the garden to join them. The sun was hot now, the bees were buzzing. 'If Freddy Hungerford was the other man in Pansy Westerham's life, it links him to her death – just as there's a link between him and the death of Mirabel Clifford.'

'You're not suggesting Hungerford killed Mrs Clifford?'

'Well, I thought about that – but it's not possible. The connection has to be Sirraway.'

'I can't see how. He would never have mixed in those social circles before the war – not the type. He could never have known someone like Pansy Westerham.'

'But he *is* implicated in Mirabel's murder – I'm sure of that.'

'Why are you trying to link these two deaths anyway?' said Auriol, collecting up the cups. 'Twenty-five years apart, two entirely different victims, two very different means of death. The common factor, I'll grant you, is Hungerford. But that's all.'

'Just a moment,' said Judy, and disappeared inside the house. Auriol remained behind to have a short discussion with Mulligatawny about whether it was a sign of content-ment when he lay with his paws crossed. The question was still unresolved when Miss Dimont returned.

'Come on,' she said. 'Get your tiara out!'

Tanfield Castle near Tavistock lay in a small valley fringed with oak trees and carpeted with early summer flowers. An avenue of poplars led to an ornate doorway with an elaborate coat of arms, while underneath stood the proud bearer of those arms, a bent but jolly old fellow clutching a bunch of delphiniums.

'Have you ever *seen* such joy!' he said, as the two women emerged from Auriol's car. 'Come in!'

In the space of five minutes the friends had learned that the Thurloes could trace their line back to the Norman Conquest, for nine centuries they'd made it a family policy to keep their noses clean and avoid political argument, they were well-off but not rich, and the roof tended to leak but only in extreme weather. There was a new vicar in the local church who wouldn't stick, he rattled on too much for Bobbety's liking, and flowers were his lifetime's passion.

They were on to the Madeira pretty quickly – Judy knew she'd regret it but couldn't resist the cut-glass goblet it came in – and quite soon came to the point.

'Pansy Westerham.'

'Yes,' said Bobbety, leaning back and stretching his legs, 'I remember her well – an absolute corker. There was something extraordinarily mysterious about her eyes – I can see them even now – she laughed a lot, but there was pain there. Not enough for you to want to ask questions, but enough for you to take notice when you were waltzing her round the dancefloor.'

'I get the impression nobody knew where she came from,' said Judy.

'Oh, she was perfectly well-brought-up. And, you know, they didn't need a copy of *Debrett's* in the Embassy lobby to check your credentials, they could always tell. She was a lady all right.'

'I think, Lord Thurloe,' said Auriol, 'that Miss Dimont was saying…'

'For heaven's sake, call me Bobbety – let us, with our second glass, dispense with formality. They call this stuff Rainwater, y'know, doesn't taste like it, does it?'

'Auriol,' said Auriol, smilingly accepting his offer.

'Huguette,' said Judy. The opulent salon in which they sat somehow called for it.

'How delicious that sounds,' said Bobbety. 'French, of course – no doubt we're related, via the Norman Conquest.'

'I would like to think so,' replied Judy with a nod to the old gentleman's courtesy, 'but I doubt it. We are Belgian.'

'A wonderful country, though perhaps I did not see it at

its best when I was there in 1915. Now, what more about the extraordinary Pansy?'

'Freddy Hungerford.'

'Ah, yes,' said the old man, wrinkling his nose. 'Not a popular figure in our circle. Too harum scarum. An inveterate gambler both on the racetrack and in, ah, the boudoir. Enormous push, of course, and perfectly charming to talk to, but a bad 'un.

'Back in the old Embassy days there were social circles, like rings on a duck pond. The tightest, the innermost circle, was the royal family – or the ones you saw, anyway – the Prince of Wales, Prince Bertie, Prince Harry, Prince George. Even Princess Mary occasionally.

'The next ring out were the close friends of the royals, the ring after that the friends of the friends, and so on. Hungerford was about three rows back but acted as though he was right at the epicentre of our group. He wasn't.'

'Go on,' said Judy, enjoying the moment so much she forgot her pledge not to touch the second glass.

'Prince George was having an affair with Pansy, but then he was having affairs with others, too, even though he was married. A very naughty boy but, oh, so adorable! Anyway, while Georgy was otherwise occupied, Pansy was with Freddy. Who did what he always did – encouraged her to buy a racehorse, took her to Ascot and made her lose a fortune on bad bets, urged her to buy risky investments through broker friends of his which never paid off. And in the space of a couple of years, she was broke.

'When she came to London she bought a small house in Knightsbridge, and the day she died she had been told it would be taken away from her to pay her debts. And, as Geraldine Phipps has told you, it is my belief she was murdered.'

'Do you think Freddy Hungerford killed her? I can't see why he would, but do you?'

'It's hard to say. He lived life so near the margins in those days and he'd always been pretty ruthless. But by that time he was an MP – would he risk a political career by murdering someone?'

'If only there was a way to find out more.'

'Well,' said Bobbety, 'the one person who knows where all the bodies are buried – I'm speaking figuratively, of course – is Lady Hungerford. You know, the German woman – she knows everything. It's why he's stayed with her all this time and never sought a divorce – a wife not being able to testify and all that, while a divorced wife is free to sing like a canary. He wouldn't dare leave her.'

'If she's kept quiet all these years, she's not likely to speak up now,' said Auriol.

'I imagine you're right.'

'You heard about the death of Mirabel Clifford?' asked Miss Dimont.

'Most regrettable. I heard it on the radio. She sounded a fine person – a welcome relief to voters after years and years of that charlatan.'

'Do you see any similarities – any link – between the two deaths,' asked Judy, 'Mirabel and Pansy? Even though they were twenty-five years apart?'

The old gent climbed to his feet. 'I don't believe I do,' he said, putting down his Madeira glass. 'In fact not at all. But come and have some lunch.'

Oh, drat, thought Judy. Just for a moment I'd hoped…

Fortunately, Tubby Clayton had brought a spare set of notes for his Austerity Lunch speech, and Betty was able to charm them off him. 'Wish I could stay,' she trilled as she waved goodbye, 'but it's a busy week. Let me know if the lunch goes up in flames!'

This is just the sort of behaviour which can get local journalism a bad name, and Rudyard Rhys frowned on it – Betty was there to sit through the lunch, like it or lump it. But she'd used her wits – first rule of journalism – to get what was needed, and nobody could object to that.

She was in no hurry to get back to the office, however, and decided on a sandwich in the Signal Box Café. The bliss of not having to swallow that gruel and listen to ghastly talk about self-sacrifice!

As the café door opened with a *ting*, she saw Lovely Mary and David Renishaw huddled at a table over by the old signal levers.

'Oh! Hello, everybody!'

'Betty,' said Renishaw, neither a greeting nor friendly.

'Er – I just came in for a sandwich, Mary, but if you're busy…'

'It's OK, I'm off,' said Renishaw and almost rudely pushed past her. And when she thought of their night together in The Chinese Singing Teacher – what cheek!

'Come you over here, maid,' said Mary, 'nice egg and cress, do you? Pot o' tea?'

'Oh yes please, Mary – sorry – was I intruding?'

'No, no, we was just settling up.'

'Oh, OK, thank you.'

Betty sat down and inspected her nail varnish which, as usual, had taken a battering from the old Underwood, wondering if Revlon made a special line for factory workers that she could get her hands on.

'Here y'are,' said Mary, and plonked a plump sandwich in front of her. She sat down opposite.

'What's wrong, Mary? You look upset.'

'Yore Mr Renishaw. Just handed in his notice, off at the end of next week. Told me not to tell anybody, but seeing as it's you, Betty.'

'Has he found somewhere...?' Betty was going to say 'nicer', Lovely Mary's accommodation being a bit on the spartan side.

'Off up back to Lunnun. A shame – he was a difficult one, but he always paid on time and made his own bed. Left the bathroom spick and span, like.'

Betty put down her sandwich. 'He's *going*, Mary? He never told me!'

'He allus pays a week in advance. He just says, *This is the last one Mary, I'm off.*'

'Why? What?'

'Had a row with your editor. Editor told him what to do, Mr Renishaw told the editor he couldn't run a bicycle shop let alone a paper.'

'I had supper with him only the other... he never mentioned it to me!'

Lovely Mary was looking at the sandwich on Betty's plate with pride; she took pleasure in her handiwork. 'Eat up now, I put a bit of extra in there just for you.'

'It's a wonderful sandwich, Mary, but I can't – how could he leave without telling me?'

If Mary had an answer to that she kept it to herself. 'He's very disillusioned,' she said. 'He told me he had hopes of staying here for ever, but in the end he felt there were too many things in his way. He was never going to get forward.'

'A bit too clever for us, Lovely.'

'I wouldn't altogether say that,' said Mary, without elucidating.

'He came with secrets, he's going with secrets,' replied Betty, testing.

'You could certainly say *that*,' said Mary and got up. There was something she wasn't telling.

Betty followed her over to the kitchen. 'Did he say where he was going? What his plans were?'

Mary gave her a searching look.

'We went out a few times,' explained Betty. 'I'd like…'

'Oh, like that, was it? You do surprise me! I didn't think he liked women – not the other thing, you know, just not interested. Didn't look at my Molly once, and *everyone* looks at my Molly, more's the worry.'

'No, Mary, not like that, but I had hopes he'd help me get to Fleet Street. He has connections.'

'Does 'e?' said Mary gruffly.

'There's something you're not telling me, Mary.'

'There's lots I don' share about, maid. A still tongue makes a wise head.'

'You're dying to tell me.'

'Oh, go on then. There's a daughter, see, who writes. Would be about twelve or thirteen. Lives with her aunt, or something, calls her Aunty anyway. Talks about her dead mother a lot.'

'No, no, that can't be right – he *divorced* Mrs Renishaw. He told me. Unless she died recently.'

'A couple of years ago by the sound of it.'

Betty stared at her. 'You've been going through his…!' she started, but then bit her tongue. Wasn't she guilty of the self-same crime?

'Though personally I'll miss the money,' said Lovely Mary. 'I think you'll find quite a lot of people will be happy when our Mr Renishaw leaves town.'

Will I? thought Betty mournfully.

Oh hell, I'll have to give Dud another whirl…

TWENTY-TWO

Like a church congregation, the massed ranks of the Fleet Street press corps sat silently, as if in prayer. Their reverence was directed not towards some celestial being, however, but the lavish dinner which had just been laid before them.

Their leader rose to say grace: 'Thank God for a murder!' and was greeted with a gale of raucous laughter.

Behind the hilarity, however, lay a serious concern. The general election was eating up virtually every square inch of their newspapers' pages, which meant that the parliamentary writers had their hands full and were pleading with their bosses for a few extra hands on deck. These men of crime, under-utilised, were in danger of being seconded to election duties which as far as they were concerned was a step down – severely reduced expenses, no Page One bylines, and having to mix with politicians, a type of person they neither knew nor trusted. Life was much safer among criminals.

'The Gevrey Chambertin '54!' commanded Guy Brace of the *Daily Herald*.

The wine waiter Peter Potts leaned anxiously forward. 'If

I'm not mistaken, sir, it did not find favour with yourself last time you was here.'

'What? Nonsense!' barked Brace. 'It's a very fine wine, though I don't expect you to know that. The largest village-named *appelation* in the Côte de Nuits, pure sunshine in a bottle!'

'At the price we're charging, I wouldn't want you to be disappointed again, Mr Brace.'

'What? Bring me the bottle, there's a good fellow – in fact bring two while you're at it!'

With the summer season not quite on its feet, a good murder in Temple Regis was a wonderful boost for the Grand. Other hoteliers in the resort looked on in envy whenever anything newsworthy occurred because as far as Fleet Street was concerned, there was no other place to stay, to eat, to drink, and to tell each other age-old stories they'd heard a million times before.

'That's when I bought the camel on expenses. Technically, of course, I still own it...'

'The judge at the Old Bailey instantly cleared the court and ordered me to stay behind. What I told him then – well, it changed the whole course of the trial...'

'General Montgomery... it was after El Alamein. He told me – in strictest confidence, of course...'

'That Rachman, call him a slum landlord if you must, but he pours the finest single malt, I can tell you...'

If the peerless Peter Potts had been listening, he could have supplied the punchline to each and every one of these shaggy dog stories – they were hauled out in the Palm Court or the dining room every time Fleet Street rode into town, which was often. The yarns never changed, though those who told them sometimes did. But who cared, in the safety and comfort of his five-star hotel, whether they ever set foot in the desert or advised a High Court judge? It was the way you told 'em that counted.

The cheers and shouts rang down the hall and through the doorway into the private bar, where Sid was applying his customary elbow grease to a couple of dozen wine glasses, in anticipation of breakages next door.

Against the bar, watching idly, leaned Inkpen of the *News Chronicle*.

'Has he been in?'

'He'll be along soon.'

'Here's a tenner. Keep us happy, will you?'

Sid smiled and bowed very slightly.

'And no interruptions – not like last time when you let that woman from the local rag come and interfere.'

'Yers, Mr Inkpen. Was you thinking of having some champagne this evening, like yesterday?'

Now he had a real story, not like at Christmas when he was here on a fishing expedition, there would be less scrutiny of Inkpen's expenses. 'Why not,' he said. 'That Pol Roger was a bit on the dry side, though.'

'Known for it, sir. Why don't you plump for the Moët & Chandon? Always a safe bet.'

'Make sure it's nice and cold.'

At that moment Frank Topham appeared in the doorway but on spotting Inkpen started to back out again.

'Frank! Welcome! I was hoping to see you.'

'You again,' said the Inspector moodily. 'I've only got ten minutes and I like to drink my pint in peace.'

Despite this, Inkpen skilfully guided the policeman to a banquette where a freshly pulled pint of Portlemouth already awaited. Behind them could be heard the crack of a champagne cork.

'Shame nothing ever came of that murder series we were planning for the paper,' said Inkpen engagingly. 'Yet here we are, back again, another death on the doorstep.'

'I may live very far from London but I'm not a complete idiot,' replied Topham. 'You wanted to turn this town into the Murder Capital of Great Britain – that rubbish about my brilliant sleuthing skills was all my eye and Betty Martin.'

'On the contrary, Inspector, on the contrary! But water under the bridge now. How's that Portlemouth?' Without waiting for a reply he blustered on: 'We know each other, Frank, we can trust one another.'

The policeman emitted a noise from the back of his throat.

'More than you can trust any of those jackals out there who'd sell their mothers for a handful of small change. No, Frank, the best way for us to cover this murder – this poor, unfortunate woman – is for you to brief me privately, and I will then circulate the info to the rest of the press pack. That way, if we can establish an agreement, I can keep them out of your hair.'

'I doubt that.'

'Club rules, Frank, club rules!'

'Let's just take it as it comes,' said the Inspector, drinking but refusing to be led up the rosy path.

'Then, of course, what I was saying to you at Christmas – a holiday! Maybe a small boat to potter round the harbour. There's always a...'

'I told you,' snarled Topham, 'I don't take bribes!'

Inkpen didn't blink. 'Ah yes, silly me. A misunderstanding. I'm sure the Widows and Orphans Fund could do with a few extra pounds, though.'

'Whaddya want?'

'You do realise, don't you, that this is a unique occurrence? No political candidate has been murdered before during a general election campaign. Ever! This will put Temple Regis on the map!'

And in just the way the Mayor, the Chief Constable and the Coroner would love to see it, thought Topham bitterly, but said nothing.

'I gather Mrs Clifford had no close family,' probed Inkpen, 'so no husband or jealous boyfriend as the prime suspect?'

'She was upright. Pillar of the community,' replied Topham, showing his contempt. 'Much liked, very efficient as a solicitor, devoted to the idea of improving things. A truly worthwhile human being.' Unlike some I could name.

The implied insult missed its target. 'Obviously the main suspects, then, have to be the Labour candidate and the Liberal – they have the most to gain.'

'Don't be ridiculous – they're women!'

'It's been known,' said Inkpen. 'You've heard the name Lizzie Borden, I'm sure.'

'There are others,' teased Topham.

'Such as?'

'Use your loaf, man!'

Inkpen struggled with this for a moment while Topham downed his pint. Finally the penny dropped: 'What?! Are you saying that Freddy Hungerford could be a suspect? He didn't want to retire so he killed his successor to get the seat back again?'

'If you like. You could try walking that round the block, see where it gets you.'

'Ha! Ha! Inspector, do you know how long I've been a crime reporter? I've lost count of the years! In my time I've dealt with bank robbers, rapists, extortionists, torturers – you name it. But the trickiest people to deal with are slippery coppers like you. Coppers, until they've been smoothed over, who are prepared to taradiddle their way from here to Timbuktu!'

'Does *smoothing over* include buying them a boat?'

'Usually.'

'My wife's a bad sailor.'

'I told you, the Widows and Orphans Fund.'

'Gets taken bad even if she steps in a puddle.'

'Yes, yes, I get the message.'

'She gets *sick*,' pressed Topham, his voice increasing in volume. 'But not as sick as I get when I come across people like you. We aren't here to take free holidays, or boats, or sugar-bags filled with cash – we're here to protect the public and uphold the law. That may sound strange to you, but that's how it is in this manor.'

Inkpen didn't even blink. 'Interpol,' he said.

'What?'

'Interpol, Inspector. You remember we talked about them when we last met. They were due to come and pay you a visit.'

'I don't recall anything like that.'

'Yes, you do,' said Inkpen, shaking his head.

'Another pint, Frank?' It was Sid looking unctuous, the tenner warming nicely in his breast pocket.

'Nah.'

'Sure, Frank?'

The copper was torn. The Portlemouth had quickly disappeared and he was ready to go. On the other hand he couldn't leave without learning what intrigues Interpol were planning on his patch.

'Here y'are, Sid,' he said, and emptied a pocketful of half crowns, shillings and sixpences onto the table. 'Have one yourself.' He didn't ask if Inkpen wanted more champagne – the glass had already been refilled.

'Go on then,' he said to the reporter.

'One good turn deserves another,' said Inkpen smiling.

Holding back his irritation, Topham replied with a forced wink, 'I'm sure we can come to some arrangement.'

'Only on that condition, and that alone, I'll tell you what I know,' said Inkpen. He really was a stinker.

Topham nodded vaguely.

'They were due to come here at Christmas but, like everybody else, they have budget constraints. At the same time they were hunting down a big gang that was importing drugs and weapons, all sorts, from France. This case got sidelined, but they're on their way back now, I'm told.'

'Who are they after?'

'A man murdered his wife and fled the country. He changed his name and hopped about the Continent for a bit, finally they think they've got him.'

'Name? Age? Description? And what's he doing in Temple Regis – *if* he's in Temple Regis.'

'I haven't been told any more for the moment. This comes from… a friend, in London. I'm assuming that when the time's right they'll let you know. Which is why we're having this cosy little chat, Inspector.'

Topham looked at him, stony-faced.

'This may sound a bit far-fetched,' went on Inkpen, 'but I'm the kind of chap who likes to take a long shot on the gee-gees. While my colleagues next door are stumbling around looking for the home-town killer of your Mrs Clifford, I have this other theory.'

'Which is?'

'That the Interpol candidate came here to kill her. Came from a long, long way away, and with one purpose – to do away with Mirabel Clifford, the squeaky-clean parliamentary candidate with a skeleton in her closet.'

'What makes you say that?' said Topham, sharply. 'You don't know the man's name or anything about his background – this is just make-believe.'

'Let's just say I have an instinct, Frank,' said Inkpen, sipping his champagne. 'Look,' he went on, 'don't let me sound critical. But for years I've travelled the world in search of criminals for my newspaper, and I have the huge financial backing to pursue the stories I do, in the way I want, and not be interfered with. Can the same be said of you?'

'Five minutes ago you were talking about what an amazingly successful detective I was.'

'*You* know what I mean,' Inkpen riposted. 'This is a hunch, but it's one I believe in and one I'm pursuing. I'm looking into Mrs Clifford's background, and when I find that skeleton I'll find the person who killed her. If it's a race between us, Inspector, I'll get to the finish line before you do.'

Topham stood up. 'Thank you,' he said, slowly, 'for the drink, and for the lecture on successful policing. I can tell you now that I've heard nothing from Interpol, and until I do, I'll stick to what we do best down here – routine policing. It's routine which will uncover the wretch who did away with a much-loved member of our community.'

'Well,' said Inkpen, serenely pouring himself another glass of Moët, 'good luck, Frank. I can tell from where I sit that you're barking up the wrong tree.'

Across town the process of persuading people it is possible to walk on water was well under way. The Labour candidate was earnestly promising a startling number of changes, all of which would benefit Temple Regis directly the moment she was elected. It truly was remarkable what benefits political change could bring in such a short time.

'The joy of rhetoric,' said David Renishaw acidly. 'Just like marshmallow – pop it in your mouth, gone in a matter of seconds.'

'Mm?' said Terry, who was using the Hassleblad today. He had a love-hate relationship with it and it occupied a disproportionate amount of his thinking time.

'They're all the same,' went on Renishaw, as if Terry was listening. 'No real commitment. No desire to help... the underdog. Why do we bother? Why... do... we...'

They were standing on the edge of a crowd watching Lilian Smee giving a very creditable speech, but the reporter didn't have his notebook out; instead he moved his feet around in jerky fashion and bobbed his head up and down.

'You OK?' said Terry, noticing his agitation.

'It's all such a waste of time. The whole process. You can't believe in politicians – they're liars and cheats. Murderers.'

'Not round here they're not,' replied Terry, levelling his camera at an earnest-looking young married with her toddler. 'This is Devon, mate.'

'You'd be surprised,' growled Renishaw. 'Anyway, I've got all I want here, what about you?'

'Yup.'

'On to the Town Hall then.'

The two men, with absolutely nothing in common beyond receiving their wages from the same source, made their way from Up Street round to the Civic Centre. As they marched up the steps, a man in a pinstripe suit stopped them.

'Press? I'm Hamish Madden, part of Sir Freddy's team. Thanks for coming – there'll be some drinks afterwards which I'm sure you'll appreciate. Be quick, though – he's about to start!'

It was extraordinary how many people could find time, during their working day, to listen to an old gasbag run through a gamut of old jokes, patronising remarks and hopeless dreams of the future, but the crowd was plentiful and Sir Freddy Hungerford was playing up to them.

'Look!' hissed Renishaw as Hungerford launched into a list of his lifetime achievements. 'Over there, Terry! It's Sirraway!'

Indeed, there was the disgruntled academic, wedged in at the front of the crowd waving a placard. 'Watch out for him, Terry, he's going to do something. He will!'

Terry obligingly pointed his camera at the miscreant and waited. Renishaw was right – Sirraway seemed to be working himself up, repeatedly challenging Sir Freddy's remarks.

'The advantage of having continuity in your sitting MP...' burbled Hungerford.

'Cheat!'

'The advantage of having continuity in...'

'*Liar!*'

'As I was saying – but really, ladies and gentlemen – don't you agree? Isn't it utterly appalling to come all the way here just to be...'

'THIEF!'

What happened next was a blur – to Terry, and to most of the audience. One moment David Renishaw was by his side, but the next—

'*Watch out, he's got a knife!*' shouted the reporter at the top of his voice, launching himself through the crowd towards Sirraway. The tightly bunched bodies gave way only gradually, so that Renishaw had to punch and barge his way through to get to the front, almost as if in slow motion.

Somehow sensing he was in danger, Sirraway tossed his placard into the crowd and tried to get away, but Renishaw finally burst through and floored the academic with a single punch. The old boy was having none of it, however, and fought back vigorously – for a moment it was hard to tell who would emerge victorious. Renishaw was shouting '*Knife! Knife!*' which deterred most of the crowd from separating them, but finally they were pulled apart.

'You're crazy,' panted Renishaw, facing his opponent, 'wanting to kill an old man like that!'

'It's you who's crazy,' panted the professor, tearing off the necktie which had been pulled tight during the mêlée and whose knot was now under his left ear. 'I haven't got

a knife – what the devil were you doing saying that I had?'
He pocketed the tie and looked ready to come at Renishaw.

The reporter stepped back. 'Well, it looked like it,' he snarled. 'And don't tell me you didn't want to kill that old man up on the stage!' He looked round, appealing to the circle of people surrounding him, then up at the microphone. 'It's OK, Sir Frederick, you're safe now!'

The MP peered down with a mixture of disgust and amusement on his face. 'Get those people out of here!' he ordered, careless of who was the assailant and who his defender. 'I have a speech to make!'

The two men stood staring at each other when Renishaw suddenly broke free and threw himself at Sirraway. Again the men were parted, then frogmarched out the room.

Terry stood there nonplussed, his cameras swinging helplessly around his neck. Never in all his years in newspapers had he seen anything like it – a reporter attacking a member of the public!

'Nothing to do with me,' he told startled bystanders, and pushed his way out of the hall in disgust.

He missed what happened next. A mighty round of applause greeted the conclusion of Hungerford's speech – extra cheers for his being so brave in the face of a violent attack – but by that stage Terry was well on his way to cover the Liberal candidate, Helena Copplestone, who was speechifying outside the public library.

Everyone else had adjourned to the anteroom in the Town Hall where, strictly against the rules, Hamish Madden was handing out free drinks. He looked as though he'd had a few himself already.

'Excellent, excellent, what a good speech,' the Mayor, Sam Brough, was saying to Hamish. He was wearing his mayoral chain and had a blue delphinium in his buttonhole.

'Another, Mr Mayor, go on!'

'No thanks. Three's enough at lunchtime.'

'Will you come this evening? The Con Club? Slap-up dinner, don't forget.'

'If I can. Now, where's Sir Freddy? I'll just say goodbye – work to do!'

'I think he just stepped down to the men's room.'

'I'm going that way myself.'

And so it was that the Mayor of Temple Regis, the most worshipful Samuel Brough, was the one to discover the body of Sir Frederick Patrick Slingsby Hungerford KBE sprawled out on the floor of the men's room of the Temple Regis Conservative Club.

His open eyes told the story well enough, that all life had been extinguished by a necktie drawn tight around his throat.

TWENTY-THREE

The chase after Hector Sirraway was chaotic, mismanaged, determined and very angry. The police, the *crème de la crème* of Fleet Street's crime correspondents, local constituency party workers – even the beleagured staff of the *Rivera Express* – all set off in hot pursuit.

The difficulty was in finding the man.

As in most murder cases, the trail went cold almost instantly. The shock of discovering Sir Freddy's body consumed the early minutes of police thinking, and by the time a co-ordinated plan had been established, Sirraway could well have whistled his way down the street to Regis Junction, bought a ticket, hopped on the first Pullman Express and steamed cheerily off to the other side of the world.

That it was Sirraway who committed the foul deed was beyond question – the murder weapon had been round his neck only minutes earlier, witnessed by dozens who were elbowed aside in the fight. The party faithful were quick to recall the professor's feverish attacks on Hungerford, not only at today's meeting, but back in December when he barracked them noisily outside the Christmas party.

And Hamish Madden, interviewed by one of Topham's assistants, confirmed the extent of Sirraway's hatred: 'I feel an intense personal responsibility,' he said emotionally, clutching a large glass of whisky. 'I saw him in the crowd, I had a further warning when he pulled out that banner and started waving it about. And when he started shouting abuse, I should have had him thrown out immediately. But Sir Freddy likes – liked! – a spot of rough-and-tumble at his meetings; he got the idea from Oswald Mosley and the Blackshirts. So I just let it go.'

'Did you have any previous intimation that he might do something like this?' asked the copper laboriously.

'Well, I'll be frank, officer. He'd been writing to Sir Freddy for the past two years, claiming this and claiming that – all lies, of course! – so much so that we were forced to create a special file on him. He came to the House of Commons and kicked up a terrible stink. And if things had gone any further, Sir Freddy was going to have him arrested. He was a terrible nuisance – mad as a hatter.'

'Shame you didn't move sooner,' said the policeman with scant sympathy. 'Was he just as anti Mrs Clifford?'

'I can't tell you that.' Madden paused a moment. 'You think he killed them both?'

'Looks like it, dunnit,' said the copper, lifting his eyes to heaven as if talking to a particularly stupid child.

'I heard somebody shouting he'd got a knife. Odd that he should strangle poor old Freddy if he had a knife.'

'There's no telling,' said the copper, shutting the conversation down. Madden raised the whisky to his lips and drained it in one.

Back at police HQ, Frank Topham had just returned to the

CID room after a deeply unpleasant interview with the Chief Constable. That's me finished, he thought, as he pictured the national newspaper headlines tomorrow morning – why the devil did Fleet Street have to be in town when *this* happened? The MURDER CAPITAL OF GREAT BRITAIN headline would be on all their front pages tomorrow – and just when the holiday season was getting under way!

'I want you to take four men and go up to Hatherleigh,' he told Sergeant Gull, whose policing in recent years had been restricted to the pencils on his desk. 'I have to stay here and co-ordinate things. If he's got any sense he won't be going anywhere near the place, but you can go and have a sniff round.'

'Lift the latch, so to speak?' said Gull with a wink.

'I didn't tell you to do that,' replied the Inspector, though instead of shaking his head he gave an affirmative nod. 'Now I need to find Mrs Clifford's secretary – surely she must have some clues as to the connection between these two killings?'

Sergeant Gull was in no position to advise – he was already out of the door and on his way, the prospect of a nice spot of overtime speeding him onwards.

At the murder scene, Topham's men interviewed the key witnesses and got the body away, while in his office the Chief Constable pondered the vital question of whether to wear his uniform or a nice suit when he came before the Press cameras. He strolled into his anteroom, put on his trilby, and tried a few experimental phrases into the mirror before rejecting it for the peaked cap.

Fleet Street's finest were at full throttle. Once the news of the assassination broke, Guy Brace jumped on a chair in the Old Jawbones and started dishing out orders. 'Mulchrone – up to Hatherleigh! Crossley – find Inspector Topham! Brittenden – find the Prof's university and get his file from them, no arguments! And Lamb…' But here the instructions petered out, for the red-nosed Lamb had fallen asleep cradling his brandy glass and would be no use to anybody for a couple of hours at least.

He looked round the serried ranks of reporters and caught the eye of Inkpen.

'And what are you going to do, Inks?' The *News Chronicle* man was a bit of a lone wolf.

'Whatever's best,' came the reply. Though he'd had a brilliant idea about the Interpol angle, there'd been no time to develop it and for once he was at a loose end. 'That chap, wossisname, Hamey McGamey, Hungerford's right-hand man. I'll give him the treatment.'

'OK. Off you go.'

The highly disciplined cadre of hacks evaporated like the morning mist, each hunting down their quarry, assured of space on their front pages the following morning. Two murders in one resort! Two parliamentary candidates, one after the other, bam bam! And both from the same party – how could they miss!

Brace wandered over to the recumbent form of the *News of the World* man and stole his brandy. All he had to do was wait till the boys came back and together they would pool their information and file their stories.

No such battle plan was being enacted over at the *Riviera Express*. In his editor's office Rudyard Rhys sat in a chair by the window and looked vacantly out at the seascape while, behind him, what remnants of staff that could be found on a Friday afternoon filed in and sat down quietly. As if by unspoken agreement, Miss Dimont assumed the chair behind the editor's desk and started proceedings, since Mr Rhys was known to equivocate in times of trouble.

'Where's Renishaw?' she said.

Silence.

'Terry?'

The chief photographer explained again what had happened – the agitated Sirraway, the anxious Renishaw, the dash through the crowd, the fight.

'It was just disgraceful. Same as what happened up at Hatherleigh, only worse! I reckon he was looking for Sirraway from the moment we came in and was determined to knock his block off.'

'Did Sirraway actually have a knife? Did you see a knife?'

'Nah, I think it was David's imagination. He wasn't in a right frame of mind, if you ask me.'

'Was Sirraway making a move towards the stage – did it look as though he was going to attack Hungerford?'

'No, and I had my lens trained on him after David spotted him. It was more like he was barracking – shouting, trying to throw Hungerford off his speech. Taunting, like – yes, that's it, he was taunting him. Hungerford looked as though he was enjoying it.'

'So why did Sirraway suddenly launch an attack on him?'

'He didn't launch an attack, Judy. The only person who attacked anybody was Renishaw.'

'Well, that really is shocking!' gasped Peter Pomeroy.

'What *will* people think of this newspaper if we send people out to report, and they do that sort of thing!'

'No need to worry about him anymore,' came a voice from the window. 'I dismissed him this morning.'

'Good Lord, Richard!' said Miss Dimont. 'What happened?'

'Disobedient, obstructive, too clever by half. Covering today's hustings was his last job for the *Express* – I told him to write it up, pack up his things and leave quietly. But obviously he was angry at being sacked and it caused him to act that way. He wanted to get back at me.'

'Didn't look that way to me,' said Terry.

'So,' said Judy, 'he's just gone? That's it?'

'Just as well,' said Peter Pomeroy, the deputy editor. 'And good riddance. Even so, think of the damage done to the reputation of the *Express*.' He was really quite upset.

'I doubt people will pay too much attention to Renishaw's behaviour. I think mainly people will be asking who let the murderer in,' said Judy soothingly. 'Anyway, everybody, we have a breathing space before our next edition – and of course those boys from the nationals will have stolen all the juiciest bits for their newspapers tomorrow and on Sunday.

'But they don't have what we have, which is local knowledge, so we have the chance to show them all up when the next *Express* comes out.

'So now here's what I think we should do…'

Much later Judy was sitting with Auriol in her back garden. The light was going, the air was clear, the church clock striking the hour, a noisy blackbird going through his night-time repertoire. It was getting chilly, though.

'We'll have to go in. Will you stay the night?'

'That would be lovely,' said Auriol, 'it'll give us more time to chat. Anyway, go on with it – you've told me once, I want to hear it all again. Things get clearer in my mind the more I hear them.'

Judy talked as she made a salad. 'We have to accept that Hector Sirraway was the murderer of both Freddy Hungerford and Mirabel Clifford – I saw the letters where he was trying to drag Mirabel into his dispute with Hungerford. Sure enough he had a genuine complaint, but he was allowing it to skew his judgement – he was trying to implicate Mirabel, determined that she should suffer, too.'

'I wonder though,' said Auriol, the wise owl. 'Two murders, but so very different. Mirabel is stabbed to death, Sir Freddy – well, I suppose you'd use the word *garroted*. It just doesn't sound right to me. Did Sirraway lose his knife in the fight with your Mr Renishaw, d'you think, and had to improvise in order to finish Sir Freddy off?'

'I asked Terry that. He said he never saw a knife. Remember, Renishaw says to him, *There's Sirraway*, and Terry focuses his long lens on him. So though they're not near each other and there's a crowd between them, Terry can see quite clearly what's going on. Sirraway's got his placard in *both hands*.'

'So no knife.'

'Can't be certain, but pretty sure not.'

'So Renishaw made that bit up? As an excuse to launch an attack on the professor? Could that be the case?'

'Always possible. He's had a thing about Sirraway ever since that dust-up in Hatherleigh. Says he's mad and violent even if nobody else seems to have got that impression.'

Judy opened the kitchen door to encourage Mulligatawny to go out for his evening prowl. Instead, the rebel clung tight to his special cushion on a kitchen chair and refused to budge. He gave a low growl.

'Cats,' sighed Auriol with exasperation. 'Why I could never have one – they never do what you tell them.'

'You don't understand,' replied Judy happily, 'that's the point about them! Glass of wine? There's some delicious rosé.'

'Yes, please. I was wondering, can we turn this thing inside out – could it be *Renishaw* who's the murderer? From what you say, his behaviour has become, well, bizarre to say the least.'

'It always was. I thought about that, but he can't have killed Mirabel because he was with Denise, our sub-editor, the whole evening – she told me that when I saw her the other day. So that won't fit. Also, Hungerford was killed with Sirraway's tie – Terry saw Sirraway rip it off after the fight and stuff it in his pocket.'

'Two murderers, then,' said Auriol.

'Ha! Why not three? *Four?*'

Together they finished preparing the salad, and Judy switched on the lamps in the sitting room. 'We'll have it on our knees,' she said, and Mulligatawny strolled in to see if there was a morsel for him.

'Let's start again. Let's go back to Sir Freddy – go back to that time Geraldine Phipps was talking about. He stole the money from that poor woman.'

'Pansy Westerham,' said Auriol.

'Yes.'

'Then she died.'

'Yes.'

'He killed her.'

'Might have.'

'Well then,' said Auriol, 'couldn't he have killed Mirabel? If he had the capacity to kill once, he could always do it again.'

'I doubt,' said Judy, 'that he then strangled himself in remorse. With someone else's necktie. Though I suppose it's always possible.'

'Ha, ha, very funny.'

'No, I'm going back to the idea of two killers,' said Judy. 'Freddy kills Mirabel because he's been denied his seat in the Lords. Someone then kills him.'

'Who d'you have in mind for that?'

'Hamish Madden, his assistant.' She explained Madden's confession of giving his boss a biffing outside the House of Commons. 'He told me himself he doesn't know his own strength – although it was meant to be a set-up, he overdid it.'

'Why would he want to kill the man who pays his wages?'

'He wouldn't be the first. Haven't you ever wanted to kill your boss? *I* have…'

'You mean when we were at the Admiralty together?' laughed Auriol. 'Thanks very much, chum!'

'I was thinking more of Richard Rhys, actually. Anyway, there's just something not quite right in Madden's eye. And you know, you could see the way Hungerford treated him as a dogsbody, so contemptuous of him.'

'All fine and dandy, but wasn't this Mr Madden in the hall serving drinks while Sir Freddy was being strangled?'

'You have a point there.'

'As for Freddy killing Mirabel, think about it – he's

seventy-plus. He's going to walk her, or drag her, up that tall lighthouse tower and then, against her will, stick a knife into her? She was comparatively young and fit – really, Hugue, if I had to go up all those stairs I'd be on my hands and knees by the time I got to the top!'

Judy shook her head. 'These two murders are linked, they have to be! Come on, have another glass, let's walk this thing round the block once more. Just like we used to in the old days.'

'I wish Arthur was here. I don't know what it is – he says a word here, a phrase there. Asks a question which seems to have no meaning, and then it all falls into place.'

'Well, he isn't – so let's jolly well get on with it.'

The two women sat silent for a moment, then Judy said, 'I'm thinking back to something that fellow from the *News Chronicle* mentioned at the Grand Hotel, when I caught him with Frank Topham before Christmas. He said that Interpol was looking for a man who was hiding in Temple Regis.

'Well,' she went on, 'we didn't hear any more about that, so it was probably just a line he was throwing at the Inspector. On the other hand, if there *was* some truth in it then suddenly it might all make sense. These deaths are linked, unquestionably – but we can't find a suspect who could have done them both.

'If there was someone else, that person could have done both. But where would they be coming from, for Interpol to be involved? Why would he – or she, come to that – have such a close interest in two political candidates from the same party?'

'Trying to destroy their chances of winning the election,

maybe?' suggested Auriol. 'After all, they'll be hard pressed to find a third prospective candidate in the time left before the ballot.'

'That's a bit far-fetched.'

'You think of something better, Hugue.'

'Hmm. Mirabel told me herself her chances of getting elected were slim. The Labour or the Liberal is likely to take the seat.'

'This isn't going terribly well, is it?' said Auriol. 'More wine, Hugue. My glass doesn't seem to be doing its job.'

TWENTY-FOUR

Murder may make big headlines, but it's marriage that sells newspapers. Next morning Miss Dimont was back at her desk helping boost the *Express*'s circulation in time-honoured-style:

```
It was separate beds for Dawn Playfair
and Ernie Pool after their marriage at St
Margaret's Church on Tuesday. Dawn returned
home to her parents' house in Creamery
Close, while Ernie climbed into his hammock
aboard HMS Antilles, which set sail from
Plymouth in the early evening.

The couple, who met at Temple's British
Legion…
```

But here, inspiration failed. The mesmerising tale of a sailor and the girl who would wait for him while he went about defending the world against itself failed to catch fire. Heaving a sigh she pushed back her chair and picked up the kettle.

'Have some of my special!' came the dulcet tones of

Athene, hidden behind her ostrich-feathered screen on the other side of the newsroom.

'Oh! I didn't notice you were there,' said Judy, glad of the distraction, weaving her way through the empty desks to where Devon's number one astrologer sat. 'How's everything?'

'Look in your cup when you've finished your tea and see if you can tell me!' joked Athene. 'Anyway, what was all that fuss about when I came into the office yesterday?'

'Everybody blaming everybody else for the death of Freddy Hungerford,' said Judy sourly. 'Our supreme commander Mr Rhys all at sea, as usual.'

'That sounds harsh, Judy, not like you.'

Just then a telephone rang on an unoccupied desk. With reluctance Miss Dimont wandered over, hoping it would stop before she reached it.

'Hello, newsroom.'

'I want to speak to a reporter.'

'There's nobody much around at the moment, I wonder if you could call back on Monday when…'

'Are *you* a reporter?' The voice was distant, but firm.

'Well, yes but…'

'My name is Gertrude Atherton,' said the voice. 'I live in the Lake District but for many years I was resident in Tuppenny Row.'

Judy sat down and idly reached for a piece of copy paper to scribble on: 'How can I help, Mrs Atherton?'

'Miss Atherton. I heard on the news this morning about the death of Sir Frederick Hungerford.'

'Yes,' said Miss Dimont. This lady sounds old, and no doubt wants to recall when he came to open her church fête, or judged her petunias to be the best in Devon. Or maybe she was his mistress a hundred years ago, she thought wickedly. 'Yes, very sad, Miss Atherton. We're all very saddened.'

'Well, I'm not,' said the distant voice. 'The man was a mountebank.'

Well, this sounds interesting, thought Judy – more interesting than separate beds for Dawn and Ernie!

'Well, of course,' she replied, 'not everybody voted for him.'

'Nor would I ever! A lifelong Liberal, I am, and I very much hope our candidate Mrs Copplestone will win the seat.'

'Is there something I can help you with, Miss Atherton?'

'I rather think the boot may be on the other foot,' said the old lady. 'It concerns an old carrier bag. Brown with, as I recall, a red vertical stripe.'

'Yes?'

'It should be in your office somewhere. If you can locate it I think it may bear fruit, from a news point of view.'

Miss Dimont's enthusiasm collapsed. What the man in the street deems newsworthy rarely turns out to be so, and in any event, where would she find an old carrier bag?

'I used to work with Margery Greenway at the library,' went on the caller. 'Twenty years we worked together.'

'Oh yes, I must have seen you when I popped in,' said Judy, 'only I never knew your name.'

'We had thousands through our door. We once spent a whole Thursday afternoon trying to work out how many library books we had issued over the years and…'

'The carrier bag?' reminded Judy gently.

'I was coming to that. As you know, poor Margery died in a fall just before Christmas. I've never understood it, because she'd gone up the ladder and she was afraid of heights. I always did the ladder and she made the tea in return.'

'I remember it very well.'

'Two weeks before she died she had a visit from a man who said he worked for the *Express*. He came to ask about a man called Sirraway and they had a nice long chat. Margery was keen to know whether the professor's book was coming out soon, and the man said he would find out. Sirraway had spent a long time in the library researching this and that and, to be frank, making a bit of a nuisance of himself – he complained about the Christmas tree! I ask you!

'So I was glad when he finally finished whatever he was doing, though of course it was always nice to have the library used as a place of reference, not just a book-lending shop.'

'Do go on,' said Judy, battling to keep Miss Atherton on the straight and narrow. 'This sounds very interesting.' She wasn't sure whether it was.

'I was on holiday that week, packing up my cottage to move up here, so I never saw him, but Margery said they had a nice long chat and while they were talking she remembered that the man Sirraway had left a carrier bag behind. We always thought he would come back for it but he never did.'

'What was in it?'

'Well, a lot of paper, notes, research – that sort of thing. It was all about Sir Frederick Hungerford. Anyway, the man said he was interested and could he take it away and have a look at it. The bag was lost property as far as we were concerned, cluttering up the place, so Margery told him he could have it and if he ever found this man Sirraway, would he promise to give it back? And he said he would.'

'Can you describe the man, Miss Atherton?'

'Like I say, I never saw him. But Margery and I had a chat about him one day when we weren't busy. She says although he sounded convincing at the time, afterwards she didn't think he *could* be working for you – she'd never seen him around town. And he had an unusual manner.'

'Well, people do sometimes pretend to be something they're not. I must say the whole thing does sound peculiar.'

'Oh, one thing. Margery said he had a slight accent – sort of American, she thought.'

'Was his name Renishaw?' said Miss Dimont, slowly.

'I simply couldn't say, I don't think Margery ever told me. What she did say was he was very interested in some other notes Sirraway had made, about people who – well, I may as well be frank, Miss, er…'

'Dimont, Judy Dimont.'

'Some of the notes – Margery read them all – were about people who Hungerford had apparently stolen money from. Women mostly. I told her it was none of our business, I personally don't deal in gossip. But she was frightfully keen and I think got quite a kick over talking about her discoveries with this man.'

'Well,' said Judy, who'd been furiously scribbling shorthand notes on the copy paper in front of her, 'I'll have to go and see if I can find this bag. Brown, you say, with a red stripe?'

'Yes,' said Miss Atherton.

'Did he come back again? The so-called reporter?'

'I don't know. There was an odd moment a few days later, just before – you know, Margery's fall – when a man came into the library but when he saw me, turned round and walked out again. A strange thing to do, I thought.'

'What did he look like?'

'I would gauge him to be in his late thirties – slim, energetic. Tell me, is that him? Does this man work for you?'

'Not any more,' came the grim reply.

'Geraldine, this is Hugue. Are you sitting comfortably?'

'I have a gin by my side, dear, if that's what you're asking.'

'Excellent. I'm working in the office or I would have popped over to see you.'

'That's all right.'

'Do you remember when we had that lovely evening in Wistman's Hotel before Christmas, all that snow?'

'Oh yes.'

'And we talked about your friend Pansy. Then I went to see Bobbety after you wangled the invitation.'

'Yes, dear.'

'You told me a man came to see you about Pansy. Works here, at this office.'

'I didn't like him. He was peculiar.'

'David Renishaw.'

'He said his mother was Serenata Forbes – you remember, dear, she was a famous Gaiety Girl same as me, though I didn't know her well. Anyway, he said he wanted to see me because he was thinking of writing a memoir of her and could I help.

'Well, we started chatting and I told him what I recalled, like when Nata slipped over on a wet patch on the stage and gave the men in the stalls an eyeful – but after a bit he started asking about Pansy. He said that Pansy was a friend of his mother and he wanted to write her into the story.'

'So what did you tell him?'

'Not much. The way he kept on about her made me doubt he was interested in Nata at all – it was all Pansy, Pansy, Pansy. After a bit I made an excuse and said I couldn't talk any more, could he come back some other time. He telephoned me a couple of times after that but I said I was busy.'

'I think I'm beginning to see the light,' said Judy, more to herself than to her friend. 'David Renishaw told me that his mother was married to a hotel doorman in Paris and ran away to be in London. Serenata Forbes, as I recall, was the wife of the explorer Sir Gibson Forbes. They lived in some style in Chelsea as I recall. Not Paris.'

'*Such* a handsome man, Hugue, not the doorman type at all.'

'On the other hand, Pansy Westerham *did* live in Paris, *did* have a child, *did* run away. Think again, Geraldine, as a mother this time – think about Renishaw asking you those questions about Pansy.'

'You mean…?'

'Yes,' said Judy, 'I definitely *do* mean.'

It was rather lovely, really: Terry was taking Judy out for Sunday lunch in his green Morgan two-seater. On the plus side it was a glorious day and it meant they could have the hood down, on the minus she was sure to have to endure a ten-minute lecture on the car's patented sliding pillar front suspension, as far as one could judge one of the wonders of the Western world.

This morning the king of the open road seemed awfully proud of his string-backed driving gloves which made it difficult for him to open the map; but they were obviously new so Judy made no comment and let him struggle.

'Where are we off to, then?'

Finally Terry managed to wrestle the map flat on the bonnet and waved a glove. 'Thought we'd go across the moor up to Bridestowe, then follow the old railway line to the peat works,' he said. 'Then Southerly Down, the Lyd Valley, Great Nodden – there you are.' The string-backed finger was so fat it completely obscured the route and Judy, as navigator, could see trouble ahead. She'd have to concentrate hard.

The Morgan roared them away from the sea and up onto Dartmoor, where vast empty expanses were already rejoicing in the coming summer with a riot of greens and purples and blues. Terry had managed to complete his description of the sliding pillar front suspension without hesitation, repetition or deviation, and quite soon the conversation turned to the inevitable.

'Sirraway,' said Terry, showily double-declutching. 'We could just nip across to Hatherleigh – only take a quarter of an hour – and take a look around. There's a nice pub there, too.'

'We could,' said Judy, happy to let Terry take the lead. 'Only thing is, won't the police have the place surrounded? If Sirraway went back there they'll have arrested him by now and he'll be back in Temple Regis. But they'll leave a police guard, so I doubt we'd be able to get in.'

'When he went missing before, he said he'd gone up to Ilfracombe – I wonder if there's any point in driving around up there on the off-chance?'

'Oho!' said Judy. 'So you didn't want to take me to the

pub for lunch, after all – you only came out here to track down the professor!'

'Anything wrong with that?'

'Police job, Terry.'

Terry snorted. 'With old Topham in charge, how long's that going to take?'

'Until Scotland Yard gets down here, I should think. Losing a hopeful parliamentary candidate is one thing, losing two is quite something else. Especially when the second one's as famous as Freddy Hungerford.'

'Topham won't like that,' said Terry, slowing and swerving expertly as a couple of Dartmoor ponies jumped friskily into their path.

'There is one thing,' said Judy, 'since I can see I'm going to have to forget about lunch.'

'Mm?'

'I had a call yesterday from Miss Atherton – she used to work in the public library with the lady who died, Miss Greenway, d'you remember? That strange business of her falling off the ladder when she was afraid of heights. Well, Miss Atherton told me that Sirraway had spent the best part of a week in the library researching things just before Christmas.'

'And?'

'Think about it.'

Terry slowed the car. 'Are you suggesting that Sirraway killed that Miss Greenway *as well* as Mirabel Clifford and Freddy Hungerford?'

'Good Lord! Am I? It had never even occurred...'

Terry stopped the car and pulled up the handbrake. 'Don't

let me put words in your mouth, Judy,' he said – was there a touch of acid there? – 'but Sirraway now appears to be a multi-murderer – whadyoucallit?'

'Serial killer.'

'Yes.'

'No, I'm not saying that. Or—'

'Make up your mind, Judy!'

'I don't think it was like that, Terry, though you could be right. It's complicated, but there are other suspects besides Sirraway. Did you bring the Thermos?'

They wandered over to a massive rock and settled themselves comfortably on its layers, looking out at the sun-splashed landscape.

'As of this moment, Hector Sirraway could be in the frame for two murders – OK, three, if we're going to include Miss Greenway. That's if she *was* murdered, we don't know that, and maybe we're getting things out of proportion – seeing murder where there isn't any, Reds-under-the-beds kind of thing. So maybe better to discount her for the moment.'

Terry was disappointed by this. He felt he'd just made a breakthrough and expected applause for it.

Miss Dimont revisited the theories she and Auriol Hedley had wrestled with on Friday evening. 'You see, it's by no means certain Sirraway killed Sir Freddy.'

'It was his tie that strangled the old boy, Judy.'

'You said yourself he didn't look particularly threatening when he was waving his placard around.'

'Mood swings,' said Terry. He couldn't think of anything better.

'He certainly could have killed Mirabel, though how he

lured her up the Templeton Light I have no idea. We don't know where he was at the time – did he have an alibi? We don't know.'

'Visiting that friend in Ilfracombe, I expect!'

'I saw his letters to Mirabel but they never threatened violence. Exposure, yes – he felt she was covering up Hungerford's misdeeds including the illegal appropriation of his property…' her voice trailed off. 'Wait a minute! *Wait a minute!* Where's that map?'

She raced over to the car and whisked it out of the map pocket – made of string, just like Terry's gloves!

'Over here, Terry, help me! Can you find Gorse Down? Somewhere near Chagford.'

Terry laid the map on the bonnet and quickly found the place. 'Want to go there? It's about fifteen minutes away. But why?'

'Tell you on the way.'

As they drove, Miss Dimont explained to her chauffeur some of the mysteries of womankind. When a person says she does not deal in gossip, for example, it does not mean she is immune to its allure, just that she never *repeats* gossip. The starchy-sounding Miss Atherton made it clear to Judy only yesterday that she was a firm believer in keeping her mouth shut.

'But her ears open,' Judy added. 'And so, though she claimed she never looked inside the carrier bag Professor Sirraway left behind in her library, she certainly listened hard when Miss Greenway told her what was inside. And she could remember it, word for word.

Not only the business about Sir Freddy's fortune-hunting

with the ladies, but the real reason for Sirraway's visit – to search for deeds or papers or references to a place called Rattlepark Mill. This, apparently, was one of the derelict properties Hungerford had surreptitiously stolen from its rightful owners.

'He had a bee in his bonnet about that place, according to Miss Greenway,' said Judy. 'Turn left here!'

It took them not fifteen minutes, but over an hour to find what they were looking for. Hidden away in a fold in the moor, approached by a worn-out track, they discovered the massive stone building set against a fast-flowing river. The mill wheel no longer turned, the roof had caved in, and the windows sagged and stared blindly across the landscape. None the less there were definite signs of life – from the back of the building came the smell of woodsmoke.

They looked at each other.

'Well,' said Terry, 'you've done it again, Judy. We've found the hidey hole of your double murderer.'

He squared his shoulders.

'You'd better let me handle this,' he said grimly.

TWENTY-FIVE

Terry rounded the corner, armed only with his courage and the Morgan's cast-iron starting handle. There, sitting on the ground near the mill race, with the remnants of a brushwood fire before him, sat Professor Hector Sirraway.

He looked up, quite unperturbed. After a pause he said:

'That one way of the few there were
Would hide her and would leave no mark:
Black water, smooth above the weir
Like starry velvet in the night...'

'Er, Prof... er, Mr Sirraway,' broke in Terry. Something told him to drop the starting handle before the fugitive spotted it. It fell with a quiet thud into the grass.

'A poem about the death of a mill,' said the professor dreamily, 'and the death of its owners. The mill is no longer needed, and neither are they. There is only one route for them both.' He turned back to look at the black water rushing close to his feet.

'I wonder if you remember me?' Terry said gently. 'We

had a cup of tea and a chat up at your place – oh, ages ago.' He didn't want to say, 'When my colleague decided to have a go at you.'

The professor eyed him mildly. 'These thoughts run through your mind, don't they? This place… all mine, but to what purpose? They stopped milling wool here even before my parents were born. For all their lives, and all of mine, it's been rotting away here – forgotten, abandoned. It's tragic really, don't you think, when you consider the tons and tons and tons of wool that came through this place, clothing and warming a whole nation?'

This was not really Terry's general line in chit-chat, and he was glad when Judy poked her nose round the corner. In gentlemanly fashion, Sirraway rose in the presence of a lady. 'Would you like tea?'

'Oh no, thank you, Professor, we had some recently. Are you all right?'

'Clever of you to find me here.'

'I imagine life must be difficult back at Hatherleigh – your place.'

'This is where I come when I want to see things clearly,' said Sirraway. 'Let them make a fuss. I doubt they will find me here before…'

Miss Dimont didn't like the sound of this. 'I *will* have that cup of tea,' she said, wanting to stir him into action and push his thoughts in another direction. 'And didn't you bring some biscuits, Terry?'

'In the Morgan. But are you sure…?' He was concerned Sirraway might produce that knife.

Miss Dimont smiled, 'That's OK, Terry,' and went to sit next to the professor. 'Nothing to worry about.'

'Why should I worry?'

'Well, yes. I think you know why we're here.'

'Local press,' he laughed bitterly. 'Want an exclusive. What d'you call it – a scoop?'

'Only up to a point – we're human beings, too. Just wanted to make sure you were all right. That must have been a terrible business with Sir Freddy.'

'I still don't understand it. All I've ever tried to do is prove he does *not* own Rattlepark Mill – it's been in my family for a hundred years and it… is… *mine*! If he conceded that point I would go away and leave him alone.'

'Too late now, Professor.'

'Well, yes. A shameful business. Nobody has the right to take someone else's life.'

Miss Dimont weighed this response up, deciding what she would say next and the likely consequences of provoking her quarry. 'Professor,' she said quietly, 'you know the police are after you?'

'Yes.'

'Why are they after you?'

'Well, it might have been better not to leave the scene of a fatality, but I…'

'It's more than that.'

'What d'you mean?'

'You *do* realise that all the evidence points to your having murdered Sir Frederick Hungerford?'

'Me? What do you mean?'

'Professor Sirraway,' said Judy, softly, 'where is your tie?'

'My tie?' He felt vaguely around his neck. 'I hardly need one out here – I don't expect the Queen will be paying me a call this morning.' He seemed genuinely bewildered Miss Dimont should want to take an interest in his personal apparel.

'The one you were wearing the other day. At the Conservative Club. Do you recall it?'

'Of course I do! I only have two – the other one's for funerals.'

'Where is it?'

Just then Terry returned with the biscuits in one hand, his Hassleblad in the other. One sharp look from Judy sent him scurrying to photograph some of the more interesting aspects of eighteenth-century mill design seen from the Dartmoor perspective – but he kept a watchful eye out as he wasted a precious roll of film.

'Professor, I get the impression you haven't the first idea of what serious trouble you're in. The police are looking for you, not because you ran away from a murder scene, but because they believe you killed Sir Freddy with your necktie.'

'Ridiculous.' He dabbed at his pockets with his hands.

'Because,' went on Judy remorselessly, 'of the way you tried to involve Mirabel Clifford in your pursuit of Hungerford, and because she's now dead, they believe you murdered her as well.'

Sirraway jumped to his feet. 'This is sheer lunacy!' he shouted. 'How could I possibly have murdered her? And him as well, you're saying? Where's the logic…'

'*Logic has nothing to do with it, Professor!* Suspicion is all that's needed in a murder inquiry, followed by proof of motive and method. However you view these two events, you are at the heart of the police's investigations – their number one suspect.'

He sat down on the grass with a bump. 'You sound like a cheap television programme.'

Taking not the slightest offence, Miss Dimont leaned over and handed him a biscuit. 'Look, it's not me who's accusing you. I'm a reporter – we have no part in the process, we just report things. But you do need to see that you're in terrible, terrible trouble.'

Sirraway looked away into the river. 'I don't know that I care that much, one way or the other. What do you want to know?'

'Tell me what happened after you were attacked at the hustings by… by… you know.'

'There was a fight. He was vicious. He kept shouting I had a knife – I *didn't* have a knife! I wasn't going to let him get the better of me, but he'd got hold of my tie and was trying to throttle me with it. I managed to pull away and tore it off and stuffed it in my pocket – and just at that moment people came in, got us apart, and that was that. Well, almost – he had one more go at me when everything had subsided, but they got him off me pretty quick.'

'And your tie?'

'Didn't give it a thought. I have no idea where it is. I'd made my point with Hungerford – I could see him looking at me from the corner of his eye while he was making his speech – so I decided enough was enough, and I left the building.'

'Didn't go down to the men's room?'

'I don't know where that is. I've never been there before.'

'And then you did what?'

'Well, I was thinking about going home, but I was upset. So I came out here.'

'And spent Friday night and Saturday night here?'

'I've made one room in the mill quite comfy – no good in winter, of course, but heavenly at this time of year. Have you ever seen dawn rise over Hunt Tor?'

'It must be extraordinarily beautiful.'

'It is,' said Professor Sirraway. 'And I have my books.'

Terry had moved round behind the couple and was getting some nice angles of the killer – nothing Judy could do about it except privately condemn his opportunism.

'Let's turn to Mirabel Clifford.'

'Nice woman, but, you know, part of the political class. Ready to cover for her fellow politicians, give them the benefit of the doubt. She knew all about Hungerford's extortion, and theft, *and* blackmail – all those terrible things he did – but she wasn't prepared to do anything about it.'

'Some would say it wasn't her job. She was hoping to bring a new style of representation to Temple Regis – as far removed from Hungerford's approach as could be imagined.'

'Huh!' said Sirraway. 'That's all you know! She was just like the rest – corrupt, and corruptible.'

'Did you dislike her enough to kill her?'

'What, with the knife I didn't have when I murdered Freddy Hungerford? Don't make me laugh!'

'Then where were you the night she was killed?'

The professor smiled and the creases on his forehead disappeared.

'Hatherleigh Bridge Club. At my house. Until the early hours. My guests included the vicar, the chairman of the parish council, and the distinguished leader of our Women's

Institute – she got the OBE recently. Do you think between them they might provide a sufficiently good alibi?'

Despite the success of their mission there was a fierce argument between reporter and photographer as they sped across Dartmoor on their way home.

'Should have done it.'

'Nah.'

'Terry! I'm going to do it when we get home!'

'Leave 'im alone and 'e'll come home, wagging his tail behind 'im.'

'He's a murder suspect! We have to tell Topham!'

'Ho, yus?' said Terry in a mocking voice. 'Is this the same Hugue-noh Dimont-oh who just two minutes ago told me the man was innocent of both crimes?'

'Well, yes, but…'

'Look, Judy, you said yourself on Friday we have to have something the national press doesn't have. We have exclusive pictures and an interview with the man accused of murdering two political candidates in one town. That's dynamite.

'But,' he went on, 'if you call up Inspector Topham and tell him where Sirraway's hiding, it's his job to go and arrest him. With no other suspect in sight, Topham will charge Sirraway with murder. The moment he does that, we can't use the interview – and *phut!* – the exclusive you were demanding will have gone.'

'There's such a thing as the law, Terry!' shouted Miss Dimont, whose hair was all over the place because of the way Terry was driving. 'Look out!'

They missed the farm tractor by a squeak but Terry didn't

slow down, he was all revved up. 'You've got your scoop!' he cried. 'Hang onto it!'

'We've got to hand him over!'

Terry stopped the car. They were coming down into Temple Regis and the sight of the estuary sparkling beneath them had the magical effect of creating a ceasefire.

'Well, do what you feel is right, Judy, but you can forget about lunch in the future.'

'I didn't get lunch today,' she smiled. 'But we did get something better, Ter, didn't we?'

She gave him a look. And casting aside all inter-office protocol, Terry leaned over and gave her a smacker on the cheek.

Miss Dimont remained perturbed. If he was to be believed, and his alibi sounded pretty cast iron, Sirraway was in the clear over Mirabel's murder. But that still left Hungerford's killer unaccounted for, and all the while Judy failed to pass on his whereabouts to the police, she remained guilty of harbouring a murder suspect.

Unless she could quickly prove a theory that had been growing at the back of her mind, she could find herself in jail and her career as a local reporter in ruins. And so an hour later, in answer to the emergency call-out, Auriol waited for her in their favourite seat on the Promenade.

The heat of the evening sun had galvanised the silver band into giving their all to a selection from *South Pacific* – their favourite seeming to be the thumpingly good 'Bloody Mary', which had come round for the third time in an hour.

'Bit noisy,' said Judy, who was thinking about Terry and hoping for a quieter spot.

'Oh, go on,' said Auriol. 'I'm waiting for them to do "Some Enchanted Evening" – brings a tear to the eye every time.'

'Not mine. Anyway, this is urgent and as I said, I need your help to work it out. Shall we move away?'

The pair strolled further from the bandstand and took a seat looking out to sea. The horizon was ablaze in the sunset, the occasional ship disappearing into it as if into a fiery furnace.

'I think I have the answer,' said Judy, slowly. 'But I need that brain of yours to work overtime on seeing what's wrong with this theory.'

'Go on.'

'Of *course* it wasn't Professor Sirraway. He's the victim of an elaborate set-up.'

'Tell that to the police! All they want is a name and a number – they let the courts do the rest.'

'Not necessarily. He had a real beef against Sir Freddy for stealing what was rightfully his. That mill, patched up, is worth a lot of money. But I'm convinced by what he said about the necktie. First, because I don't believe he's a killer – honestly, Auriol, if you could have looked into his eyes you would say the same – and second because a necktie, dangling out of a pocket in a crowd, is the easiest thing in the world to whip away without the owner noticing.'

'Who would do that?'

'Only one person, Auriol, only one.'

'*Who?*'

'David Renishaw.'

'What? What on earth makes you pick on him?'

'Just listen. Renishaw arrives at the *Riviera Express* last

November. His purpose is to kill Freddy Hungerford – the reason I'll explain in a minute.' She raised her hand to prevent Auriol butting in.

'He's not what he seems. Yes, he's an outstanding journalist, but he's also a very troubled man. This is a hunch, but it fits the timescale – he plans to do the murder when Hungerford comes down to Temple Regis for his leaving do. But at the last moment Mr Rhys takes Renishaw off the job and gives it to Betty. He goes along anyway, and hangs around outside in the crowd – and there he sees Professor Sirraway protesting like mad, stirring up the party faithful.

'And that's when he gets the idea of laying suspicion on Sirraway for Sir Freddy's death.'

'You'd better go on, I'm confused.'

'My hunch is based on what Geraldine Phipps told me yesterday – that when Renishaw came to visit her, he was fixated on Pansy Westerham. He told Geraldine that his mother was Serenata Forbes, but he told *me* his mother had come from Paris.

'Nata Forbes was born, currently lives, and will beyond a shadow of doubt die in Chelsea. Pansy, on the other hand, lived in Paris just as David Renishaw described. David's mother had one child – just as Pansy had; and she disappeared – just as Pansy did.'

'Yes, but…'

'I think Pansy Westerham was David Renishaw's mother. No proof, just a feeling – but it takes us further along the road of this hunch.

'When the departed librarian, Miss Greenway, read the carrier-bag file on the various people Hungerford had extorted money from over the years, Pansy's name was on the list – and, she told her colleague Miss Atherton, the notes went into detail on how Hungerford had squeezed every last penny out of Pansy so that she had to sell her house.

'She was made bankrupt, she died. And as we know, Renishaw got hold of those notes – can you imagine how much that must have enraged him, to read how his mother had been milked of her last penny, to the point where she had to throw herself from the top floor?'

'Or was pushed,' reminded Auriol.

'Or was pushed,' agreed Judy. 'But wouldn't he have wanted to kill the monster who caused his mother's death?'

'But hold on a minute,' countered Auriol. 'Surely you're mixing up fact and supposition here – that's always a dangerous combination! Why would Renishaw wait twenty-five years after his mother's death before suddenly wanting to avenge it?'

'I've thought about that. The most likely reason is he only recently discovered it wasn't an accident. Or maybe he never knew what had happened to her – if you recall, he said she just upped sticks one day, left Paris and never came home. How would he ever manage to find her?

'He also said she was married to a hotel concierge, but I have my doubts about that. If you'd seen the photos of her, my dear, dressed up to the nines and weighed down in jewels!'

'It's a long time to bear a grudge.'

'A *grudge*? Auriol, that was his mother – she died! Whatever fortune she had, it'd been stolen by Freddy Hungerford! That's grounds enough, surely – especially if you think she disappeared when he was twelve – the most vulnerable age, psychologically, for a boy.'

Just at that moment Auriol got her wish – the band broke into 'Some Enchanted Evening', and for a moment the pair fell silent, each imagining their own particular stranger across a crowded room.

'OK,' said Judy after a moment or two, 'let's move onto the murder itself. When Renishaw and Sirraway were parted, the professor put his necktie in his pocket. Terry saw that. Sirraway told me he only hurriedly pushed it halfway in, it was dangling out. After they'd been parted and the dust had settled, Renishaw launched himself at the professor again – and that's when he could have snatched it, it wouldn't have taken much skill.

'So now Renishaw's got the murder weapon – *and* he's laid suspicion on Sirraway by shouting he's got a knife.'

Auriol nodded. 'What happened to the knife, by the way?'

'There wasn't one.'

'Well, so far you've got me half-believing this, but why did Renishaw murder Mirabel Clifford? It seems a bit extreme to kill someone in cold blood just to divert suspicion to another quarter.'

'No, no, that wasn't him,' Judy said, half to herself. 'He was with Denise, the sub-editor, the night Mirabel was killed.'

'Ha!' laughed Auriol. 'That blows the whole theory apart, then. For you to be right, there would have to be not one, but two killers.'

'You said that the other night,' said Judy, 'and now I think you're right.'

'Who's the other killer, then?'

'The late Sir Frederick Hungerford.'

TWENTY-SIX

In an anteroom just off the Grand Hotel's Palm Court, the morning conference of Fleet Street's finest kicked off with unwonted urgency.

'Purple Perfidy for the two o'clock at Haydock Park,' called Brittenden.

'Call My Bluff, Newmarket 2.45,' shouted Crossley.

'Has to be a two-way at Uttoxeter,' yodelled Mulchrone. 'Foolish Pride and Damaging Expense, absolute certainty!'

They were pooling their information not about the Temple Regis murders, but on which nag they favoured from their gleanings of the Sunday newspaper tipsters.

The important work of the day done, and with the newest member of the pack dispatched to the bookmaker with their orders, Guy Brace looked around his colleagues and heaved a contented sigh.

'We seem to be making progress,' he said genially. 'But not too much – this should last the week out! Meantime there's a meeting on at Exeter this afternoon, any of you gentlemen care to join me?'

A murmur of assent spread through the room. Life on

the road away from loved ones, away from El Vino and the Cheshire Cheese and the Mucky Duck, could be hard on a middle-aged reporter and they were forced to take their comforts where they could. Though Exeter may not be among the front rank of racecourses, it would do at a pinch.

'So what have we got?' said Brace. 'On the murders? Inks?'

'Off to see Hamish Madden, Freddy Hungerford's major-domo,' replied Inkpen. 'He was away over the weekend. He should have something useful to add.' Inks would come back with a lively backgrounder on the MP, helping to fill the void until the murderer was found. This much he would share – what he didn't say was he'd be doing a little digging over the business of Mrs Baines.

He may look snootily down on the dregs of humanity who staffed local newspapers, but Inkpen was no fool – he'd been storing up the info on the MP's mistress ever since Miss Dimont teased him with it when he was last in town. Without her help he'd discovered Mrs Baines' name, and once given the fuller story by Madden, would be up to town to nail her sob story while his colleagues swilled champagne and squandered their expense accounts on the gee-gees.

'Progress on Sirraway, anybody?'

'Nothing, Guy. He just waltzed off down the Promenade, probably bought himself an ice cream and a ticket for the dodgems.'

'His house?'

'I was up there yesterday,' said Brittenden. 'Had a long chat with Sergeant Gull, not the sharpest tool in the box, but he hasn't been back there. So I guess by now he's in Timbuktu.'

Brace opened the debate to the floor, and within an hour the team had collectively devised their tomorrow's article, based on a mad professor theme. Each would write it up differently so that if anybody compared newspapers the next day, it would look as though each of them had gained their own insight into the character and nature of this murderer on the loose.

'Mr Inkpen? A telephone call for you, sir.'

The reporter strolled out to the lobby and picked up the house phone.

'Inks, it's Charlie Berry.'

'Charlie.'

'In case you're still interested, I've got a name now. For the Interpol suspect.'

'Blimey, I thought they'd given up on that.'

'Budgetary constraints, old man. But it's all been cleared now – the Interpol boys'll be coming down today.'

'Back up a little bit,' said Inkpen, pulling a pencil from his top pocket. 'Who is he? What's he done? I've written a million stories since we had that conversation, Charlie, and I can't remember what—'

'The name on the passport is D. P. Ouistreham, don't know his first name. Wanted for murder, and they're pretty determined to get him – so you can bet your bottom dollar they'll be making their presence felt when they arrive.'

'Hmm, interesting.'

'Come to think of it, you've had a couple of murders in Temple Regis recently, haven't you? Well, don't let me make two and two equal five, mate, but it looks like a bit more than a coincidence.'

'Much obliged,' said Inkpen. 'The usual two hundred in a nice brown envelope.'

'Mind how you go,' said the copper, and hung up.

Inkpen returned to the anteroom and promised Guy Brace he'd report back at the cocktail hour. Stepping out of the hotel lobby, it took him five minutes to reach the Old Jawbones where he found Hamish Madden already waiting in the upstairs bar.

'Thanks for seeing me,' said Inkpen. 'Coffee?'

'Just the ticket. Put something in it, though, will you?'

Inkpen ordered a double brandy and poured it in. 'Mmm,' said Madden, breathing in the fumes, 'Heart starter!' It was not yet eleven o'clock.

The reporter spent the customary quarter hour asking after Madden's welfare, his background, his school, his lack of a wife, and his long and devoted service at Westminster.

'It's funny,' Madden said, 'after today I shall never see this place again. Funny how things turn out, isn't it?' He did not seem like a man in mourning.

Inkpen had his notebook out, but rested his pencil while the brandy went to work. His exclusive on the MP, the widow, and the Chelsea love nest was just around the corner – it was only a matter of patience.

'Another?'

'Thank you. Don't bother with the coffee.'

'Now,' said Inkpen when they were settled again, 'tell me all about Mrs Baines.'

Madden sang like a canary. Sir Freddy was married to a brute of a wife – German, after all – and had patiently endured this state for nigh on fifty years. Recently he had found true love in the arms of Mrs Baines, and who could deny him that consolation?

For appearance's sake he and Lady Hungerford maintained a united front, but the storm clouds were about to burst, with Mrs Baines angling to become Lady Hungerford while the present Lady Hungerford was only waiting to claim her social advancement when Freddy took his seat in the House of Lords before dumping him.

This seemed interesting but hardly earth-shattering, and before long Inkpen's thoughts were meandering. He was thinking about Interpol.

'Well, thank you Mr Madden – let's hope they find the killer soon.'

'For all our sakes!' said the fellow, looking mournfully towards the bar. Inkpen made a hasty exit but mercifully for Madden, who hated to drink alone, he didn't have long to wait to find a new companion.

'Hello there, I heard you were in here. Judy Dimont, d'you remember?'

'Would you care to join me in a drink?' said Madden, half rising to his feet.

'No, let me.'

The formalities dispensed with, Miss Dimont employed much the same warm-up technique as Inkpen – only judging by the pinkness of her interviewee's cheeks, she needn't wait so long before getting to the point.

'You see, I find it perplexing that Sir Freddy was on his way to the House of Lords, then suddenly did a complete turnaround and came back to fight this election.'

'He did it for the party, and for Miriam.'

'Mirabel.'

'Yes. He was deeply concerned that her death meant the seat would go to Labour or the Liberals. He *had* to come back, d'you see, to save it.'

'That's not my understanding,' said Judy, sweetly enough. 'I've been told he'd been promised the peerage and so stepped down, only for the peerage to be rescinded.'

'You seem remarkably well informed. But I assure you—'

'I don't think Sir Freddy ever had any intention of standing as an MP again – but the prospect of not having a seat at Westminster, for a man like that… Quite impossible!'

'He came back to save the constituency.'

'He came back because he wasn't going to get his peerage after all. It was kyboshed by the Palace.'

'How d'you know *that*?'

'Private information.' Thank you, Arthur, for drinking with those gasbags at your club.

'But,' Judy went on, 'by the time he got the bad news Mirabel Clifford was already well established as his successor. What was he to do? Suddenly he was faced with political oblivion – and he couldn't bear it.

'Most men in his circumstances would just sigh and accept their fate – but not Freddy! He was too big, too important a man, to be beaten like that. And the easiest route to staying in power was to get rid of Mirabel, and stand once more in the constituency which, after all, had elected him many times before.'

'What absolute piffle,' said Madden in a muffled voice, and got up to go to the bar. Judy wasn't sure whether he would come back.

'The problem with you journalists is, you don't know things so you make them up,' said Madden, loftily. 'It's complete horse-poo, all of it – you don't know anything!'

'Well, I'm going to tell you something *you* don't know, Mr Madden. Do you know the name Pansy Westerham?'

'No.'

'You should. Your Sir Freddy had a hand in her death. It was many years ago, but just because a person dies doesn't mean they're forgotten – by friends, by people who may be related to them.'

Miss Dimont turned her face up to Madden.

'And maybe that's why his longed-for peerage bit the dust – because people remember. Whether he killed Pansy, or whether he merely caused her death, it's impossible to say. But she died, and he was responsible – she'd become an embarrassment once he'd milked her of all her money.'

'I have *no* idea what you're talking about.'

'What I'm saying is that he was ruthless. And, given what happened to Pansy Westerham, it's my belief Freddy Hungerford also killed Mirabel Clifford.'

Madden's pink cheeks turned bright red. 'How dare you! How dare you speak ill of the dead? Of a man who gave his life to public service and was the backbone of Parliament! You're a disgrace – I'm going to report you to your editor!'

'Report away, Mr Madden, only I haven't finished yet. I think it was his intention to kill her, and to frame an innocent man, Professor Sirraway.'

'Ah! Now *there* you're wrong! Sirraway was nothing to do with…' Madden paused, his mouth open.

'Oh,' said Judy, seizing this. 'So Sirraway *wasn't* part of your plan! What *was* it, then?'

Madden reached across the bar and picked up a brandy bottle. 'You've no idea,' he started, 'no idea at all...'

'I think I do.'

'Really? *Really?* You think someone of Freddy's age could haul a protesting woman halfway up a winding staircase? With her shouting and screaming and struggling as she went?' His voice was suddenly agitated, uncontrolled. 'You think he'd have the strength to do that? You think he'd have the *nerve* to do that?'

He sloshed the brandy into his glass. 'You think he had the *stamina* and the *guts* to do such a thing? To drag her up and out onto the platform before shoving the knife into her? D'you think that old bully could manage all that? Well, you're wrong, Miss... er... you have no idea. You reporters – you just make it up. *You make it up!*'

The man stood rigid, as if to attention. The whites of his eyes shone bright.

'I have to go now,' said Judy, after a long silence. 'Sorry if I upset you. Why don't you sit here with your nice glass of brandy, it's been such a stressful time for you.'

She slipped quickly down the stairs, pausing to see if he was following her. Then stepping out into the bright sunlight, a miracle occurred – a policeman was to be found standing in the Market Square. Better still, it was the redoubtable Inspector Topham. With intense relief, Judy raced up to him.

'Inspector.'

'Miss Dimont. I haven't anything more to add at the moment, if that's what you're—'

'Inspector. We've known each other a long time. Our views differ quite a lot, but we do have one thing in common – a desire to see the right thing done.'

'If you put it that way, I…'

'I'm going to ask you to do something which is completely counter to your police training, and probably against your gut instinct, too.'

'What's that?'

'Up there, in the top bar of the Jawbones, is Hamish Madden, the assistant to Sir Freddy Hungerford. I ask you, based on our joint passion for the right thing, to go up there and arrest him on suspicion of murder.'

'I can't do that.'

'If you want to, you can.'

'He killed his own boss? Sir Freddy? Ridiculous – he was serving drinks when—'

'Not Hungerford, Inspector! Madden killed Mirabel Clifford! On Hungerford's instructions maybe, or maybe just to please his boss. But he killed her all right.'

'You got the evidence?' said Topham, sizing up the task ahead and raising his eyes to the top window of the Jawbones.

'Enough. And it's all right, Inspector, he's had a few. Actually, he's had far more than a few. Judging by his demeanour, he's ready to call it a day.' Though not to a mere woman, she thought with asperity.

'I'll need to get a couple of men,' said Topham, still hesitant.

'Don't bother. I think he'll come like a lamb.'

As she walked off into the Market Square, Miss Dimont saw Inkpen striding towards her. 'Hello,' she said, stepping in front of him, 'thinking about interviewing our Mr Madden? You might be just a moment too late.'

'Did him earlier,' said Inkpen importantly. 'You were right about Hungerford's mistress. But also wrong – the story's a bit ho-hum.'

'Why don't you break the habits of a lifetime and share some information with a local journalist for a change?' said Judy, teasing. 'I've got something to offer in return – something far better than Freddy Hungerford's popsy.'

Inkpen looked about the empty square, then back at Judy. Though he'd been given the Interpol tip by Charlie Berry, so far he hadn't been able to get any further with it. Desperation had driven him back to the Jawbones in the hope Madden would juice up what he'd said about Mrs Baines – ho-hum or not.

'What information?' said Inkpen suspiciously.

'About Mirabel Clifford's murderer. I think there may be an arrest soon.'

'Arrest? Are you sure?' The boys were all up at Exeter Racecourse – they won't like this, he thought. On the other hand, it'll be *my* scoop!

'OK,' said Inkpen slowly, strapping on an insincere smile. 'Why don't we sit over here in the sun?'

'You go first,' encouraged Miss Dimont, as they settled on a bench. 'You know what I'm going to tell you, it'll just be a name.'

'How can I assist you?' said Inkpen, not meaning a word of it. 'Anything I can do…'

'Interpol,' she said. 'I just want to be sure I haven't done something terribly wrong. I wondered, since you were telling me about it before, whether anything more had come of that particular line of inquiry?'

'Are you hoping Interpol may have a lead on who did the double murder? That they're chasing the murderer? That they know who he is?'

'In a nutshell.'

'Which might then discount the imminent arrest of the suspect whose name you're about to give me?'

Gosh, thought Miss Dimont, you're cleverer than you look.

'Looks like we're evens,' he said. 'A name for a name. You go first.'

'No, you.'

'It won't mean anything, it's a foreigner.'

'Go on anyway.'

He got out his notebook and flipped back a page or two. 'The man Interpol is after is a D. P. Ouistreham. Wanted for murder. My source thinks he could be responsible for the two down here but I doubt it myself.'

'Can you spell that?'

He did. 'Sounds Dutch to me.'

'Ouistreham is a port in Normandy,' said Judy. 'Famous for its Calvados, famous for its D-Day. You must have heard of Pegasus Bridge, surely.'

'Mm.'

'Anything else you can tell me about this Frenchman?'

'Nothing more, that's it – but I should've thought it'd be a piece of cake to find someone with a Froggy accent in a place like this.'

'*You* don't seem to have had much success yet, though?' said Miss Dimont sweetly.

'Your turn,' said Inkpen sourly. 'Haven't got all day.'

'Well, you're in for a thrill,' said Judy, waving her hand towards the Old Jawbones. 'Oh look, here comes Terry, aren't I lucky to have a photographer! Where's *your* snapper, Mr Inkpen?'

Up at ruddy Exeter Racecourse he thought, but bit his lip. 'So what am I looking for?'

'Unless I'm much mistaken, out of that door, very shortly, will emerge Inspector Topham of the local CID accompanied by your friend Hamish Madden.'

'You mean…'

'Yes. Madden killed Mirabel Clifford.'

'Wow!' said Inkpen, shedding his professional cool. 'That's terrific!' He turned to Judy, beaming. 'Sorry, I didn't have much to give you by way of exchange – just the name of some Frenchman who can't possibly have anything to do with all this.'

'You're wrong,' said Judy slowly. 'You've just given me something very precious.'

TWENTY-SEVEN

It was all over Page One next morning, with every national newspaper carrying Terry's exclusive picture of Hamish Madden being led away by Topham.

DOUBLE MURDERER NABBED brayed most of the headlines – phrased differently according to readers' tastes, naturally, and with only *The Times* using the word 'apprehended'.

Though inaccurate, the body-count was of less interest to the headline writers than the fact the police had cuffed their man. And since Madden had not yet been charged, reporters and editors were free to write follow-up pieces describing the background to the case.

Which was just as well since, with the exception of Inkpen, Fleet Street's finest had been caught on the hop and so far hadn't written a single word. When the murderer they were supposed to be hunting was collared, they'd all been on a distant racecourse celebrating Mulchrone's double in the 4.30 which had made them all rich as Rockefeller. What with the popping of corks and this and that, their bus did not deposit them back at the Grand until 6.30 p.m. – by which time Inkpen had written and dispatched their copy for them.

'Brilliant job, Inks – shampoo on me tonight!' they all cried, relieved their bylines would be on the front page tomorrow morning; fearful of the inevitable where-were-you call from their news editors.

It was the photographers who were really in the soup – not a single one had a photo of the mass killer, and picture editors up and down Fleet Street had to buy in Terry's brilliant shot, one in which he contrived to make Hamish Madden look very guilty indeed. It meant a nice bonus for him, and a useful few quid in the *Riviera Express* coffers, too.

Back at the newspaper in question there was another, more urgent, murder conference going on. Once again the editor took his seat by the window and let Judy do the talking.

'The job isn't over yet,' she said commandingly to her troops. 'And now we have a real chance to beat the nationals at their own game – show them what we're made of!'

'Nae a chance o' that,' drawled John Ross from the back of the room, 'it's Tuesday. We don't come out till Friday. That gives them two days' start on us. They have the money. They have the manpower. They have the...' But here he paused – even a cynical, embittered, clapped-out old Glaswegian with a whisky bottle in his bottom drawer couldn't betray his colleagues by saying, 'they have the talent, and we don't.'

But the silence which followed said it for him.

Judy's leadership was greeted in two ways – to the younger members of staff, it was a thrilling call to action. To the time servers it inspired nothing more than a mixture of guilt, disbelief and denial – the *Express* wasn't there to provide nationwide scoops, it was the home of Athene, and Mothers

Union reports, football results, and the latest harebrained scheme of the Mayor, Sam Brough.

But Miss Dimont rose above their trepidation.

'Our main task is to find David Renishaw,' she ordered. 'As you know, he has left the staff, but I believe he has information which can help us. It can help us *a great deal*. So I want everyone to put on their thinking caps and come up with some idea of where he might be found – if he's still in Temple Regis, that is. Terry and I have a job to do for the next hour or two, so I'm leaving Betty in charge of co-ordinating your search ideas.'

Betty put her nail file down and blushed.

'We'll be back at lunchtime and I hope we'll all have made some good progress by then.' As Miss Dimont stood, she could see smiles on the faces of some of the staff, and one or two clustered excitedly around her as she headed towards the darkroom.

'Get a move on there, Terry,' she called, though she could see her partner in crime was up to his elbows in developer fluid. 'Some unfinished business!'

The Minor could go at quite a zip when it wanted, but even so the journey back to Dartmoor was less exhilarating than in the Morgan. 'What are you hoping for?' Terry was saying as they whizzed past Bonehill Rocks.

'There's something worrying me that needs sorting out,' she replied. 'At the same time I want to reassure Sirraway. If he can hold out a couple of days more at the mill, he won't be arrested and we'll have our scoop for Friday's paper.'

'Slight shift of tack from the other day. You were all for handing him over, putting him in chains.'

'A lady's privilege to change her mind, Ter, you know that.'

That raised a sardonic laugh.

When they reached Rattlepark Mill, they discovered the professor had spent his time erecting an awning out from the back door to the edge of the lawn, and was sitting contentedly under it, reading a book. He looked like a holidaymaker, not one of the most wanted men in Britain.

'Looks like you're going to have a garden party, Hector!'

'Oh, hello. I've been experimenting with dandelion tea but I won't offer you any, I don't think I've got it right yet.'

'Are you keeping up with what's going on?'

'I have my portable radio, but the signal here only gives me the *Third Programme* – lots of elegant Elgar and delicious Delibes, but not much news.'

Judy filled in the missing details. 'So you see, if you keep your head down you'll be in the clear in a couple of days. We just have one or two things to tie up first of all.' Meaning, we still have to catch the murderer of Sir Freddy, but I know it wasn't you.

'Just one thing I want to ask you,' she went on. 'To set my mind at rest.'

'Go ahead.'

'Before Christmas, you did some research in the public library and were helped out by the two ladies there – Miss Greenway and Miss Atherton.'

'Yes.'

'Miss Greenway died, you know.'

'I did know. Very sad, a nice lady – though I must confess she was not so good with her reference books. Mislabelled, badly indexed, I had the devil of a time finding what I wanted.'

'She fell off her ladder.'

'Most unfortunate. I heard about it when I got back from France – I looked in at the library to try to retrieve a carrier bag I'd left but it was all a bit chaotic, they couldn't find it.'

'You were in France, then, when she died?'

'Yes.'

'And you can prove it?'

'Of course. D'you want my passport? They stamped it, y'know.'

'No, that's all I need to know.'

'Peculiar question,' said Sirraway, but just then he caught sight of a mistle thrush skating across the lawn and his thoughts flew away with it.

'Come on, Terry.' Miss Dimont swung her bag over her shoulder. 'Oh, I brought you some more biscuits, Hector. Ratafia this time.'

'What's wrong with good old digestives?' said Terry witheringly as they got back in the Minor. 'Ratafia, indeed!'

As they drove across the moor the photographer asked – as photographers often do, because nobody ever bothers to give them in-depth briefings – exactly what that was all about. 'It's a long drive there and back,' he said, 'with nothing to show for it.'

'I'll tell you why I had to do it,' said Judy. 'This whole saga was spiralling out of control. Two murders in Temple Regis, and beyond them, a death in Knightsbridge twenty-five years ago. Interpol coming after a man who killed someone, we don't know the circumstances, and the unanswered question about Miss Greenway – did she fall or was she pushed? Is it all one thing? Or many different things?'

'I'm just the driver. You tell me.'

'We went to see Sirraway because I was uneasy about Miss Greenway's death. Was it an accident, as Dr Rudkin decreed? When we saw Sirraway last, I came away convinced he was an innocent enough fellow but there's something so strange about the man, so peculiar. I woke up this morning convinced that when he went back to collect that carrier bag, he did away with poor Miss Greenway.'

'And now?'

'If he says he was in France and can prove it, he's off the hook. It leaves only one other suspect.'

'David Renishaw,' Terry nodded.

'Was he trying to implicate Sirraway again? Trying to get him arrested, charged with murder – what has he got against the man?'

'I've seen it twice,' said Terry, 'the violence. He needs to be found, and quickly.'

'Well, let's see what Betty's come up with while we've been away.' They were almost back in Temple Regis. 'We've *got* to find him.'

Terry suddenly made a surprise right turn. 'I just want to try one thing,' he said. 'It won't take a minute.'

He drove the Minor into Yondertown Square, a little redbrick street backing onto Regis Junction Station, and into view came the red front door of Lovely Mary's cottage.

'Let's go and have a quick look,' said Terry. The way he slipped out of the car reminded her of the way boxers get into the ring – lithe, supple, ready for a fight.

'He won't be here,' said Judy, right behind him, 'he'll be in London by now.'

'I wonder.'

They were walking up to the front door when Terry suddenly swerved off. 'Round the back,' he ordered. They went through a side gate and found the back door open.

In the kitchen sat Lovely Mary and David Renishaw. Between them on the table lay a worn-looking pistol.

''E's all right, Terry,' said Mary, cautiously looking up. ''E's all right. Just a bit upset.'

Terry looked from one to the other and then grinned. 'David,' he said, 'we're friends, right? I'm going to help you, mate. I'm going to take away that gun.'

Renishaw looked up at the photographer, his eyes full of tears.

'But David, d'you hear? If you try to do anything to stop me, I'll knock your block off.'

Renishaw made a movement, but only to reach for a handkerchief. 'A bit upset,' repeated Mary, ''e's been telling me all about it, 'aven't you, David?'

Terry leaned over the table, perhaps a little too menacingly, and Judy stepped forward to give him a nudge as if to say, *back off.* 'I'm glad you're safe, David. All over now.'

'For you maybe,' mumbled Renishaw. 'Not for me. I thought it would make things better, but it hasn't.'

'That's why 'e come back,' said Lovely Mary. ''E was going off to Lunnun, but got to Exeter, turned round and come back. Said 'e didn't know where to go to now, 'cept Temple Regis. I said 'e could have his old room back. I put some clean sheets on.'

Judy thought before the day was out, other less comfortable accommodation would probably be made available to the ex-reporter – rent-free and with breakfast thrown in – but said nothing. She nudged Terry again and he lifted the pistol nimbly from the table.

'Will you make some tea, Lovely?'

'Kettle's just boiled, maid.'

Judy sat down, took off her glasses and polished them. 'Terry, you sit too.' Just as well to have him close to hand.

'David, you're very upset and I understand why – I think,' she said gently. 'I can see you don't want to talk much, so I'm going to tell you what I think has happened, and I hope you'll correct me if I go wrong.'

Renishaw wiped his eyes and looked up as Lovely Mary handed him a cup of tea. True to her name, she smiled and kissed the top of his head.

'I talked to Interpol in Paris first thing this morning,' Judy began. 'They told me they're on the lookout for a David Ouistreham – your height, age and description – they have a warrant for his arrest for the murder of his wife in Toronto, Canada.'

'Isn't me, wasn't me,' he said tiredly.

'Let's get this straight,' said Judy. 'It *is* you they're after, and that is your name – your real name? It finally came to me yesterday when the *News Chronicle* reporter first mentioned it. It was the way he pronounced it which finally put things in place.

'Then I remembered Bobbety Thurloe talking to me about Mrs Phipps' friend Pansy. Nobody was sure where she came from, but she was a lady all right,' she said. 'She used to say when introduced, *I'm Mrs Westerham when I'm in England*, as if she had a foreign title she didn't use here – Westerham sounds almost the same and is easier to spell. Her husband, your father, was Philippe Ouistreham. Am I right so far?'

'Yes,' said Renishaw.

'And Renishaw was her maiden name.'

'Yes.'

'Your father was not a concierge at the Palace Hotel, but a racing driver.'

'Yes.'

'He relied on her for money to keep his cars going; he otherwise did no work.'

'I don't see why this is of interest, but yes.'

'Again, early this morning I talked to a friend in Paris who remembered Philippe. Very distinguished, she said, very well known, but not terribly successful in his chosen field.'

Renishaw was staring into his tea. Lovely Mary gave his shoulders a rub and sat down next to him.

'Now I'm guessing,' continued Judy, 'but from the various pieces of information which have come my way it looks like the story goes like this. Your mother despaired of your father ever finding a job which would pay the bills, and when you were twelve she finally left the family home – left you and your father – never to return. She moved to London taking with her what remained of her fortune.

'She had enough left to buy a small house and keep herself in style. Soon she gravitated to that circle which revolved round the Embassy Club in Mayfair, and because of her exceptional looks and her poise, she was soon taken up by... let's say, a certain prince.'

'Wrong. They met in Paris.'

'Ah. So she knew him when she arrived in London.

Very good. For a time everything went well, but the prince had other fish to fry – and that's when Pansy fell under the spell of Freddy Hungerford. They had an affair and, as was Hungerford's habit, he started sucking what money she had out of her bank accounts. Within two years she'd lost everything and was bankrupt.'

'He used her and used her until there was nothing left to use,' mumbled Renishaw. 'Then he killed her.'

'Do you know that?'

'Yes. No. I don't know – all the evidence points that way.'

'David, I'd love to know what evidence you were able to dredge up on a death which took place twenty-five years ago. Because I've tried and failed to establish whether Hungerford murdered your mother or whether it was a case of…' She would not use the word, for fear of it hurting him more.

'He killed her. I killed him. That's enough, isn't it?' He looked up and the tears had stopped.

'Tell me, then, what happened after she left home.'

'My father tried to find her, obviously. Came to London, went to see the police. Went to see my grandparents in Cambridge, but they disapproved of him and his lifestyle and refused to help. Maybe they knew where my mother was and agreed to keep it secret, I don't know.

'He is – was – French, and knew nobody in England. She'd changed her name and he couldn't find her, so he came home and life went on without her. When the war broke out I was still at school, so he sent me off to Canada to live with some cousins. I started college but then went to work on a local newspaper. After the war I came to London and worked for a time, off and on, in Fleet Street.'

'Then you went back to Canada?'

'My grandparents both died and left me a little money and I thought I could do better with it over there, so I went to Toronto, met my wife and got married.'

'Let's talk about your wife in a moment.' Terry had got up from the table and had taken a small pocket Leica from his coat and was aiming it at Renishaw. He didn't seem to notice.

'So your life went on. Then, suddenly, you decided to come back to England and go in pursuit of Freddy Hungerford – why? Why, after twenty-five years?'

'You may find this extraordinary,' said Renishaw, 'but a couple of years ago I was sitting in the dentist's waiting room and I picked up a copy of an old magazine – *Tatler*, I think it was. Years out of date, but that's the war for you. I opened it up and there was a picture of my mother, all dressed up to the nines, at some society affair in London. The picture caption said her name was Pansy Westerham – no wonder my father couldn't find her!'

'What was her name, then, when she was married to him?'

'Pamela Ouistreham; I have no idea where the Pansy comes from. It was a terrible shock – to see this face you knew so well, but with another name attached to it, in a country far from home, surrounded by people you've never heard of.

'I sat and thought about it. Then I called friends I'd made in Fleet Street during my short time there, and over the next few months they delved into cuttings and picture libraries and put together a portfolio which, for the first time, told me something about my mother's London life.'

'That must have been painful, seeing her enjoying herself while you and your father...'

Renishaw wiped his eyes. 'She was obviously never cut out for motherhood. A woman, it seems, can live her life without her child, but the child without his mother…'

'What did you learn about her life?'

'Not much, but one thing I gathered quite quickly – she featured in a lot of society columns and glossy magazines, but when I looked at the informal group shots, time and again somewhere near her was this figure, Freddy Hungerford. Handsome, moustachioed, wealthy-looking. They were careful not to be photographed as a couple, but when you saw that many photos from so many different events, it was obvious that they were an item.'

'And?' said Judy. She could see he was ready to unburden himself of the whole story – glad of it, in fact.

'Again, with the help of my friends I looked into Hungerford. He was married, of course. There were lots of sniping little paragraphs in the gossip columns – he obviously wasn't much liked even then, except by the ladies. And when you pieced all the cuttings and stories together, a pattern emerged which led me to believe something I was only able to confirm later, when I got my hands on that man Sirraway's research notes.'

'Which was?'

'That Hungerford had made his fortune out of wooing – if that's the word – rich women.'

'So what did you do?'

'By that stage I'd tired of journalism and I was running an outfit called Underdog. It was a very well-intentioned organisation with one simple aim – to help those who couldn't help themselves. I had enough money from my inheritance to do that and still make ends meet. I just wanted to *do* something for these people.'

Lovely Mary poured him another cup. 'You have a good heart, David,' she said, 'even if you're a bit strange.'

'Wouldn't *you* be, Mary? If you lost your mother like that?'

'I do see that, my dear, I do.' She reached out and lightly touched his hand.

'That was at the beginning of last year,' he went on. 'At about the same time my wife was killed – and that upset me, greatly. We hadn't been getting on and the marriage was effectively over, but we still shared the same house. I was away doing my Underdogging in a town called Hamilton, and someone I'd been after on an earlier case came round and beat her up. Her injuries weren't that bad but she had a weak heart, and that's what killed her.'

'Interpol say *you* killed her, David,' said Judy quietly.

'They know I didn't. I was an hour's drive away, even though I couldn't prove it. They had me in for questioning and gave me a very hard time, and I took it badly. Very badly. What with that and discovering about my mother, I must have gone a bit crazy. I packed a bag and left.'

'Leaving your daughter behind?'

'Staying with her best friend – they are very good people, they take care of her. I just had to go, I didn't care where.'

'How did you get out of the country?'

'Two passports. My French one is in the name of Ouistreham, the Canadian in the name of Renishaw. I left Canada as Ouistreham – they were looking for Renishaw.'

'Didn't take long for Interpol to catch up with you, though. They were practically knocking on your door at Christmas.'

'Well,' said Renishaw wryly, 'it doesn't exactly take a genius to work out that the "David Renishaw", Devon journalist, is very similar to "David Renishaw", ex-journalist, of Toronto. You might say I like living dangerously – I didn't exactly go out of my way to disappear from view. For goodness' sake, I had my name on the front page of the *Riviera Express* most weeks!'

Pushing my own byline out of the way, thought Judy, but now I'm obliged to forgive you.

'If I'm ever brought to trial for my wife's death, the evidence will clearly point to who did it – not me. They just didn't like me hopping it, and wanted to make an example of me.'

'I think, though,' replied Miss Dimont, 'there's another trial you are going to have to face first.'

'Yes,' said Renishaw, and his eyes disappeared into his teacup again. 'Yes. I came to London and sat alone for a week in a boarding house, looking at the cuttings, looking at the pictures, and it was then I decided I had to see Hungerford. To judge for myself. It didn't matter whether he murdered her or she committed suicide or it was just a terrible accident. He was responsible, and I had to face him with it.'

'For once,' said Judy, 'you were the underdog.'

'You could say that, but I didn't see it that way. I thought I would stand a better chance of getting away with it – whatever *it* was, I hadn't made up my mind – if I came down to Temple Regis, his constituency, and disappeared into the woodwork. So I applied to Rhys for a job and he took me on.'

'Hah! You did all that research,' said Judy, 'but you failed to discover he barely ever visited the constituency!'

'Correct. I got down here and only then found out what an absentee MP he was. But I'd got the job and was rather enjoying the change of scene. And I got the chance to get close to him when he came down for his farewell Christmas party.

'I saw Sirraway shouting his head off in the crowd about Hungerford and that gave me an idea. One of the people near me said they'd seen him a couple of days in a row in the library, and so I dropped in, hoping to find out something more. That's when Miss Greenway gave me the carrier bag with Sirraway's notes.'

'And you realised then,' said Judy, 'that you could pin the murder on him. The dossier he'd created was in itself almost enough to incriminate him – the fact that he'd amassed all those details, that he was so vocal in his opposition to Hungerford. That he was stalking him.'

Renishaw reached out for Mary's hand. 'I wasn't thinking straight. By that time, I knew what had to be done – Hungerford had done nothing but harm in his life, he'd left a trail of destruction in his rise to the top, and it was time to put an end to it. Nothing mattered now except to find the best way to kill Hungerford, then get away. I had a daughter to go home to, you know.'

'You said.'

'Well, it didn't work. I did my best to implicate him but I failed. But I did succeed in what I set out to do – I killed the man who killed my mother. There's a price to pay for that, I suppose.

'But,' he added, 'since I got hold of Sirraway's dossier I've gathered even more evidence about Hungerford fleecing innocent people, and I know the judge will take that into account when we get to the end of the trial. Really, Judy, I've amassed hundreds of documents, you'd be amazed!'

His eyes were twitching from side to side. 'She may have made the latter part of my childhood wretched,' he went on. 'She may have broken my heart by abandoning me. But my mother was a wonderful woman, unique – and *nobody* had the right to do what they did to her. Nobody!'

'I'm going to go and call Inspector Topham, David,' said Judy gently. 'Terry will stay with you, won't you, Terry? And Lovely Mary.'

'That's all right,' said Renishaw in an exhausted voice. 'I think I'll just go and lie down.'

Miss Dimont stole out into the hall and picked up the phone.

'Inspector Topham? If you come quickly, you can beat Interpol at their own game!'

TWENTY-EIGHT

'So you see,' said Judy, 'if Hamish Madden's trial goes ahead first, it'll help David Renishaw no end. Just think – a long-standing Member of Parliament ordering the murder of his successor! Plus he was an embezzler, a fraud, a thief! Just think of the waves of sympathy that'll come wafting David's way!'

'I wouldn't bank on it,' said Terry grimly, 'the man's still a murderer.' He hadn't got over the reporter's disgraceful behaviour at the Con Club – in Terry's book, damaging the good name of the *Riviera Express* was a far graver crime than topping Freddy Hungerford.

Not everyone shared his bleak view. Athene was making her special this morning, and her aura was positively golden. 'I have the feeling,' she said dreamily, making circles in the air with her hands, 'they'll treat him leniently. Once they see what a positive *avalanche* of troubles his stars lined up for him.'

They'd all gathered in the editor's office, though the great eminence himself was absent; he'd gone off somewhere, probably to get his bad temper trimmed.

'Is there any gin?' croaked Mrs Phipps, who'd been invited

in to celebrate but was never terribly keen on a plain cup of tea.

'No,' said Judy, 'but I think I can find some whisky, will that do?' She made in the direction of John Ross's desk – he'd never open that bottle again – and returned triumphant. Mrs Phipps poured a hefty belt into her teacup.

Auriol, sitting close by, lifted an eyebrow and turned away.

'Go on, then,' urged Peter Pomeroy. 'The best bits are always the ones that don't get into print.'

'I hardly know how to say this,' said Judy, abashed. 'But I was sitting on the evidence all the time.'

'What?' said Auriol, shocked. 'And you let these things happen? *Judy!* I can't believe it of you!'

'There's nothing I could have done. It's just that when Mirabel Clifford handed me that folder of Sirraway's, I didn't read it thoroughly – I was looking for recent events, not something that had happened pre-war. So there, inside, was a full report on Hungerford's relationship with Pansy Westerham, and it passed me by.

'When it comes to the murders, Sirraway had done a magnificent research job on our MP, but he wasn't blessed with second sight – he couldn't foretell that Hungerford was going to have his rival killed. Or that David would kill him. Nobody could.'

Except Athene, thought Auriol starchily. Isn't that her job, what she's paid to do by the *Express*?

'If I'd read Sirraway's report, maybe something would have come to me – maybe I could have worked out the link between Pansy and David, but still I wouldn't have been able to see he intended to kill Hungerford.'

'Well, I think you did a magnificent job,' said Mrs Phipps, approvingly. 'Even if you aren't able to say whether Freddy Hungerford killed Pansy.'

'Oh, I think he did, no question. I telephoned Bobbety Thurloe last night to let him know about Pansy – he made me promise – and he told me something he'd learned from his cousin. Apparently, it was well known by some – though obviously not Bobbety – that in her last weeks alive, Pansy had become something of a nuisance. She threatened to go to the newspapers if Freddy Hungerford didn't pay her back some of her money.'

'A *nuisance* – I think we all know what that means when it comes to Sir Frederick.'

'Oh, Judy,' cooed Athene, 'you're *so* brilliant!'

'I don't know,' said Judy. 'Everybody had a hand in this one. It's our joint success.'

But the laurel leaves were all hers this morning. 'Dashed good show,' wheezed Ray Bennett, the bow-tied arts editor, who wouldn't know a crime story if it came and cracked him over the head.

'Will David be allowed visitors in prison? A hot water bottle? Time alone with those who wish to comfort him?' said Betty, who would do anything for a lame dog. 'Oh, congrats, by the way.'

'Don't let this success run away with your expenses claims,' warned Rhys, putting his head round the door. 'I'll be keeping a close eye.'

Judy was pleased with her victory, if surprised that so far there'd been no word from Inspector Topham, to whom she'd handed not one but two murderers on a plate. On the other hand, the paperwork involved, and the meddlesome interference of Interpol, make a copper far busier than when he's merely hunting down killers.

Mrs Phipps, who found she liked the taste of whisky more than she realised, helped herself to more. She was especially pleased that her ancient cobwebbed mystery had played such an important part in the whole drama.

'When I look back on those days... the fun we had,' she sighed.

'Can't have been much fun for Pansy Westerham. Married to a bad 'un, intrigued by another. Abandoned her child, her money all gone. Her house taken away from her,' reminded Auriol. 'And then...'

'My dear, all of that is true. But think of the excitement we've had – almost as thrilling as being back on the stage! You *are* a bit of a genius, Judy! And I talked to Bobbety, too – he says come for dinner and stay the night. White tie and tiaras!'

'Just tell me this,' said Terry. 'Because I didn't like that Renishaw, I'll be frank. I see what his problem was, but what I can't understand is why he attacked that man Sirraway so viciously. Why he tried to set him up.'

'I think he'd gone a bit mad by that stage,' said Judy. 'We thought Sirraway was mad when he was sane. We thought David was sane when clearly he wasn't.

'There's no excuse for what he did to a perfectly innocent man. But he knew Interpol was closing in, and he only had a very short time to achieve what he'd set out to do. When you went up to Hatherleigh that first time, Terry, he suddenly saw he could paint Sirraway as a likely murder suspect because the man behaved so oddly.

'By the time he tackled him at the hustings, shouting he'd got a knife, he'd got the plan clear in his mind. He saw Sirraway as his means of escape – Sirraway would get arrested and he could make his getaway.'

'Well, like I said, I don't like him. I'm glad Mr Rhys fired him.'

'Oh no, Terry, don't you see? He *made* the editor fire him! By that stage he'd decided he would lead Interpol a merry dance – *I like living dangerously* he told me – and he wanted to get back to Canada to his daughter. So he engineered a row – a row he would lose – with Mr Rhys. So Rhys fires him, and David has a legitimate excuse to leave town.'

'Ur,' said Terry. He hadn't seen that one. It made him grumpy.

'Anyway, Terry, if anyone's the star of this show, it's you. Your gut instinct told you that Renishaw had gone back to Lovely Mary's and we got there just at the right moment. I didn't like the look of that gun.'

'It was loaded all right, five rounds.'

'You never told me that! He has mood swings, you can see that. The only place he felt safe was with Lovely Mary, but I worried about the way he was looking at her when we walked in the room. Not in control. And the way you took the gun away from him, faultless. So brave.'

Terry slurped his tea.

'The people that come to work here, how strange they can be,' said Athene, not realising she was perhaps the strangest of them all. 'I'm thinking of David, but all the others too – I wonder where they all are now?'

Perhaps she was thinking of Valentine Waterford, the

lovely young reporter who got in his bubble car one day and drove off over the horizon. But there had been so many, using the *Express* as their staging post or springboard – some remembered for years to come, others forgotten instantly.

'Wherever they are, they're not in a better place than here,' said loyal Peter Pomeroy, who'd been on the paper since the Dark Ages.

'I wonder, though,' said Judy. 'Aren't the best journalists the gypsies among us, the ones with a pebble in their shoe, the ones who always have to move on?' Maybe she was thinking of Valentine too.

'Don't start that,' advised Auriol. 'The next thing we'll hear is that you're packing it in – rolling up your tent, moving on.'

'Maybe one day soon. I sat in the garden last night with the church bells tolling and the blackbirds singing and asked myself whether there wasn't something else I should be doing. Another newspaper, a fresh start. We all need a change in life. What should I do next?

'And then I realised what it was.

'I have to find out who killed Miss Greenway.'

THE END
(for now...)

If you enjoyed this Miss Dimont mystery, then read on for an extract from her first adventure, *The Riviera Express*...

ONE

When Miss Dimont smiled, which she did a lot, she was beautiful. There was something mystical about the arrangement of her face-furniture – the grey eyes, the broad forehead, the thin lips wide spread, her dainty perfect teeth. In that smile was a *joie de vivre* which encouraged people to believe that good must be just around the corner.

But there were two faces to Miss Dimont. When hunched over her typewriter, rattling out the latest episode of life in Temple Regis, she seemed not so sunny. Her corkscrew hair fell out of its makeshift pinnings, her glasses slipped down the convex nose, those self-same lips pinched themselves into a tight little knot and a general air of mild chaos and discontent emanated like puffs of smoke from her desk.

Life on the *Riviera Express* was no party. The newspaper's offices, situated at the bottom of the hill next door to the brewery, maintained their dreary pre-war combination of uprightness and formality. The front hall, the only area of access permitted to townsfolk, spoke with its oak panelling and heavy desks of decorum, gentility, continuity.

But the most momentous events in Temple Regis in 1958

– its births, marriages and deaths, its council ordinances, its police court and its occasional encounters with celebrity – were channelled through a less august set of rooms, inadequately lit and peopled by journalism's flotsam and jetsam, up a back corridor and far from the public gaze.

Lately there'd been a number of black-and-white 'B' features at the Picturedrome, but these always portrayed the heady excitements of Fleet Street. Behind the green baize door, beyond the stout oak panelling, the making of this particular local journal was decidedly less ritzy.

Far from Miss Dimont lifting an ivory telephone to her ear while partaking of a genteel breakfast in her silk-sheeted bed, the real-life reporter started her day with an apple and 'The Calls' – humdrum visits to Temple's police station, its council offices, fire station, and sundry other sources of bread-and-butter material whose everyday occurrences would, next Friday, fill the heart of the *Express*.

Like a laden beachcomber she would return mid-morning to her desk to write up her gleanings before leaving for the Magistrates' Court, where the bulk of her work, from that bottomless well of human misdeeds and misfortunes, daily bubbled up.

After luncheon, usually taken alone with her crossword in the Signal Box Café, she would return briefly to court before preparing for an evening meeting of the Town Council, the Townswomen's Guild, or – light relief – a performance by the Temple Regis Amateur Operatic Society.

Then it would be home on her moped, corkscrew hair

blowing in the wind, to Mulligatawny, whose sleek head would be staring out of the mullioned window awaiting his supper and her pithy account of the day's events.

Miss Dimont, now unaccountably beyond the age of forty, had the fastest shorthand note in the West Country. In addition, she could charm the birds out of the trees when she chose – her capacity to get people to talk about themselves, it was said, could make even the dead speak. She was shy but she was shrewd; and if perhaps she was comfortably proportioned she was, everyone agreed, quite lovely.

Why Betty Featherstone, her so-called friend, got the front-page stories and Miss Dimont did not was lost in the mists of time. Suffice to say that on press day, when everyone's temper shortened, it was Judy who got it in the neck from her editor. Betty wrote what he wanted, while Judy wrote the truth – and it did not always make comfortable reading. She didn't mind the fusillades aimed in her direction for having overturned a civic reputation or two, for ever since she had known him, and it had been a long time, Rudyard Rhys had lacked consistency. Furthermore, his ancient socks smelt. Miss Dimont rose above.

Unquestionably Devon's prettiest town, Temple Regis took itself very seriously. Its beaches, giving out on to the turquoise and indigo waters which inspired some wily publicist to coin the phrase 'England's Riviera', were white and pristine. Broad lawns encircling the bandstand and flowing down towards the pier were scrupulously shaved, immaculately edged. Out in the estuary, the water was an impossible shade

of aquamarine, its colour a magical invention of the gods –
and since everyone in Temple agreed their little town was the
sunniest spot in England, it really was very beautiful.

It was far too nice a place to be murdered.

*

Confusingly, the *Riviera Express* was both newspaper and
railway train. Which came first was occasionally the cause
for heated debate down in the snug of the Cap'n Fortescue,
but the laws of copyright had not yet been invented when the
two rivals were born; and an ambitious rail company serving
the dreams of holidaymakers heading for the South West was
certainly not giving way to a tinpot local rag when it came to
claiming the title. Similarly, with a rock-solid local readership
and a justifiable claim to both 'Riviera' and 'Express' – a
popular newspaper title – the weekly journal snootily toler-
ated its more famous namesake. If neither would admit it,
each benefited from the other's existence.

Before the war successive editors lived in constant turmoil,
sometimes printing glowing lists of the visitors from another
world who spilled from the brown and cream liveried railway
carriages ('The Hon. Mrs Gerald Legge and her mother, the
novelist Barbara Cartland, are here for the week'). At other
times, Princess Margaret Rose herself could have puffed into
town and the old codgers would have ignored it. Rudyard
Rhys saw both points of view so there was no telling what
he would think one week to the next – to greet the afternoon
arrival? Or not to bother?

'Mr Rhys, we could go to meet the 4.30,' warned his chief reporter on this particular Tuesday. 'But – also – there's a cycling-without-lights case in court which could turn nasty. The curate from St Margaret's. He told me he's going to challenge his prosecution on the grounds that British Summer Time has no substantive legal basis. It could be very interesting.'

'Rrrr.'

'Don't you see? The Chairman of the Bench is one of his parishioners! Sure to be an almighty dust-up!'

'Rrrr . . . rrr.'

'A clash between the Church and the Law, Mr Rhys! We haven't had one of those for a while!'

Rudyard Rhys lit his pipe. An unpleasant smell filled the room. Miss Dimont stepped back but otherwise held her ground. She was all too familiar with this fence-sitting by her editor.

'Bit of a waste going to meet the 4.30,' she persisted. 'There's only Gerald Hennessy on board . . .' (and an encounter with a garrulous, prosy, self-obsessed matinée idol might make me late for my choir practice, she might have added).

'Hennessy?' The editor put down his pipe with a clunk. 'Now *that's* news!'

'Oh?' snipped Miss Dimont. 'You said you hated *The Conqueror and the Conquered*. "Not very manly for a VC", I think were your words. You objected to the length of his hair.'

'Rrrr.'

'Even though he had been lost in the Burmese jungle for three years.'

Mr Rhys performed his usual backflip. 'Hennessy,' he ordered.

It was enough. Miss Dimont noted that, once again, the editor had deserted his journalistic principles in favour of celebrity worship. Rhys enjoyed the perquisite accorded him by the Picturedrome of two back stalls seats each week. He had actually enjoyed *The Conqueror and the Conquered* so much he sat through it twice.

Miss Dimont did not know this, but anyone who had played as many square-jawed warriors as Gerald Hennessy was always likely to find space in the pages of the *Riviera Express*. Something about heroism by association, she had noted in the past, was at the root of her editor's lofty decisions. That all went back to the War, of course.

'Four-thirty it is, then,' she said a trifle bitterly. 'But *Church* v. *Law* – now there's a story that might have been followed up by the nationals,' and with that she swept out, notebook flapping from her raffia bag.

This parting shot was a reference to the long-standing feud between the editor and his senior reporter. After all, Rudyard Rhys had made the wrong call on not only the Hamilton Biscuit Case, but the Vicar's Longboat Party, the Temple Regis Tennis Scandal and the Football Pools Farrago. Each of these exclusives from the pen of Judy Dimont had been picked up by the repulsive Arthur Shrimsley, an out-to-grass former Fleet Street type who made a killing by selling them on to the national papers, at the same time showing up the *Riviera Express* for the newspaper it was – hesitant, and slow to spot its own scoops when it had them.

On each occasion the editor's decision had been final – and wrong. But Judy was no saint either, and the cat's cradle of complaint triggered by her coverage of the Regis Conservative Ball last winter still made for a chuckle or two in the sub-editors' room on wet Thursday afternoons.

With her raffia bag swinging furiously, she stalked out to the car park, for Judy Dimont was resolute in almost everything she did, and her walk was merely the outer manifestation of that doughty inner being – a purposeful march which sent out radar-like warnings to flag-day sellers, tin-can rattlers, and other such supplicants and cleared her path as if by miracle. It was not manly, for Miss Dimont was nothing if not feminine, but it was no-nonsense.

She took no nonsense, either, from Herbert, her trusty moped, who sat expectantly, awaiting her arrival. With one cough, Herbert was kicked into life and the magnificent Miss Dimont flew away towards Temple Regis railway station, corkscrew hair flapping in the wind, a happy smile upon her lips. For there was nothing she liked more than to go in search of new adventures – whether they were to be found in the Magistrates' Court, the Horticultural Society, or the railway station.

Her favourite route took in Tuppenny Row, the elegant terrace of Regency cottages whose brickwork had turned a pale pink with the passage of time, bleached by Temple

Regis sun and washed by its soft rains. She turned into Cable Street, then came down the long run to the station, whose yellow-and-chocolate bargeboard frontage you could glimpse from the top of the hill, and Miss Dimont, with practice born of long experience, started her descent just as the sooty, steamy clouds of vapour from the *Riviera Express* slowed in preparation for its arrival at Regis Junction.

She had done her homework on Gerald Hennessy and, despite her misgivings about missing the choir practice, she was looking forward to their encounter, for Miss Dimont was far from immune to the charms of the opposite sex. Since the War, Hennessy had become the perfect English hero in the nation's collective imagination – square-jawed, crinkle-eyed, wavy-haired and fair. He spoke so nicely when asked to deliver his lines, and there was always about him an air of amused self-deprecation which made the nation's mothers wish him for their daughters, if not secretly for themselves.

Miss Dimont brought Herbert to a halt, his final splutter of complaint lost in the clanking, wheezing riot of sooty chaos which signals the arrival of every self-regarding Pullman Express. Across the station courtyard she spotted Terry Eagleton, the *Express*'s photographer, and made towards him as she pulled the purple gloves from her hands.

'Anyone apart from Hennessy?'

'Just 'im, Miss Dim.'

'I've told you before, call me Judy,' she said stuffily. The dreaded nickname had been born out of an angry tussle with Rudyard Rhys, long ago, over a front-page story which had gone wrong. Somehow it stuck, and the editor took a fiendish delight in roaring it out in times of stress. Bad enough having to put up with it from him – though invariably she rose above – but no need to be cheeked by this impertinent snapper. She had mixed feelings about Terry Eagleton.

'Call me Judy,' she repeated sternly, and got out her notebook.

'Ain't your handle, anyways,' parried Terry swiftly, and he was right – for Miss Dimont had a far more euphonious name, one she kept very quiet and for a number of good reasons.

Terry busily shifted his camera bag from one shoulder to the other. Employed by his newspaper as a trained observer, he could see before him a bespectacled woman of a certain age – heading towards fifty, surely – raffia bag slung over one shoulder, notebook flapping out of its top, with a distinctly harassed air and a permanently peppery riposte. Though she was much loved by all who knew her, Terry sometimes found it difficult to see why. It made him sigh for Doreen, the sweet young blonde newly employed on the front desk, who had difficulty remembering people's names but was indeed an adornment to life.

Miss Dimont led the way on to Platform 1.

'Pics first,' said Terry.

'No, Terry,' countered Miss Dim. 'You take so long there's never time left for the interview.'

'Picture's worth a thousand words, they always say. How many words are you goin' to write – *two hundred*?'

The same old story. In Fleet Street, always the old battle between monkeys and blunts, and even here in sweetest Devon the same old manoeuvring based on jealousy, rivalry and the belief that pictures counted more than words or, conversely, words enhanced pictures and gave them the meaning and substance they otherwise lacked.

And so this warring pair went to work, arriving on the platform just as the doors started to swing open and the holidaymakers began to alight. It was always a joyous moment, thought Miss Dimont, this happy release from confinement into sunshine, the promise of uncountable pleasures ahead. A small girl raced past, her face a picture of joy, pigtails given an extra bounce by the skip in her step.

The routine on these occasions was always the same – if a single celebrity was to be interviewed, he or she would be ushered into the first-class waiting room in order to be relieved of their innermost secrets. If more than one, the likeliest candidate would be pushed in by Terry, while Judy quickly handed the others her card, enquiring discreetly where they were staying and arranging a suitable time for their interrogation.

This manoeuvring took some skill and required a deftness of touch in which Miss Dimont excelled. On a day like today, no such juggling was required – just an invitation to old Gerald to step inside for a moment and explain away his presence in Devon's prettiest town.

The late holiday crowds swiftly dispersed, the guard completed the task of unloading from his van the precious goods entrusted to his care – a basket of somnolent homing pigeons, another of chicks tweeting furiously, the usual assortment of brown paper parcels. Then the engine driver climbed aboard to prepare for his next destination, Exbridge.

A moment of stillness descended. A blackbird sang. Dust settled in gentle folds and the reporter and photographer looked at each other.

'No ruddy Hennessy,' said Terry Eagleton.

Miss Dimont screwed up her pretty features into a scowl. In her mind was the lost scoop of *Church* v. *Law*, the clerical challenge to the authority of the redoubtable Mrs Marchbank. The uncomfortable explanation to Rudyard Rhys of how she had missed not one, but two stories in an afternoon – and with press day only two days away.

Mr Rhys was unforgiving about such things.

Just then, a shout was heard from the other end of Platform 1 up by the first-class carriages. A porter was waving his hands. Inarticulate shouts spewed forth from his shaking face. He appeared, for a moment, to be running on the spot. It was as if a small tornado had descended and hit the platform where he stood.

Terry had it in an instant. Without a word he launched himself down the platform, past the bewildered guard, racing towards the porter. The urgency with which he took off sprang in Miss Dimont an inner terror and the certain knowledge that she must run too – run like the wind . . .

By the time she reached the other end of the platform Terry was already on board. She could see him racing through the first-class corridor, checking each compartment, moving swiftly on. As fast as she could, she followed alongside him on the platform.

They reached the last compartment almost simultaneously, but Terry was a pace or two ahead of Judy. There, perfectly composed, immaculately clad in country tweeds, his oxblood brogues twinkling in the sunlight, sat their interviewee, Gerald Hennessy.

You did not have to be an expert to know he was dead.

TWO

You had to hand it to Terry – no Einstein he, but in an emergency as cool as ice. He was photographing the lifeless form of a famous man barely before the reality of the situation hit home. Miss Dimont watched through the carriage window, momentarily rooted to the spot, as he went about his work efficiently, quickly, dextrously. But then, as Terry switched positions to get another angle, his eye caught her immobile form.

'Call the office,' he snapped through the window. 'Call the police. In that order.'

But Judy could not take her eyes off the man who so recently had graced the Picturedrome's silver screen. His hair, now restored to a more conventional length, flopped forward across his brow. The tweed suit was immaculate. The foulard tie lay gently across what looked like a cream silk shirt, pink socks disappeared into those twinkling brogues. She had to admit that in death Gerald Hennessy, when viewed this close, looked almost more gorgeous than in life . . .

'The phone!' barked Terry.

Miss Dimont started, then, recovering herself, raced to the

nearby telephone box, pushed four pennies urgently into the slot and dialled the news desk. To her surprise she was met with the grim tones of Rudyard Rhys himself. It was rare for the editor to answer a phone – or do anything else useful around the office, thought Miss Dimont in a fleeting aperçu.

'Mr Rhys,' she hicupped, 'Mr Rhys! Gerald Hennessy . . . the . . . dead . . .' Then she realised she had forgotten to press Button A to connect the call. That technicality righted, she repeated her message with rather more coherence, only to be greeted by a lion-like roar from her editor.

'Rrr-rrr-rrrr . . .'

'What's that, Mr Rhys?'

'Damn fellow! Damn him, damn the man. Damn damn damn!'

'Well, Mr Rhys, I don't really think you can speak like that. He's . . . dead . . . Gerald Hennessy – the actor, you know – he is dead.'

'He's not the only one,' bellowed Rudyard. 'You'll have to come away. Something more important.'

Just for the moment Miss Dim lived up to her soubriquet, her brilliant brain grinding to a halt. What did he mean? Was she missing something? What could be more important than the country's number-one matinée idol sitting dead in a railway carriage, here in Temple Regis?

Had Rudyard Rhys done it again? The old Vicar's Longboat Party tale all over again? Walking away from the biggest story to come the *Express*'s way in a decade? How typical of the man!

She glanced over her shoulder to see Terry, now out of the compartment of death and standing on the platform, talking to the porter. That's *my* job, she thought, hotly. In a second she had dropped the phone and raced to Terry's side, her flapping notebook ready to soak up every detail of the poor man's testimony.

The extraordinary thing about death is it makes you repeat things, thought Miss Dimont calmly. You say it once, then you say it again – you go on saying it until you have run out of people to say it to. So though technically Terry had the scoop (a) he wasn't taking notes and (b) he wasn't going to be writing the tale so (c) the story would still be hers. In the sharply competitive world of Devon journalism, ownership of a scoop was all and everything.

'There 'e was,' said the porter, whose name was Mudge. 'There 'e was.'

So far so good, thought Miss Dimont. This one's a talker. 'So then you . . .?'

'I told 'im,' said Mudge, pointing at Terry. 'I already told 'im.' And with that he clamped his uneven jaws together.

Oh Lord, thought Miss Dimont, this one's *not* a talker.

But not for nothing was the *Express*'s corkscrew-haired reporter renowned for charming the birds out of the trees. 'He doesn't listen,' she said, nodding towards the photographer. 'Deaf to anything but praise. You'll need to tell me. The train came in and . . .'

'I told 'im.'

There was a pause.

'Mr Mudge,' responded Miss Dimont slowly and perfectly reasonably, 'if you're unable to assist me, I shall have to ask Mrs Mudge when I see her at choir practice this evening.'

This surprisingly bland statement came down on the ancient porter as if a Damoclean sword had slipped its fastenings and pierced his bald head.

'You'm no need botherin' her,' he said fiercely, but you could see he was on the turn. Mrs Mudge's soprano, an eldritch screech whether in the church hall or at home, had weakened the poor man's resolve over half a century. All he asked now was a quiet life.

'The 4.30 come in,' he conceded swiftly.

'Always full,' said Miss Dimont, jollying the old bore along. 'Keeping you busy.'

'People got out.'

Oh, come *on*, Mudge!

'Missus Charteris arsk me to take 'er bags to the car. Gave me thruppence.'

'That chauffeur of hers is so idle,' observed Miss Dimont serenely. Things were moving along. 'So then . . .?'

'I come back to furs clars see if anyone else wanted porterin'. That's when I saw 'im. Just like lookin' at a photograph of 'im in the paper.' Mr Mudge was warming to his theme. ''E wasn't movin'.'

Suddenly the truth had dawned – first, who the well-dressed figure was; second, that he was very dead. The shocking combination had caused him to dance his tarantella on the platform edge.

The rest of the story was down to Terry Eagleton. 'Yep, looks like a heart attack. What was he – forty-five? Bit young for that sort of thing.'

As Judy turned this over in her mind Terry started quizzing Mudge again – they seemed to share an arcane lingo which mistrusted verbs, adjectives, and many of the finer adornments which make the English language the envy of the civilised world. It was a wonder to listen to.

'Werm coddit?'

'Ur, nemmer be.'

'C'rubble.'

Miss Dimont was too absorbed by the drama to pay much attention to these linguistic dinosaurs and their game of semantic shove-ha'penny; she sidled back to the railway carriage and then, pausing for a moment, heart in mouth, stepped aboard.

The silent Pullman coach was the *dernier cri* in luxury, a handsome relic of pre-war days and a reassuring memory of antebellum prosperity. Heavily carpeted and lined with exotic African woods, it smelt of leather and beeswax and smoke, its surfaces uniformly coated in a layer of dust so fine it was impossible to see: only by rubbing her sleeve on the corridor's handrail did the house-proud reporter discover what all seasoned railway passengers know – that travelling by steam locomotive is a dirty business.

She cautiously advanced from the far end of the carriage towards the dead man's compartment, her journalist's eye taking in the debris common to the end of all long-distance journeys – discarded newspapers, old wrappers, a teacup or two, an abandoned novel. On she stepped, her eyes a camera, recording each detail; her heart may be pounding but her head was clear.

Gerald Hennessy sat in the corner seat with his back to the engine. He looked pretty relaxed for a dead man – she wondered briefly if, called on to play a corpse by his director, Gerald would have done such a convincing job in life. One arm was extended, a finger pointing towards who knows what, as if the star was himself directing a scene. He looked rather heroic.

Above him in the luggage rack sat an important-looking suitcase, by his side a copy of *The Times*. The compartment smelt of . . . limes? Lemons? Something both sweet and sharp – presumably the actor's eau de cologne. But unlike Terry Eagleton Miss Dimont did not cross the threshold, for this was not the first death scene she had encountered in her lengthy and unusual career, and from long experience she knew better than to interfere.

She looked around, she didn't know why, for signs of violence – ridiculous, really, given Terry's confident reading of the cause of death – but Gerald's untroubled features offered nothing by way of fear or hurt.

And yet something was not quite right.

As her eyes took in the finer detail of the compartment, she spotted something near the doorway beneath another seat – it looked like a sandwich wrapper or a piece of litter of some kind. Just then Terry's angry face appeared at the compartment window and his fist knocked hard on the pane. She could hear him through the thick glass ordering her out on to the platform and she guessed that the police were about to arrive.

Without pausing to think why, she whisked up the litter from the floor – somehow it made the place look tidier, more dignified. It was how she would recall seeing the last of Gerald Hennessy, and how she would describe to her readers his final scene – the matinée idol as elegant in death as in life. Her introductory paragraph was already forming itself in her mind.

Terry stood on the platform, red-faced and hopping from foot to foot. 'Thought I told you to call the police.'

'Oh,' said Miss Dimont, downcast, 'I . . . oh . . . I'll go and do it now but then we've got another—'

'Done it,' he snapped back. 'And, yes we've got another fatality. I've talked to the desk. Come on.'

That was what was so irritating about Terry. You wanted to call him a know-it-all, but know-it-alls, by virtue of their irritating natures, do *not* know it all and frequently get things wrong. But Terry rarely did – it was what made him so infuriating.

'You know,' he said, as he slung his heavy camera bag over his shoulder and headed towards his car, 'sometimes you really *can* be quite dim.'

*

Bedlington-on-Sea was the exclusive end of Temple Regis,

more formal and less engagingly pretty than its big sister. Here houses of substance stood on improbably small plots, with large Edwardian rooms giving on to pocket-handkerchief gardens and huge windows looking out over a small bay.

Holidaymakers might occasionally spill into Bedlington but despite its apparent charm, they did not stay long. There was no pub and no beach, no ice-cream vendors, no pier, and a general frowning upon people who looked like they might want to have fun. It would be wrong to say that Bedlingtonians were stuffy and self-regarding, but people said it all the same.

The journey from the railway station took no more than six or seven minutes but it was like entering another world, thought Miss Dimont, as she and Herbert puttered behind the *Riviera Express*'s smart new Morris Minor. There was never any news in Bedlington – the townsfolk kept whatever they knew to themselves, and did not like publicity of any sort. If indeed there was a dead body on its streets this afternoon, you could put money on its not lying there for more than a few minutes before some civic-minded resident had it swept away. That's the way Bedlingtonians were.

And so Miss Dimont rather dreaded the inevitable 'knocks' she would have to undertake once the body was located. Usually this was a task at which she excelled – a tap on the door, regrets issued, brief words exchanged, the odd intimacy unveiled, the gradual jigsaw of half-information built up over maybe a dozen or so doorsteps – but in Bedlington she knew the chances of learning anything of use were remote. Snooty wasn't in it.

They had been in such a rush she hadn't been able to get out of Terry where exactly the body was to be found, but as they rounded the bend of Clarenceux Avenue there was no need for further questions. Ahead was the trusty black Wolseley of the Temple Regis police force, a horseshoe of spectators and an atmosphere electric with curiosity.

At the end of the avenue there rose a cliff of Himalayan proportions, a tower of deep red Devonian soil and rock, at the top of which one could just glimpse the evidence of a recent cliff fall. As one's eye moved down the sharp slope it was possible to pinpoint the trajectory of the deceased's involuntary descent; and in an instant it was clear to even the most casual observer that this was a tragic accident, a case of Man Overboard, where rocks and earth had given way under his feet.

Terry and Miss Dimont parked and made their way through to where Sergeant Hernaford was standing, facing the crowd, urging them hopelessly, pointlessly, that there was nothing to see and that they should move on.

The sergeant spoke with forked tongue, for there *was* something to see before they went home to tea – there, under a police blanket, lay a body a-sprawl, as if still in the act of trying to save itself. But it was chillingly still.

'Oh dear,' said Miss Dimont, conversationally, to Sergeant Hernaford, 'how tragic.'

''Oo was it?' said Terry, a bit more to the point.

Hernaford slowly turned his gaze towards the official representatives of the fourth estate. He had seen them many times before in many different circumstances, and here they were again – these purveyors of truth and of history, these curators of local legend, these *nosy parkers*.

'Back be'ind the line,' rasped Hernaford in a most unfriendly manner, for just like the haughty Bedlingtonians he did not like journalists. 'Get *back*!'

'Now Sergeant Hernaford,' said Miss Dimont, stiffening, for she did not like his tone. 'Here we have a man of late middle age – I can see his shoes, he's a man of late middle age – who has walked too close to the cliff edge. When I was up there at the top last week there were signs explicitly warning that there had been a rockfall and that people should keep away. So, man of late middle age, tragic accident. Coroner will say he was a BF for ignoring the warnings; the *Riviera Express* will say what a loss to the community. An extra paragraph listing his bereaved relations, there's the story.

'All that's missing,' she added, magnificently, edging closer to the sergeant, 'is his name. I expect you know it. I expect he had a wallet or something. Or maybe one of these good people—' she looked round, smiling at the horseshoe but her words taking on a steely edge '—has assisted you in your identification. He has clearly been here for a while – your blanket is damp and it stopped raining an hour ago – so in that time you must have had a chance to find out who he is.'

She smiled tightly and her voice became quite stern.

'I expect you have already informed your inspector and,

rather than drive all the way over to Temple Regis police station and take up his *very precious time* getting two words out of him – a Christian name and a surname, after all that is all I am asking – I imagine you would rather he did not complain to you about my wasting his *very precious time*.

'So, Sergeant,' she said, 'please spare us all that further pain.'

It was at times like this that Terry had to confess she may be a bit scatty but Miss Dimont could be, well, remarkable. He watched Sergeant Hernaford, a barnacle of the old school, crumble before his very eyes.

'Name, Arthur Shrimsley. Address, Tide Cottage, Exbridge. Now move on. Move *on*!'

Judy Dimont gazed owlishly, her spectacles sliding down her convex nose and resting precariously at its tip. 'Not *the* Arthur . . .?' she enquired, but before she could finish, Terry had whisked her away, for Hernaford was not a man to exchange pleasantries with – that was as much as they were going to get. As they retreated, he pushed Miss Dimont aside with his elbow while turning to take snaps of the corpse and its abrasive custodian before pulling open the car door.

'Let's go,' he urged. 'Lots to do.'

Miss Dimont obliged. Dear Herbert would have to wait. She pulled out her notebook and started to scribble as Terry noisily let in the clutch and they headed for the office.

Already the complexity of the situation was becoming clear; and no matter what happened next, disaster was about to befall her. Two deaths, two very different sets of journalistic values. And only Judy Dimont to adjudicate between the rival tales as to which served her readers best.

If she favoured the death of Gerald Hennessy over the sad loss of Arthur Shrimsley, local readers would never forgive her, for Arthur Shrimsley had made a big name for himself in the local community. The *Express* printed his letters most weeks, even at the moment when he was stealing their stories and selling them to Fleet Street. Rudyard Rhys, in thrall to Shrimsley's superior journalistic skills, had even allowed him to write a column for a time. But narcissistic and self-regarding it turned out to be, and of late he was permitted merely to see his name in print at the foot of a letter which would excoriate the local council, or the town brass band, or the ladies at the WI for failing to keep his cup full at the local flower show.

There was nothing nice about Arthur Shrimsley, yet he had invented a persona which his readers were all too ready to believe in and even love. His loss would be a genuine one to the community.

On the other hand, thought Miss Dimont feverishly, as Terry manoeuvred expertly round the tight corner of Tuppenny Row, we have a story of national importance here. Gerald Hennessy, star of *Heroes at Dawn* and *The First of the Few*, husband of the equally famous Prudence Aubrey, has died on our patch. Gerald *Hennessy*!

The question was, which sad passing should lead the *Express*'s front page? And who would take the blame when, as was inevitable, the wrong choice was made?

ONE PLACE. MANY STORIES

Bold, innovative and
empowering publishing.

FOLLOW US ON:

@HQStories